Di Morrissey is one of Australia's most successful writers. She began writing as a young woman, training and working as a journalist for Australian Consolidated Press in Sydney and Northcliffe Newspapers in London. She has worked in television in Australia and in the USA as a presenter, reporter, producer and actress. After her marriage to a US diplomat, Peter Morrissey, she lived in Singapore, Japan, Thailand, South America and Washington. Returning to Australia, Di continued to work in television before publishing her first novel in 1991.

Di has a daughter, Dr Gabrielle Morrissey Hansen, a human sexuality and relationship expert and academic. Di's son, Dr Nicolas Morrissey, is a lecturer in South East Asian Art History and Buddhist Studies at the University of Georgia, USA. Di has three grandchildren: Sonoma Grace and Everton Peter Hansen and William James Bodhi Morrissey.

Di and her partner, Boris Janjic, live in the Manning Valley in New South Wales when not travelling to research her novels, which are all inspired by a particular landscape.

www.dimorrissey.com

Di Morrissey
The Islands

PAN
Pan Macmillan Australia

*In memory of
my dearest mother, Kay, with whom I first visited
The Islands.*

First published 2008 by Pan Macmillan Australia Pty Limited
1 Market Street, Sydney

978-1-250-05333-6

Internal map by Laurie Whiddon
Internal illustrations by Donald K. Hall, Hawaii
Photographs on pages 1 and 446 by Getty Images

'Memory' from *Cats* by Andrew Lloyd Webber, Tim Rice and
T.S. Eliot © Faber and Faber Ltd / Reprinted with permission.

The Islands is a work of fiction. The characters in this book are
fictitious and any resemblance to real persons,
living or dead, is purely coincidental.

Acknowledgments

As always, hugs to my amazing children who give me such love, support and joy – Gabrielle and Nick.

My darling partner, Boris, who makes each day so wonderful.

My dear family, Jim and Ron Revitt, Ro, Pauline, David, Damien, Julie, Emma and all my lovely cousins. And a big happy 95th to darling Dorothy Morrissey.

Thank you to friends who were so helpful – Lloyd and Margaret Wood and their network in Honolulu, Peter Morrissey, former USA surf champion, Rusty Miller and some special soul surfers who wish to be anonymous. And not forgetting my old friend, Ted Johnston.

Thanks and love to my non-surfing lawyer, Ian Robertson and my pal and publisher, James Fraser.

To everyone at Pan Macmillan – Ross Gibb, Roxarne Burns, Jeannine Fowler, Jane Novak, Katie Crawford, Elizabeth Foster, Millie Shilland. And thanks to eagle-eyed copyeditor Rowena Lennox.

And a special thanks to Liz Adams (and Richard) for your friendship, patience and for being such a wonderful editor!

And to the late legendary waterman, Tom Blake, who inspired the character of Lester.

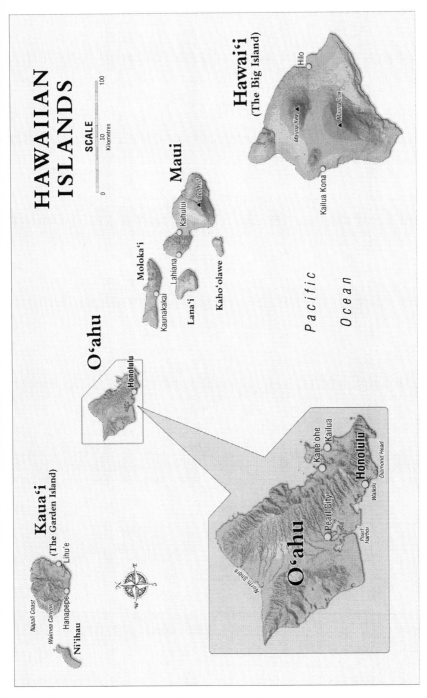

I

THE SKY-BLUE HOLDEN STATION wagon wound along the freshly graded dirt road lined by elderly eucalypts, a firmly anchored landmark for nearly one hundred years. The landscape was familiar to the man driving and the girl beside him. Catherine Moreland and Robert Turner were neighbours. Robert, his sisters and parents lived on a large property settled by his great-grandfather. Catherine's grandfather had started grazing sheep in the same district. Catherine and Robert had known each other since childhood.

Mollie Aitken, Catherine's girlfriend, sat in the back seat looking at countryside unfamiliar to her, as the two old friends in front chatted about local news and the big party that night for Catherine's twenty-first birthday. For Mollie it'd been a bit of a shock flying from Sydney into the rural district where there seemed to be nothing but paddocks, hills and a river. From the twin-engined, propellered plane, towns below looked to be small and few and far between. After living in trendy, inner city suburbs these open spaces made her feel very isolated.

Mollie had heard stories about bush bashes and how fantastic the parties were, so she'd been excited to be asked to Catherine's twenty-first. Catherine had told her that there were lots of single boys in the district but now, having seen where they lived, Mollie knew she could never survive so far away from shops, restaurants, bars and entertainment. But she was looking forward to the weekend house party, especially tonight's big celebration.

The Peel Airport was basic – a dressed-up shed really – and Mollie had been amused to walk outside to collect her bag from a trolley wheeled from the plane to the side of the terminal.

The drive seemed interminable although Rob and Catherine kept her entertained, describing some of the people coming to the party and giving sketchy, sometimes lurid, details of previous escapades at parties and balls over the years.

Mollie had met Catherine during a holiday on the Great Barrier Reef and they had kept in touch. On visits to Sydney Catherine stayed with Mollie. Now it was Catherine's turn to host her. Mollie had never been to a rural property in north-western New South Wales or anywhere else in the countryside before this visit. She knew that this property had been part of Catherine's grandfather's much larger holding. Over the years it had been broken up and had gone from raising sheep to become a smaller property where Catherine's father Keith raised stud Murray Grey cattle. He might be a solicitor working in Peel, the nearby regional town, but these cattle were his passion.

Mollie had been told that while other friends were

coming from Sydney and Brisbane for Catherine's twenty-first, the majority of the guests would be neighbours and friends from school days.

Mollie was relieved when Catherine pointed out the enormous mailbox with *Heatherbrae* painted on its side and announced that they'd arrived as they turned into a narrow dusty road. Yet they continued to drive for what seemed ages past fences and dusty paddocks and the occasional head of Keith Moreland's prized cattle.

Rob glanced in the rear-vision mirror noting a truck following them, keeping well clear of the plume of orange dust kicked up by the station wagon.

'So how many are coming tonight?' asked Rob. 'Seems like everyone and their dog from the district.'

'Well, it is Cathy's twenty-first,' Mollie reminded him. 'And she's an only child.'

'It's looking like a B and S ball without the ball,' grinned Catherine. 'I have a sinking feeling the two hundred people I asked are all going to turn up.'

'What's B and S?' asked Mollie.

'Bachelors and Spinsters . . . meaning anyone who's single and under thirty generally.'

'Oh, I see. Sounds a bit old fashioned, who calls themself a spinster in 1971?'

'It's a term,' said Catherine. 'I'm glad it's not going to rain,' she added, looking at the cloudless blue sky.

'We could do with some follow-up rain,' sighed Rob.

'Spoken like a true farmer,' laughed Catherine.

Mollie leant forward as the house came into view. Several vehicles, muddy and dusty, were already parked close to the big shed behind the gracious white homestead.

The house was an old building, with French doors opening onto the long latticed and colonnaded verandah. A sleep-out with striped canvas blinds ran along one side and the sandstone steps from the verandah led to a length of well watered lawn and thick flowering shrubbery. The house had an air of permanence, of solid respectability, of having survived hard seasons, a place where children were born, raised and played. An extension built in the 1960s blended in. The fresh white paint and startling bright aqua pool announced that, although this was a classic building, it was also a modern home.

They got out of the station wagon and Rob reached for Mollie's bag as Rosemary, Catherine's mother, came to greet them.

'Plane must have been on time. Thanks for doing the airport run, Rob. All our vehicles are running about the countryside either working or on party business.'

'No trouble at all, Mrs Moreland.'

'And welcome to you, Mollie. I suppose you're hanging out for a cup of tea?' She led the way into the house followed by Robert and Catherine.

'I certainly wouldn't say no,' sighed Mollie. 'Oh, it's so nice and cool in here.'

'It's the thick walls, Dad says it's like a wine cellar, constant temperature. Even in winter,' said Catherine. 'My grandfather built the house of mud bricks.'

'I've put you in the little spare room at the back of the house.' Rosemary headed down the cool dark hallway of polished wood where family photographs were hung next to photos of prize-winning bulls and horses.

'I suppose the early arrivals are getting stuck into the beer,' said Rob with some longing.

'Probably. But I've given those fellows a few jobs to do, so I hope they get them finished before getting onto the grog,' said Rosemary. 'Make yourself at home, Rob, there's a bed or two left in the sleep-out.'

'I'm okay. I have my swag, thanks, Mrs Moreland. At least the weather is holding.'

'It's going to be a lovely night. Perfect for you, Catherine.'

4

Rob swung Mollie's bag onto the bed and grinned at the girls. 'There you go. I'll be off then and see if there's anything I can do out where they're setting up.'

Catherine laughed. 'You do that. See you later. Thanks again for the ride.' As she helped Mollie hang up her dresses she whispered, 'He'll be straight over to the boys at the keg.'

'What time does it all start?' asked Mollie.

'Seems like it already has,' said Rosemary. 'I'll leave you girls to it. Shout if you need anything, Mollie, dear.'

'Rob is nice, I see what you mean about country boys – very polite. Good looking too. Have you and Rob, ever, you know, been boyfriend girlfriend?' asked Mollie, keen to sort out which boys might be available. She intended to make the most of her long weekend in the country.

'Heavens, no!' exclaimed Catherine. 'He's like a brother. We had to sit in kindergarten classes together.'

'Where was the kindergarten?' wondered Mollie. 'It must have been a long trip.'

'Oh Mum ran it here at *Heatherbrae*, there were quite a few of us. There was always a family or two with kids. Later we went into Peel on a bus but Rob went to boarding school in Sydney. Now, let's get some tea and I'll show you around.'

'What room is the party in? Or is it on the verandah?' Mollie hadn't seen anywhere that could hold a large group.

Catherine burst out laughing. 'It's down in the paddock . . . as far away from the house as possible. The oldies stay up here. We'll come up here later in the evening for the official toast and to cut the cake.'

'A paddock! But I brought a new lace outfit and high heels!'

'Don't worry, everyone dresses up. Like I told you, these parties can last till sunrise! Or until the booze runs out. We can make as much noise as we want to – the nearest neighbours are miles away and they are all here anyway! I've got a few chores to do. I'm going to help Dad move our horses further away so the party doesn't upset them. Want to come?'

'I'm not very horsey,' said Mollie. 'I might have a bit of a rest and freshen up. Remember, I left home very early this morning!'

Catherine rode beside her father as they led a young horse behind them. The horses walked slowly side by side allowing Catherine and her father to talk.

'Thanks for throwing the party, Dad.'

'Got to celebrate the big occasion. Hope everyone has a good time. Not too good a time,' he added. 'I know some of the boys can drink a dam dry.'

'They'll be okay, Dad. At least everyone is staying the night. Glad it's not raining, though we could've moved it to the shed I guess.'

'Yeah, like we did for my fiftieth.' Keith Moreland was quiet for a moment, then asked, 'So, anyone special here? In the man department?'

'You know better than that, Dad. They're all just friends. Some are engaged, a couple married, I've known most of them since I was little.'

'Doesn't mean you can't fall in love with them. It's the best way, starting out as friends first, knowing their family background, liking the same things. Country people tend to marry country people. It's a different way of life to city people. And as for these new flower-power hippie types, well, I'm blowed if I know what they're on about. Or where they fit in.'

Catherine chuckled. 'None of them round these parts, Dad.'

They rode in silence for a few more moments, but Keith persisted probing into his daughter's love life. 'So no-one special, eh? I thought that Brian Grimshaw was a bit keen on you.'

'Oh, we had a few dates. Nothing serious. Anyway he's brought up a girl from Sydney for tonight's party.'

'And your friend Mollie, she got her eye on some of our bush boys?'

'If she does it will only be for the short term. There's no way she'd live out here.'

'And you? What are you going to do with your life, eh, love? Twenty-one is the time to think about these things.'

'I don't know, Dad. I can't think of living anywhere but here. I had a couple of months in Sydney and that was enough for me.'

They busied themselves getting the horses into a small paddock, unsaddled them and threw the gear into the farm ute that Keith had earlier left by the fence. Catherine was thinking about what her father had said. Just where would she end up? Mollie had once said to her that she had to get off the property or she'd end up an old maid looking after her ageing parents. But this threat didn't worry Catherine as she felt a deep attachment to her home and the country around it. The beauty of the landscape, its familiarity, was close to her heart. It was a lifestyle she appreciated. She couldn't imagine living in a city, in suburbia. While she still worked in her father's office in Peel, she knew she had the freedom to move on or do something else any time she wanted. She was amused by her parents' interest in her love life but, unlike her girlfriends, she wasn't worried that she didn't have a regular boyfriend or any immediate prospects of settling down.

She was happy with life the way it was.

*

In the far paddock, surrounded by vehicles, long trestle tables and chairs were placed near an old bathtub filled with drinks cooling in ice under wet hessian bags. Close by was a keg of beer and a newly erected bush barbecue. A bonfire was ready to light even though the weather was warm, for by evening it would provide welcome light.

Closer to the homestead a guesthouse that had been the shearers' quarters in Catherine's grandfather's day had been taken over by a group of girls who were early arrivals. There was an understood demarcation between the adults, who would be staying in the house, and the young people in the paddock, so that the groups didn't encroach on each other.

After the party people would crash in swags on the ground or sleep in their cars. Many would be so drunk that they'd sleep anywhere and not notice any discomfort.

Perched on bales of hay, on chairs and benches and on blankets on the patchy grass, Catherine's friends talked and laughed, catching up with news and acquaintances they hadn't seen in months. Two couples had a toddler and a baby, another girl was showing off her engagement ring. No-one was older than twenty-four and most had known each other forever.

At the main house the women who were friends of the Morelands helped Rosemary in the kitchen. The men had taken over the verandah, perched on the railing under the wisteria vine that in spring dripped bunches of lavender blooms. Other men sat in the old cane verandah chairs and on the front steps, beers in hand, discussing cattle prices, the economy, Prime Minister Billy McMahon, rain and rabbits.

Everyone was dressed up – ties and jackets, highly polished good boots for the men, the young women choosing mini skirts or halter-neck patio dresses, or colourful palazzo pyjamas. Most of the mothers had opted for maxi skirts, which they topped with frilled or satin blouses. Rosemary had wanted to hire some young people who worked in the pub in town to help serve drinks at the house party, but Keith told her it wasn't necessary. 'And those kids don't need a bartender either. They'll look after themselves.'

Down in the paddock, there was some dancing, with a lot of stumbling on the roughly cleared ground, but it was mostly drinking, talking and much laughter. Catherine was hugged, kissed and teased by her friends. Occasionally she got into intense conversations she suspected wouldn't be recalled in the morning. But mostly she found herself looking around at the gathering as if just an observer. The firelight and lanterns flickered light and shadows across familiar faces. There was an atmosphere of friendship, nearly everybody knew and liked everybody else. Sometimes Catherine thought it was like being part of a clan.

Keith came into the kitchen and found his wife supervising trays of hot sausage rolls, meatballs and meat pies. 'I'd better do the honours and get the young people up here for the birthday toast.'

'Well, since you're doing the speech,' she answered, 'I'll get the camera.'

With everybody gathered and overflowing from the lounge room onto the screened verandah, Keith stepped forward and raised his voice.

'Ladies and gentleman . . . your attention. Please charge your glasses.'

As bottles of champagne were passed and glasses topped up, Rosemary studied their only child and realised that Catherine really was grown up. She'd always been such a tomboy around the farm and she never looked her age. But now with carefully applied make-up, her hair teased and piled on top of her head and high-heeled sandals peeping below her silky green and purple Pucci print palazzo outfit, she looked elegant and sophisticated, a change from her usual outdoorsy-look of windswept burnished brown curls. Her skin was creamy, with a dusting of freckles, her hazel-green eyes clear and wide. Catherine's upturned mouth always seemed to be smiling and while not tall, she was shapely, slim and sporty fit.

'She looks lovely. Is there a special boy around tonight?' asked Glenys, Rosemary's old school friend.

'A couple I think,' whispered Rosemary.

'She needs a serious boyfriend. Half her friends are engaged or married,' said Glenys. 'But she deserves someone very special.'

Rosemary put her finger to her lips as Keith continued.

'Thank you all for coming tonight to celebrate our Catherine's coming of age. I hope you agree with me how beautiful she looks and we all know what a beautiful person she is as well.'

There was a hearty cheer at this and Catherine blushed.

'It's difficult for a father to admit that his daughter is now a grown woman and setting out in the world to make her own life.' Keith gave Catherine a fond smile. 'Because you'll always be our little girl. But in addition to this great party – thanks to her mother, Rosemary, her team of helpers and friends – I'd like to give Catherine a little extra gift.' He drew an envelope from his pocket and smiled at his daughter. 'You give us more joy than you'll ever know, Catherine, and while I know you'll eventually choose some lucky boy . . .'

More comments greeted this remark with a few calls for attention from a couple of lads sporting long sideburns.

'Before you settle down in the good old district of Russell Plains, your mother and I would like you to see a bit more of the world – just to confirm we live in the best damn country in the universe.'

Another loud cheer greeted this comment.

'And so here is a ticket to London – return of course! But with a bit of a stopover holiday in Hawaii when you choose to come back. Enjoy it, sweetheart.' He leant down to kiss Catherine as she took the envelope from her father to big applause.

Rosemary had given Rob her camera to take pictures and Rob now eased to one side to get a better angle of Catherine.

'Come on, love, say a few words.' Keith helped Catherine onto a chair so everyone could see and hear her.

Catherine gazed out at her friends and family, their smiling faces lit by the moonlight and reflections from the strings of coloured lights strung around the roof outside and she felt a rush of gratitude and love for the life she had.

'Thank you all so much for being here to share this evening. Thank you, Mum and Dad, for being . . . just so great. London . . .' She fingered the envelope. 'I've always wanted to travel, but tonight, I have to agree with Dad, we are lucky to be here. We live in such a peaceful and beautiful place. With good neighbours, good friends . . . it's exciting to think about seeing the world, but it's always going to be good to come home. I hope you're all having a great night – I am!' She raised her arms and everyone applauded as she hugged her parents.

Rob circled the crowd and edged outside to cut through the kitchen.

'Mum, I don't know what to say. This is too much,' said Catherine to her mother.

'Nonsense, go now, before you settle down. Travelling isn't the same with kids and a husband. Have fun.' She raised an eyebrow. 'Is Brian Grimshaw here?'

11

'Yeah, he's here,' said Catherine, knowing her mother hoped their friendship would bloom into an engagement. 'He's here with friends.' She didn't add that her ex-boyfriend had brought along a new girl he'd met at the picnic races a few weeks back.

Catherine was very glad she had something to look forward to and plans to make. She'd saved a bit of money working in her father's office, and now with the plane tickets she knew she'd be leaving the district for a few months.

As she embraced her mother's friend, Glenys, there was a sudden shout from outside.

'Christ, someone's in the pool!' It was Rob's voice.

Catherine grinned at her mother. They'd had a bet someone would jump in the pool at some stage of the night.

But Rob's shouting was urgent and people were rushing to the patio.

As Catherine pushed through the crowd she knew something was wrong by the sudden change in atmosphere and the alarmed shouts calling for Doctor Haybourne. In the bright blue floodlit pool she saw Rob, dripping wet, dragging a young man from the water. He was fully clothed and seemed to be unconscious.

Rob knelt over him, trying to resuscitate him. Her father was kneeling beside him. An older man pushed through and hurried to join them.

'Thank God, the doc is here,' said a guest.

As Doctor Haybourne leant over the young man, Rob turned the youth's head, and he began to cough and splutter.

'C'mon, Dave, spew it up,' said Rob. 'He's okay, he's coming to. How is he, Doc?'

They helped the young man sit up. 'Let me check him, seems you got to him in time, Rob. You're a very lucky young man, I'd say,' he said to the dazed boy. Clearly he had drunk too much and had either passed out or tripped and fallen into the pool. 'Rob's quick actions got you out before any damage was done.'

'You booze too much, Davo,' said Rob cheerfully.

Keith headed back into the house. 'Righto, show's over. Doc Haybourne has everything under control. Everyone inside, it's all okay.' In an aside to Rosemary he muttered, 'Some of these boys drink themselves into oblivion. No bloody control.' He raised his voice and said brightly, 'Now where were we?'

'Are we cutting the cake?' asked Rosemary.

'Good idea, love. Okay, everyone, cake time, gather round.' Keith tried to revive the jovial atmosphere as people were talking among themselves.

Rosemary put the large cake lit with twenty-one candles on the table. 'Over here, everyone. I hope there's enough to go round. Blow out the candles and make a wish, darling,' she said, holding her daughter's hand.

Now that the drama was over, Catherine squeezed her eyes shut and blew the candles out in a rush, but to her surprise she couldn't think of a wish. It seemed to her that she had all she wanted in the world at this very moment.

Her father handed her a silver knife to cut the cake as the guests roared out the words of 'Happy Birthday'.

Catherine sought Rob out after he'd dried himself and borrowed some clothes from her father.

'Thanks, Rob. That could have been an awful accident.'

'Just lucky I was trying to get to the front to get a good shot. Thought it'd be quicker to go round the outside than trying to squeeze through the mob inside. Then I spotted him. Gave me a shock when I saw him face down, thought he was a goner.'

'Thanks again. Hope you haven't suffered any damage. Is your watch waterproof?'

'Hope so.'

Rob's date rushed up and handed him a glass of beer. 'Here you go. Wasn't he wonderful?' she gushed to Catherine. 'Such a shame it nearly ruined your party.'

'Aw, cut it out, Barb, it was no big drama.'

'He would've drowned if you hadn't been there,' she exclaimed.

'Yes, well, anyone would've done the same thing. Lucky I was on the spot, so to speak. Cheers, Catherine. It's a great party,' he said cheerfully.

'Thanks, Rob. Enjoy yourselves.'

In the early hours of the morning as a cool breeze brought relief to those in swags and sleeping bags under the night sky, Catherine walked softly outside. Soon her parents and their friends would be in the kitchen brewing tea, starting breakfast. The hair-of-the-dog party would see the hungover young people hitting the bloody marys and beer again, until a big barbecue helped sober them up so they could start the long trek back to their properties.

Dawn wasn't far off and she could smell the earth under its layer of fine dew. A horse whinnied and the distant ridge of hills was a smudge against the lightening sky. This was home, everything familiar for as long as she could remember. She'd reached a milestone and she filed away these moments to take with her into the next stage of her life.

Catherine thought she'd never get used to the cold. And the drizzling rain of London never seemed to make its mind up to stop. She wished it would just get it over and done with and pour down in a weighty blanket of water.

She missed the wild storms at home that swept across the paddocks in torrential streaming rain.

She picked her way between puddles, holding her coat to her throat and clutching her umbrella as she bumped into pedestrians with the same intent. It was grey, night closing in, yet it was still early afternoon. Lights were on in shops and pubs, car headlights shone on the wet pavement and roads. At the end of Aldwych she turned into The Strand and entered the grey stone building where the Australian flag flapped damply above the sign – Australia House.

With her name ticked off the list at the main desk she was directed to the small reception room where a drinks party hosted by Brian Lord, the Australian cultural attaché, was underway. He was an old school friend of her father's and had sent her an invitation when he knew she was staying in London. Shyly Catherine edged into the room with its dark panelling and sombre leather furniture. People were talking quietly in subdued groups. She glanced at the bright photographs of Australian beaches and landscapes and thought they looked almost garish compared to the grey afternoon outside.

A waiter proffered a tray of drinks – sherry, beer, lemonade or wine. She took a glass of wine and stood at the fringe of people around the attaché, who quickly stepped aside and drew her into the group. She introduced herself and he greeted her warmly.

'Good to see you, Catherine, how's your dad? Had any rain up your way?'

'He sends his regards and as usual they're hoping for follow-up rain. Thank you for inviting me.'

'Pleasure. Hope you're enjoying Londontown. Working holiday?'

'Bit of both. I'm planning to go to the continent soon.'

'Wonderful. Now, let's see, do you know anyone here?

A few expats and a couple of Peace Corps volunteers from the US. Few military bods. Mainly people involved in the arts here and from home.' He gestured at the young people around him. 'These fine fellows are from a theatre based in Melbourne and are currently touring the provinces.'

They smiled and nodded and Catherine glanced at their name tags but didn't recognise any names.

'We host these little events every few months,' continued the attaché. 'Now if you'll excuse me . . .' He headed to another group leaving Catherine with the actors.

Catherine made small talk, where are you from, how long are you here for, what is the play you're doing – though she had to confess she'd never seen it. 'I live in the country, it's hard to get to the theatre.'

A man appeared beside her. 'I hope you're making the most of your time here, the theatre is wonderful.'

He had an American accent and was wearing a smart US naval uniform. He smoothly joined their group, extending his hand. 'Hello, I'm Lieutenant Bradley Connor, pleased to meet you.'

Catherine was last to shake his hand and introduce herself.

'So you're not an actor? You're a country girl, you said. How long are you staying in London?' he asked.

'Oh, it's flexible. I'm staying in a flat with friends and we all come and go. I'm trying to see as much as possible. What about you? Holiday or working?' asked Catherine.

'I'm trying to do a bit of both. Although I'm with the US navy, I have a desk job at the consulate at present. What about you? What are you doing here?' asked Bradley.

'Mr Lord went to school with my father. I doubt they've seen each other in years and years but, you know, the old school tie and all that.'

'Oh, I think I understand what you mean.' He looked around. 'This is a bit dull. Would you like to go for a decent drink and a bite to eat nearby? There're some great pubs around here.'

Catherine only hesitated for an instant. Bradley seemed charming, was very handsome, and she had nothing else planned. 'I'd love to. Where'd you have in mind?'

'The Cheshire Cheese in Fleet Street. It's always full of interesting characters. Journalists and the like.'

Catherine had a terrific evening. After the pub, Bradley took her to a small Italian restaurant and they talked for hours over a bottle of red wine. She'd told him about living on a property, small by Australian standards, and described her lifestyle. He was from California, had a brother and a sister at college and had joined the navy not just to follow in his father's footsteps, but also because he loved to travel.

Bradley dropped her off in a taxi after they'd exchanged phone numbers. Catherine bounced into the flat she was sharing to tell her flatmates about her great time only to find the other girls were out. The next morning she described her evening and the girls agreed that it sounded as though Catherine had the highest score in the date department for that week.

Her date rating went through the roof when the following Friday evening Bradley called at the flat in South Kensington to take her to dinner and gave her a posy of tiny pink rosebuds. Catherine introduced him to her flatmates, who told her later that he looked like a movie star.

And so Friday night dinner became a regular event and soon Saturday night as well. Bradley played tennis with fellow officers on Sundays and during the week his schedule was busy. Catherine could well imagine Bradley would be an attractive asset at the many events the consulate participated in and hosted.

While she enjoyed Bradley's company, she didn't want to limit her own experiences in swinging London. Bradley, she found, didn't like the disco scene, but they both enjoyed walking the streets of London exploring its nooks and crannies.

She planned trips to Paris, Spain and Greece. Bradley listened, offered advice and suggestions and gave her the impression that he'd be waiting and available in London when she returned.

'Have you slept with him?' asked Donna, one of the girls in the flat Catherine shared.

'No! Of course not. I mean, he's not like that.'

'What's wrong with him? He's so attractive.'

Catherine smiled. 'Yes, he is. But he's so . . . polite, gentle . . . considerate.'

'Conservative, you mean,' said Donna. 'I'd be seducing him if I were you.'

'And have him think I'm cheap? I'd like him to be around for a bit.'

'Aw, come on, Catherine. Make the most of it. You're not going to land this man on a permanent basis.'

'Why do you say that?' asked Catherine huffily.

'No offence, sweetie, but he's an officer in the US navy and going places. Up the ladder. He's probably got a girl back in California. He's too . . . different. Not our sort of fellow. Not the sort you settle down with. Can you imagine him in Peel?'

'And you can't imagine me in California?' retorted Catherine.

'Come on, Catherine, men like Bradley . . . well, they're different from us. And why do you always call him Bradley? What's wrong with Brad?'

'Well,' said Catherine, 'I don't think he likes his name shortened. He's not a Brad sort of person.'

'Okay then, just enjoy yourself. He's generous, takes

you nice places. Get on the pill, have a good time. Make the most of it while you can, I say,' finished Donna.

Catherine just smiled and thought that although Donna's comments were well meant, they contained a few sour grapes, but they challenged her. Bradley hadn't given any indication of wanting to take her to bed, but he kissed her quite nicely and he'd never mentioned another girl back home. He was always so decent and thoughtful, she felt sure he would have mentioned any other girl so as not to lead her on.

Catherine couldn't help comparing him to some of the boys back home. Bradley was so sophisticated, he'd certainly never get drunk. He wouldn't fall in a pool, or make a fool of himself. He'd once told her how naval officers were always on show, representing the navy, in or out of uniform. He didn't often talk about his work, instead they talked about the world in general, things that interested them, the shows, films and theatre that they saw in London. And they shared stories of their families and growing up.

'So what are you going to do in Paris?' Bradley asked over dinner two nights later. 'Have you friends there? Is anyone going with you?'

'No. I thought I'd strike out on my own. I've been surrounded by friends here. I have a very detailed list of places to go and see, things to do. I'm looking forward to it.'

'To Paris? Or being on your own?' he asked.

'Why Paris, of course,' she laughed.

He took a mouthful of food. 'It doesn't seem right – going to Paris on your own. Unless of course you're looking for a romantic interlude . . .'

'With a stranger? I don't think so.'

'What about me?'

Catherine blinked. 'You? You mean, come to Paris with me?'

'I've never been. I didn't like the idea of seeing the city of lights on my own. Perhaps we could . . . well, do it together. I'll find my own pension or something. Where are you staying by the way?' When Catherine didn't answer straight away, he hastily added, 'That's only if you'd like some company. Purely platonic of course.'

'Of course,' she smiled. 'I think it's a great idea.'

'You do? Fantastic.' He sounded relieved. 'I hope you don't have the wrong idea or anything.'

'Of course not. But I insist we split expenses. Meals and travel and so on.'

He went to protest, but then nodded. 'Agreed. That's very fair. And it's only for a week. I'll have to see if I can get leave.'

The next day he phoned her to say he couldn't get time off. 'I'm very disappointed.'

'Me too,' said Catherine and realised how much she'd been looking forward to their trip together. Bradley was such good company.

She adored Paris but occasionally as she sat in a café watching the crowds she wished Bradley was with her. She wished she could talk to him and share her feelings and experiences of the beautiful city. She dutifully worked her way through her list of must-see places, but occasionally she just followed a boulevard, wandered through a park or along the Seine to see where she ended up.

On her way to join the queues at the Louvre, Catherine passed a small gallery that was holding a photographic exhibition. Intrigued by the poster and the photograph on display she decided to go in and look around.

She was riveted by the photographs – mostly black and white images of people, places and streets scenes in a grainy, gritty Paris she'd never imagined. A bed on a floor with rumpled white sheets beneath a curtainless window that framed a chimney stack. A beautiful naked Indian woman in an old white claw-foot bath. A long-haired man in a doorway in a shaggy sheepskin jacket smoking a joint. Two girls in beads and kaftans behind a stall selling knick-knacks, old lace and books. A wet cobblestone street with a hunched figure in a bulky coat beneath a large black umbrella.

The exhibition was titled *A Slice of Life* and it made her think of the contrast with her own life – clean, comfortable, safe. As she continued on her walk she filed away the idea that maybe one day she'd pick up something more than her instamatic camera and document her home, its town, landscape and people.

Back at the flat in London, there was an envelope on her bed. She didn't recognise the writing, and there was no stamp. It was from Bradley.

> *Dear Catherine,*
> *Terrible news! I've had to leave London. Been transferred to Pearl Harbor in Hawaii as an urgent replacement for an officer. It's a far more interesting assignment than London and I'll get back to the sunshine which appeals! However I am so very disappointed to miss seeing you to say goodbye. Or au revoir. I hope you had a wonderful time in Paris. You said you had a ticket home via Honolulu . . . so I hope you'll let me know and plan to stop over as I would very much like to see you again. If I may, I'll call you. My contact address is below. I haven't a home phone as I'm in quarters.*
> *Warmest wishes,*
> *Bradley*

'Well, that's that then,' said Donna after Catherine showed the girls the letter.

'Why do you say that? I'll definitely look him up in Honolulu,' said Catherine.

'A fling maybe. Listen, don't hold your breath over that one. We met some groovy blokes who're in a band. Come with us to the pub tonight. They're playing in the back room and they're terrific. We can all hang out with them afterwards.'

'I'm tired. Maybe some other time.'

'Yeah, righto.' Donna left Catherine and whispered to the other two girls, 'Let her get over the Yank sailor.'

'American officer,' Catherine called out before shutting her door. Loudly.

She lay on her bed and fingered the blue notepaper with Bradley's curling, tidy handwriting. She'd go to Greece and Spain, she'd go to the Lake District as she'd planned, and go to Hawaii on the way home. She was not going to mope about the handsome American. Anyway, two boys from home were due in London and she'd promised to show them around. One of them was Dave who'd fallen in the pool at her party. She hoped he wouldn't get drunk, or fight, or fall over in her company. But she was glad to be seeing someone from home.

Catherine sent Bradley a polite note telling him a little of her trip to Paris, that she was sorry she missed saying goodbye, she wished him well and said she might just stop into Honolulu on her way back to Australia in several months time.

She then booked her flight to Hawaii just to be sure. But she didn't tell anyone. Even if Bradley wasn't there, her parents had given her a week in a nice hotel as part of her twenty-first birthday trip.

Knowing sunny Hawaii was booked made the greyness of London more bearable.

2

THE AIR WAS PUNGENT. Sweet. A tradewind lifted the damp curls on Catherine's neck. The sun was warm. In the background she heard Hawaiian steel guitars playing. Her body was relaxing after the long flight. The snowy stopover in New York had been tiring and the weather had been freezing. Here in Honolulu the bright sunlight, the colourful clothes, the flowers, made her feel the plane had landed on a different planet. These initial sensations would stay with her the rest of her life.

In the airport terminal everyone was smiling, welcoming, greeting people with 'Aloha, aloha'. Walking through the exit Catherine saw waving palms outside the glass doors and a blur of faces.

And there was Bradley, just as he'd promised.

In the last few months, Bradley had surprised Catherine

with letters and occasional phone calls and this had strengthened the bond between them. The distance had given them time to develop a different relationship where they'd exchanged thoughts and feelings on all kinds of subjects, the kind of things that might be difficult to say face to face. And without the physical closeness there wasn't any pressure to move their friendship to an intimate level.

Strangely, she felt she knew Bradley better because of this space between them, rather than if he'd been by her side. He wrote to her about his new job, telling her that he might be based in Pearl Harbor for the next few years or so. He described his commanding officer and his organising wife. In his letters Bradley summed up his colleagues and the people he met in a few pithy sentences that were often quite hilarious. Catherine really enjoyed his sense of humour, which she hadn't appreciated in the short time they'd known each other in London.

They had arranged to meet on her way back to Australia so that he could show her round Honolulu and take her to dinner and a show. Catherine's father had insisted on treating her to a final fling before she came home and 'got back to work', so here she was booked into an old but stylish hotel on Waikiki Beach.

Catherine walked towards Bradley and found she was shaking at the sight of him. He stood out from the crowd not only because he was so tall, but he also looked handsome in his crisp white naval uniform. His arms showing from under the short sleeves of his shirt were tanned and he held his peaked officer's cap under one arm while he carried a lei made of perfumed creamy flowers. He was smiling broadly and Catherine couldn't help noticing the second glances he got from other women.

'Hello, hello!' He embraced Catherine, kissed her cheek, took her luggage and put it down beside them as he lifted the lei over her head. 'Local custom.' He smiled and kissed her lightly on the lips.

She lifted the lei and inhaled deeply. 'How gorgeous. Are they frangipani?'

'Plumeria. Slightly different. Is this all your luggage? I'm parked out the front. You must be exhausted. Such a long flight.'

As they drove to the Moana Hotel they fell into easy conversation, picking up where they'd left off in their last phone call. She felt as if she'd known him for years. Bradley pulled up under the Corinthian columns of the portico at the hotel entrance as a smiling bellboy opened the car door and took her hand luggage.

'I'll see if I can park out on Kalakaua Avenue,' called Bradley as Catherine followed the young Hawaiian into the lobby.

As she looked about her, she realised that the hotel had gone through many stages – the old wood panelling, the touches of art deco, some fifties modernisation and the Italianate entrance made it an odd mixture, but the breezy open plan looking out to a courtyard flanked by wide verandahs was definitely tropical.

'First order of the day – a drink under the banyan tree,' said Bradley as she signed the registration card.

'I don't know what time of night or day it is,' laughed Catherine.

'A fresh pineapple juice, with a splash of coconut milk,' suggested Bradley. 'Or a coffee?'

'Juice sounds wonderful, thanks. Wow!' Catherine gasped as they came to the steps leading to the courtyard flanked by the polished wood floor verandahs. The hotel was at the edge of the beach and the sand was swept and lined with deck chairs where holiday makers lounged. Beyond them glittered the blue ocean where long low breakers lazily rolled towards the shore. Further along the beach jutted the unmistakable outline of Diamond Head. In the centre of the courtyard was a magnificent banyan tree, its branches shading several tables and chairs.

'The tree's very historic. Been here since 1904, planted a few years after the hotel opened.' Bradley drew out a chair. 'Great spot for an evening cocktail.'

'I don't think I'll move from here the whole week of my stay,' sighed Catherine.

Bradley had to work the next day so Catherine used the time to explore a little on her own, though all she did was walk along the beach and browse in the shops on Kalakaua Avenue. She preferred to sit in the shade of the banyan tree in the hotel courtyard watching the people on the sands of Waikiki. This was such a long way from Peel and from London. It all felt so exotic and romantic. The locals stood out. Fit and tanned wearing colourful – if sometimes sun-faded – casual clothes. She decided she had to buy a beach sarong. She noticed the women hotel staff, generally older and all smiling and friendly, wore long full and loose muu-muus that fell from a yoke at the top. Most of the women were plump but looked cool and comfortable in the flowered print dresses.

When Bradley arrived that evening to take her to dinner, she was wearing flowers from the lei he had given her in her hair.

'Glad to see you're getting into the aloha spirit,' he said, giving her a light kiss.

'I went shopping in that International Marketplace but got utterly confused with all the different Hawaiian prints.' She pointed to a woman in a bright muu-muu. 'Is that the traditional dress?'

'Now it is. They were originally introduced by the missionaries to cover up all that decadent naked flesh. No more grass skirts and bare breasts.'

They sat on the terrace at the Ilikai Hotel which was

further down the avenue and watched the sunset ceremony of lighting the tiki torches as an Hawaiian warrior blew a large conch shell to summon the men and women dancers to gather on the outdoor terrace. Musicians appeared and as the sky glowed red and orange and the sun sank below the horizon the dancers performed popular hulas.

'It's a bit hokey, but it's kind of nice,' said Bradley.

'I like it. Where else are tourists going to see this kind of thing?' said Catherine.

'Oh, lots of touristy places do cultural shows. One drink and we'll head back to Waikiki for dinner and we'll see some wonderful classical dancing.'

'In the heart of Waikiki?' Catherine was hoping they'd head away from the tourist strip and go somewhere more local, though there was time for that she figured. It was nice of him to show her the glamorous side of the city. Waikiki was what everyone came to Honolulu to see.

Bradley took her to yet another famous old hotel – the Moonflower – explaining, 'There's a woman I want you to see, and it's a lovely setting. The hotel is named after a sweet-smelling flower that only blooms at night.'

They walked onto the terrace that faced the sea and settled at a table and Bradley ordered two mai tais. 'Also a tradition. Basically pineapple juice and rum.'

'This is gorgeous.' Catherine sighed as the ever present tradewind wafted across the terrace, still glowing in the remains of the sunset. The moon was rising as a band set up and a beautiful woman wearing a figure-hugging Hawaiian dress and draped in long flower leis walked between the tables, pausing to greet the scattering of people around the terrace and verandah of the restaurant.

'Who's that?' whispered Catherine. She was struck by the beauty of the Hawaiian girl and her interesting blend of features, tawny olive skin and dark rippling hair. 'Is she pure Hawaiian?'

'She's just called Kiann'e. I think she's pure Hawaiian. Wait till you see her dance.'

The dancer smiled at them and made her way to the raised dais in front of the band. She chatted to the musicians and then moved to the centre of the stage as they began to play 'Lovely Hula Hands'. In her bare feet Kiann'e began to sway, her hips circling, her arms lifted in a graceful curve, her eyes on her fingertips. She moved slowly, like an unfolding flower.

'Watch her hands, they tell the story,' said Bradley. 'I know it's all a bit old fashioned, but this is so popular.'

'I was thinking of those rattling grass skirts and shaking fast swinging hips,' said Catherine. 'This is exquisite. I suppose you have to be born to it to dance like that.'

'For sure. They learn as toddlers.' Bradley sipped his drink served in half a small pineapple decorated with a bright red cherry and paper umbrella.

Catherine was entranced by the dancing.

After the show they moved into the restaurant for dinner and Bradley talked about his work, living in Honolulu and how much he enjoyed it.

'What about a nightcap?' he suggested after their meal. 'Take in a couple of the old Hawaiian institutions – the tiki lounges.'

'Maybe just one bar or club will do tonight. And no more mai tais, they sneak up on you.'

She wondered where he was driving them as they wound down a lane past a cement plant and came to a lagoon, finally parking near a sign pointing to the Mariana Sailing Club.

Catherine glanced at the marina in the distance. 'Is this a club?'

'Yes, but people come here for the Hawaiian atmosphere. It's been run since the 1950s by this lady. She bought all kinds of memorabilia from some of the old establishments like Trader Vic, Don the Beachcomber, the Kon Tiki Room. Are you familiar with Exotica music? Tourists love it.'

'No. I only know the latest London groups.'

'This is the old music started by Martin Denny, Arthur Lyman, Les Baxter and it's a kind of Polynesian cultural mix of Hawaiian music, jazz, drums and sound effects like frogs and waterfalls. You might recognise it when you hear it.'

Catherine doubted it. This was another world and a long way from the country music back in Peel.

The lounge bar was strung with coloured lights, the ceiling and walls were of bamboo and large carved tiki gods scowled from the doorway. Coloured glass balls on ropes were strung around the room next to plastic palm trees and in one corner a small waterfall splashed into a miniature pond where coloured lights played across the water. A large artificial frog sat on a plastic lily pad. The waiters wore bright Hawaiian shirts and white shorts and the waitresses wore Hawaiian-print strapless dresses with the mini skirts showing lots of tanned legs.

'A lot of the staff here are from California,' said Bradley. 'The surf thing, you know.'

'You know a lot about Honolulu in a short time,' said Catherine.

He smiled. 'Ah, sailors. They find the hot spots pretty quickly so I get to hear about them. Not that I frequent some of the joints they recommend.'

They ordered drinks but when the music started conversation was difficult so they leaned close to talk and at one point, while Catherine was trying to explain how different London disco clubs were, Bradley moved closer and kissed her on the lips. A lingering kiss that made her tingle.

They danced to a slow song, Bradley didn't like fast dancing.

'My mother made me go to ballroom dancing classes.

I earned some money during college teaching ballroom. Assisting the lady teacher as her partner.' He pulled her tighter to him. 'I didn't want any of my fraternity brothers to know about that. They were on the football team. There, I've told you my darkest secret.'

Catherine laughed.

They danced through another song holding each other close, aware of the building sexual attraction between them. The music finished and he took her hand, leading her from the little dance floor.

'Another drink?'

'No, I'm ready to go if you don't mind. I'm still a bit jet lagged.'

He opened the car door for her at the hotel. It was late, no staff appeared. A low branch of a large plumeria tree bowed over them. He plucked one of the creamy sweet flowers and handed it to her.

'Put it on your pillow and you'll know you're in the tropics.'

Catherine drew a deep breath inhaling the scent of flowers, the soft breeze, the tang of salt. In the lull of music and voices they could hear the soft splash of waves lapping on the beach in front of the hotel. 'It's been wonderful. Thanks so much, Bradley.'

'It's been wonderful for me too.' He leant forward to kiss her goodnight but this time he wrapped his arms around her and kissed her with more passion than he'd ever shown before. Catherine curled her arms around his neck and returned his kiss. They pulled apart somewhat breathless. Bradley smiled and touched her cheek.

'Sleep well. See you after work tomorrow. If I can get away early there's somewhere I'd like to take you.'

'I'm in your hands. You're being very generous,' said Catherine.

'I wish I could spend every minute with you . . . while

you're here.' He took a step towards the car. 'We'll make the most of it, shall we?'

Catherine nodded and walked up the white stone steps into the hotel lobby knowing he was watching her. He waited until she was out of sight before pulling away from the portico.

The next morning Catherine caught a bus down to the Ala Moana shopping centre and lost herself among the stores – Liberty House, Sears and Shirokiya – as well as browsing among the proliferation of shops selling Hawaiiana looking for gifts to take home. She bought bottles of Hawaiian flower perfume and quilted potholders and cushion covers featuring brightly coloured flowers and palm trees, which she thought her mother would love. She wandered into a boutique called Carol and Mary and tried on dresses and bought a new swimsuit. As she was paying for it Kiann'e, the dancer from the Moonflower, came in and the woman in charge hurried to greet her. Kiann'e smiled at Catherine.

Catherine smiled back. 'Excuse me, but I saw you dancing last night and I thought you were just wonderful.'

'Thank you,' replied the beautiful young woman. 'Have you found something to buy here?'

Catherine held up her pink carry bag. 'A new swimsuit.'

'Terrific. They have lovely things in here,' said Kiann'e.

'Yes. I love the dresses you wear in your show. Do you buy them here?'

'Why, thank you. No, my aunty makes my holomuus. Based on the old style. I come in here to feel modern.'

Catherine laughed. 'Well at least you'll never go out of fashion.'

'I hope not. The dances I mean. We teach the little ones so it gets handed down.'

She had a lilting accent and Catherine thought she was the most beautiful woman she'd ever seen. She guessed Kiann'e was around her own age, perhaps a little older. With her smooth olive skin and classical looks it was hard to tell.

Kiann'e smiled her wide infectious smile. 'Enjoy your swimsuit. Enjoy Hawai'i.'

'Where are we going then?' she asked late that afternoon as Bradley drove past the multistorey Kaiser Hospital at the Ala Wai yacht harbour.

'I'd like you to see Pearl Harbor – the *Arizona* memorial,' he said quietly.

'Oh, the American battleship that was sunk. It got America into the war didn't it?' said Catherine.

'Certainly did. The whole Seventh Fleet was attacked. December 1941. I think this is a very special memorial. Being a naval man, it has a lot of meaning for me.'

'Of course.' It was obvious that Bradley loved the navy, as had his father and grandfather.

Catherine was silent as they parked near the visitors' centre where the tenders departed to take visitors out to the odd-shaped white memorial floating in the harbour.

It was late in the day and there were only two other couples boarding the tender. It was manned by smartly dressed naval personnel and cruised across the bay to the sunken remains of the USS *Arizona*.

The six visitors clambered onto the memorial and as they went through to the midsection one of the men took a bunch of flowers from his wife, dropped it into the water and saluted. Bradley stood to attention, and everyone fell silent. After a few moments Bradley took Catherine's hand and pointed out the remains of the sunken vessel below them.

'The memorial doesn't touch the ship below . . . it's where more than a thousand men are entombed,' said Bradley. 'If you look carefully, you can see oil from the *Arizona* still rising to the surface.'

Catherine shivered. The thought she was standing on the grave of those young men was so sad.

At the far end of the memorial, in the Shrine Room, they stood before the marble wall where the names of all those lost were carved. Everyone spoke in whispers.

Catherine glanced at the solemn-faced Bradley. 'Do you ever think about going to war?'

He thought for a moment then said, 'I think if you choose to serve your country, you accept whatever comes along.'

'Whether or not you agree with the reasons behind it?' she asked, thinking of the protest demonstrations against the Vietnam War she'd seen on television at home and in London.

'Like I said, you choose to serve. I believe in what our government is doing. The public doesn't always know what goes on behind the scenes.' He took her arm. 'Thanks for coming along. I thought it might give you a sense of the history that's here.'

'Yes. Thanks for bringing me.' The visit had given Catherine a sense of how important the navy was to Bradley. As the tender ferried them back to the visitors' centre, Bradley put his arm around her.

'Are you up for another Hawaiian institution?' he asked. 'Something romantic.'

'Of course. Where're we going?'

'It's a show – Don Ho at the Beachcomber Lounge. But I thought we'd have a cocktail under the banyan tree first. You can change into something else for the show as it doesn't start till later. Or you can go as you are of course. You look lovely whatever you wear.'

'I bought some things today including a dress, so I'd like to wear it tonight. That's thoughtful of you.' She was learning Bradley was thoughtful – and a planner.

They took their regular spot under the banyan tree and a waiter appeared and Bradley ordered a mai tai for Catherine and a Tom Collins for himself. She wondered what that was and would have preferred something other than the sweet and sneaky mai tai but she didn't want to hurt Bradley's feelings.

'And bring us a platter of pupus as well, please,' added Bradley.

Catherine lifted an eyebrow.

'Little snacks, Hawaiian hors d'oeuvres,' he explained.

They picked at the tasty food, Catherine had a second mai tai, which she sipped slowly as she was already feeling somewhat mellow from the first one and they talked and talked. She found Bradley immensely entertaining and interesting. Their conversation always flowed easily and fluently without her having to think of a subject to discuss or wonder what to say next.

Bradley glanced at his watch. 'Do you want to slip upstairs and change?' Catherine would have preferred to stay where they were as the sun had set and it was cool, the courtyard and beach almost deserted.

'Is your room okay?' asked Bradley as he pulled out her chair.

'Yes. It has a wonderful view of Diamond Head from the little balcony, or lanai rather. Why don't you come up? I'll only take a minute to change.'

Bradley grinned. 'Now that's something I like to hear. None of this fussing and primping and messing with hair-dos that takes hours.'

The room was neat, spartan almost, with dark wood, crisp white sheets, a mosquito net looped above the bed and a stiff arrangement of waxy red anthuriums with spiky green leaves was arranged on the coffee table. A bowl of plumeria sat on the bedside table. Catherine suddenly felt a little uncomfortable at the intimacy of the small space. Bradley didn't seem to notice and strolled onto the small lanai and looked at Diamond Head, a glimpse of Waikiki Beach and the lights from the hotels illuminating the sand.

'Won't be a minute.' Catherine scooped up her dress and sandals and shut the bathroom door. She slipped out of her clothes and took off her bra. The new dress was daring and backless. She brushed her hair and swept it up in a ponytail that she twisted into a knot, wisps curling around her face. She touched up her make-up, sprayed her new pikake perfume in a mist around her head, added some dangly earrings and slipped her feet into silver sandals.

Bradley was leaning on the lanai railing and straightened up as he heard Catherine behind him. He turned and stopped. 'Catherine, you look lovely, utterly gorgeous. I love the dress.'

She was pleased and twirled before him. 'Just trying to fit in with the locals.'

'You need a flower in your hair.' He took her hand and led her into the room and took one of the plumeria blooms from the bowl. He tucked it in her hair. 'There. Perfect.' He leaned forward and kissed her gently.

But his lips lingered and Catherine found she was winding her arms about him, clinging to him as their kisses became more passionate. They fell back on the bed, wrapped in each other's arms, desire and longing overwhelming them. Catherine kicked off her shoes and pulled at Bradley's shirt as he tugged at the straps of her dress. But as they clung together, naked in the soft light, Bradley pulled back, searching her face.

'I'm not so sure we should be doing this.'

'Why not? It's all right,' she murmured.

He was still hesitant, shy even, and let Catherine lead.

She felt powerful and it heightened her desire to feel she was in charge. Such a caring man, not wanting to push himself on her, but she ached to have him make love. She pulled him on top of her and Bradley surrendered.

They lay together, warm wet bodies side by side as they came back to reality.

Bradley nuzzled her neck. 'That was wonderful. I can't tell you how wonderful.'

'Mmm, yes, it was.' She smiled and ran her finger down his firm lean chest.

'I'm sorry if I've ruined your make-up, crushed your clothes.'

'Who cares! It was fun.' She laughed. She felt full of energy. 'Hey, I'm starving, can we still make that show?'

Bradley sat up and looked at his watch. 'Yes, the late one. It's only over the road. You still want to go?'

'If you do. Though I'm *very* happy to stay here,' she said giving him a cheeky look.

He laughed, swung his legs over the side of the bed and began to dress. 'I have the tickets. You shouldn't miss Don Ho.'

As they left the hotel Catherine felt different. She had the feeling the staff, the taxi drivers waiting out the front of the hotel, passers-by in the street, were giving them knowing glances. Bradley held her hand as they ran across the road.

Inside the lounge Catherine felt she was entering another world, but one with which she was becoming familiar. In the time she'd been in Honolulu Bradley had introduced her to cocktail lounges, piano bars, garden terraces, resort hotels and beachside cafés. Drinks, food, entertainment amidst stylised Hawaiiana with slick American overtones was so new, so different, from what she had known at home and in cold wet London. It was not hard to take. As they settled into a booth under starry lights where a candle flickered in pink glass surrounded by flowers, she asked Bradley if he'd lived like this before he came to Hawaii.

'Californians like their bars and nice eateries. My parents dine out every week at their club and try new places with their friends. My father retired early with ideas of dabbling in real estate but really my parents just enjoy themselves.'

'What about holidays? Where do they go?' Catherine was thinking of the camping trips she was used to where they piled into the car and headed along the river to a quiet spot to pitch a tent, or out into the hills where her father fished quiet streams or panned for gold. Their nights were spent talking around the campfire or the bush barbecue. Sometimes her cousins Peter and Suzanne were invited and the bush would ring with their laughter and excitement.

'Oh, my folks like Lake Tahoe. There's a lodge that's lovely in the winter, not that they ski or skate, we kids did though. And in the summer the lake was fun, but the water is really cold. My folks liked the casinos and the nightlife. Lots of big-name entertainers go to the casinos.'

'Sounds fun,' said Catherine politely. 'Our parents sound quite different.'

'Are you liking it here?' He leant over and took her hand, looking concerned.

'Of course! This is a dream. Fantastic. It's going to be hard going home to the humdrum.'

He squeezed her hand. 'I don't live like this normally, either. That's the magic of Hawaii. It's the ultimate romantic getaway,' said Bradley softly.

His words stung her. 'Is that what this is? How often do you have romantic getaways?'

'Oh, I didn't mean it like that. This is a first for me too,' he said quickly and earnestly. 'In every way.' He took both her hands in his. 'Can I kiss you?'

They leant across the small table and he kissed her

quickly but fiercely, trying to erase his words. They drew apart as the waiter put their drinks on the table.

'Catherine . . . these past few days, well, it seems like months . . . they've been very special. This is the first time I've really had someone to share Honolulu with and, well, it's just wonderful.'

Catherine didn't speak, but nodded, feeling rather lost for words. It had been a wonderful magical time. And their lovemaking had brought them closer together.

Bradley continued. 'Do you think you could stay on here a little longer? Change your booking?'

'Heavens, I have no idea. But, yes, what a fabulous plan.'

'I want to spend more time with you,' said Bradley softly. 'As well as show you Hawaii. Maybe we could go to another island.'

'How many islands are there in Hawaii?'

'Well, hundreds, but most of them are really tiny. The main ones are Oahu, that we're on now, the Big Island of Hawaii with its volcanoes, Maui, and the one that's supposed to be the most beautiful of all, Kauai. And the smaller ones are Lanai and Molokai.'

'Volcanoes. Won't that be dangerous?'

'No, not really. They're not the explosive type. More damage is done by tsunamis.'

'What's a tsunami?'

'A tidal wave. The Hawaiian islands are in the middle of the Pacific Ocean, so if there's an earthquake anywhere out there, the effect is felt in Hawaii. Luckily, most of the tsunamis are quite small.'

'That's a relief.' She squeezed his hand. The islands sounded beguiling and exciting and to see them with Bradley made them even more appealing.

He handed her the menu. 'Let's order dinner, the show is about to start.'

Catherine enjoyed Don Ho's show. His throaty voice,

his humour and flirtatious manner, the bevy of Hawaiian dancers and singers was unlike anything she'd seen before. The last big show she'd seen had been an outdoor concert by the Who in London where it had rained.

She whispered to Bradley, 'Not like the Who, is it?'

'Certainly not. Do you want to dance? This is his signature tune.' He pulled her to her feet as several couples went onto the small dance floor. 'Know the two-step?'

'Kind of.' She allowed Bradley to lead her as the singer began.

Tiny bubbles . . .

Bradley was a great dancer and, being tall, he swept her easily around the floor holding her close, singing softly along in her ear.

So here's to the golden moon
And here's to the silver sea
And mostly here's a toast
To you and me
So here's to the ginger lei
I give to you today
And here's a kiss
That will not fade away . . .

He kissed her gently and led her from the dance floor. 'Shall we leave now? Do you want to go somewhere else?'

He looked at her with such longing that Catherine picked up her purse. 'A nightcap on my lanai?'

He stayed the night. And in the morning when she awakened he was sitting on the lanai, wrapped in a white towel, smoking a cigarette. She looked at his strong back, the outline of his head and thought he was the most handsome man she'd ever seen.

'Good morning. Sorry I slept in, how long have you been awake?' she called.

He put out his cigarette and came towards her. 'Not long. I watched you sleep for a while. You look like a little girl.' He dropped the towel and slid into bed beside her. 'You in a rush to go anywhere?'

She giggled and reached for him. 'No, sir. Are you?'

'My day off. We could stay here all day . . .'

Bradley and Catherine spent as much time together as they could for the next few days, while Bradley arranged time off work for a trip to Maui. She phoned her parents to tell them she'd be spending a bit longer in Hawaii.

'I'm moving into a cheaper hotel when I get back from Maui.'

'Sounds like you're having a good time. You like Hawaii, eh?' said her father.

'It's fabulous,' said Catherine, knowing her voice was very upbeat.

Her father seemed amused. 'Sounds like it. Well, you enjoy yourself, love. You sound very happy. Must be nice to be in the sun after London. We can't wait to have you home though. Your mother is making all kinds of plans.'

'Oh that's nice of her but, Dad, I really just want to relax. Be with you, ride around the place, settle in, you know. No parties, please. You know what Mum's like.'

'I understand, sweetheart. Send us a telegram when you know you're coming home. Cheaper than these phone calls.'

Catherine couldn't stop smiling and she couldn't stop thinking of Bradley. He arrived at her hotel room after work each day with a lei, chocolates, macadamia nuts and a nice bottle of wine. They fell into bed and made love with an eagerness and enthusiasm that left both of them gasping, laughing, hugging and exclaiming that neither had enjoyed making love so much before.

She found Maui interesting and not as touristy as Honolulu, though Bradley pointed out that holiday apartment complexes were beginning to be built.

Wandering around the old whaling port of Lahaina, Bradley came out of a shop and pressed a small package into her hands.

Catherine exclaimed in delight at the tiny pretty coral earrings. 'How sweet, I love them. Thank you so much.' She gave him a kiss and they linked arms.

'Let's eat at one of these seafood places overlooking the water and you can put them on,' he suggested.

They were sharing the cost of their hotel – Catherine had insisted – and she was quite surprised at how easy and comfortable the arrangement was. She thought it would be awkward living with a stranger but Bradley was so easy to be with. He didn't snore, he was attentive and sensitive to her needs, excusing himself to go and buy something if he sensed she wanted privacy or time alone. They walked on the beach and went for a swim before breakfast, he planned their day's sightseeing, made suggestions about where to go for dinner. The days sped past. She was pleased that she'd extended her holiday. They returned to Honolulu and she moved into a smaller hotel set back from the beach but with a view of the ocean from the top floor where she was staying. Bradley returned to work but spent every evening with her.

Sometimes during the day she opened the closet and touched Bradley's crisp white spare uniform hanging beside her clothes. She felt a sense of proprietary togetherness seeing his toiletries in the bathroom.

*

A few days before she was due to fly back to Australia, Bradley said he had something to ask her. He sounded slightly hesitant.

'It's about tomorrow night . . . I was wondering if you'd like to come to a dinner . . . It's with my superior officer. They have these social get-togethers. His wife is a great hostess and they have a house on the base at Pearl Harbor. Of course, you might find it a bit boring . . .'

'Why would I find it boring? It'd be nice to meet people who live here. Is it for a special reason?' she asked.

'Not really. The idea is for us all to maintain close links, keep in touch socially, which is supposed to help us work together.'

'Sounds a good idea.' She wondered why he sounded so formal. 'Is there anything I should know? What to wear? Who's who?'

Bradley grinned. 'You always look nice. They're just a bit conservative . . . older ladies, you know. It'll give you a taste of the other side of my life here.' He wrapped his arms around her and lifted her off the ground. 'So you know what I'm putting up with while you're galloping around Peel.'

'My other life,' mused Catherine. 'I only gallop around *Heatherbrae*. Not much to get excited about in Peel.' She kissed him thinking how dull Peel would seem after all the glamour and fun of Hawaii. And Bradley. It was going to be hard to say goodbye. She refused to think about that moment.

Commander and Mrs Goodwin were gracious and made a fuss of Catherine. She was introduced to the other wives who were gathered on the terrace. The men, dressed in smart casual clothes, were bunched on the lawn by the pool. The immaculate grass was dotted with palms and its elevated position boasted a lovely view of the harbour.

'What a spectacular place,' said Catherine.

'The senior officers and families are housed in that section over there, the single officers are in an apartment block. It has lovely views,' said Mrs Goodwin. Then turning to several other wives she said, 'Don't you just love Catherine's accent?'

'It's darling. I've always wanted to go to Australia. My husband visited there on his way to Vietnam. Where's your home, dear?' asked a woman with bright red hair lacquered into a helmet that flipped up on her shoulders but didn't move.

'Oh, it's in the country. Nowhere anyone's heard of,' answered Catherine.

'You mean like a ranch, honey?'

'A small one. Just horses and stud cattle. A hobby for my father. He's a solicitor. A lawyer,' she added as Bradley had explained that solicitor wasn't an American term.

'And how long have you known Bradley?' asked another wife, joining the growing circle around Catherine.

She sensed their curiosity. Their glances flicked up and down from her shoes to her hair, and she felt she was being judged. Had Bradley brought other girls to meet the boss's wife?

'Oh, we met in London, at a reception at Australia House,' she threw in for good measure. 'We've kept in touch and as I'd planned to stop over in Hawaii – a twenty-first birthday present from my father – we were able to catch up again.'

'How nice. I suppose you're looking forward to seeing your family. How long have you been away, Catherine?' asked Mrs Goodwin. 'Do you have a job waiting or are you going to college?'

Bradley suddenly appeared behind her. 'Mrs Goodwin, ladies.' He smiled at the women who all gave him big smiles in return. 'Would you excuse us if I stole Catherine for a moment? Commander Goodwin and Jim Bensen have a dispute about Australia. We're hoping Catherine can settle the question.'

'I'll try.' Catherine made her escape.

'Sorry. Hope they didn't grill you too much,' whispered Bradley.

'It's all right. What's going on?'

'Oh, it's just an argument of semantics really. You say tom-mah-toe, we say too-may-toe . . . kinda thing. I just thought I'd rescue you.'

'Thanks.'

She was introduced to several other naval officers about Bradley's age. They made cheerful talk, happy to chat with someone more interesting than the older men. Catherine enjoyed their company but she kept an ear tuned to what Bradley was saying. He was obviously regarded with some esteem by his fellow officers and held his own in most of the discussions.

Later in the evening as they drove back to Catherine's hotel, Bradley apologised. 'I hope it wasn't too painful. They're all well meaning, it was a bit unusual for me to turn up with a date. I haven't done that before.'

'They did seem to check me out, but as soon as I told them I was going back to Australia, they lost interest.'

Bradley chuckled. 'You were terrific. All the guys thought you were great.'

'So how often do you have to go to an evening like that?'

'Ah, not often. I owe you one for coming along and making it less painful for me.'

'So why go, if you find these things painful?' asked Catherine.

Bradley looked genuinely surprised. 'Ah, well. It's the done thing. When one's commanding officer invites, one doesn't have a choice.' He changed the subject. 'It's not too late, anywhere you'd like to go?'

'I've had my fill of fancy food. She must've worked for hours on all those fiddly pupus and things,' sighed Catherine.

'Oh, no. I'm sure she had them made by the cook at the officers' mess. How about a drink? Somewhere we haven't been?'

Catherine rested her hand on his thigh. 'No, but thanks. We have cocktail makings at the hotel, wine and some beer. We'd better drink it or you'll have to take it home with you when I leave.'

He laid his hand over hers. 'Good thinking.'

They had a drink, went to bed, made love and Bradley turned on his side and slept soundly.

Catherine lay beside him, wondering how she was going to adjust to being without him. This sojourn had been like playing houses, playing at being married. She'd never had a relationship like this, brief as it was. Her relationships with various boyfriends had been sporadic and fragmented. She'd never spent as much intimate time with anyone else before. But she knew it was coming to an end. Their lives were so different and no matter what promises they made of meeting again, keeping in touch, distance would make the relationship dissipate. They would go on and lead very different lives. Live for the moment, she told herself. But the moments were running out. She turned on her side and silent tears ran down her cheeks.

In the morning, she felt calmer and she lay quietly, not wanting to wake Bradley as the sun rose and light filled the small room.

He woke, stretched and reached for her, drawing her close to him. Sleepily he held her, stroking her hair. 'Want to go for a swim? A walk on the beach?' he murmured.

45

Catherine snuggled into him. 'Not this morning. Do you want coffee?'

'Not yet.'

They lay quietly, their bodies wrapped together, each caught in their own thoughts.

Suddenly Bradley rolled on his back. 'I have to go to work. Hell.'

'What's up? A bad day looming?' It occurred to Catherine she was very hazy about what he did every day.

'No.' He hugged her tightly. 'I want to stay with you and make love and eat and drink and make love and never get out of bed all day.'

She laughed softly. 'Sounds like a good kind of day to me.'

He smiled, looking into her eyes and slowly lowered his face to hers and kissed her gently.

It was a kiss that went on and on, ranging from touching lightly, to deep passionate lingering, reluctant to part.

They drew apart, staring deeply into each others' eyes.

Bradley traced the outline of her face, as if memorising it. 'I love you,' he said softly.

'Me too,' said Catherine, closing her eyes and lifting her mouth to his. The words came easily, with no emphasis or deep thought or implication. She wanted to taste his lips again, lose herself in his kiss.

But Bradley didn't return her kiss. He looked thoughtful, concerned almost, and she was suddenly worried that she shouldn't have said what she did, that it might place some sense of obligation on him. The words 'Me too' had slipped out. She was not analysing whether it was Bradley, Hawaii, or how serious she felt about Bradley. She'd spoken spontaneously from the heart.

But the words had resonated with him. 'Do you? Love me?'

She nodded. Not trusting herself to speak, not wanting to be clingy, get teary, have their parting uncomfortable by making heartfelt promises they wouldn't keep. Keep it clean, keep it tidy, don't make it hard for him. For me, she chided herself. She closed her eyes.

'Then will you marry me?'

Her eyes snapped open in shock. 'What! What did you say?'

He looked sheepish. 'I think I just proposed. Well, will you?'

'Marry you?' Catherine was swamped with a wall of emotion as the floodgates fell and all the feelings she'd been storing up, afraid to show him, overcame her. She grabbed him in a giant hug, squeezing him to her as hard as she could, afraid he'd disappear. 'Yes. Oh, yes. Oh, Bradley . . .'

They kissed through smiling lips, hugging, laughing, kissing. She flung a leg over him pinning him on the bed, running her hands over his body, feeling him respond. But Bradley gently lifted her arm.

'Don't do that or I'll never leave. I have to get to work. I'm running a training program for some new guys. But tonight . . . tonight we celebrate!'

'Wonderful.' Catherine watched him get out of bed. 'I guess we have plans to make . . .'

'We'll talk about the future over dinner, shall we? First thing is a ring. What's your favourite stone?'

'Ah, I don't know. I've never thought about it.'

'A diamond of course, but maybe we can find something special. Do a little browsing today.' He jumped in the shower. He was off and running into another day.

Extract from The Biography of

THE WATERMAN

1918

Red Hawk, Nebraska, was swathed in snow. The wind that swept in from the prairie sent icy flurries along the near-deserted main street. Snow, splashed with mud, piled in mounds against the corners of buildings.

The young man, head bent, hugging his coat around him, kicked his boots along the soggy sidewalk. He stepped off the street into the foyer of a small movie theatre to stare at the film posters. He dug deep into his trouser pocket, counted out several coins and slid them under the grille to the girl in the ticket booth. She was reading a fan magazine and chewing gum. As she pushed the ticket to the boy she glanced up and gave him a big smile as if to acknowledge that he was even better looking than the movie stars she was reading about.

Still shivering, he slid into a seat in the dark where several other figures were slumped, thawing in the warmth of the small theatre. The young man knew nothing about the movie that was playing, but the old wooden theatre was cosy, a good place to pass the time until he met his father at the general store.

The movie newsreels flickered across the screen, pictures of American soldiers marching into France. He closed his eyes, dozing in the warmth. When he re-opened them, the screen was showing the most amazing sight he'd ever seen.

Even in the scratchy black and white images he could imagine the colours of the scene: the blue ocean, the green headland, the emerald palm trees and the golden sand.

But the miracle that mesmerised him was the sight of the tall dark men riding on the curling waves, standing on long wooden planks. They made it look so easy, the way they nonchalantly glided across the top of the ocean. Pretty girls with long hair, coconut halves on their breasts and long leaf skirts swayed their hips, lifting their arms to the sky as they danced on the sand.

He could feel the sun and tried to imagine what it would be like to walk on water like that. The film titles on the screen explained that this was surfboard riding in the islands of Hawaii. It was an art once practised only by the kings and chiefs, but now it was the sport of champions and in Waikiki it seemed anyone could learn it.

He never remembered the main feature showing in the movie house that day. But from the moment he walked out of the dark theatre into the bleak afternoon, the young man promised himself one day that he would ride the waves at Waikiki.

There wasn't much to entertain young people in Red Hawk, Nebraska, but this young man liked to keep himself fit. In the summer he swam in the mountain lakes far out of town. When it became too cold for that, he enjoyed running. People thought he was strange to run for miles across the plains or along the lonely roads. There was nowhere to run to, they reasoned, just the prairie that met the Indian reservation on the outskirts of Muskosha in the foothills of the Rockies. And then he'd turn around and run right back again, through the moonlight to reach home. His endurance was such that he could travel for days with little food.

The young man had worked on his father's farm, done odd jobs for tradespeople in the town of Red Hawk. He talked to people passing through, from travelling entertainers, to circus performers, to itinerant families looking to make a home on the great plains.

He wanted to travel as well, so he started moving around the country, taking odd jobs for food. And everywhere he went he seemed to find a benefactor willing to help him when he had nowhere to turn and hunger and cold claimed him.

He became adept at riding the freight trains across the plains and mountains. He quickly learned to avoid the railyard 'bulls' hired to beat anyone sneaking into a boxcar. He learned to fight hunger and discomfort by mentally removing himself to another place. In his mind he saw again the Islands of Hawaii.

A hobo, sharing a freight car, told him to go west. California was where dreams came true. A paradise, home of Califia, the Queen of the Island of California. As they rattled over the tracks, the hobo spun the tale of the island ruled by beautiful black Amazonian women, dressed in gold armour, who raided the seas, stole the men they favoured, ravished them and put them and any male children to death by feeding them to giant man-eating griffins.

The young man decided California would be his next stop. And eventually he made his way to the City of the Angels.

It was close to paradise. The air was clear, he could see the distant Santa Ana mountains, the sun was warm, the streets had palm trees. And there was the beach and the ocean almost as beautiful and magical as he imagined the Islands of Hawaii to be.

Come the summer he took a job as a lifeguard at the beach. He soon became known as the strongest swimmer at the beach and he saved several people from drowning, stroking strongly to reach them and pull them back to shore.

It was one such grateful survivor who handed the shy young man a wad of money. And that gesture of thanks allowed him to live through another winter in LA when there was no work. He was able to concentrate on swimming and running, keeping his body fit, his mind clear and dreams intact.

3

MOLLIE DROVE THROUGH THE morning peak hour Sydney traffic, which was slower than normal due to a slight drizzle.

Beside her Catherine looked at the rows of neat suburban red-roofed houses and remarked, 'Everything looks so tidy, so straight-laced after the rampant greenery and casualness of Hawaii.'

'Hawaii sounds lovely. You'll notice a difference when you get to Peel. It's been dry. Your mum said *Heatherbrae* needs rain.'

Catherine nodded. Hawaii had stolen her heart. She'd thought about it on the flight home and while she knew her love of Hawaii was bound up in her love for Bradley, there was still a pull about the Islands that held her. A promise of so much to discover. She couldn't wait to get back there.

She hadn't yet told Mollie about her engagement. When Mollie had offered to meet her, Catherine had planned to rush straight to her from Arrivals and wave her hand in her face and cry, 'I'm engaged!' But her bag had been lost and by the time it'd been located and she'd exited the customs hall, Mollie was there, jumping up and down and grabbed the bag from her, saying, 'Quick, quick, I'll get booked. I'm parked illegally.'

So they'd rushed to the car, Mollie chattering non-stop about her new job, a fellow she'd met and mutual friends, then she'd needed to concentrate on driving out of the jammed airport and the moment had been lost. Catherine began to plan a little scenario about how she'd break her news to Mollie. She also wanted her advice as to how she could tell her parents. She knew her mum would have very mixed emotions, primarily because she would be marrying a foreigner and wouldn't be living close by.

Settled in Mollie's flat, Catherine had a shower while Mollie boiled the kettle for a cup of tea.

'So what would you like to do for the rest of the day?' asked Mollie. 'They say it's best to stay awake till bedtime to get on local time.'

'I'd love a snooze, you could wake me up in an hour and then we could go out. I'm so sleepy.' Catherine stifled a yawn.

'What's that?' Mollie grabbed Catherine's hand away from her mouth and bent over the ring on her left hand.

'Oh. I've been trying to find a way to tell you. I'm engaged.'

'Oh my God! *Oh my God!*' shrieked Mollie. 'Who? Where? When? How could you keep this a secret? Is it that American?' she demanded. She leaned closer to examine the ring. 'It's just beautiful.' She sat back and folded her arms. 'Okay, tell me everything.'

Catherine smiled and settled back with her cup of tea, anxious to recount once again every detail of meeting Bradley and their friendship in London, despite what she'd already told Mollie in her letters.

'Were you lovers?' interjected Mollie.

'In London? No. He was very courteous. Very proper. We went slowly. We became friends first off.'

'Boring,' sighed Mollie. 'Get to the exciting stuff.'

Their mugs of tea sat untouched as Catherine talked and talked.

'And so were you expecting him to propose?' asked Mollie finally.

'No. Not all. But I was getting sad at the idea of leaving him. And Hawaii.'

'And then he popped the question and flourished the ring.'

'The ring came afterwards. He chose it. He asked me my favourite stone and did I want something big and flashy or smaller and good quality.'

'I'd have asked for big,' said Mollie. 'Not that yours is tiny. An emerald and two diamonds. I didn't know emeralds were your favourite stone.'

'I always thought I'd have a sapphire and diamond engagement ring. Bradley chose this and I love it.'

'I'd rather choose my own,' said Mollie. 'Though I 'spose if he's paying for it you can't very well say give me that big rock of a diamond. Is he rich?'

'I don't think wildly so. His parents are comfortable by the sound of them. Middle-class Californians.'

'Does he know you are a lady of some means? After all, your father has a good legal practice and is a highly respected citizen of Peel and of course there's *Heatherbrae*,' said Mollie. 'Anyway, everyone is going to be mightily impressed. And a bit jealous. You've outclassed Trudy Rowle who thought she was the bees knees when she snared Adam Thomas with his grandparents' Point Piper house.'

'It's not a competition, Mollie,' laughed Catherine. But secretly she was rather pleased she had broken the mould of her contemporaries and was marrying outside the familiar circle.

'So where and when is the wedding? At *Heatherbrae*? Your mother is going to be beside herself! Does she know? Hey, am I going to be a bridesmaid?'

'Of course you are. But you'll have to come to Hawaii. We're getting married in the Islands.'

'Wow! Ooh, is your mum okay with that? You're not eloping are you?'

'Mollie, really. No. But I haven't told my parents yet. Thought it would be better in person and Bradley only proposed two days before I left. He's writing to his folks.'

'Folks?' exclaimed Mollie. 'Don't you go all Yankee on us. Well, let's get to the important stuff. What are you going to wear? Let's go look at wedding dresses this afternoon!' She jumped up.

Catherine laughed. Mollie's enthusiasm was nice. And it did give her a tingle in the pit of her stomach. A wedding dress, trousseau stuff, she'd need to get some nice things together. And what personal pieces would she take to their home in Honolulu?

Catching her train of thought Mollie asked, 'So where are you going to live? Will you have a beach house in Waikiki so we can all come and visit?'

'Kind of. I think so,' said Catherine thinking of the naval compound around the Goodwins'.

Mollie stared at her. 'I was kidding. Are you serious? He must be rich. I thought there were only big hotels at Waikiki.'

'It's the navy base at Pearl Harbor. The navy have the best spots on the island Bradley says. There are different quarters for the married and single officers, the enlisted men, and the senior brass.'

'Ooh, I don't like the sound of that too much. Do you? Living and working with the same people. Can you get your own place?' asked Mollie.

'I thought of that and mentioned it to Bradley but if we want to save money, living on the base is better. But he says he's looking into things,' said Catherine. 'My next issue is calling Mum. She'll be wanting to know if I've arrived safely.'

'Oh, I forgot. Yes, she rang here just before I left for the airport. Look, you can't tell her your big news over the phone. Give her a call and say you're jet lagged and want to stay here for a day or so and see old friends before going home,' said Mollie.

'That's a good idea. Otherwise she'll be jumping in the car and coming down to get me.' Catherine reached for the phone.

Her mother was excited. 'I can't wait to see you. You're going to love your room, Dad painted . . . oh dear, he wanted it to be a surprise, don't let on. We thought we'd have a party on the weekend to welcome you home. So many people we haven't seen since the races . . .'

'Mum, that's all lovely. But let's hold off a bit. A party sounds great . . .' Catherine rolled her eyes at Mollie and wagged her ring finger. 'I just want to enjoy being at home again. On my own. Go for a ride, maybe a picnic, just us.'

'Of course, dear. Lovely. Though so many friends keep asking after you.'

'Sure, Mum, we'll work out something. Anyway, I want to stay here with Mollie for a day or so. I'll come up on the Saturday morning flight. Love you.'

It was cloudy when the small plane took off from

Sydney but within minutes they were in sunshine and had left the coast behind. Catherine kept looking out the window trying to recognise the country below.

Once they started to descend she felt a lump come to her throat and she had to blink quickly, surprised at the sudden tears in her eyes as she recognised the gorge country from where the Home River flowed onto the plains around Peel. The wheat paddocks were brown stubble, cattle clustered in blotchy brown and black groups, tin roofs shimmered in the bright light and the miles of fences below delineated the borders of family properties. She was pretty sure she recognised the ribbon of road that headed towards the north-west and *Heatherbrae*.

They flew over the compact township of Peel and came in to land at the airstrip. As she got up from her seat she could see her parents among the group standing in front of the glass doors of the airport building, waving madly at the plane.

On the drive back to their property, her mother chattered from the front seat to bring Catherine up to date with all the local news. 'And Rob's got engaged to that nice girl, Barbara, but I'm not sure that she's all that keen on living in the country.' Her father occasionally glanced at Catherine in the rear-vision mirror, giving her a small smile and a 'be patient' look.

Catherine exclaimed in delight at her freshly painted room and admired her mother's garden.

'How's Parker doing? And your cattle, Dad?'

'They're great. Feed was a bit of a worry for a bit, but I handled a case for a client who paid me in feed,' he replied. 'I rode Parker a few times and so did Rob when he came over to tell us about his engagement.' He shook his head. 'Not sure how that girl is going to settle down out here. City girl, like your friend Mollie.'

'Now then, Keith, you don't know how girls can adapt

to please their man. How about a cup of tea, dear, and Dad will take you round the paddocks, up to the knoll? Or we could take lunch up there, like we used to. What would you like to do, pet?' asked her mother.

'Er, sure, Mum, whatever you'd like.'

'Don't rush her, love. Let her adjust to being back here. Must seem quiet after the big cities you've seen, eh?' said her father.

Catherine saw a chance to raise the subject of her engagement. 'Well, London was great, but I really loved Hawaii . . .'

'Certainly must have,' interjected her mother. 'Extending your stay like you did . . .'

Her father interrupted his wife. 'You throw that picnic together and I'll take Catherine down to see her horse.'

They drove past the dam and stopped to watch several head of cattle and calves in the best paddock.

'They're looking good, Dad. It's a bit dry though isn't it?'

'It certainly is, nothing like the green of Hawaii, I suppose.'

'That's for sure,' answered Catherine. She touched her father's shoulder. 'Giving me that holiday in Hawaii for my twenty-first was the best thing you've ever done, Dad.' She paused. 'Dad, there's something I have to tell you. And Mum.'

He flicked an amused glance at his daughter as he started the car. 'Wouldn't have anything to do with that ring you're wearing, would it?'

'Oh, Dad! You're a smart old thing,' said Catherine with relief, lifting her hand to admire her engagement ring. 'Yes, I got engaged. Happened just before I left Honolulu. Bradley's living there. Oh, Dad, I'm so happy. But I just don't know how Mum is going to react. About not knowing Bradley, not living here . . .'

'Hang on, pet, start at the beginning. Has he got a job? Not some dropout is he?'

'Of course not! He's a naval officer. Very impressive, well educated, handsome, his family lives in California . . .'

'He's American?'

Catherine saw the slight frown cross her father's face. 'Well, yes. Charming, warm, caring. He's very sensible. You'll really like him, Dad.'

'Mmm. Never thought you'd choose a foreign bloke. Never thought you'd live far from *Heatherbrae* and us.'

'Nor did I, Dad. Is that going to be a problem for you and Mum?'

'You have to make your own life, sweetie. And if this is the way the cards have fallen, well, we'll make the best of it.' He glanced at his daughter, his heart had filled with love at seeing Catherine so glowing and happy. 'Be hard on your mum having you so far away. Still, I suppose the wedding will keep her occupied for a bit.'

Catherine was silent a moment. 'We're planning on getting married in Hawaii. His parents will come out and you and Mum can have a holiday at the same time. Be less work for everyone,' she added brightly.

'Your mother might be disappointed. She'd always hoped you'd be married here, in the garden. Maybe when he comes and sees this place, you might get him to change his mind.'

'We hadn't planned on that. Coming out here first,' said Catherine quietly. 'Bradley really wants to get married in the naval chapel, he's so much a navy man.'

'Seems like you've made all your plans, then,' said her father, turning the truck around.

'Oh, Dad. I'm sorry.' Tears sprang to Catherine's eyes.

He patted her arm. 'We just want you to be happy. As

58

long as you're sure about this. It's a big step. Come on, let's find that horse of yours. He's as fat as a pig. Needs some serious riding.' Her engagement was put to one side.

Catherine had always loved the small knoll at the back of *Heatherbrae* as it was a place away from everything and where she could sit and dream. Yet she never felt alone up on the knoll. Perhaps because there had been so many family gatherings on the grass plateau with its sweeping views: picnics and barbecues, bonfires and fireworks. Other times she sat alone while Parker picked at the grass and she watched the birds swoop, a lizard sun itself or a wallaby hop through the tall grass at the edge of the trees further down the hillside. It was a place where problems were solved, where dark moods lifted and where anything seemed possible. She always rode away cheered, invigorated and enthused. It seemed right that her engagement should be celebrated at this outdoor family sanctum.

After initial dismay, her mother had become more accepting of the news of her daughter's engagement. As the sandwiches were passed and Rosemary poured the tea from the thermos into mugs, she became more enthusiastic about the wedding, raising details that Catherine hadn't yet considered.

'What about bridesmaids? It's a long way to go, who can afford such a trip? Does Bradley have a sister?'

'Yes. But I don't know her. I only need one bridesmaid – and that's Mollie. She's already agreed. She's been saving for a holiday so she's keen on Hawaii. I guess Bradley will ask his brother to be best man. We want to keep it small. Simple,' said Catherine. 'Mr and Mrs Connor want to throw a party for us in California later at Thanksgiving. Be wonderful if you could go over too.'

'I don't know about a trip to Hawaii then a couple of

months later a trip to California,' said her father. 'Plane travel is expensive and I can't be away from the office too long.'

'We can spend time with Bradley's family after the wedding. They're staying for a bit longer aren't they? Of course, we should really go over early to help with arrangements, it's the bride's family's obligation,' added her mother.

'Mum, the whole idea is to keep this low key and simple so we don't get into all the mother of the bride stuff . . . flowers, cars, who pays for what . . . Bradley wants to pay for everything just so we can do things our way.'

'If he wants to run the show let him, love,' said Keith to Rosemary. 'I think I'll have a quiet word with Bradley about the financial arrangements when I meet him in Honolulu. But the boy clearly takes his responsibilities seriously and that's a good thing.'

Nevertheless Rosemary was determined that part of the celebrations would take place at *Heatherbrae* and a welcome home party was rearranged into a kitchen tea and an early evening drinks party.

So, while the women gathered in the house to watch Catherine unwrap gifts and show photos of Bradley taken in Hawaii, the men sat around the barbecue and pool area talking farming, politics and the weather.

Before the last guests left, Rob found Catherine in the kitchen stacking glasses, cups and plates at the sink.

'Hey, congratulations. You caught everyone by surprise,' he said warmly.

'Thanks. I hope you and Barbara will be happy. How're plans going for your big day?'

Rob rolled his eyes. 'Bloody dramas every day from the smallest thing like the colour of the corsages to someone who's not invited because they don't get on with someone else. I'm keeping out of it. If you and your bloke can pull off a simple, easy event, good on you. I suppose getting married on a tropical island away from everybody is the smart way to do it.'

'I'll miss all my friends, but what you describe is what Bradley is trying to avoid. It might be hard for us with families on opposite sides of the world, but it's simplified the wedding.'

'Yeah, I suppose so. Aren't you going to miss being here though? You're a long way from those who love you, Cath. And Aussie-land. You always seemed more attached to this place than many of us.'

'Except you, Rob. I hope Barbara settles into country life,' said Catherine, changing the subject. Rob had touched a nerve. 'I'll try to come back as often as I can and Mum and Dad plan to come over and see us as well. Anytime you and Barbara want an Hawaiian holiday – just yell,' she said lightly.

'Takes a few bob to dash across the Pacific at the drop of a hat. You know us farmers. If there's any spare cash it goes into the land or a new ute.' He smiled. 'This chap must be pretty special. Good luck, Cath.'

'Thanks, Rob. Same to you and Barbara. I'm sure our families will swap wedding photos so we can see how it went.'

Bradley picked up an orange pottery canister with a cork lid. 'Catherine, this is truly ugly. I can't believe you paid to ship all this stuff over here.'

'They're our wedding presents.'

'Right, but most of them are awful. Or things we don't need.'

'I didn't have time to go through everything before I left. I thought this would be fun,' said Catherine miserably. Compared to what was available in American shops and displayed in magazines, the selection of gifts from family and friends did not seem very inspired. She didn't want to be mercenary about things, but tea towels, pottery canisters and a Corning Ware lasagne dish were never going to be kept as family heirlooms. Moreover, Bradley was right, it had cost a lot to ship over the box of gifts.

'I should have waited. But I was anxious to get here and set up our first home.'

Bradley had bought a small apartment in which they could live while they waited for married quarters to become available on the base. While the apartment in the TradeWinds building was small, it was across the street from the Ilikai Hotel and marina and Catherine loved sitting on their lanai watching all the activity and hearing the jingle of the rigging of the moored yachts. The apartment was furnished with the basics, which Bradley had decorated with his personal effects collected during his time at college and his travels with the navy. There was nothing very feminine about it and Catherine wished she'd brought more of her personal memorabilia. She decided to ask her mother to bring some photos she had taken of Parker, her friends and scenes of *Heatherbrae*.

Catherine had arrived two weeks before the big day, but found that Bradley, true to his word, had arranged everything. She'd bought a wedding dress in Sydney with her mother and Mollie but now she fretted that it wouldn't look right on the day. It seemed too formal, too stiff and stylised. Bradley had his dress uniform to wear, which suited any occasion. She pored over magazines, the social pages, and looked in the stores at the Ala Moana centre, feeling that her choice was not quite right for the Islands. But, she didn't discuss her concerns with Bradley as she'd told him she had everything organised and didn't want to appear as insecure as she suddenly felt.

Bradley was working longer hours than usual, partly because it was the nature of the job and partly because he wanted to get everything up to date before he left for the honeymoon, so Catherine was not surprised when one day he told her that he had a function to go to after work. It was only for naval personnel so she was not invited and, as he would miss dinner, he suggested that she walk across to the Ilikai and treat herself to a meal.

Catherine didn't want to eat alone at a tourist spot so she decided to walk the length of Waikiki Beach at sunset and grab a hamburger at a small restaurant on the way back. She knew she could get on the bus that ran past their apartment and hoped to be back by dark.

The beach was almost deserted save for a few surfers standing by their boards. The flame torches around the hotels' gardens were already alight and people were gathering for sunset cocktails. Walking past the Moonflower she saw the band setting up and as she walked closer to see if Kiann'e was there, she was hailed.

'Hello again.'

Catherine turned to see Kiann'e on the beach ahead of her being professionally photographed. 'Hello! I was just wondering if your show was about to start.'

'Shortly. We wanted a sunset picture for a new album cover. How are you? Are you still on vacation, or have you been home and come back? Can't keep away? It's been awhile since I saw you in Carol and Marys.'

'You have a good memory! Actually I have been back to Australia but I'm here now to get married.'

'Wonderful. A beach wedding? And then back to Australia?' Kiann'e joined Catherine as the photographer set up a silver umbrella on a small stand.

'No, we're going to live here. For a while anyway. He's with the navy.'

'Great. Then we'll probably see each other again. I'm Kiann'e Schultz. I married a German,' she added by explanation. 'Are you living at the base?'

'I'm Catherine Moreland soon to be Connor. We're living in a small apartment near the Ilikai while we wait for quarters on the base. Is Honolulu your home?'

'No, Kauai. But we live on Oahu because of the work. Where're you getting married?'

'At the naval chapel. His commanding officer and his wife are giving us a small reception at their home. It's a pretty setting.'

'Is your family coming from Australia?'

'Just my parents and my best friend. Bradley's parents and brother are coming from California. I don't know many people here yet.'

'You know me now. Would you like to get together one day for coffee?'

'I'd love to!' exclaimed Catherine. 'This might sound crazy but I brought a wedding dress with me and now it doesn't seem right. Would you know anywhere I might find something . . . not too formal but not too . . . extreme?' she finished.

'You mean not too Hawaiian, but a bit of the flavour of the Islands?' asked Kiann'e. 'Don't want your family to think you've gone too tropical! I'll be glad to give you my suggestions. I'll give you my number.' She went to fetch her small basket beside the photographer's gear.

'Can we get this shot before all the light goes?' he asked.

'Here's my card. Give me a call. We'll make it a project. Aloha.' Kiann'e handed Catherine a business card and then took her position in front of the camera.

Catherine waved, tucked the card in her wallet and retraced her steps along the beach, wondering at the ease with which she'd made a friend of the beautiful Hawaiian girl. People were shopping, strolling along the colourful strip and the bars were jammed. She saw a bus marked Kalakaua Avenue, jumped onto it and got off at the

International Marketplace. Later she caught a bus to the Ilikai Hotel, crossed the street to the TradeWinds and caught the elevator to the seventh floor.

The phone was ringing as she got inside.

'Where have you been? I was starting to worry. Did you go across the road for dinner?'

'No. I walked down the beachfront to Waikiki.'

'You what? At night, that could be dangerous. There're a lot of hustlers round that International Marketplace. You're still a bit of an innocent in Honolulu,' exclaimed Bradley. 'Where did you eat?'

'Oh, I bought an ice cream. There's stuff here. Hey, guess who I met?'

'Who?' asked Bradley still sounding worried.

She told him about Kiann'e and he was slightly surprised until Catherine explained they'd met before in a shop at Ala Moana.

'That's nice. Hey, maybe she'd dance at our wedding! No, forget that, the arrangements are already made. So you're okay then? I'll be another half hour or so and then I'll be home. Shall I bring some food?'

'No, thanks. I'm fine. See you soon.'

'Watch some TV. Johnny Carson'll be on soon.'

'Okay, darling.'

Catherine put a record on the stereo. She wasn't as addicted to American television as Bradley was.

Both families arrived a few days before the wedding. Catherine moved out of Bradley's apartment into the Moana, where her parents and Mollie were staying. She enjoyed a late breakfast with her parents on the verandah by the courtyard while she told them how sitting under the banyan tree at sunset had played a role in her and Bradley's courtship.

Catherine was to meet Bradley's parents at the classic Royal Hawaiian Hotel for a celebratory drink, before being joined later by her parents and Bradley's brother, Joel, for dinner in the hotel's restaurant. She felt apprehensive about this first meeting, but was quickly put at ease by her future in-laws.

Bradley's mother, Angela, was attractive in a polished, beauty-shop way. His father, Richard, wore a cream golf shirt under a blue linen jacket. Both were gregarious, laughed loudly and 'joshed' each other.

'Don't take any notice of Richard,' said Angela. 'He's such a tease. We're just so thrilled for Bradley. For you both. We always hoped he'd find a darling like you. How wonderful for you both to start married life in paradise!' She waved her arms around the cocktail lounge with its rows of orchids, potted palms and views out to Waikiki Beach.

'It is a rather special place,' agreed Catherine. 'It's like being on holiday all the time. Though I hope I can find some kind of job.'

'Work? Whatever for, honey? That Bradley is earning enough for you to stay on permanent vacation,' declared Richard. 'Don't you let him kid you into taking a job. You enjoy yourself, sweetie. Soon enough there'll be little bambinos, other postings. Not every assignment is as luxurious as Hawaii,' he said. 'Angela and I had some tough early posts. Not so bad for the men at sea, harder on the gals. So you enjoy your time here.'

'He's right, Catherine. You set up your little nest, be there for him. You'll find you have plenty to do just running a home. Friends are the secret. Other women in the same boat! Besides, what kind of work could you possibly do here?' said Angela who'd been a navy wife for thirty-five years.

Catherine bristled. 'I'm sure I could find a job. I don't want to be totally dependent on Bradley.'

'Darling, the navy is his life and you'll quickly discover it will be yours too. As a navy wife you'll have obligations and duties,' said Angela.

Bradley appeared with a waiter carrying a tray with champagne and four glasses. 'Here we are . . . time to celebrate.' He glanced at Catherine who gave him a smile.

The waiter filled the glasses and Richard lifted his champagne. 'Here's to you, Catherine. Welcome to the family. I hope you and Bradley will be as happy as you can be.'

'Indeed, darlings. This is so exciting. Bradley, dear, to you and Catherine.' Angela delicately sipped her champagne.

'To you, son,' said Richard. 'Congratulations. Pleased to see you settling down at last. Always thought you were too picky. But you've found a little gem in your Aussie gal here.'

Bradley winked at Catherine as he raised his glass.

'See the world first, we told him,' Angela said to Catherine. 'And that's what he's doing. You wait till you come visit our home and see Marin County. God's own country. You'll adore California.'

Bradley caught the expression on Catherine's face and said quickly, 'Catherine is hoping you'll visit Australia too.'

'Well, of course we will, dear. Shame it's so far away,' said Angela.

'You can bank on it, sweetheart. We'll make sure we head Down Under one of these days.' Bradley's father downed the last of his champagne and handed his glass to Bradley. 'How about getting your old man a decent belt? Scotch and soda with lots of ice.'

The dinner where the two sets of parents met was a great success, though, as Catherine said to Bradley, it would be hard not to like his very gregarious parents.

'Americans are a friendly bunch, aren't they,' said Keith at breakfast to Catherine and Rosemary.

'They'll be very easy to get along with as in-laws,' her mother added.

'Especially when they're miles away,' commented Keith.

'Same goes for us,' said Rosemary. 'Now, they are coming to visit Australia and stay at *Heatherbrae*, I hope. We'll have to make sure we show them a good time. I don't think they're really country people by the sound of it.'

'Mum, that's not going to be for a while, so don't start planning just yet,' said Catherine. She didn't like to remind them that Bradley had already arranged for the two of them to spend Thanksgiving in California to meet the rest of his family.

'Well, I'd like to spend some more time with Bradley, on his own. Just the four of us. Get to know him better,' said Rosemary.

'I'm not going to give the poor chap the rounds of the kitchen,' said Keith. 'If Catherine's picked him then that's all there is it to it.'

'And it is a small wedding, Mum. There'll be plenty of time to get to know him.'

'If it were at home it would be a full-on event with a hundred people and four bridesmaids and so on,' sighed her mother.

'More like two hundred,' said her father. 'You've got a good bloke in Bradley. So what're you wearing? A grass skirt?'

Catherine laughed. 'No, you know I'm not. I have a new friend here, a lovely girl, in fact you'll see her tonight. It's our turn to host dinner so I thought we'd go to the Moonflower and see Kiann'e dance. I'm so glad Mollie has arrived, she's going to love Kiann'e.'

She wanted her parents to meet Kiann'e as well as see her perform. She was happy that she had made a friend here already. She and Kiann'e had got together twice since they'd met on the beach. After a coffee and exchanging life histories, Kiann'e had come to the apartment one morning and Catherine had tried on her wedding dress to get the dancer's reaction.

'I just feel it's a bit formal, stiff, you know, after seeing what people wear here,' said Catherine. 'But I couldn't not wear it. My mum and girlfriend Mollie and I had a huge shopping expedition one day in Sydney to find it.'

'Of course you can't not wear it and you look dreamy,' exclaimed Kiann'e. 'From what you've told me, you'd have had a huge wedding at home and this would be perfect.' She walked around Catherine who stood still in the tiny lounge room in her cream wedding dress. 'It's kind of Elizabethan, very romantic,' said Kiann'e. 'But it's the little crown and the veil, I think, that makes it so formal.'

'I'll pin up my hair, pull it back in a smooth bun,' said Catherine, trying to control her flyaway curls.

'No. I like that casual hair,' said Kiann'e. 'If you like I'll get you an Hawaiian tiara . . . made of fresh flowers. Keep your hair soft and I'll bring over a wedding lei of tiny pikake flowers, strands and strands that hang down almost to your knees. Then you'll look more like an Hawaiian princess. Just a touch, yet still a regal bride.'

'That sounds perfect. I can't thank you enough, Kiann'e. I wish you could be there. I'll ask Bradley.'

'No, no. Not at this late stage, and while I'd love to be there . . . this is a family thing. I'll see you on the morning.' She hugged Catherine.

That evening with Bradley, Catherine raised the idea of inviting Kiann'e to their wedding but Bradley was definite and shook his head. 'No, we couldn't possibly.

Mrs Goodwin would have a seizure. If she'd been booked to come and dance as a performer, well, okay, I guess, but Mrs G has every minute of the reception planned.'

'But what about just as a guest, as my friend?' persisted Catherine.

'Sorry, sweetheart. Not how things are done. You can see her socially, and I love watching her dance at the Moonflower . . . but, well, there's just a protocol thing. She wouldn't feel comfortable either.'

Catherine didn't argue. She knew it was a very last-minute request but she sensed there was more to the issue than that. She decided not to tell Bradley about Kiann'e's change to her wedding outfit. She'd told him she'd bought her dress at a bridal salon in Sydney with her mother and girlfriend and that was it quite traditional. He'd seemed pleased.

The day of the wedding was another perfect day. Catherine went out on the hotel lanai with a glass of pineapple juice and watched the sky turn from cloudless pink to clear blue and the tops of palm trees begin to shiver awake in the first breath of a breeze. Her father appeared behind her wrapped in the kimono provided by the hotel.

'Morning, princess. Another top day. Do you suppose you'll get sick of this endless summer, though by the looks of the greenery they get their share of rain. Hope it's raining back home.'

Catherine linked her arm through her father's and leant against him. 'I'll miss home. Miss you and Mum too. Look after Parker for me. I can't believe I'm not going back there for ages and ages.'

'It's a big step in life, love. Getting married. You sure about this bloke? The kind of life he's offering? You're leaving your family, friends and your country. But if he's the one, thems the breaks, eh?' He patted her hand. 'If you're as happy as your mother and I have been, well, you'll be all right.'

'I hope so, Dad. Bradley is terribly considerate and caring. You have any advice? Putting on your legal hat as well as your dad's hat.'

'Your grandmother always told us, never go to bed on an argument. And while you have to make your own decisions together, I don't have to tell you I'm here whenever you want an ear. Just to run things past. I know you're not one of those bra-burning feminists, but you stick up for yourself. Put your side forward as well when it comes to making those big decisions.'

'Thanks, Dad. You're the best. Look after Mum. I don't think it's hit her yet – that I'm off in the world and not just on a holiday trip. Although I'm getting married, I want to do something else that's fulfilling as well. I'd like to get a job so I can save up and come and visit as often as I can.'

'Any time you want to do that, we'll always stake you the fare. Just make sure Bradley understands how much your home and family mean to you. It's different for fellows, and Bradley seems very content here, travelling, his job, now a lovely wife. He won't feel the same pull to go back to Californ-eye-a the same way you'll miss Peel.' He gave her a quick hug. 'Don't worry about your mum. She'll be busy helping out with Rob's wedding, and I thought I'd try a few angora goats. It's a new thing. Make it her little project. I'd better wake her up. She's still complaining about these tea bags. First thing we'll do when we get home is make a decent cuppa.'

'Oh Dad, I'm going to miss you. I love you so much.'

Catherine remembered some moments quite vividly but other parts of her wedding day were a blur. Her mother became teary and upset over a misplaced earring and everyone was relieved when Mollie burst in to help dress the bride and diffused the tension, cheering them up with her bubbling excitement. Not long before Catherine and her father were due to leave, Kiann'e arrived as she promised, dazzling them with an armful of beautiful flowers.

When Catherine emerged from her bedroom wearing the tiara of tiny flowers threaded with delicate ferns and leaves and the long lei of pikake flowers, her parents and Mollie applauded.

'Stunning, perfect. What a lovely touch,' exclaimed her mother. 'Keith, quick get the camera and take a photo of the girls.'

Kiann'e kissed Catherine on the cheek. 'Ho'omaikai hauoli ame akaaka. It means blessings, joy and laughter for your married life.'

'I can't thank you enough. Promise you'll come and have dinner with us after we're back from our honeymoon?'

'Of course. Now where are you staying on Kauai? The Plantation House? The Cottages? Or the Palm Grove?'

'The Palm Grove, of course. Bradley is such a movie buff and apparently some famous old movies were made there in the fifties.'

Kiann'e smiled. 'It's wonderful, you'll love it. Be sure and tell Eleanor you're my friend. She's been like a best aunty to me.'

'Is she the manager?' asked Keith.

'The owner. She's run the place for twenty years and really made it the attraction it is. Her husband bought it along with the Moonflower but it's the real gem – thanks to Eleanor's inspiration. The Palm Grove is her life, she still has big plans for it. She always has a big dream. She's amazing.'

'My, she sounds an energetic person,' said Rosemary. 'Now you two relax and enjoy yourselves over there.'

'Kauai is a very romantic island. It's my home,' said Kiann'e. 'You'll fall under its spell I'm sure. Now one more thing before I go.' She gave Rosemary and Mollie beautiful leis that matched their dresses and then held up a length of dark green leaves that she put over Keith's shoulders. 'Maile leaves, worn by the kings and princes,' said Kiann'e. 'I've made one for Bradley as well. All the flowers were picked early this morning.'

'How about that? Well, we look a pretty smart group. Very thoughtful of you, Kiann'e,' said Keith. 'And there's one more adornment for the bride.' He took two small boxes from his pocket. 'One from Bradley and one from us.'

Too surprised to speak, Catherine opened the box from Bradley and found a string of tiny perfect pearls with a card: 'May each pearl represent years and years ahead with you. My love. B' And from her parents there were matching earrings.

Kiann'e took photos of them all and then left as Keith glanced at his watch.

'Right. Can't keep Commander Goodwin waiting.'

'The car will be there. You and Dad follow Mollie and me. Give us time to get out of the car and be ready to help you.' Rosemary dabbed at her eyes. 'Oh dear, I'm going to ruin my make-up.'

The ceremony was short, the padre's advice to the couple brief and practical reminding them to serve each other, God and country and as they left the chapel as husband and wife, they walked through an honour guard of Bradley's fellow officers.

The formal atmosphere continued at the reception at the Goodwin's lovely home. The small group gathered on the terrace and two waiters in white mess jackets served champagne from silver trays. There were several officers with their wives also at the reception. Two of these couples were the same age as Bradley and Catherine sensed they would be an integral part of their social circle. All were charming, socially graceful and made courteous if dull conversation.

After a few polite questions about Australia, their interest waned and Keith gallantly asked about the American economy and various parts of America. He and Rosemary listened as the virtues of the USA were extolled at length.

Mollie received attention from two single officers but she managed to whisper to Catherine, 'Hell, what a dead dull bunch. Wish Kiann'e had come along.'

Bradley took Catherine's hand. 'It's time to do the rounds and thank everyone. We're supposed to be out of here by six as it stipulated on the invitations. And we have a plane to catch.' He squeezed her arm.

They'd changed back at the Moana, their bags were waiting and Catherine carefully packed their leis and flowers in a box to take with her. Bradley didn't want to wear the wedding leis because he thought they would draw unwanted attention.

Outside the hotel, as they put their bags in a taxi, Mollie said she wanted to go to the airport with them.

Bradley smiled at her and told her politely that it was unnecessary. 'It's only a forty minute inter-island hop. You've done enough and it's been such a big day. Enjoy your vacation.'

Rosemary was holding Keith's hand as it dawned on her that her daughter was not just leaving on her honeymoon but was moving on from their shared life. 'I can't believe we won't be seeing you after the honeymoon,' she began. 'We should have gone to Kauai too.'

'Darling, it's their honeymoon, they don't want us oldies around. We'll be seeing them before you know it,' said Keith.

'We'll phone you, Mum. Tomorrow, I promise.' Catherine's eyes filled with tears as she hugged her parents.

Mollie grabbed her and gave her a kiss. 'I'll look after your mum and dad. You get on with the rest of your life. But call me, okay?'

Catherine nodded as Bradley shook hands with her father and ushered her into the taxi. It all seemed so rushed. She looked out of the taxi to see the three waving figures in the soft light, silhouetted against the white columns of the portico of the Moana.

Bradley put his arm around her shoulders and drew her close. 'Well, I'm glad that's all over. We mustn't forget to send a thank you to the Goodwins.' He kissed her. 'So, Mrs Connor. Are you happy? You looked beautiful. I was a bit surprised at the Hawaiian touch, but it was very appropriate, seeing how Hawaii is your home now.'

He pulled the airline tickets from his pocket to check them and didn't notice the tears trickle down Catherine's cheeks.

4

IT WAS EVERYTHING A honeymoon should be. Catherine
and Bradley spent hazy hours lazing in bed, making love,
talking, wandering along the beach holding hands and
swimming in the warm blue water. It was tropical, exotic,
utterly romantic. Barefoot, flowers in her hair, wrapped
in a sarong, it was unlike anything Catherine had ever
imagined her honeymoon would be. She also was unprepared for the magical experience of the Palm Grove
Hotel. She had an image of a tropical resort in her head,
but it was not just the hotel's setting and layout, its staff
and service, the daily events and entertainment, that had
her attention, but the powerhouse behind it all – Eleanor
Lang.

Kiann'e had contacted Eleanor to tell her that Catherine and Bradley would be there on their honeymoon.

There had been a spectacular flower arrangement in their Princess Bungalow and a chilled bottle of champagne waiting for them, with a note: *'Aloha! E komo mai. Congratulations and welcome.'* They opened the champagne as they explored their thatched bungalow sheltering in the magnificent gardens.

'Bradley, look in the bathroom – we have a basin each, but it's a giant clam shell! And there's an indoor and outdoor private shower.'

Bradley was looking at the bedhead, which was rattan inlaid with an intricate design of peacock feathers. The bed cover was a traditional Hawaiian quilt of appliquéd hibiscus and anthurium flowers entwined with dark green leaves. On the wall was a beautifully framed sepia photograph of an early Hawaiian princess.

'Seems like all the cottages are named after Hawaiian royalty,' said Bradley. 'Mrs Lang is obviously keen on the old traditions as well as the architecture.'

'Well, let's go to the evening torch ceremony tonight then,' said Catherine.

Eleanor Lang, dressed in a brightly coloured muu-muu and a fresh lei, greeted her guests at sunset. They were offered complimentary fruit juice or the evening's special cocktail and directed from the terrace along the pathway beside the row of interconnecting man-made lagoons to chairs set up at the edge of the grove of coconut trees that had been stripped of their coconuts.

Catherine and Bradley chatted to some of the other guests, many of whom were returnees who swore that there was no place anywhere in the Islands like the Palm Grove and it was all because of Eleanor.

'What happened to her husband?' wondered Catherine aloud.

'He died very suddenly just after they bought this place about twenty years ago. It was a run-down old hotel and Eleanor has transformed it. It's her life,' confided one woman.

Catherine wished she had their little camera with her at that moment. The last rays of the sun streamed through the hundreds of coconut palms, gilding the waters of the lagoons silvery gold.

Everyone suddenly fell silent as a wooden canoe slid into view on the furthest lagoon. Standing in its centre was a tall, well-built Hawaiian with a red and orange cloak over his naked shoulders. He wore a short red lava lava around his waist and on his head was an elaborate feather headdress. He carried a large conch shell.

The canoe was paddled by an older man wearing just a lava lava and a shell lei around his neck. Catherine recognised him as the man she'd seen earlier tending the gardens. He guided the canoe into the centre of the lagoon and stopped, steadying it carefully as the other man, standing stiffly, lifted the conch shell and blew a long deep musical note. The sound of the conch shell rang through the darkening grove and was followed by one more haunting call.

There was a murmur from the guests as flickering lights emerged through the palms. And then Eleanor's voice echoed from a microphone on the terrace.

'As the sun slips from day to welcome the stars of night, we rejoice in the passing of the day and the release of the spirits of the moon. These are the spirits of days past who protect and watch over the land, its creatures and all who shelter here. Enjoy this special part of Kaua'i as all who have shared the bounty and beauty of the place that was once the kingdom of kings, queens, princes and princesses and which we now know as the Palm Grove.'

Drum beats rang through the grounds and from out of the grove came two young men, lean, brown, bare-chested and smiling. They each carried a flaming torch and darted between the palms, and along the canal and lagoon as far as the hotel terrace, sprinting to light the flame torches speared at intervals into the ground. Within minutes the grove had become a twinkling fairyland. To the rapid beat of the drums, the runners, the drummers and the canoe with its heroic conch shell caller, all disappeared. Later they were to reappear in the guise of waiters, bellhops and gardeners.

'Well, that was pretty spectacular,' admitted Bradley as everyone rose and headed for pre-dinner cocktails, or to other parts of the hotel.

'Let's go for a walk around the lagoon. It's so pretty,' said Catherine. She didn't want to break the spell of the brief ceremony and the strong emotions it had aroused in her. Nor was she ready to make small talk with strangers.

They wandered into the heart of the palm grove and in the fading light saw there were plaques at the base of many of the coconut palms. Some of the trees were tall, old ones, others were young, more recently planted. In the fading light Catherine and Bradley read the names and the dates on the plaques. Some names they recognised, others they didn't – but all commemorated a tree planting here in the last twenty years.

'There must be hundreds of trees planted in here,' said Catherine. 'By everyone from movie stars to mavericks by the look of it.'

'A lot of big Hollywood movies were filmed at this hotel in the fifties,' said Bradley. 'In fact lots of films were shot on this island. Elvis, Frank Sinatra, Esther Williams, they all stayed here.

'They all seem to have contributed something to Hawaii or had a connection to the island,' said Catherine. 'Who's Duke Kahanamoku?'

'Duke was an American hero, as much for who he was

as for his prowess in popularising the sport of Hawaii's kings. He was a great Hawaiian gentleman. You should know about him, he's the father of modern surfing. I thought all Australians surfed,' said Bradley.

'I wouldn't know. I'm a bush girl,' said Catherine. 'How come you know about him? Were you a surfer?'

'Not at all. But living in California, surfing has become huge in the last few years. The Beach Boys, surfing music, that kind of thing.'

They held hands as they walked from the grove back towards the hotel dining room. As they reached the terrace Eleanor appeared with one of the young torch bearers.

'Good evening to you both. Did you enjoy our evening ceremony?'

'Wonderful. A great idea,' said Bradley.

'Do you do it every night?' asked Catherine.

'Haven't missed since we started,' replied Eleanor. 'Even when there was a hurricane! Isn't that right, Kane?'

The torch bearer beside her nodded vigorously. 'I was trying to run through water past my knees. But da torches no go out.'

Eleanor Lang looked at Catherine and said seriously, 'I like to think of it as the spirit of our island, lighting the way no matter what happens around us. I hope while you're in the Islands you learn something of our Hawaiian culture.'

Catherine studied the American woman who spoke with a cultured accent and whose bright blue eyes seemed to take in everything around her at a glance. That probably accounted for the attention to detail at the hotel that Catherine had already observed. The Palm Grove proprietor had an air of authority and a firmness in her manner which commanded respect.

'Yes, I'd like to do that. I feel very ignorant about my

new home,' said Catherine. She suddenly realised that this would be something she'd really like to pursue. Hawaii intrigued her.

Eleanor studied her for a moment. 'Make the most of your time here. I can introduce you to some of our staff, you'll learn a lot from them.'

Bradley gave a small laugh. 'Darling, it is our honeymoon, don't forget.'

Eleanor glanced at him with a polite smile. 'Of course it is. Catherine, when you return to Oahu, spend time with Kiann'e. She's a very special person. Now, I do hope you'll be joining us for dinner this evening. Our chef has prepared his famous kalua pig on the spit and coconut cream pie.'

'Looking forward to it,' said Bradley.

'And tomorrow evening, I hope you'll come to my cocktail party after the torch-lighting ceremony.'

'Thank you, we'd be delighted,' said Catherine.

'Why did you accept her drinks invitation?' said Bradley in a low voice as they walked away. 'We might want to do something else. Or just be together.'

'Come on, Bradley. You're always telling me how important it is to socialise and meet new people.'

'Well, you're probably right about Mrs Lang, she's a legend, isn't she? But we'll never see any of these other people again. And you're not really interested in hearing some gardener's story of his family or whatever, are you?'

'You make it sound like this is a one-off experience and we'll never come back here,' said Catherine.

'Oh, you mean you want to come back here for our anniversary? I'd rather explore another of the Islands. The Big Island is great, you'd like it.'

She took his arm. 'Let's enjoy being here and make the most of it, eh?'

He grinned. 'Okay. Want to forgo dinner in the Palm Palace?'

Catherine laughed. 'No way. I'm starving. Let's try the Lagoon Room.'

The main dining room was crowded. On the little stage near the dance floor an Hawaiian band played, dwarfed by the soaring peaked ceiling of thatched palm fronds and hung with coloured lights. The conch shell caller, now dressed in the hotel staff uniform of a bright aloha shirt and a lei made of shells and seeds, greeted them and showed them to their table.

'Welcome, Mr and Mrs Connor. So glad you are joining us this evening.' He gave Bradley a broad smile, showing large white teeth. 'I'm Abel John. Any time you have any request, want to go anywhere, see the island, join in our hotel activities, please, you call me.'

'Thank you. We enjoyed the torch ceremony tonight,' said Catherine.

'It's a tradition at the hotel. Mrs Lang has made the Palm Grove a very special place by paying tribute to old Hawai'i.' He gave the islands' name its traditional pronunciation. 'Enjoy your time on our beautiful island. This is Narita – she will look after you this evening.'

A short plump waitress of Japanese descent bustled around them, pouring water into glasses, unfolding their napkins, handing them menus.

As Bradley studied the menu, Catherine asked her, 'Have you been working here a long time?'

'Five years only. Many people have been with Mrs L much longer. Except the young ones. But they part of da family too. The Palm Grove family,' she explained.

'Is everyone from Kauai or do people come and work here from the other islands?' asked Bradley. 'There seem to be plenty of staff.'

'We are all from Kauai, this hotel has helped many

families. Wherever possible Mrs Lang uses local people to do things. My mother make all da staff uniforms, even Mrs L's muu-muus,' she said proudly. 'If you want some made, I can ask for you,' she said to Catherine. 'And you get one special cheap price.'

'Thanks. I'd love that,' said Catherine. 'I'll talk to you after dinner perhaps.'

'You enjoy your dinner. We have delicious ahi caught today.'

As Narita bustled away Bradley shook his head. 'Surely you're not serious, Catherine?'

'About the ahi? Here it is . . .' She read from the menu. 'Seared ahi with okra and ginger.'

'About the dresses. It's like aloha shirts – an impulse buy you never wear when you get home.'

Catherine glanced at Eleanor Lang who, dressed in her muu-muu with long sleeves, was making her elegant way around the room, greeting people at each table. 'I know, but they are very practical, flattering, you don't have to think what to wear. Add sandals or high heels and you're casual or formal. I love them. And the flowers . . .' Catherine patted the hibiscus she'd pinned in her hair.

'I like what you're wearing now,' said Bradley.

Catherine glanced down at her simple sundress, but just the same she decided that she'd buy an aloha shirt for Bradley and order a muu-muu for herself.

The meal was fresh and delicious, much of the produce was grown and brought in by local farmers, Narita told them.

During dinner there were performances by a singer nicknamed Mouse and his band and a hula dancer. Abel John acted as the MC and he called out the names of those celebrating a birthday or an anniversary and introduced Bradley and Catherine, 'Who are here on their honeymoon. We wish you many years of joy and hope you will celebrate every anniversary with us here at the Palm Grove. And bring the little keikis with you too!'

There was a round of applause and laughter and Bradley cringed and said he didn't want to dance after dinner and they left soon after their coconut cream pie was served.

It was almost their last day . . . the ten days had melted away too quickly. They had succumbed to many enticements: a waterfall picnic in the high lush hills. Abel John had given them directions to Secret Beach, where they hiked down to a pristine empty beach save for a few surfers riding the long breakers off the point; they had gone snorkelling in a beautiful bay; and Catherine had beat Bradley at a game of tennis. He was a bit put out, saying he hadn't been trying.

'You underestimated a female opponent,' laughed Catherine.

When Catherine spotted a sign 'Horse Riding' she couldn't resist the chance to go for a ride. Mouse, whose cousin owned the horses, offered to go with her as Bradley refused to sit on a horse.

Catherine was elated to be riding again and it was the perfect way to explore the ravine rising above the fields of pineapples and sugar cane. Mouse told her a little of his family history. 'Me a mix of Hawaiian Portugee and Chinese'. The latter had come to the Islands as indentured workers and they still worked the same land as their ancestors. Mouse told Catherine that he had been hired to work in the gardens and to care for the coconut palms at the Palm Grove and one day while he was singing as he worked, Eleanor overheard him and asked if he sang in public.

'I tell her, my family, we all sing,' he said. 'So she got

me singing to the guests. Sometimes my sisters sing, too. Mrs L, she even get me on a record. I made three now. We have a Palm Grove choir. Do shows and make big concert at Christmas for guests. It good fun.'

The horses broke out of the heavy foliage and picked their way along a lava rock path where Catherine stopped to admire the breathtaking views from the peaks across to the ocean.

'This island is so beautiful, so tropical and unspoiled,' said Catherine. 'No wonder it's called the Garden Isle.'

'We get plenty rain, so there are many rainbows, mists and flowers. Some of the places around here are sacred places. There's a special heiau, a temple, I could show you. Abel John knows much stories 'bout this place. He tell Mrs Lang all the old stories and she use them in the shows. She's always putting on some Hawaiian story for the guests.'

'The local people, do they know the stories, the history?' asked Catherine. This outer island, where the landscape was so untouched, made her realise there was a society with a mixed cultural heritage linked to old Hawaii that appeared to be very vibrant.

'We Hawaiian people are all mix up, but the pure Hawaiians, like Abel John, they are very proud of their people, their royalty. Mrs L, she knew the last princess of the Kauai royal family, she let the old lady live in one of the cottages till she die, 'bout ten years ago. Mrs L has been given plenty knowledge, more than many local people.' He paused, then picked up the reins of his horse. 'People here now more interested in making money from tourists.'

'It's good then that the Palm Grove gives visitors a taste of the old traditions,' said Catherine. She wished she and Bradley would be there for some of the other ceremonies she'd heard happened at the Palm Grove – the honouring of the last princess, a special tree planting and the great king's birthday.

'Yep. It's good that people know Hawaii isn't just like the rest of America. We have a special history. But that Mrs L, maybe she dress them legends and ceremonies up some. They go way back, so who's to say, eh?' He grinned and clicked his tongue and their horses moved on.

Bradley was in the swimming pool doing as many lengths as he could to work off what he considered to be his overindulgence in the copious food on offer when Catherine got back. 'Buffets are my downfall,' he confessed. 'We'll diet when we get home. Just a couple more laps and I'll be with you.'

Catherine wandered off through the coconut palms, a peaceful place she found fascinating. Bradley's comment about going 'home' had made her realise that home was now their little Honolulu apartment.

While they'd lived together before the wedding, it had seemed a temporary arrangement and it had all been fun and exciting. Now, with Bradley returning to work, she wondered what her life would be like. Cleaning, shopping, planning meals, making friends, fitting into navy life. They'd have to sort out their lifestyles, tastes, social roles and finances. It worried her that she would have no income and Bradley seemed disinclined to let her look for work. Nor was a family on their immediate agenda. Bradley had made sure she was on the pill so that they wouldn't start a family until the time was right.

It was still and steamy. No midday breeze stirred the drooping palm fronds. The soil beneath her feet smelt dank, the grass a crumpled carpet. No birds swooped or rustled the dry leaves, though behind the grove she could hear the grunt of Eleanor's pet water buffalo near the hotel zoo, a fenced section you could walk through that housed some exotic birds.

Catherine stepped onto the paved path that wound through the main part of the grove and stopped in surprise, wondering for a moment if what she saw was a hallucination. A couple were standing together, he staring into the distance as she gazed up at him.

The huge bronzed man was wearing the royal regalia of an Hawaiian king. His cloak was of feathers, as was his helmet, a great collar of shells and feathers lay against his bare skin, a skein of maile leaves was draped around his neck and he held a large carved wooden staff. His lava lava wrapped around his hips was painted like tapa cloth. His feet were bare.

His queen was dressed in a shimmering fabric, her dress long with a train, a tight bodice, high neck, the sleeves flounced over her shoulders covering her arms to the wrists edged in lace. She wore a crown of fern leaves and flowers, a thick lei of blossoms and the long royal maile leaves draped around her neck fell to her knees. It was the painting that hung in the Palm Palace dining room come to life.

As Catherine gasped, expecting the apparition to disappear in the wavering heat haze, a man's voice spoke and the royal couple relaxed their rigid pose.

'Great, move to the right and we try one more.'

Catherine walked closer and saw the Palm Grove photographer, a dark-skinned Japanese man, resetting his shot of the pair. Now, as Catherine approached, she recognised the queen as Talia, one of the housekeepers who cleaned their bungalow and the king was none other than Abel John.

'Aloha,' he called. 'How're you, Mrs Connor?'

'Good . . . What's going on?'

'Mr Kitamura is taking a picture for Mrs Lang's Christmas card. She always do something special for her cards.'

'She send out hundreds,' added Talia.

Catherine watched the photographer move his tripod and peer through the camera. Around his neck dangled another camera, which he decided to remove. He handed it to Catherine. 'Would you like to assist, ma'am?'

'Of course,' she said. For the next half an hour she stood behind the photographer as he worked, stepping in to adjust the king's cape or the queen's train as Mr Kitamura directed. Occasionally Catherine peered through the viewfinder of the solid SLR camera he'd given her to hold, framing her own version of the photograph.

'You like to take pictures?' Mr Kitamura asked as he began to pack up.

'Oh, only happy snaps,' said Catherine thinking of the photos she had taken of *Heatherbrae* and Parker. 'Though since being in Hawaii I've been thinking I should buy a good camera. There are so many stunning sights to photograph.'

'You can buy that one. I grading up to this one,' said Mr Kitamura quaintly. He held up the expensive Leica large-format camera he'd been using. 'That one you have, it very good one. Single lens reflex, good brand, strong make. It has big zoom lens too.'

'Oh, I don't think so, this looks too professional for me,' said Catherine.

'The mo better da camera the mo better da pictures,' said Abel John. 'Take a few lessons. Mr Kitamura will show you.'

Catherine turned the solid black camera over in her hands. It felt weighty and comfortable. When she looked through it, the world was reduced to a controllable image with limitations, or she could frame what she wanted and exclude what didn't please her. Or, with a twist of the lens she could make the image blurry and soft, sending it into another dimension, or bring it back into sharp-focus reality; another twist of the zoom lens and she could push the image far away or draw it as close as she chose.

Catherine lowered the camera. 'Is it expensive, Mr Kitamura?'

'Yes, when I bought it. But now . . .' he shrugged. 'I will give it to you for a fair price.'

Catherine wanted to buy the camera. But immediately she felt guilty and hated her confusion. In her single life she wouldn't have thought twice about it, but now she was unsure about her financial situation and she wasn't earning any money. How would Bradley feel about an impulse – and unnecessary – purchase like a big camera? He'd talked in general terms about a budget, housekeeping expenses and investments 'after they were married' but the talk hadn't yet eventuated. She assumed they'd sort it out when they settled into their new life. Nevertheless, she rationalised that she still had some of her own spending money left over from her holiday and so she could still do as she pleased. She nodded to Mr Kitamura. Yes, she would buy the camera. Just the same, she packed it at the bottom of her suitcase and decided not to tell Bradley but keep it as a surprise.

On their last day Catherine collected two Hawaiian dresses and Bradley's new shirt from Narita's mother in her little sewing room at the back of the housekeeper's quarters. She was pleasantly surprised at the price, which wouldn't dent her budget. She said goodbye to Mouse, Mr Kitamura, Abel John, the housekeeper Talia, the waiters and Mr Hong, the Chinese chef at the Lagoon Room, where they'd breakfasted most mornings.

Eleanor was there to see them off and she gave Catherine a kiss on the cheek. 'You'll come back to Kauai again and you are always welcome here,' she said warmly. 'Please say hello to Kiann'e and ask when is she coming over.'

'If you come to Oahu, please give us a call, we'd love to see you,' said Catherine.

'Thank you, my dear.' She shook Bradley's hand. 'Good luck to you both.'

'It's been a delightful experience,' he answered.

They drove down the driveway marked by the spreading fans of old traveller's palm trees and at the gates, where Palm Grove was spelled out in shells glued to the black lava rock wall, Catherine sighed. 'You feel like you've been visiting a family who are friends – they don't seem like staff – and you don't feel like paying guests.'

'That's Mrs Lang's recipe for success, I'd say. She probably makes the staff sit up at night memorising guests' names. One couple who'd been there before said the staff remembered their names, their children's details and their favourite cocktail and food. Everything we ate and said has probably been noted in a book for our next visit,' said Bradley.

'Oh good, we're coming back then?' said Catherine.

'Do you really want to? It was lovely, very romantic and a beautiful setting, but maybe a bit homespun, too much of the community spirit if you ask me,' he answered. 'And you can see it's getting a bit run down. Some of the furnishings need replacing. I think the place could do with an overhaul.'

'Mmm. I'd rather be here than at a cold, impersonal, big international hotel,' said Catherine.

'I'm glad you liked it.' He patted her knee. 'It was a wonderful interlude. But real life beckons, sweetheart. For me anyway.'

'What about me? What's my real life going to be, Bradley?' she asked lightly, but with some concern.

'Whatever you make of it, Catherine. Of course I'd hoped you would see your role as wife as a new challenge. And you mentioned dressing up our apartment somewhat. Not that we need to totally re-decorate, as I'm sure we'll get bigger quarters on the base and then we can rent out the TradeWinds apartment.'

'Then there's not much point in my making a nest, is there?' said Catherine. 'I should look for a job.'

'That's not necessary. I have some money put aside in investments, but we should stick to a budget.'

'And how does that work?' asked Catherine.

'I'll set aside an amount each week for our expenses, food, utilities, travel, a dinner out on Friday nights, entertainment like movies. You can manage that can't you?'

'Of course, I just want to contribute,' answered Catherine.

'Keeping the house, making meals, dropping and picking me up from work – so you'll have the car all day – attending the Wives' Club and social functions . . . sounds like a pretty full life to me.' When she didn't answer, he took her hand. 'I'm sure you'll miss your parents and this is a new place and a new routine, but I just want you to be happy, Catherine. You will tell me if there's anything . . . wrong, if you're not happy?'

'I couldn't ask for anyone more thoughtful. You've thought of everything,' said Catherine. 'I'm just a bit nervous about the Wives' Club thing . . .'

'Oh, it's just a bit of fun. And the other women will sweep you up and you'll settle in with a bunch of girlfriends and tennis and goodness knows what before you know it.'

'Great,' said Catherine. 'I just hope your navy friends are going to like me.'

Bradley turned his attention to the signs to Lihue Airport and then began talking about their trip to California to his family for Thanksgiving.

Within a few weeks a routine was quickly established. Bradley only had black coffee for breakfast and a cigarette.

91

On weekends he'd eat the fresh red papaya with lime juice squeezed over it that Catherine prepared. Then he would walk down to the mini mart on the corner for the morning paper and bring back some of Mrs Hing's freshly made malasadas, fried donuts with cinnamon and powdered sugar on top, to eat with his coffee as he read. Weekday mornings he dressed in his naval whites – crisply ironed pants and short-sleeved white shirt with the naval insignia on it – which Catherine had struggled to iron to perfection. The laundry in the basement of the building required perseverance and after a disaster with his naval dress pants they'd settled on sending those to the cleaners. Catherine also sent off a few of his dress shirts as well then hung them in his closet minus their plastic covering as they had defeated her pressing capabilities.

Meals, too, were a challenge. Catherine thought back on the parties at *Heatherbrae* where her parents had entertained and fed up to one hundred people at a gathering. Throwing half a cow on the barbecue with the men in charge and enlisting the talents of the women who were good country cooks and always brought along a casserole, salad or cake to share had made feeding everyone seem easy.

Catherine hadn't had much practice in making a candlelit dinner for two. American recipes cut from the *Honolulu Advertiser* confused her when they talked about broiling and using Crisco as a softener – was that butter, margarine or lard? she wondered. The name of the white shortening rang a bell. She'd commented to Narita at the Palm Grove about her beautiful skin and she told Catherine she used Crisco as a night cream. Catherine couldn't bring herself to cook with it after that.

Bradley sometimes liked pancakes with eggs, bacon and maple syrup – a crazy combination as far as Catherine was concerned. She was unfamiliar with the local seafood and the names of fruit and vegetables – aubergine for eggplant, bell pepper for capsicum – took getting used to. The idea that the salad was served before the meal rather than as an accompaniment threw her entirely. She could hear her dad saying 'So what's it matter?' but Bradley hinted, with a small frown, that she'd better get one meal down pat so that they could entertain guests at their first dinner party.

'Well, who are we going to invite?' she asked. 'Kiann'e and her husband? Someone from your work? None of them is going to be fussed about what we eat. In fact, why don't we get one of those hibachi things I've seen everywhere. You know, it's like a little barbecue with coals and a hot plate and we could set it up on our lanai and grill satay sticks or prawns or something.'

Bradley gave her a look. 'Our lanai can seat two people. One small table and a pot plant and it's full. It's not an entertaining area. We have enough room inside to have a dinner for six people, maximum, with drinks and hors d'oeuvres in the living area. It's tight but it can work. It's expected of us, Catherine. We owe Jim and Julia, Lance and Melanie an invitation. They've had us over twice, at least.'

'Oh. I didn't realise it was kind of tit for tat. I thought they were just being friendly, showing me the ropes, doing the right thing,' said Catherine, who'd found Bradley's colleagues and their wives saccharine and superficial. Entertaining them would be a duty rather than a pleasure. The men always talked baseball and football, the wives, well, she couldn't recall what they'd talked about really . . . the Liberty House sale, the Christmas fundraiser, one poor family's problem with a miscreant teenager. She'd tuned out. It wasn't conversation but chit chat. Someone had asked about their honeymoon on Kauai and when Catherine had launched into the characters, especially Eleanor, the ethos at the hotel, the emphasis on Hawaiian traditions, the women had lost interest, asking, yes, but what about the food? And what was there to do? To buy?

Bradley broke into her thoughts. 'That's it – doing the right thing. What my mom calls a nice gesture. We have to reciprocate, Catherine. They are trying to make you feel welcome, included. Included in my world. It's all very well feeling comfortable and relaxed here in Hawaii, which is peaceful, beautiful and has nice people who speak the same language and is part of the USA. In other posts, other situations, it can be a lot more difficult. So whom do we turn to for support, for help, for information, for fun? Our navy family.'

Catherine couldn't argue with him. Just the same, even though American culture wasn't entirely alien, the small differences between it and her own became picky and petty issues. It was similar and familiar enough not to present huge adjustments so she found she was whingeing about the way a formal table was set, how food was served. The tiny social observances that, in her normal life, were of no consequence, now became frustrating, numbing problems. At *Heatherbrae* they wouldn't have mattered to anyone. But here, in Bradley's world, the navy world, and among his friends, these little things really mattered. Table settings, flower arrangements, the latest trendy food fad – fondue and parfaits – were somehow important. Catherine wilted under the inaneness of it and the fact these things were of consequence to her husband.

She rang her mother and unburdened herself.

'Oh, sweetie, that's all quite normal. You know what a wonderful cook Granny Moreland was, and Dad had all his favourite dishes and of course I never made them as well as his mother.'

'But, Mum, this food is so foreign . . . I would expect it if I was living in Hungary or Greece, but I didn't think American food was so different to ours!'

'In what way, sweetie?'

'Bradley complains about his weight, but can't see that toasty tarts with jam – excuse me, jelly – are bad for you, and everything here has so much fat, artificial cream, and they serve just so much food on a dish, no-one can eat it all . . . the waste is shocking.'

'What about Hawaiian food? Don't they eat lots of fruit? Seafood?' asked Rosemary.

'Yes, but it's dressed up with so much decoration, trimmings, sauces and side things like chips – not French fries, crisps. I'm told real Hawaiian food is starchy and fattening. I tried poi and it's horrible – grey glue.'

Her mother laughed. 'You're overreacting. At least you're not starving. Start a new trend and eat and serve Aussie tucker. Keep it simple, plain meat and salads.'

'Mum! Meat comes cooked in lots of ways with a zillion sauces and there are a hundred types of salads from waldorf to caesar with honey cream dressing, ranch to roquefort cheese, you name it. Simple and plain doesn't exist in American cooking,' wailed Catherine. 'I'm going to gain weight and be a failure as a hostess.'

'Then, when in Rome, do as they do or just do your own thing. I'll send you some Australian cookbooks,' advised Rosemary 'Really, I can't imagine this is such an important issue. Just watch what others do, look in magazines and cookbooks. If you can read you can cook. You'll be fine.'

'Thanks, Mum,' said Catherine, not feeling all that much better.

She hoped entertaining was far off. Serving Bradley a meal each evening when he was tired, preoccupied and talking about people and plans she knew nothing about didn't make for a jolly evening. He was polite though, and complimented her on her cooking whether the meal had worked or was a rescued disaster. She began to wonder if she'd ever be up to doing a dinner for six people.

She wrote to Mollie who sent back a swift reply – 'Get a caterer or buy in ready-made on the quiet and tip it into a dish in the oven. Who's to know?'

Catherine dropped Bradley off at the entrance to the base where two sailors, smartly turned out with impassive faces under their peaked caps, manned the sentry boxes at the gate. She watched them salute and wave Bradley through. As he crossed the emerald lawn in his white uniform, she felt her heartbeat quicken at how handsome and striking he was.

She collected the dry cleaning and some of Mrs Hing's just-cooked malasadas and returned home to change for her first Wives' Club meeting, being held at the Goodwins. She put on a pretty aloha print sundress that showed off her tan. On the way to the car she picked up a plumeria flower that had fallen from a tree and tucked it in her hair.

By the time Catherine arrived, feeling slightly flustered as she'd had difficulty finding the right place to park and had taken a short cut and got lost, all the other women were there. The housekeeper greeted her and showed her into the large living room where about twenty women were gathered, standing and holding glasses of juice or cups of coffee. A long buffet table was set with food, beautifully presented on pretty dishes and decorated with slices of fruit, flowers, or radish and carrot rosettes.

Connie Goodwin came forward with a smile. 'My dear. You made it at last. I was worried you'd got lost. Oh, and you brought something, how nice.' She took the plastic box of buns from Catherine and handed them to the housekeeper. 'Put these out – on a platter, please, Amber.'

Catherine glanced at the table. 'How beautifully laid out the food is. My, I thought it was just morning tea.'

'Oh, our girls are so talented. Very artistic too.'

It suddenly dawned on Catherine that everyone had taken 'bring a plate' rather seriously, vying to outdo each other with elaborate presentations. All presumably homemade. Well, at least she'd taken the buns out of Mrs Hing's takeaway carton and put them in her own plastic box, even if it wasn't Tupperware.

'Come and meet our current club president, and the other members of the committee,' said Mrs Goodwin steering her towards one group who were wearing ribbons above their name tags. 'You'll be given your name tag at our little welcome to the club ceremony,' she added.

Catherine's heart sank. She had thought that this was to be an informal morning tea but it had all the hallmarks of a political rally, a class reunion of some private girls' school and a church supper rolled into one. Catherine had been to a lot of meetings of the Country Women's Association with her mother and had found them great fun, efficient, practical and welcoming. She now felt she was on show and being studied, assessed, judged and found wanting.

And she was dressed inappropriately. Despite the sunshine and soft breeze outside, the Goodwin's home was closed up and air conditioners hummed, sending an icy blast through the rooms. Catherine shivered and saw that the other women were dressed as if they were going to a smart lunch in San Francisco. Jackets, pencil-line skirts, high heels, nylons. Who wore stockings in Hawaii? Smart dresses were accessorised with elegantly knotted scarves or strands of pearls and gold chains. All had been to the hairdresser and their make-up was immaculate. Each woman was clearly trying to impress the others. Catherine felt completely inadequate.

She shook hands and smiled as she was introduced to the committee members. And the awkward newcomer smalltalk began.

'Yes, that's right, just married. Met in London. Kauai

was lovely. Yes, we'll be in California for Thanksgiving. His family are delightful. Yes, we hope to be living on the base very soon.' On it went. When it was her turn to ask questions she asked, 'What exactly does the Wives' Club committee do? Does anyone work?'

'We all work, Catherine. That's the idea of the committee, to share the workload,' said Elizabeth, the president.

'Workload? I meant does anyone have a job? Is anyone employed in Honolulu?'

'Not that I'm aware,' said Mrs Goodwin in a tone that implied that if she did know she would not approve. 'You'll discover all our committee and the club work very hard, not just for our own community but for those less fortunate around the world. Our country, as I'm sure you are aware, has a social conscience to help little children and their suffering mothers in those countries not as fortunate as our own.'

Catherine held her tongue and nodded approvingly, while trying to think what to say next. She came up with, 'How long do committee members hold office?'

This was safe ground and there followed a detailed explanation of the voting procedures.

Eventually Mrs Goodwin went to the middle of the room and rang a small bell and there was immediate silence. She said a few words of welcome, called the meeting to order and handed over to the president. The women all sat down on the circle of chairs as Elizabeth consulted her notes and ran through some 'housekeeping' about the next meeting, asking for volunteers to put their name down for the school and hospital visits and a proposed outing to tour the Dole pineapple plantation.

'We now come to some very pleasant business. And that is to welcome our new member – Catherine Connor.' She beckoned Catherine to stand up and join her, which Catherine did with a nervous smile.

Elizabeth handed Catherine a gold name tag pin with a small ribbon attached. 'Welcome and wear this badge with pride. As wives of the officers of the United States Navy, whose men so gallantly uphold the American flag, its honour, tradition and all that America stands for, join us in saying the pledge: *We pledge to honour our country, its fighting men, those who work and serve in every capacity to make this world a better place. We stand by those who serve. God bless America.* All stood with their hands on their hearts and Catherine mumbled along. She vaguely recalled some paperwork in the welcome kit the navy had sent home with Bradley but she hadn't had the time, or inclination, to study it. Obviously she was supposed to do so and be word perfect with all this.

Elizabeth turned to Catherine. 'And now we'll hear from Catherine.' As Catherine shot her a shocked blank look, she said, 'Tell us about yourself. Your background, your interests, your hobbies. It doesn't have to be very long,' she added in a stage whisper.

Catherine wished even more that she'd paid attention to those briefing papers in the welcome kit. 'I'm from Australia, from a small country town surrounded by very beautiful countryside,' she began in a quavering voice. 'My father's a solicitor – lawyer – and runs a small cattle stud called *Heatherbrae*. I'm an only child, so it's very hard for my parents having me live so far away but I've been brought up to follow my heart . . .' Here she gave a small smile as there were encouraging smiles on several faces. 'And Bradley is a wonderful man, very special and so . . . here I am. Oh, I have worked as a secretary, personal assistant, in my father's office and as a general dogsbody on our property.'

'Hobbies?' prompted Elizabeth.

'Riding. I have a horse, Parker, that I miss very much. I'm still adjusting to being a bride, well, a new wife. I'm not much of a cook, I don't do any craft or sew, but I'm hoping now I have the time, I might improve my skills,' she finished quickly, not wanting to appear a handicap to the group.

There was polite applause. 'Thank you, Catherine. I'm sure over the coming months we'll hear more about your homeland and we can all share our favourite recipes and handy tips with you. And, of course, we are all here to support you in any way we can. My goodness, I don't know where I would have been without my sorority sisters when I first got married,' trilled Elizabeth.

Catherine decided not to mention that she hadn't gone to university as it was not as commonplace in Australia as it was in America. The fact that Mollie and half their friends hadn't gone to university wouldn't be understood by these women, most of whom had gone to college at eighteen to 'find a husband'. Few, Catherine discovered, had done anything career-wise with their degrees.

The morning dragged on and at the time appointed on the invitation, they rose to make their goodbyes and thank Mrs Goodwin effusively. The food they'd brought had disappeared and a pile of clean plates, platters and bowls were stacked on the table for their owners to retrieve. The housekeeper stood to one side ready to answer Mrs Goodwin's sudden demands . . .

'Amber, fetch some leftover cakes for Mrs Hand's driver's family. Amber, where are the brochures for Mrs Gordon? Did everyone get their information sheets? I'm so glad you've volunteered for the Christmas craft roster, Catherine,' she said as Catherine stood in line to bid her hostess farewell.

Catherine had not wanted to volunteer for anything specific, but had become aware that one had to sign up for something and so had put her name on the first sheet handed to her. Craft. She had no craft skills. Well, she'd deal with that later. She just wanted to get out of the freezing house and claustrophobic atmosphere.

Driving home Catherine broke into peals of laughter in the car and wished that Mollie was with her to hear her mimic the president and some of the other women.

Over a drink before dinner she began to regale Bradley with her now hilarious morning, but he stood up and cut her short.

'Catherine, I don't find it at all amusing. You're being childish and quite unappreciative. These women mean well, they are trying to help you fit in, and, remember, their husbands are my work colleagues and fellow officers and, indeed, superiors. If you offend them you harm my professional standing. Please be aware of that.'

'Oh, come on, Bradley. It was a morning tea party with a bunch of women with nothing but time on their hands trying to feel important,' she retorted.

'Catherine, that's not the right attitude at all. You have to stop being so critical. Have you considered those women probably feel sorry for you? They consider you a country girl from Down Under who has a lot to learn about how things are done in the USA?'

'What rubbish!'

Bradley sighed. 'Look, just fit in, be sweet, listen, do what it takes. Don't rock the boat. It's my career and the wives play an important role, even when it comes to promotion. This marriage is a partnership. I thought you understood that.' He spoke in a serious voice as if to an errant child.

Catherine didn't know whether to laugh or cry. She wanted to raise her voice and tell him he was being ridiculous. When Bradley had talked about his career, the support of the other wives, the navy community – the navy family – she'd thought in general terms, in the big scheme of things: some social events and if there was a problem, then the other women were there to support you. She hadn't considered that she would have to play a role in the minutiae of a weekly social club with women whose focus was so narrow.

'Okay, Bradley. If it means so much to you and my baking cakes and going to craft classes will help your career path then of course, I'll do whatever you say.'

He gave her a sharp look to see if she was being facetious though her tone was meek. 'I'm not telling you what to do, Catherine. I'm assuming you will make that call yourself and know what is the correct thing to do.'

She changed the subject and busied herself in the kitchen wondering if they'd just had their first fight.

It was a relief when she had a chance to meet Kiann'e for coffee and the two hours they spent together disappeared in a flash. Catherine told her how wonderful she thought Eleanor and the Palm Grove were and Kiann'e told her more about Eleanor, Abel John, Mouse and the ethos of working for the hotel.

'Eleanor can be a tyrant in some ways, things just have to be done her way, there is no other. But you can't deny she's what makes it work. She took me under her wing and encouraged me and she arranged a job for me at the Moonflower.'

'I find it strange that a woman from the East Coast should be so steeped in the culture and traditions of Hawaii. How, why did she come to the Islands?'

'I think she ran away from a broken romance somewhere. She doesn't like to talk about herself. She married Ed Lang who was older and they were so happy. I know she desperately wanted a child but it didn't happen, then Ed died so suddenly and everyone thought she'd sell their hotels they'd bought and go back East. But she threw herself into the Palm Grove and it was like she was reborn. It *is* her life.'

'She seems very knowledgeable about the old traditions, the history and so on,' said Catherine. 'I was fascinated. All I knew about Hawaii was Waikiki Beach and that Captain Cook was killed on the Big Island.'

Kiann'e swirled the last of the coffee in the bottom of her cup. 'There's a lot to know. Many of the kids today have no interest in the old days; it's past history, they say. A few quaint traditions linger that are trotted out for tourists . . . But there's a lot happening in some quarters,' said Kiann'e carefully.

'Like what? I'm really interested,' said Catherine, aware that Kiann'e was hesitant about going into details.

The dancer smiled. 'Slowly, slowly. If you're really interested we can visit a few people, special places. I think you'd appreciate and understand there's a lot more to learn.'

'I'd like that, really I would,' said Catherine eagerly. 'I need more in my life than craft classes, tea parties and talking to women who are adornments to their husbands' careers.'

Kiann'e gave a soft laugh. 'You're Australian, so you're a straight shooter, Catherine. I like that. In the coming weeks and months, let's just tell your husband you're out with a girlfriend. But really, you and I . . . we're going on a journey.' She reached across the table and the two young women clasped hands.

THE WATERMAN

For the young man, swimming was not just a way of earning a meagre living as a lifeguard. Swimming was a challenge like running, a sport and a pleasure. It became the focus of each day. Something he looked forward to, an earned gift after the boredom of sitting on the beach and fulfilling his lifeguard duties.

When he was running he found himself as much a novelty in the suburbs of Los Angeles as he had back in Red Hawk. Residents didn't walk about much because the popularity of automobiles was increasing. Sometimes he was regarded with curiosity, but a second glance at the fit and handsome young man, determinedly running at an even steady pace and taking no notice of passing traffic, soon settled any doubts. Sometimes passers-by waved or called a greeting but most ignored him and sped past.

After the barren plains of Red Hawk, the geography of Los Angeles intrigued him and he never noticed the distances he covered. He came to know the sprawl of the town, areas of adobe houses, farm fields, the west-side mansions, the orchards of the San Fernando Valley and the cluster of buildings and movie studios known as Hollywood.

He discovered small pockets populated by foreign people and in one section, five miles from Hollywood, he discovered a dark-skinned man with heavily accented English who had opened a small shop and baked heavy wholewheat bread for ten cents a loaf. Three loaves of this wonderful bread and a bag of groceries from a local farm shop kept the young man going for nearly a week.

When he was running and swimming the young man came alive. He tested his body, felt every muscle, every fibre, every breath and every heartbeat. His feet and arms moved as a machine, but his mind whirled free as his feet pounded over the miles.

Sometimes he imagined he was zooming over the Rockies like one of the great eagles, or the hawks of his home town. Sometimes he was sliding in snow, skimming over an icy lake, or taking the first spring plunge in a frosty river. And always his fantasy, the movie in his mind, ended with him, upright, standing on a board, riding the waves of Hawaii.

The ocean at Santa Monica was unpredictable and not always suitable for serious swimming so when he heard that the smart new private sports and athletic club was about to open he managed to slip in to watch the extravagant opening ceremony.

He had never seen a building so grand. The beautiful swimming pool was on an upper floor – a first for the city – and decorated in the beaux-arts style with etched coloured-glass windows, chandeliers, lamps in the shape of swans and marble floors. On the ground floor a forty-piece band was playing and waiters in sharp suits passed around food and drinks to the movie stars and other celebrities. He was amazed when he realised that the initial 'plunge' into the pool would be taken by the Hawaiian king of swimming and surfing – Duke Kahanamoku, the very man he had seen in that newsreel in Red Hawk.

He pushed forward and was there, waiting to shake the Duke's hand as he left the pool. Breathlessly the young man, less than a decade the Duke's junior, told him how he'd seen him one day in the movie theatre and how he now dreamed of going to Hawaii.

'Look me up at the Outrigger Canoe Club when you get there,' the Duke said kindly before he was swept away by officials.

In the weeks that followed, the young man made the

acquaintance of one of the security guards of the club who allowed him to go into the pool late at night to swim by himself. With no day job other than being a lifeguard at the beach in summer and using the money from his grateful benefactor in winter, he spent every spare moment lapping the pool. He began to compete against others and frequently won. When he heard of a competition he'd turn up, dive in and win. The club began to notice his success and the club coach explained there was a system to these events and he needed to represent a club. He suggested the young man represent theirs. He no longer had to train at night by himself.

The coach persuaded him to swim for the club at the long-distance swimming championship in Philadelphia. The coach accompanied him and this time he travelled as a legitimate train passenger. Second class wasn't luxurious but it was vastly superior to the boxcar of the freight trains.

While the coach had befriended him, the young man had no illusions their friendship was based on anything more than his winning for the club. Should he fail to do so, he would once again be alone and at a loose end. He did not have close friends among the club's members or the other competitors. He kept to himself and his drive and determination isolated him.

The race was along the chilly and choppy Delaware River but when he dived in he imaged he was swimming in the tepid waters of Waikiki. He won the race by yards and found his face on the sports pages of the local newspaper the next day. The newspaper account hailed the champ from the west who had annexed the local titles in his debut long-distance swimming meet. He carefully cut out his first newspaper photo, wrote the date on it and slipped it into his wallet. He was asked to stay in the east and compete in several more events from a one-mile invitational to a ten-mile race, and he won them all. He was starting to become famous not only as a long-distance swimmer but for winning any event he entered. His name now appeared regularly in newspapers and so it came as no surprise to him that he was asked to try out for the Olympic Games.

When the Princess Matoika *sailed from New York with the US Olympic team bound for the Games in Antwerp, the young man was amazed to find himself sharing a cabin with his hero and the star of the swimming team, Duke Paoa Kahanamoku.*

5

THE SUN HAD YET to appear but already fierce gold light was piercing the soft skirts of fading night. Catherine waited on the street outside the TradeWinds watching the early morning shift workers head for hotels, coffee shops and businesses. Even though Honolulu was a holiday place, where, on a morning like this, you could tell already from the gentle breeze, the warmth in the air and the clear sky that it was going to be a picture-postcard day, life for many was as humdrum as in any city in America. Children to get ready for school, breakfasts to prepare, news programs on television, people planning their day, going to jobs and generally focusing on the daily issues of their lives. And yet, decided Catherine, there was a difference here. The casual way people dressed, the mixture of races, the smiling demeanour on their faces. Glance upward in any direction and you glimpsed a palm tree with the knowledge that not far away you'd strike a strip of beautiful beach and stunning scenery. Yes, Hawaii was different. Living here she couldn't escape or ignore the fact she was part of this 'island paradise' and, as everyone reminded her, she was lucky to be part of it.

Kiann'e had suggested that Catherine join her on one of her early morning outings where she walked on the beach, had a swim and was home in time to make her husband's breakfast before he went to work. Catherine agreed, though she admitted to being not much of a beach person.

She recognised Kiann'e's little red truck as it pulled into the curb.

'Morning. Have I kept you waiting?' asked Kiann'e.

'No, I didn't want you to have to wait so I was a few minutes early.'

'Is Bradley up? You should bring him along.'

'He was just waking up . . . but he needs a cigarette and black coffee before he gets going. How about your husband, Willi, isn't it?' Catherine hadn't met Kiann'e's husband who ran a small factory making some sort of light industrial equipment that Catherine didn't quite understand. She knew he made frequent trips to Germany where his father had an engineering business. Kiann'e didn't talk about Willi's business or her home life very much and Catherine hadn't wanted to pry. Besides, she was far more interested in Kiann'e's dancing career and her stories about growing up on Kauai.

Kiann'e drove below the rugged peak of Diamond Head, circling Kapiolani Park and pulled into a small apartment building of dark wood with lanai railings all painted bright turquoise. The wooden shuttered screen doors gave the Ambassador Apartments a Japanese flavour. She parked underneath in a resident's parking place and got out.

'Follow me.'

'Who lives here? Anyone you know or do you just park here?' asked Catherine as she followed her out of the underground car park to a narrow strip of lawn and small swimming pool. A low rock wall separated the grounds from the beach with several steps leading onto the sand. The beach was deserted save for two men walking. An older woman was sitting by the pool reading a newspaper. She nodded at Kiann'e as they went down onto the sand.

'Let's walk first.' Kiann'e pointed up at one of the apartments that faced the beach. 'Lester Manning lives up there. He doesn't drive anymore so he doesn't mind me using his spot. A couple of times a week I pick up some groceries for him.'

'Handy. And who's Lester Manning?' asked Catherine as they began walking along the water's edge.

'Lester Manning? He was a world champion surfer for years. A legend. Like Duke Kahanamoku. And Tom Blake. Made some radical changes to surfboard designs. Very famous in his day,' said Kiann'e.

'Oh. I see. How do you know him?' asked Catherine. 'Is he a relative?'

'No. But I've kind of adopted him. He doesn't have any family. Abel John looks out for him too, when he comes to Honolulu.'

'You don't take him out?'

'Sometimes. He's in his seventies and has terrible arthritis so he finds it difficult to move around now. It's hard for a man who was so active, such an athlete who loved the water so much not to be able to enjoy it. Eleanor looks after him too. I heard she owns the apartment and lets him live there for free.'

'He didn't make money as a world champion surfer?' Catherine wasn't very interested in surfing, but even she'd read about its becoming commercialised with movies, magazines and surf shops.

Kiann'e knew what she was thinking. 'In the old days there wasn't the money to be made as is starting to be now. Mind you, very few make a living at it even now. Surfers are a special breed anyway. They do it for the love of surfing and hope they can pay a few expenses. That hasn't changed. I'll introduce you to Lester later if you like. C'mon, let's go as far as that palm tree bending over, and swim back.'

'Ah, that's why we left everything back on the beach,' said Catherine as Kiann'e sprinted ahead before wading into the clear water.

There were no waves, just a gentle wash that slapped in and out onto the sand. Catherine waded out to her waist then dived underwater as she'd seen Kiann'e do. She stroked behind Kiann'e who was swimming like a fish, her head down, arms barely making a splash as she cleaved through the water. It was like being in a huge pool protected by a reef, which suited Catherine. Large pound-ing waves like those at beaches in Australia didn't appeal to her. There were several other early morning swimmers stroking lazily through the water or floating on their backs, almost looking to be asleep. All were older people who perhaps were retirees from the mainland. Bradley had told her it was the dream of all his parents' friends in California to retire to the Islands.

Holidaymakers were stirring, sitting on their bal-conies, appearing at the open-air dining rooms of the beachfront hotels.

'Hey,' said Kiann'e, 'you're a good swimmer.'

'Well,' laughed Catherine, 'I mightn't have lived anywhere near the sea, but we did have a pool in our backyard.'

'Got time for a coffee with Lester?' asked Kiann'e.

'Why not? Bradley is taking the car today as he has a few other things to do so I don't have to race back.'

'That's terrific. Maybe we could go out for lunch. Or I could show you some of Oahu,' suggested Kiann'e.

'Sounds great. Our apartment is so small, I feel a bit claustrophobic at times, after the wide open spaces at home.'

They got out of the compact elevator on the third floor and Kiann'e rapped on the door of the end apartment then let herself in. 'Hi, Lester, it's me. I've brought a friend to meet you.'

The two women walked into the small apartment to be met by an older man leaning heavily on his walking stick. Catherine was struck by the man's straight posture and forceful presence. He had silver hair but his face and upper body were tanned. His skinny legs looked like those of a bird poking beneath his voluminous shorts. He wore a yellow singlet and his bright blue eyes and cheerful smile made Catherine think of a cheeky canary.

'Hello, hello. Who have we here? Another pretty girl. What a lucky man am I. What's your name, girl?' He held out his hand.

Catherine took his hand to shake it and was impressed by his firm and friendly grip. 'I'm Catherine. I'm so very pleased to meet you. Kiann'e has told me a lot about you.'

'Has she now? She exaggerates. So, where're you from, Miss Catherine? You a malahini?'

'A newcomer to the island? That's me,' she smiled, glad she'd heard the expression before. 'I'm from Australia. Western New South Wales. Near a town called Peel.'

'Australia! Went there with the Duke once. My, those Down Under boys took to surfing like ducks to water,' he chuckled. 'Captain Cook, after he discovered Australia and came to Hawaii, was the first person to write about surfing.'

'He was?' said Catherine. 'It goes back that far?'

'Way, way back. The Hawaiian kings were the first surfers. Royalty and the chiefs used to ride wooden planks on the waves. Show off to the villagers.'

'Lester is an encyclopedia on surfing. How are you feeling this morning?' asked Kiann'e. 'Ready for some coffee?'

'You girls go ahead. I've had my quota. But you can make me one of those concoctions of yours, Kiann'e.'

'I whip him up a milkshake in the blender with plenty of fruit and vitamins,' she said to Catherine. 'You guys sit and chat.'

'So what brings you to the Islands, young lady? Pull out a chair.'

Catherine sat on a cane chair opposite Lester. 'I just married an American, he's here with the navy.'

'Uh huh. And what do you do with yourself while he's at sea?'

'He's onshore, at the base. Administration. So I'm not on my own.'

'You've got a good friend in Miss Kiann'e. She been showing you round? You been to Kauai? That's one beautiful island.'

'Yes. I had my honeymoon there. At the Palm Grove.'

The old man's face lit up. 'Ah, that's a magic place. Eleanor and Ed had a dream and that Eleanor, she's made it happen. She's a hard worker and a tough boss but, by golly, that place is one in a million.'

'She seems an amazing woman. I really liked her,' agreed Catherine.

'Heart as big as Hawaii, too. She sure been good to me,' said Lester. 'This is her place, y'know. Belonged to her and Ed and she lets me stay here. And I'm not the only one. She don't talk about it, but I know she helped that Abel John. Put him through some school.'

Kiann'e handed Lester his milkshake. 'I'm not surprised that Eleanor helps you. You're a somebody, for sure.'

'I'm just an old kamaaina.'

Kiann'e wagged her finger at him. 'You're more than an old timer in the Islands and you know it. They call him an Hawaiian treasure,' she said to Catherine.

'Have you always lived here?' asked Catherine as Kiann'e made their coffee.

'No. Would've been 1918. Our boys were fighting in France and I was a young man. It was winter in Nebraska and I was watching a newsreel in a little movie house trying to get warm and they showed a clip of the Duke standing up on a board off Waikiki, his arms crossed, cruising down a wave like he was standing still, with sand and palm trees in the background. And I said to myself that's where I'm going.'

'And you never left?'

'Oh, occasionally. When my father died – my mom died when I was a baby – and a couple of times I had to scratch around for some money.' He paused. 'And once or twice I went to the desert. Arizona. When I needed to think about things. Sitting on a mountain, out there in the wilderness, on your own, helps me think. I reckon it's the air . . . so clear and sharp, the light so bright, nothing gets in the way between you and a conversation with God.'

'I know what you mean,' said Catherine. 'There's a small hill, a knoll, at the back of my parents' property and I like to ride my horse up there and sit and look at all the empty countryside. It's so beautiful, so peaceful. A good place for thinking.'

Lester nodded. 'Yep. The desert and the sea. Very important places in my life.'

Kiann'e brought in two mugs of coffee. 'Bet you never imagined you'd end up staying here and becoming a surf champ like the Duke, eh? He helped you a lot didn't he?'

'He was a mighty man. Helped many kids. But we became pals, real good pals. He died a few years ago and I miss him. He was an Olympic gold medallist swim champ, but he'll always be remembered as the father of modern surfing. That's right, isn't it, Kiann'e?'

'Sure thing, Lester. But you racked up a few achievements yourself. Now where's your shopping list?'

'On the kitchen counter. Say, Kiann'e, you taken Catherine to some special places? She met your family?'

'Not yet, Lester. But we'll do that.' She turned to Catherine. 'Now that's something we could do today. Go and visit my family on the windward side. I have to take some things to them anyway. My aunty will make us lunch.'

'I don't want to put her to any trouble,' began Catherine, but Lester and Kiann'e both laughed.

'Wait till you meet my family, there's always a small tribe hanging around. Nothing's ever any trouble. C'mon, I'll drop you back at your place and you can change, I'll go home and feed Willi, then we'll head over the Pali.' She dropped a kiss on Lester's head. 'Take care, I'll bring your groceries over tomorrow.'

'Aloha to your aunty. Nice to meet you, Catherine. I know I'll see you again. Say, any time you want to swim here, you know the ropes now.'

'Really? That's lovely of you, Lester. Thank you.'

Kiann'e's little red pick-up wound up the Pali and she turned off at the sign pointing to the Pali lookout.

'Have you stopped at the lookout?'

'No. I'd love to stop, we seem to be very high,' said Catherine.

'Hold onto your hat. It's always unbelievably windy,' said Kiann'e.

'What happened to the day?' said Catherine as she got out of the pick-up and felt the cool wind whip around her. They were shrouded in mist and as they walked to

115

the edge of the lookout Catherine could just make out the coastline below.

'Pali weather. We're about a thousand feet up here.'

'It's a spectacular view,' said Catherine. 'But kind of creepy. The weather I guess.'

'You're tuning in to the landscape. King Kamehameha the First conquered this island by forcing his enemies up here until they all went over the cliffs. There are a lot of superstitions about this place. Some silly – though my mother believes them.'

'Like what?' asked Catherine.

'Oh, not carrying pork over the mountain at night. And she swears she's seen a menehune up here one time. Says he followed her from Kauai.'

'What's a menehune?'

'Little people, as the Irish say. Spirit people. Small people with magic powers believed to live in the forests on Kauai. They've supposedly built many things.'

'So they're not just mystical, they do practical things?'

'Some academics say they are from an original race that first peopled the Islands. My mother doesn't agree,' said Kiann'e. 'She prefers the history of the ali'i, the powerful Hawaiian chieftans. Did you see Abel John enacting the role at the torch ceremony at the Palm Grove?'

Catherine laughed. 'I did. I have to say I'm with your mum. He looked so majestic, so big and strong. Is your mother pure Hawaiian?'

Kiann'e stared at the stretch of coastline, distant towns and beaches below them. 'No, but her mother was. Mom's very proud of her connection to the old royal house of Kauai rulers.' Kiann'e shrugged. 'It's a rather complicated history with marriages, deposings, wars, politics, the British, then the United States. The families of ruling royals exist in name only now. But she grew up on Kauai and won't move.'

'So your mother has royal blood! And on your father's side?'

'Ah, then we get into Chinese, Portuguese, other Europeans.' She grinned. 'Many people have washed ashore on these islands, fallen in love and chosen to stay. Not always with happy endings,' she added. 'Your Captain Cook, for example.'

'He's not my Captain Cook. He was English,' said Catherine. 'This wind is driving me nuts. Shall we go? I'm worried about being late at your aunty's.'

But when they arrived at Kiann'e's aunty's house, Catherine saw she needn't have worried about being so punctual.

The house was opposite a strip of parkland and a beach. The lawns were littered with palm fronds from the large coconut palms shading the house, which was a rambling old home surrounded by a wide terrace. The yard was crowded with cars, a playhouse and garden furniture, a couple of hammocks were strung between the trees. A faded striped awning sagged over the front windows. It was a house that looked as if it had been well lived in for many years. Two small children were playing in the front and when they recognised Kiann'e's little red pick-up they raced over shouting her name.

A tall stately woman came out of the house, calling to the children. Although her figure was more than ample, she walked with a straight-backed, regal carriage and was smiling broadly. Her dark hair was shot with silver and twisted into a braid on top of her head and a flower was tucked into the side. Bare brown feet poked from beneath her muu-muu.

'Aloha, girls. Come on, Keiki, here's Kiann'e and her friend.'

The little boy and girl ran to Kiann'e, wrapping their arms around her knees, while glancing shyly at Catherine.

'This is Catherine. Give her a hug too,' said Kiann'e. 'These are my cousin's children. One of my cousins. We're a big family. Aunty looks after them while their parents work. And those two,' she pointed at two older girls hanging by the front door, 'they're neighbours who are living here for a while . . . been a few problems in their family, so Aunty is caring for them.

'Catherine, this is my aunt, Keialani Pakula – everyone calls her Lani.'

Kiann'e's aunt opened her arms and swept Catherine into a big hug. 'Welcome to the ohana. Come, come inside. You two, cold drinks, go and pour them.' She waved at the two older girls who giggled and hurried inside. 'Kiann'e says you are a new bride and new to the Islands . . . We'd better show you some old-fashioned Hawaiian hospitality, then.'

'Everyone is being wonderful. I hope we haven't sprung this visit on you. It looks like you have your hands full.'

'Nonsense. Many hands make light work. A cold juice and a walk around the garden before we eat.'

'I've brought things you wanted, Aunty. I'll unpack them,' said Kiann'e carrying a brown paper supermarket bag inside.

Lani took Catherine's hand and, trailed by a small boy, they walked through the house to the back porch where a large brick barbecue was smouldering. There was a long table with mismatched chairs under an old thatched roof as well as an unpainted shed that was crammed with canoes, surfboards, a lawn mower, storage boxes and tools. A fish pond with water lilies and a small pit covered with wire mesh surrounded by burnt grass completed the picture.

'What's that?' asked Catherine.

'That's our imu. Nothing fancy, just an underground oven, for luaus and any time we want to cook for a big group. You had lomi pig yet?'

'We had roast pig on a spit at the Palm Grove.'

'Not the same as in the underground oven. We'll have a luau one of these days. You bring your husband.'

'That'd be great.'

'Doesn't have to be a special occasion, we just get people together, get the pig, or a goat, cook it all day and in the night we eat and sing and dance. You sing, play ukulele or do hula?'

'Oh, gosh no. I just love watching Kiann'e dance.'

'Everyone can learn hula. We teach 'em from babies. Little boys too. You show Catherine how you can dance, yes, Otis?'

The little boy nodded seriously. 'And the mele, Lani?'

'For sure. You know 'bout that, Catherine? The important things to learn? Oli, the old chants, mele, the songs, mo'oleho, storytelling, and hula, the dance. That's how we pass on our culture, from ancient times.'

'The Aborigines back home do this sort of thing too. I'm looking forward to seeing it. Not like the shows done for the tourists, I suppose.'

'The essence is there. Kiann'e dances some of the old hulas but the tourists they want the happa haole stuff, what they see in the movies, hear on the records. But that's okay, many of the old songs and dances are sacred, some that have been handed down are secret.'

'Has the hula always been just entertainment? How did it start?' asked Catherine who was beginning to realise there was more to the dance than the swaying dusky maidens in grass skirts depicted in old movies and on postcards.

'How it began is lost in the mists of old Hawai'i . . . maybe because it was a form of worship of the Gods and homage to the ali'i, the old ruling chiefs, it could have come from a spiritual base. But it's always been used to greet visitors, entertain on special occasions. But the way it was taught in the old days was very strict, very kapu, taboo.'

'I heard that the missionaries banned the hula,' said Catherine.

Lani chuckled as they walked around a bank of hibiscus bushes. 'They found it too sensual, depraved even. So, yep, they banned hula and put the women in long dresses.' She lifted the hem of her cotton, ankle length muu-muu. 'However that tradition has stuck. Most comfortable dress invented.'

By the time they had circled the house, there were several men standing around the barbecue where hamburgers were sizzling. Kiann'e and the older girls were setting the table under the thatched pergola and another woman came from the kitchen carrying a large bowl.

'Heavens, it's a party!' exclaimed Catherine.

'No, just some friends come by. Arnold Lapoka and Bill Opooku been helping me fix up the roof. That's Bill's wife, she helps me with the keikis, like little Otis here. I never know how many heads we have around a table or how many beds I got to find come night time,' chuckled Lani.

Catherine was introduced to the friendly, casual group. Salads were prepared, yams wrapped and tied in banana skins had been baked and Bill expertly slashed the tops off a bunch of green coconuts which were then handed around with straws poked in them.

'Hawaiian milkshake,' said Kiann'e. 'And after you finish the juice you scoop out the soft flesh, it's delicious.'

It was a very informal meal with lots of passing of dishes, chatter and laughter. The children climbed on laps, were hugged and kissed and teased, then given small tasks to do to help clean up. The men leaned back in their chairs. Arnold pulled a small harmonica from his pocket and Otis ran to bring Bill his ukulele. Suddenly everyone was singing.

Catherine didn't understand the Hawaiian words, but the sense of fun was contagious. The children were eventually lined up and, with the two older girls on each end, they sang and danced an old fishing song, mimicking paddling the canoe, throwing out the nets and pulling in the humuhumunukunukuapua'a.

'It's one little fish with da big name,' Otis told her.

Later the women and children walked across to the beach to watch the children swim.

'This is heavenly,' sighed Catherine. 'Is this all traditional land?'

'No,' replied Kiann'e, 'it belongs to Aunty's husband's family. They came to Hawaii as indentured labourers to work on the plantations and were given this land for their houses. Back then beachfront land was worthless. Now, of course, it's very valuable. Developers want it for hotels and expensive houses, but Aunty would never leave it. Too nice. I think we should start to drive back, don't you?'

Catherine was shocked by how quickly the day had sped by. She hadn't even thought about preparing dinner.

'We'll stop at Cheekys, they do a great saimin noodle salad and some pork satay. All you have to do is cook a bit of rice.'

'Sounds great. And easy. Kiann'e, I can't thank you enough. It's been a wonderful day. It was fun and I learnt so much. And your Aunty Lani is terrific. Amazing.'

Bradley was surprised by the meal and complimentary. 'Delicious. But tell me, you didn't make all this from scratch?'

'No. I have to confess, Kiann'e took me to one of her favourite hole-in-the-wall eateries.'

'That's fine for us – on occasion. Buying ready-made

food is expensive. But when we entertain, you must do it yourself.'

'I'm working on it,' she assured him, thinking of the lunch she'd enjoyed at Aunty Lani's house. Perhaps she might be willing to teach her how to make some of the delicious food they'd had. But on second thoughts it probably wouldn't be the kind of meal Bradley expected her to serve. She was dreading the idea of entertaining at all.

'When we go home for Thanksgiving, you'll see the sort of thing my mother prepares. Perhaps she can give you some ideas,' suggested Bradley.

Bradley's parents were waiting at the airport, scooped them up and headed homewards in their comfortable older model Cadillac. Sights were pointed out to her, the Golden Gate Bridge, the Bay Bridge, and Catherine remarked how the bay reminded her of Sydney Harbour.

Sun filtered through the fog and the skyscrapers glinted in the late afternoon light, then as the freeway cut through Marin County, Catherine thought how barren the countryside looked – brown hills and so few trees. They passed tracts of large homes and shopping malls clustered in muted-toned blocks like a child's building set.

As if reading her thoughts, Bradley said, 'It's winter. Always looks a bit dry. Soon we'll see the peaks of the Sierras. Should have snow on them.'

'Do you like skiing, Catherine?' asked Angela. 'If we have time we could drive up to Tahoe. Why don't we do that, Richard? The Roses told us we could use their house at Thunderhead any time while they're in Europe.'

'Mother, I'm not sure we'll have time. I want to show Catherine San Francisco. And I'm sure you have friends we have to see.'

'Now, Bradley, don't be like that. Of course, our

friends all want to meet Catherine. We thought a little party . . .' And as Bradley groaned, she smiled at Catherine. 'Get it all over and done with in one go. It'll be fun, don't you think?'

'I guess so,' said Catherine unsurely. 'Whatever you've planned is fine by me,' she added politely.

'There, you see, Bradley. Catherine's fine with a little reception.'

The Connors' home was in a quiet cul-de-sac in Deauville where the houses were similar in style, neatness and decoration. They all seemed to be ranch-style houses – elongated with French windows looking out onto unfenced lawns to the kerb. They all had circular driveways, neat shrubbery and trees and elaborate mail boxes sprouting the stars and stripes. The Connors' house was tastefully furnished with plush cream carpet, pale-blue velvet sofas, gilt mirrors and a polished wooden antique-style dining setting. Catherine and Bradley were shown to their room, which was filled with photos of Bradley and his siblings, stuffed toys and a large handmade patchwork quilt.

'What a cute little boy you were!' said Catherine looking at the toddler posing with a teddy bear. 'And here's the bear rug shot!' She laughed at the naked baby lying on a fur rug.

'I think we visited the photographer every year until we were old enough to object,' he answered. 'Don't let Mom go through the childhood picture albums – it will take hours.'

They joined Richard and Angela in the family room, a large comfortable room with an elaborate bar, a big TV, easy chairs and a long sofa with a generous coffee table. The walls were lined with photos: a group family portrait, family graduation photos and Christmas snaps.

'What's your pleasure, Catherine?' asked Richard from behind his bar.

'A glass of white wine, thanks.'

'Napa Valley's finest coming up. And you, son? The usual? Tom Collins?'

'That's fine, thank you.'

Angela carried in a platter with dips, cheese, crackers and olives. 'Hot hors d'oeuvres on the way. Your favourites, Bradley.'

'Your mother's been cooking up a storm for a week,' commented Richard. 'She's doing the entire catering for this party.'

'That's a lot of work,' said Catherine, hoping Bradley didn't expect her to do this sort of thing.

'Not really, I just make things and put them in the freezer. You know, little vol-au-vent, rolls, savoury things that can be heated up in a flash. A couple of big casseroles to eat with salad. Richard has ordered a whole wheel of cheese. It'll just be cocktails and a buffet. After all, Thanksgiving is only a couple of days away.'

The Connors' little cocktail party was rather overwhelming for Catherine. So many people to meet, names to remember, so many questions, so many compliments, so much food and drink. Sixty guests filled the sitting and family rooms and some stood outside on the patio, even though it was a cold evening. Catherine held onto Bradley's hand as they went from group to group, overhearing comments.

'Didn't you just know he'd marry someone like that!'

'She's just darling.'

'I love that accent.'

'Congratulations, Bradley, join the navy and see the world, huh? Well, you brought back a little champ.'

'Are you excited to be in America, Catherine?'

Earlier she'd helped Angela put the extension in the

dining room table and set out the good china, linen and silverware, paying attention to how Angela laid the cutlery in a carefully arranged fan shape next to the pile of plates at one end of the table. The crystal wine glasses and ice bucket to chill the champagne were set on the buffet next to two special champagne glasses that had ribbons and small flowers tied to their stems and 'Bradley' and 'Catherine' etched onto their rims in an entwined heart.

Catherine was glad she at least knew Bradley's brother, Joel, who'd been the best man at the wedding. His sister, Deidre, arrived late, dressed in an expensive lace dress and jacket with a fur collar. She kissed Catherine and handed her a huge bag of gifts.

'I'm so sorry I couldn't be at the wedding. So I've brought some wedding gifts and a few goodies I found at Neiman Marcus . . . I couldn't resist so I asked Bradley your size and what colours you like.'

'You shouldn't have,' said Catherine, feeling rather dazed as she pulled out a cashmere sweater.

'Deidre is a shopper,' said Bradley. 'I'm sure she and Mother will take you round the stores.'

'There's a wonderful white sale coming up and there's always a pre-Christmas special sale after Thanksgiving. You'll love it,' said Deidre.

'I don't know that I need anything,' said Catherine, worried about Bradley's budget and wondering why Deidre had bought her a winter top that she would never use in Hawaii.

'Need? Who said anything about needing things?' laughed Deidre.

'These girls send me bankrupt saving money at the sales,' said Richard, putting his arms around his daughter and his wife.

'I know Bradley hates shopping, so you come with us,' said Angela. 'Now let's serve the food.'

Richard made a toast and Angela announced supper was served.

Everybody gushed effusively about the food, told Bradley once again what a lucky man he was, extended invitations to them both to 'Call around for a drink before going back to the Islands' and commented on Catherine being such a darling gal, and when were they moving to California?

The whole trip was go-go, as Bradley described it. Shopping, meals at the Connors' club at the golf course, cocktails, shopping and shopping. Bradley had given Catherine some spending money. Angela and Deidre cruised every floor of every department store, went into every little store they found cute and checked out any new place to shop even when they had no intention of buying anything. Catherine didn't see the point. She found it tiring and boring after she'd toured just one smart store, trying on outfits Angela and Deidre insisted would be perfect for her.

Nevertheless, a small alarm did go off when Deidre asked if she had a nice outfit to wear for Thanksgiving, as Angela pointed out, 'We do dress for the occasion.'

Back at the house she asked Bradley how formal was Thanksgiving to be and he shrugged. 'Dad and I wear a tie and jacket, mother and Deidre wear something dressy – like they did for the party.'

'But that was a cocktail reception. People were very formal – lace, silk, jewels, bare backs, low fronts, glittery high heels . . . I thought this was supposed to be a family dinner. A time to give thanks.' She was thinking of her simple Hawaiian long dresses that could be quite formal in Hawaii but here, in the cold weather, where people came in furs and sequined tops, floral cotton didn't quite measure up.

'Didn't you buy something? That's what the shopping was all about, wasn't it?'

'No! I didn't know I was supposed to be looking for something fancy when it's just the family.'

'It's not just family. Mother always asks along a loner or two. You can't have Thanksgiving on your own. And of course Aunt Meredith is coming. Mother's sister from Portland.'

'That's not helpful, Bradley. I'm feeling dreadfully out of place here. Why didn't you tell me this was such a big deal? I thought that one of my Hawaiian dresses would be fine, and you're telling me it won't. Is it the same for Christmas?'

'Mother does go to town at Christmas when there are kids around but you know, Catherine, Christmas isn't celebrated everywhere here for religious reasons, so Thanksgiving is *the* annual event. The turkey, trimmings, the full schmeer.'

'I suppose it's the cold weather that makes it so formal.' She thought about their relaxed Christmases at *Heatherbrae*. 'At home it's hard to be formal when it's the middle of summer and it's boiling hot and all you want to do is lie in the pool.' Nevertheless, even though she found it bitterly cold outside, the inside of the Connors' home was excruciatingly hot. A fake fire flickered in the gas ornamental fireplace and the central heating roared, so everyone left their heavy outer-garments at the door and wandered around in lightweight party clothes.

'It's also the fact this is a special occasion,' said Bradley. 'Meredith is coming all the way to be here to meet you.'

'What's she like? She's your mum's older sister, right?' Catherine was trying to get a handle on all the family.

'Meredith is a bit of a radical. Quite different from Mother. Divorced when young, no children, had a career, rather bossy. But I suspect you two will get along quite well.'

'Nothing to do with being bossy, I hope,' said Catherine tartly.

Bradley smiled. 'Of course not. Just take everything she says with a grain of salt.'

'She exaggerates? Is less than truthful?'

'No, it's not that. She's rather opinionated.'

'Oh, I see. Well, I'll try not to say anything to set her off,' said Catherine, but she thought to herself it might be stimulating to hear a few strong opinions. Everyone around her was being so sweet, thoughtful and, well, bland. She supposed Bradley's family were on their best behaviour and didn't want to say anything to give a bad impression or make her feel uncomfortable. Politics, religion, nasty relatives, blunders one had made, all were avoided. Only the pleasant and adorable stories of Bradley as a little boy had been aired.

Richard and Angela weren't stuffy but even after quite a few cocktails, when they laughed a lot and voices were louder, nobody talked about anything of substance. They hadn't asked about Bradley's career, their plans and prospects, the situation with the war in Asia and the build up of the US fleet in the Pacific, or the rumours of an oil crisis in the Middle East. But then Catherine realised that as Richard was also a retired naval officer he would know exactly what their life was like. Angela asked how she was going to fix up their little apartment, where she did her shopping and how she got on with the other navy wives. Catherine didn't raise the subject of getting a job.

Meredith arrived on the eve of Thanksgiving and Deidre insisted that she take her room, as she was staying with a college girlfriend.

'I am perfectly happy to stay at the Deauville Lodge but, if you insist, thank you, Deidre. It will give me more time to chat to the newest member of the clan. Hello, my dear. You are obviously Catherine.' She advanced towards Catherine, holding out her hand and shook Catherine's hand vigorously. 'Good to meet you. Nice to have fresh blood in the family.'

'Meredith, really. You make us sound like two-headed hillbillies.' Angela led her sister down the hall. 'Come and drop your bag then we'll have coffee or a drink. Dinner won't be long. Just a light supper, quiche, I thought. A little caesar salad.'

'Saving our appetites for turkey day? Hope I haven't delayed proceedings. Traffic, you know. Everyone was travelling to get home for Thanksgiving. Nightmare.'

'Did you drive all the way from Portland?' asked Catherine.

'Certainly did. I'm heading to Big Sur down the coast. Extraordinary place. Interesting people. Tell Bradley to take you there.'

'In here, Meredith. I've put out fresh towels.' They disappeared into Deidre's old bedroom. Though she'd vacated it at eighteen when she went to college, it was still decorated in her childhood décor of ruffled pink and white gingham cushions, curtains and bedspread, all edged in white broderie anglaise.

Meredith's strong voice echoed down the hall. 'Lord, Angela, has Deidre still got all this junk? Must I sleep with those bears and dolls? I feel like I'm on a sugar overload.'

'I'll make you a black coffee. No sugar, then,' snapped Angela and left her sister to unpack.

Catherine carried the mug of coffee down to what Meredith called the sugar 'n' spice room.

'Come in, girl. Sit down on that rocker, move all the doo-dads.' Meredith took a sip of coffee, eyeing Catherine, who stared frankly back at her.

Meredith had the same eyes and mouth as Angela but was taller, broader and less glamorous. Her greying brown hair was trimmed neatly, parted on one side and held with a tortoiseshell clip. She sat very straight on the edge of the bed, her feet planted firmly on the ground.

'How are you finding the family? Married life all you thought it'd be?'

'I've only been here a few days. I hardly got a chance to get to know everyone at the wedding and it's been quite hectic since we arrived.'

'I know. You don't have to trawl around stores, you know. Tell them you'd rather stay here. Sit on the patio with a good book. That's what I do.'

'Everyone is so hospitable and Bradley wants to show me around.'

'Show you off, more like it. You're a pretty thing. Nice and natural looking. Stay that way. You like the Islands?'

'I do! Have you been there?'

Meredith smiled at the rush of enthusiasm in Catherine's voice and face. 'In the fifties. Took a cruise. I don't like to fly.'

'But you must come over and visit us,' said Catherine, surprising herself.

'No, you come and visit me sometime. I knew I'd like you. Bradley has done very well for himself. Thought he'd end up with one of Angela's endless parade of suitables. Glad to see the boy has a mind of his own. So what do you do with yourself while he's off playing boats?'

Catherine immediately wanted to defend Bradley's career and how seriously he took the navy, but she realised Meredith would know that, it was just her flippant manner of speaking. 'I'm still settling in, finding my way around, exploring. I've met a lovely local girl, a dancer. She's shown me a lot. I've been to her aunt's place. She's related to the Kauai royal family, one of the princesses, I think. Oh, and of course, I have my visits and duties with the navy Wives' Club.'

'Of course,' said Meredith with a wry smile. 'Listen, young lady, you get out and do what you can, as much as you can, while you have your freedom.' She drained her coffee and stood up. 'Angela will think I'm grilling you – on toast – to quote Richard. Let's face the music, cocktails at the ready. At least you must feel at home here.'

'You mean, in California?' asked Catherine as she followed Meredith down the hall.

'Yes.' She lowered her voice and pointed at the thermostat on the wall. 'They heat the place like the tropics in summer. Madness.' She promptly twisted the dial a few degrees lower. 'Open your window at night for some fresh air, this central heating dries you out like an Egyptian mummy.'

'Good tip,' answered Catherine who decided she liked the plain-speaking Meredith.

After supper, Meredith retired early. 'I'm not watching drivel and quiz games on television.'

Angela asked Catherine to help her set the table while Bradley and his father watched an old John Wayne movie. Catherine was initially surprised that they were setting the table for a meal happening late the next day. 'We'll eat at two p.m.,' Angela had explained. But Catherine could see the logic when she saw the elaborate preparations.

The extended dining table was covered with a starched linen and lace cloth with matching napkins in silver napkin rings that matched the silver candelabra. Angela had polished all the silver and shined all the crystal glasses. She showed Catherine one place setting: the white and silver dinner plates under the salad plates, bread and butter plate to one side, the napkin folded like a bird inside its ring centred on each plate. Catherine copied the setting around the table set for ten.

Bradley and Catherine had their monogrammed champagne glasses at their place on silver coasters engraved with a turkey and the silver carvers and platter were put in front of Richard. Angela had written pretty little place cards with guests' names and they sat in a small porcelain holder in front of each plate. In addition to the four of them and Meredith, there were Bradley's brother, Joel, and his girlfriend, Trudy, Deidre and a girlfriend, and Jay, a friend of Richard's from the club whose wife was away on a cruise.

Serving dishes, bowls, olive forks, spoons to dish out the condiments, a set of crystal pepper and salt shakers at each end of the table were readied. And in the centre next to the candelabra was a bowl of roses ordered from the Deauville florist. Once the table was done to Angela's satisfaction she ran through the menu with Catherine, double checking they had everything set for the final preparation the next morning.

'You have to be prepared, the day just goes. There's the Macy's Parade on TV, phone calls, and we have to be through in time for the boys to watch the game. Those Miami Dolphins are on a winning streak. Richard always wants to make daiquiris or gin fizzes and forgets to get the sourdough bread. So here's the mixture for the stuffing, I thought liver pate and marinated prunes this year, sound all right to you?'

Catherine nodded as she gazed into the shelves of the fridge and freezer where Angela had dishes and containers labelled with ingredients.

'The bacon rashers are to go on top of the turkey while it's cooking, they come off at the last minute to get it browned. I bake the yams with orange juice and brown sugar and we toast the marshmallows on top so they melt – just a second or two as they catch fire so easily. The potato salad – my mother's recipe, the waldorf salad, fresh green beans, gravy, cranberry sauce, and the hors d'oeuvres I've made ahead and frozen . . .'

'Dessert?' asked Catherine feeling weak, wondering how they'd get through all the food.

'Ice cream cake. But not just any ole ice cream cake, a friend makes them for very special occasions. It takes ages to create. I love making desserts, but even I can't make anything like this.' She pointed to the back of the freezer to where what looked to be a real basket of fruit sat. 'The basket is woven out of wafers. The bow on the handle is real, but every piece of fruit is a separate piece of ice cream with the flavour of the fruit – bananas, peaches, strawberries. It's just heaven even though it's so much work.'

'It looks amazing.'

'Of course, there's Jell-O, ice cream and chocolates. We like to string out dessert before coffee and liqueurs.'

Knowing what was coming, Catherine abstained from Richard's big breakfast. Everyone had to dress and assemble in the sitting room in front of the fire at midday for hot toddies, light snacks and photographs posing together in their new outfits.

Because she had not bought a special dress to wear and had already worn her one cocktail frock, Catherine decided to heed Meredith's advice and wear what she felt comfortable in. Most of the women were dressed in after-five fashions. Shyly Catherine joined them while Bradley was in the family room helping his father with the first round of drinks.

Catherine stood there in her long sleeveless muu-muu topped with a pale yellow silk shawl and her pearl necklace and earrings. Her dress was simple yet stylish with pale embroidered primroses scattered across the fabric and had the effect of making every other woman feel overdressed.

'Oh, honey, you look just lovely.'

'My, a real breath of the Islands. Gorgeous.'

On hearing the fuss being made over Catherine, Bradley came into the room. He blinked a moment as he saw her, then smiled and went to her side. 'You look just great, Catherine.'

She looked at her husband in his pale lemon shirt and camel wool jacket. 'We match.'

'You certainly do, a pigeon pair. Here's to you both. Cheers and may we all share many more Thanksgivings,' said Richard carrying in a tray of drinks.

The guests arrived. Deidre and Catherine, the daughter and daughter-in-law, passed trays of the dainty hors d'oeuvres that Angela had spent so much time making. There was general smalltalk and Meredith looked bored to tears.

'Catherine, come into the family room where it's quiet and we can have a little chat. From the small amount of time we've managed to spend together, I've come to the conclusion you shouldn't be wasted just on the navy. Get yourself a life of your own before children come along – not that they should kill a career – but Bradley's career will take precedence.'

'I've always known that,' said Catherine. 'I've never had much of a career. I wasn't sure what I was going to do when I got back to Australia after travelling, but meeting Bradley changed all that so I haven't had to make a decision.'

'Very romantic. But you can still do a course of some kind. The University of Hawaii is excellent, as is their East West Centre. I left it very late to do my masters degree, but I've never regretted it. I'm a school principal, due to retire in two years and I'm already making plans to keep busy and fulfilled in the next phase of my life. Just remember,

Catherine, nothing lasts forever, the good times and the bad times. Keep moving forward is the objective, don't stagnate, that's my motto.'

'Now, Meredith, don't earbash Catherine.' Richard appeared in the family room. 'Angela is ringing the bell. Time to eat.'

The conversation was general. Catherine was seated on Richard's right, Bradley was on his mother's right at the other end of the table. Dishes were passed along the table as Richard carved the huge golden turkey that Angela had fretted over as it was a self-basting one which she'd never tried before.

'Everything is absolutely delicious, glorious, Angela. You're such a great cook,' said Trudy. 'I must get your recipe for the potato salad.'

'It's my mother's. One of her secrets is sprinkling vinegar over the potatoes overnight with –'

'Not now, Angela. Now that we've finished dessert, let's have a toast,' interjected Richard who had poured the red wine, but kept his bourbon beside him. 'To family and friends, thank you for sharing this bountiful meal. We are all damned lucky to live in the best goddamned country in the world.' He lifted his glass, ignoring the frown from Angela at his cussing. 'Welcome to young Catherine, as part of our family and who'll be an American soon enough, not that we don't love those Aussies. American forces are out there fighting communism in Asia, and we pray that we clean up this mess and our boys will soon be home. So thanks to the Lord, to my dear wife, my children and friends. You too, Meredith,' he gave a nod in his sister-in-law's direction, 'thanks for coming so far, it's been too long since we shared a meal. Of course, your curiosity about Bradley's wife might have had something to do with it. So let's hear from Catherine, the new Mrs Connor, to propose the toast.' He sat down.

Catherine paled, no-one had prepared her for this ritual. She rose and lifted her glass, catching Bradley's eye who looked apologetic but gave her an encouraging smile. 'I'd just like to say thank you for the wonderful hospitality,' she smiled at Angela, 'for making me feel so welcome.' She turned to Richard. 'And yes, we all hope the men fighting in Vietnam will be home soon . . . Australians have fought beside Americans in the Second World War, just as they have done in Vietnam,' she gently reminded everyone. I think Thanksgiving is a wonderful occasion, and I look forward to being a part of this great tradition. Happy Thanksgiving.' She raised her glass and sat down as everyone chorused the toast and sipped their wine. She didn't look at Bradley but along the table Meredith gave Catherine a broad smile and raised her glass to her.

Richard leant over to her. 'Well said, young lady. We haven't forgotten the Aussies. I was there too, my ship was in the Pacific theatre. Met General MacArthur several times.' He patted her hand. 'Even had leave in Sydney once. What a town. What girls!'

'I didn't know that. But, Richard, what did you mean about me becoming an American? You mean take out citizenship? Bradley's never mentioned that,' said Catherine.

'Why, I just assumed you'd do that, honey. Especially if he wants to be stationed abroad. Much better for his career if you're an American. Anyway, I thought you'd just love to be a part of this glorious country.'

Angela stood up. 'We'll take coffee in the sitting room, shall we?'

As Catherine curled beside Bradley in bed that night, she raised the subject of citizenship as it had been bothering her. 'What did your dad mean about me taking out American citizenship? I don't have to do that do I?'

'There're a lot of advantages, darling, besides making life simpler for us. And any children, of course. And my career. Let's not worry about it now. We have to get up early. Mother wants us to be in the city by nine.'

Catherine turned over and hugged her pillow. She didn't want to spend a freezing day in San Francisco, which she'd been told was going to be wet and windy. Shopping at I Magnins and some wholesale outlet that sold designer clothes for seventy per cent reduction didn't excite her, especially as they would all be winter clothes. Lunch at the Top of the Mark and afternoon tea with some rich friends who had a beautiful home on Union Street sounded exhausting. She missed *Heatherbrae*, even though Bradley had promised her they'd take a trip back after Christmas. But most of all, she missed the warmth of the Islands.

6

THERE WAS ACTIVITY AT the harbour. A destroyer was preparing to sail. A tender with tourists aboard headed to the *Arizona* memorial. Catherine was not yet familiar with the workings of Pearl Harbor, but now, after a few weeks studying the panoramic view from her tiny kitchen, she was becoming more aware of the routines of the naval shipyard and dock.

Bradley had been excited when he'd come home and announced they could move to the base and rent out their apartment in the TradeWinds. Catherine was just starting to feel comfortable and at home there and she loved being so close to Waikiki. She'd accepted Lester's invitation to use his parking space and several mornings a week after dropping Bradley at the base she drove straight to the Ambassador apartments, parked, walked the beach and then took a leisurely swim.

Kiann'e had gone to Kauai for a few days to see her mother but Catherine still followed the routine of coffee with Lester as well as doing his grocery shopping, taking it back to his apartment and sitting to talk awhile. She loved these visits and found Lester's stories of life on the island fascinating.

At Pearl Harbor she felt isolated even though she was surrounded by other naval families. Nevertheless, the condominium was bigger than the TradeWinds apartment, with a second bedroom, and it had a view towards the harbour. The block was set in well-kept lawns and was close to the amenities on the base.

She was stunned at the big base PX, which supplied all the naval families with everything from furniture to stereos and TVs and souvenirs, especially Hawaiiana, all at what Catherine thought to be very cheap prices. The Commissary stocked favourite American food and products at lower prices than in the supermarkets in Honolulu. But, while it was convenient, Catherine preferred to buy from the smaller local markets Kiann'e had told her sold local produce, especially the food shops in Chinatown.

Bradley thought it was silly not to shop at the base where the fruit and vegetables were chilled and flown straight in from California and so inexpensive. But Bradley, apart from this advice, let Catherine run the household as she wished. 'It's your department, you're in charge of the budget and you're starting to turn out some interesting dishes,' he said. 'But sukiyaki and that Korean fish dish you made, they're not really appropriate for dinner parties.'

'Oh God, *the* dinner party . . . Do we have to?' wailed Catherine.

Bradley took her in his arms. 'Of course we do, and it'll be fine. You underestimate yourself. It goes with the territory, Catherine. You saw how Mother does things; scale it down, six people, that's all. The Goodwins are very understanding.'

He kissed her and she rested her head against his shoulder but she was concerned that, as understanding as Bradley's commanding officer and his wife may be, it appeared that Bradley's career prospects could be judged on her entertaining abilities.

Bradley released her. 'Do a beef Wellington, a crab starter. Something with mango for dessert.'

Subject closed, thought Catherine as she followed him out the door to drive him to work.

Kiann'e had returned from Kauai and as they walked the beach early the next morning, she told Catherine that her mother might be coming to Honolulu.

'She's visiting Aunty, looking into all the pilikia about the Big House that's happening out at the beach.'

'What kind of trouble is that? What's the Big House?'

'It's a development planned along the beachfront where Aunty lives, they want to move people out. A group of haole businessmen have come in and want to put up these blocks to sell condos to rich people from the mainland.'

'But that'd be terrible! Can they do that?' asked Catherine.

'Apparently, depending on the type of ownership you have. Land entitlements vary from gifts to informal arrangements to ownership if you're lucky. There's a plan to displace the locals who live along the coast. My Uncle Henry's land could be resumed and even if he's paid for it of course, he doesn't want to leave. It's his home. Aunty is very upset and worried. When you hear my mother and the old people talk of the Hawaiian kingdom, before Queen Liliokualani was overthrown, it makes me sad. The queen was setting up a constitution that protected the property of the local people.'

'What happened?'

'She was undermined by her government, known as "the missionary gang", which betrayed her to the rich white planters. Money always talks. So the foreign businessmen and their overseas supporters took control. They plotted with the American government representative who sent for the marines and declared Hawaii a US protectorate and raised the American flag in 1893.'

'It doesn't sound very constitutional to me. But Hawaii became a state of the Union?'

'In 1959. But it was much earlier, when we became a republic in 1894, that the fate of the Hawaiian people was sealed,' said Kiann'e with a grimace.

Catherine was shocked at the anger in her friend's voice. 'It seems to me that Hawaii is a great combination of island and American culture.'

'That's the problem! Mainland culture is not island culture. We were a sovereign nation with a long, long history laid down by our first rulers to cherish and protect our aina, our land, as the land is the provider of all life. It is the centre between the sky and the seas. Our land represents who we are and what we stand for, which it is why it's so important to us.'

'I think Aboriginal people feel the same,' said Catherine hesitantly, now trying to recall the stories she'd heard at home, although she really didn't know very much.

'Like American Indians and other indigenous peoples, our land and traditional customs are cherished. There's a change coming but it won't be easy and it won't be quick. Like, after hundreds of years speaking our own language it nearly died out when it was banned by the American government in 1900. But now it's undergoing a revival with Hawaiian language schools and so on. We're teaching Otis his own language as well as English.'

'So what will happen about your aunty and uncle's land?' asked Catherine.

Kiann'e stared at the ocean as they walked. 'I'd like to tell you. You seem sensitive and want to understand about the movement.'

'What movement is that?' asked Catherine. She was becoming aware that there was a whole other side to Hawaii and that she was only seeing the superficial, touristy, postcard picture.

'Let's sit down.' Kiann'e dropped to the sand and they looked at the smooth sea, slight rolling waves glinting in the early morning light. 'There's a group of us, no special leader or anything, who've banded together on Kauai to stop the eviction of families from a couple of the old farms and save a strip of land along the coast. It's a special place for surfers and they don't want to see development there either.'

'So it's the same as on this island? Once someone builds a resort or homes on a place like your aunt and uncle's land then I suppose it's open slather after that,' commented Catherine. 'Can't the state government stop it?'

'Heavens no, they're backing the offshore business people. It means money to the local government. The more buildings, the more people, the more fees, rates, tourism. Saving the land, keeping it the way it was and how it was managed by Hawaiian people for centuries, doesn't make them money.'

'I suppose they call it progress. What are you going to do about it?' asked Catherine.

'There's been a bit of action, petitions and so on, but that's done nothing. So we're planning a big protest here in Honolulu about eviction and property rights and development on all the islands.'

'Wow. When's that happening?'

'In a few days time. At Iolani Palace. Eleanor and

Abel John are coming over from Kauai, Mr Kitamura too, I think.'

'Eleanor? She's not Hawaiian. And in a way she's part of the problem isn't she? Promoting tourism?'

Kiann'e nodded. 'Yes, but Eleanor is sensitive at least to traditional Hawaiian culture and she employs Hawaiian people. Tourism is fine if it shows our culture properly, but when our culture is used to sell refrigerators or motor cars it cheapens what is sacred – the aloha spirit, our dances, our way of life.'

'Dances? Kiann'e, you dance for tourists!' Catherine smiled because she thought her Hawaiian friend was taking everything too seriously.

Kiann'e threw up her hands. 'I know, I know. But I'm trying to show people the classical and more traditional dances, not the suggestive or corny hulas that have been "westernised" by popular singers and Hollywood films.'

'You said Mr Kitamura is coming over . . . I wonder if I could meet up with him. I bought a camera from him but it's a bit complicated. I think I need some help. And I'd love to catch up with Eleanor,' said Catherine, trying to calm her friend down by changing the topic.

Kiann'e refused to be deflected. 'Come to the rally! We have a lot of people joining us. Lester is determined to be there. There're a lot of kamaianas coming along. You could bring Bradley. I like to think that once visitors and malahinis like yourself understand what's happening, you'll support us too.'

'Oh, I don't think Bradley would like that. He's so concerned about me doing the right thing for his career. He's worried enough about the dinner party I have to do for his boss and his wife and some others.'

'But you're not concerned about a dinner party, are you?' asked Kiann'e. And when Catherine didn't answer for a moment, she added gently, 'Come over to our place and see Kitamura and Eleanor. Bring Bradley, let him hear what we have to say. Willi is coming to the rally.'

'Well, I'll ask him,' said Catherine doubtfully.

But with the looming dinner party Catherine put off mentioning the rally to Bradley and arranged to meet Eleanor and Mr Kitamura at Kiann'e's house. When she read the recipe for beef Wellington she threw it to one side. Too hard, she thought. She decided to phone Mollie. She needed her sense of humour at this moment.

Mollie immediately made her feel better. 'Oh, for God's sake . . . I told you what to do, go out and buy stuff. Cosy up to your favourite restaurant.'

'Actually, I had thought of asking my friend Kiann'e to see if the chef at her hotel could do something for me.'

'There you go. Ask him and take your own pot. Buy a dessert and add to it. Easy.'

'Mollie, I feel terrible. What if Bradley says no?'

'Don't ask him, I wouldn't tell him . . . unless he asks. Get it all ready while he's at work. So what else have you been doing? You must be so tanned, lucky duck.'

'I swim early in the morning with Kiann'e.' Catherine went on to tell Mollie about Kiann'e's family, and the protest rally.

'Well, you're going aren't you?' demanded Mollie. 'That's not right that they can toss people out of their homes. And big hotels we can see anywhere. Next time, when I come to see you I want the postcard view . . . the empty beach, a handsome surfer, those amazing cliffs.'

'Okay, I'll fix it up,' replied Catherine. 'But you can't be serious about me going to the protest rally. Bradley will have a fit when I tell him.'

'Then don't tell him. Stay in the background, don't get up the front where you'll be photographed. Hey, there's an idea,' exclaimed Mollie. 'Take your fancy camera and tell anyone who asks you're a professional photographer.'

'It's been so good talking with you, Mol. Apart from Kiann'e I haven't got a close friend here. The other wives are nice but we have nothing in common. I guess I don't try very hard, though,' said Catherine.

'Listen, I'll call you next time. We'll take turns, say, every couple of weeks. How's that sound?' said Mollie.

'Great. I want to know all about this fellow you're seeing.'

'He's lots of fun. And that's important isn't it?' said Mollie. 'Good luck with the dinner. Just say it's your mother's recipe!'

Catherine took Mollie's advice and the dinner was a big success. The chef at the Moonflower had entered into the deception with glee. Catherine carried home a large pot of bouillabaisse, a tray of stuffed mushrooms to be baked in the oven as an appetiser and a key lime pie that stood five inches high. She was busy making garlic bread and a salad when Bradley came home with flowers for the table. Catherine told him she had everything under control.

'I'm fine with everything, darling, but could you fix the drinks?'

'It looks wonderful, Catherine. Smells good too.' He came up behind her and gave her a hug and kissed the top of her head. 'There'll probably be a lot of shop talk, but you'll be busy with the food anyway. Oh, and don't worry if the Commander nods off, take no notice, he tends to do that. Ten minutes later he wakes up and picks up where he left off.'

After everyone left and Catherine had stacked the dishes and Bradley had tidied away the wine glasses and ashtrays and taken the trash down to the end of the hall to the garbage chute, she sat down to enjoy a nightcap and put her feet up, and to tell him how she'd pulled off the meal. But Bradley wanted to go to bed and make love. He kept saying how wonderful the meal was, how impressed Mrs Goodwin had been and how happy he was with the whole evening that Catherine shrank from disillusioning him right then. She'd tell him at breakfast. Make a bit of a joke of it and promise to practise or take a course and cook the next dinner party herself.

But in the morning he was tired, running late and distracted so the opportunity didn't present itself. And so Catherine never did tell him. She did however tell Bradley she was meeting Mr Kitamura and was going to ask for a few lessons on how to use the camera she'd bought from him.

'That's a good idea. I thought that the camera was a bit of a white elephant. But it was your money. It will be good to get to use it properly.'

'Eleanor Lang is in town too, I'd love to have her over.'

'Whatever you like, though I'm surprised you were so concerned about entertaining the Goodwins and yet have no qualms about inviting such a hospitality queen over,' he joked.

'I know Eleanor is the hostess with the mostest, but she's friendly and I like her a lot. Besides, your career doesn't hinge on my entertaining her correctly. Kiann'e asked if we'd like to go to her house, too. A lot of Kauai people are going to be there,' began Catherine, but Bradley shook his head.

'I don't think so. Why? I don't have anything in common with them. I don't know why you spend so much time with these people, Catherine. You hardly ever mix with the other women here. Why don't you play tennis with them? Join the social club . . .'

'Darling, we've been through this before. I see them at the Wives' Club dos, I've already agreed to work on the Christmas committee,' said Catherine.

'Okay, whatever you like. I'm glad you're keeping busy and not moping. Some wives get dreadfully homesick and it can be very distracting for their husbands – especially if they have to go to sea.'

But Bradley must have thought about Catherine's feeling bored or lonely because that evening he announced, 'I have tomorrow off. How about we have a day to ourselves? Take a picnic to Hanauma Bay, go up to a waterfall, take a drive somewhere?'

Catherine was surprised, but pleased, and hugged him. 'I'll organise a picnic lunch.'

For Catherine, it was a perfect day. The pair walked down the slope to the semi-circular beach, which was beautifully protected from large waves, and settled themselves among palm trees close to the sandy beach. The water was jewel-clear and the dark shadows of the coral reef in the shallower water was already dotted with snorkellers.

'This is just glorious, what a fabulous place,' sighed Catherine as she spread out their towels and picnic basket. 'We can alternate between the beach, the water and here in the shade. And there's hardly anyone here.'

'It's still early. And the middle of the week,' said Bradley. 'There's lots of marine life to look at if you float around the reef. This is the crater of a volcano that was flooded when part of the rim collapsed. It's deeper further out and great for scuba diving. Ever tried it?'

'Not me. I grew up in a swimming pool so this suits me just fine.'

'Me, too,' said Bradley, taking off his sunglasses. 'I'm going in.'

She watched his tall lean figure in his favourite, faded batik swim shorts stride to the water. She reflected how comfortable they were together now, the strangeness of being with another person every day had worn off. They'd settled into a routine, they knew each other's habits, likes and dislikes. Bradley was always polite, kind and considerate. Their lovemaking was familiar and pleasant, although the issue of starting a family had resurfaced after they'd moved into their new home.

Bradley had looked at Catherine's side of the vanity where she always laid out her make-up and lotions, hairbrush and other personal items.

'Where's your pill packet?' he'd asked. 'I hope you're still taking them.'

'Why? Is that a problem?" she'd joked.

But Bradley had become serious. 'Catherine, your getting pregnant is something we have already discussed. It affects my postings, where we live, all manner of things. We want to be able to afford children and do it right, when the time is appropriate.'

'Okay, okay, for heaven's sake. I'm keeping them in here with other stuff.' She yanked open the top drawer. But she was cranky with him and felt she was being watched. She wished they could just let nature take its course and if she did fall pregnant, well, so be it. But she continued to take her daily contraceptive as deep down she had a niggling fear that if she became pregnant at an 'inconvenient' time Bradley might, just might, ask her to have an abortion. Maybe she was being unfair to him, but it was a hypothetical situation she wasn't prepared to raise.

They swam, drifting and floating in the warm crystal water as colourful fish darted beneath them. The steep lush hillside rose above them and Catherine could imagine they were cast adrift, the only people on this beautiful island. But she knew above them wound the Kalanianaole Highway and she thought again of Kiann'e's anger at the threat of increasing development in the Islands.

As she handed Bradley a sandwich she asked, 'What do you think this place will look like in ten, twenty years?'

'Well, this won't change, it's now a protected marine

conservation area. They might put in an aquatic museum, a restaurant, big bitumen parking lot. Mind you, there could be more houses along the coast road leading here. Hawaii is changing.'

'But is that good? Local people are getting pushed off their land and farms because rich Japanese and American developers want to build golf courses and condos.'

'Catherine, you've been listening to your friends too much. Hawaii is part of America, participating in the American dream, and it's un-American to stop progress. We Americans admire success and achievement.'

'That's fine, Bradley, but Hawaii is different from the rest of the US. It was a country of its own, with its own people, traditions, culture, language . . . and that's all being taken over.'

'Catherine, please! These people you've been seeing sound a bit radical. Development brings jobs and most Hawaiians want to have a nice home, a nice car, a good lifestyle. Have what the rest of America works towards. I hope you don't raise this in front of people like the Goodwins, or any of our friends.'

'Your friends, Bradley. My friends are Hawaiians and they're different. I don't think they do want to be like people in . . . Deauville, or wherever.'

'Catherine, an Hawaiian, is a mixture of races anyway. I don't believe you know any pure Hawaiians.'

'What about Abel John at the Palm Grove?' demanded Catherine.

'Ethnically he probably is. But look what he does for a living. He caters to tourists and trades on his background, how ethical is that?'

'There's nothing wrong with making visitors aware there was a long tradition and culture here that's being lost. I'm going back in the sea.' Catherine stomped down the beach feeling angry and frustrated. She felt she'd been chastised like a schoolgirl. She always thought she could never win an argument with Bradley, he was always calm, rational and somewhat condescending in any discussion and that infuriated her. It wasn't usually till later when she'd calmed down that she came up with a point she wished she'd made at the time.

Suddenly she decided she'd go with Kiann'e to the rally on Saturday morning. She'd make some excuse to Bradley and he'd never know where she was. Now that she'd had the discussion with Bradley, Catherine felt it was important. She just wished she was more knowledgeable and had the courage to walk at the front with her friends. She'd never been part of a protest or felt the need to participate in one. But since being in the Islands, meeting Kiann'e and her family and friends, something had stirred in Catherine.

She realised that, although she lived in rural Australia, she had had limited contact with and knowledge of Aboriginal culture. There were Aboriginal families in Peel and on the outskirts but they kept to themselves. Guiltily she began to reflect she had become far more interested in traditional Hawaiian culture than that of the first Australians. But she knew she was not alone in her ignorance of Aboriginal history, traditions and culture.

She had superficial impressions of corroboree dances, men carving canoes from tree bark, brilliant stockmen in the outback, piccaninnies with large black eyes, the names of some Aboriginal footballers as well as that of a popular singer, and the uglier side of shanties and humpies, the problems stemming from alcohol. Was this what Kiann'e meant when she described the superficial stereotypical images people outside Hawaii had of their culture?

By the time she walked out of the ocean to rejoin Bradley, who smiled and held out her towel to her, Catherine had made up her mind. If this was her new home and her future was linked to this country, she was determined she wouldn't be a bystander but would learn all she could.

Catherine left Bradley watching a football game with a bunch of his colleagues at a neighbouring apartment and drove to Kiann'e and Willi's house for what Kiann'e described as sunset drinks and a light supper. It was a charming house that Catherine, who had already visited on a couple of occasions, called 'old Hawaii' architecture – lots of white wooden trim with carved fretwork around the eaves and a front patio that was made from slabs of dark lava rock. She thought that Willi's business must be doing well for them to be able to afford such a lovely place. Its dark-red tile roof contrasted with the thick shrubbery and palms and flaming torches were lit at the front and on the rear lawn. Guests could be seen moving about inside through the large French doors.

Catherine was delighted to see Eleanor in the distance and Abel John kissed her on the cheek with warm aloha. Aunty Lani and Uncle Henry and their family were also there. Taki Kitamura was the only other person she could see who she knew and she was surprised by the number and eclectic mix of people.

Mr Kitamura greeted Catherine with a big grin and a slight bow. 'Have you been taking lots of pictures?' he asked.

'A few. But I want to learn how to use the camera properly, not just set it on automatic and hope for the best,' she answered.

'Once you begin to understand, you will enjoy the challenge. Perhaps even learn to print your own films!'

'I don't know about that,' she said.

A man joined them, shaking Mr Kitamura's hand. 'Good to see you here, Taki. Is this one of your students?'

Catherine held out her hand. 'I'm Catherine Connor, and I'm hoping to master a beautiful SLR I bought from Mr Kitamura.'

'You're a photographer? I'm looking for a back-up for Taki on Saturday.' He turned to the Japanese photographer. 'Can you show her enough to shoot some of the side action?'

Mr Kitamura nodded. 'I am sure.' He smiled at Catherine. 'You think you have the eye?'

'Er, I'm not sure what you're talking about.'

The man in the bright aloha shirt grasped her hand. 'Sorry, I'm Vince Akana, editor of the *Hawaii News*. We've started up in opposition to the *Honolulu Advertiser* and the *Honolulu Star Bulletin*. I'm hunting staff and need as much coverage as I can get of Saturday's rally. You're going I assume?'

'Yes, I am,' answered Catherine. 'I don't know about working professionally straight away,' she laughed. 'Though photography has always interested me,' she added, realising this was indeed the case, even if she'd never articulated it before. It was one of those things that she'd filed away as something to take up one day.

'I can show you enough to take pictures at the rally,' said Mr Kitamura. 'But it will be better and more rewarding for you to do the course.'

'Course? Where is that?' asked Catherine.

'Taki organises a photography course at the community college. Anyone can go, he's been doing it for ages and it's quite popular. There are some other great teachers too and he pops in and out. It runs for about six weeks. Between assignments, eh, Taki?'

'I hadn't considered a whole course,' said Catherine, 'but I'd like to find out about it. What sort of photos do you want, Mr Akana?'

'Hey, it's Vince. Well, whatever action grabs you,

Catherine. Bring it back to the office straight after and I'll get it processed . . . see if I can use it. Here's my card. Oh, this is a volunteer job to help me. Call it a trial run, okay, but I will pay you for anything I use.'

'Whatever you think,' said Catherine, rather bemused at the sudden turn of events.

Vince Akana took Taki Kitamura by the arm. 'I'll just borrow him, point out a few faces I need. Catch you later, Catherine.'

Catherine stood there, suddenly alone in a sea of people, until Eleanor came over and gave her an embrace and kiss. 'You look beautiful, how are you my dear?'

'Great, thanks, Eleanor. It's lovely to see you again.' Catherine smiled at the charming woman dressed as always in her long muu-muu. 'I'm doing really well. As a matter of fact, I think I just had a job interview!'

'Glad to hear it. With Taki?'

'No. As a freelance photographer. What's the *Hawaii News*?'

'It's new and very good. Giving the others a run and Vince is fearless. He feels it's his role to tell the locals' side of the story. But he's fair and unbiased. He's the proprietor so he doesn't have shareholders, a board or local councillors trying to influence him.'

'I'm not sure my husband will approve of me submitting pictures to it,' said Catherine.

'I thought he would be proud of you,' said Eleanor.

'I feel I'm jumping the gun, my pictures mightn't be good enough, anyway,' laughed Catherine. 'So tell me about the rally.'

'We're here to support Kiann'e and the cause. A lot of my staff are affected. They're locals who live on small holdings – pig farmers, fruit and orchid growers who do shift work at the Palm Grove. I hate the idea of their being pushed off their land.'

'How do you feel about development in general? I know the Palm Grove has been there a long time, but big resorts would be competition wouldn't they?'

'Not at all. We're unique. And we're all Hawaiian,' said Eleanor firmly. 'These Waikiki hotels have already copied a lot of my ideas, such as the fire-lighting ceremony. I don't mind, it's promoting the Islands. But throwing up glass and concrete all over the Islands, displacing people who have every right to continue their way of life on their land as they've always done, is not right. All the money they're expecting will pour into the Islands isn't going to help local people. Profits go, whoosh, shooting out there.' She waved her arm towards the sky. 'Offshore. Things need changing.' With that, she wandered onto the lawn to talk to another friend.

Just then Willi came in with a beaming Lester leaning on his arm and Catherine greeted him with a hug.

'You look great, Lester.'

'Good to see you here, Catherine. I'm glad you're coming along on Saturday.'

'I'm going to take some photographs for the paper. Well, that's the plan, not sure how expert I'll be,' she laughed.

'Be sure and get those boys in,' Lester inclined his head to a group of young men on the lawn.

'Who are they, Lester?'

'They are board riders from the islands so I've been talking to some of them. They want to save the surfing beaches. You're on a ride and you see that strip of beach with palms and mountains as you come in, it's beautiful. None of them want big hotels, houses, condos, shopping malls on the secret beaches, spoiling their rides.'

'So they're all surfers?' Catherine glanced out at the group. Save for the darker skinned local boys, the haole surfers all seemed to have long sun-bleached hair and were trim and tanned.

'Yeah, good looking bunch. Seem to be nice guys too,' said Lester. 'I used to be like them.'

'You're still a good sort, Lester. So these surfers have come here to be part of the rally?'

'You betcha. Surfers generally keep to themselves, but they feel strongly about the desecration of the shoreline. 'Course, a lot of them live on the beach, too. Just sleeping rough. Camping or living in shacks, you know how it is.'

'No, I don't. Lester, you know that I've never taken any interest in surfing,' said Catherine.

'Then it's time you started learning. It's what I keep telling you. Best place to do it, right here,' he said firmly.

'And there's no-one better to tell you all about it,' said Kiann'e. 'Come on, Lester. Catherine, come and meet my mother.' She took Catherine and Lester outside to the small terrace of the house.

There was no mistaking Kiann'e's mother. Beatrice Lo'Ohouiki was a woman held in some esteem. She had reverted to her Hawaiian name after the death of her husband. She sat, straight and proud, in a cane plantation chair listening and occasionally nodding as people talked in the group surrounding her. She wore a dark-green and white flowered muu-muu and a bright red hibiscus in her greying hair. She had deeper olive skin than Kiann'e but her wide jaw, high cheekbones and large eyes showed where Kiann'e's beauty had come from. As Catherine was led forward, Beatrice turned her attention to the shy young woman her daughter was introducing.

Catherine didn't know what to say; Beatrice had a powerful personality, a regal air, that was quite intimidating. Catherine held out her hand and Beatrice grasped it, pulling her towards her, a wide smile breaking out as she lifted her cheek for Catherine to kiss.

The group made room for Catherine to sit beside Beatrice on the rattan sofa next to her chair.

'I'm so glad you're joining us, Catherine. Kiann'e has told me all about you. I am pleased she has such a sweet new friend and it's important that newcomers like yourself are willing to learn about the true Hawaii, how it was, how it should be. Mahalo.'

'You're welcome,' said Catherine, unsure what to say and feeling silly that she was being thanked when she hadn't done anything. But then it occurred to her that the burning eyes and big smile from Beatrice were enticements and, like everyone else in the circle, Catherine was seduced. Lester, Abel John, one of the surfers, a haole couple and a young woman making notes, all wanted to do whatever they could to please and help this powerful Hawaiian woman. She glanced around the group. Mr Kitamura was discreetly in the background taking photographs, Kiann'e stood behind her mother, her hands resting on her shoulders.

'There's food inside, a buffet, help yourselves when you're ready.' Kiann'e leaned down to her mother. 'Can I bring you a plate, M'ma?'

Beatrice lightly touched her daughter's hand. 'Please.' She turned back to the man on the other side of her. 'There must be no unpleasantness. We can make our point without aggression. Double check any banners, posters. And the line-up and order of speeches. Loud hailers? Microphones? The petition to be handed over?'

Aunty Lani strode out to join them. The two sisters were striking, strong, formidable-looking women, gracious and hospitable, yet determined and passionate.

'Beatrice, let da people go. Food is waiting, no-one will eat until you come and help yourself first.' Lani waved at the group. 'Kau kau awaits.'

Lester got to his feet and, leaning on his cane, announced, 'I'm ready. Can I take your arm, Beatrice?'

'Don't you play being an old man with me, Lester.'

Beatrice got to her feet. 'Thank you, Lani, we'll eat and talk more later.'

'How about one mele or dance?' muttered Abel John with a wink at Catherine. 'You've settled in to the local scene. How's your husband?'

'Watching football. Have you come over from Kauai just for this?'

Abel John watched Beatrice and Lani make their way indoors and said, 'Royal ali'i performance! Between those two and Eleanor a man has no power.' He grinned. 'Of course I feel strongly about this too. My ohana, my family, is affected. As is my island. Mahalo for coming along.'

'Yeah. It's good that malahinis are interested in what really goes on.'

The surfer from the group nodded to Catherine. 'Tourists should be indoctrinated before landing here. The surfers love the Islands as much as Hawaiians do . . . you might think for selfish reasons, but our passion is real. When you appreciate the landscape, nature and mystique of a place, get into its soul, you can't stand by and see it raped.'

They walked into the house. 'I'm getting an inkling of the feelings people have for the Islands to remain an unspoiled paradise. But there's always the other side of the coin. I guess every tourist place can't be like the Palm Grove,' said Catherine.

'No. And those places that show themselves as Hawaiian are usually the Hollywood kind, or else they move in with modern Americana that could be straight from Vegas or Cincinnati. It's the pace these guys want to go at that worries me. By the year 2000 the Islands will be bulging with high rises up and down the coast,' said Abel John.

'What a horrible thought. I see why Kiann'e and her family are so determined to restrain things,' said Catherine.

*

157

The following day Catherine visited the classroom at the community college where Paul Collins ran his photography classes supervised by Mr Kitamura. She spent several hours learning the basics of her camera. She watched them develop a roll of film and make a set of prints.

'I'd love to do that,' said Catherine. 'I can see how you can compose your pictures, take a bit off here, blow up a bit there. Fascinating. Can I enrol in the course?'

'We would be very pleased to have you. Two evenings a week,' said Mr Kitamura. 'Paul runs the classes, but I like to help when I can get off Kauai.'

'I think that taking a photography course is a really good idea if it keeps you happy,' said Bradley when Catherine told him the next day what she was doing. 'You could become the official photographer for the Wives' Club.'

'I don't think so,' smiled Catherine. 'But the island is so beautiful I'll never get tired of taking pictures.'

'You can buy postcards, you know,' teased Bradley.

'But there's so much to explore!' Catherine paused. 'I thought I'd spend a few hours downtown, take some photos of the old buildings and so on for Mum and Dad.'

'Great. But the main reason that I think that the photography course will be good for you is because I've been given new orders. I'm going back to sea early next year.'

'Oh. That's not far off.' It took a minute to sink in. 'Bradley, I know you're pleased, but I'm going to miss you. When are you leaving?'

'I know it's going to be hard on you, but it is my job. You'll get used to it. Anyway, it's not right away, the exact date hasn't been finalised. We'll still have time together.'

'I guess I'll adjust to the idea. I mean, it's hardly a surprise. After all you are a sailor.' Catherine smiled, but she felt shocked just the same. Knowing that something was inevitable and its actually becoming a reality were two different things. 'Well, then,' she continued, sounding more cheerful than she felt, 'I suppose if you're not going straight away, you'll still be spending this afternoon with the boys at the rec canteen at Fort De Russy.'

'Yes, if that's still okay with you.' Bradley was clearly pleased at her acceptance of his news.

'You take the car, I can hop on a bus,' said Catherine. 'Don't forget we have dinner at the Bensens' tonight.'

Catherine found there were several locals on the bus who were going to the rally. They carried flags and rolled-up placards but there was only friendly banter as if they were going on a picnic.

There were hundreds of people gathered on the lawns and in the forecourt of the Iolani Palace. Kiann'e's group were all dressed in Hawaiian clothes and wore maile leaf and kukui nut leis and headdresses. They looked impressive. Catherine was moved and took out her camera to photograph them. There were several other photographers, including Mr Kitamura, focusing on the group.

Abel John had a loud hailer. He began to call everyone together and explained there would be speeches from the steps of the palace and then a march around the downtown area. The male leaders grouped and performed a chant, echoed by the women.

Catherine circled around the growing crowd, photographing the people who were listening, talking and waving placards. A few tourists stopped to watch but shook their heads when told what the rally was about.

'Progress, man. You can't stop it. You should be glad to be part of America,' said a loud man in an equally loud aloha shirt.

Catherine heard the voices of Kiann'e and Beatrice

speaking from the front and there was a roar of approval from the crowd. She moved closer to hear Beatrice.

'Here, on the sacred ground of our ancestors, on the steps of the building where our Hawaii Islands were annexed as a US territory, we demand that the lands of Hawaii be returned to our people, that there be no evictions of residents so their land can be turned over to outside interests. We call for a stop to the urbanisation of our precious wetlands, coastlines, hinterland and agricultural lands. We call for a halt to the military misuse of Hawaiian land. One day, from here, where our Queen was deposed, we will claim sovereignty once again, to be a nation within a nation!'

There was another cheer. Catherine lifted her camera and saw through the lens a photographer taking a photograph of her. She turned her head away and then looked for him again but he had disappeared in the crowd, which now numbered many hundreds. She pressed through the throngs of people and felt a tap on her shoulder. She turned to see several of the surfers who she had met at Kiann'e's dinner.

'So you made it,' called out one of them.

'Yes. It's quite something. A lot of passion and not much opposition to what's being said,' remarked Catherine.

'There will be. Say, this is Damien, he's from Down Under, too.' He introduced one of the young men who smiled at her.

'You staying here or just here surfing?' asked Catherine.

'Both. It's not "just surfing". We're on a world surfing championship safari,' he answered. 'You seen the North Shore?'

Catherine shook her head as there was another deafening roar and people around them surged forward.

'Catch ya later. Good luck with the pictures.' Damien and the other surfer plunged back into the crowd.

Catherine decided that she'd covered most of the

action and was about to head over to the *Hawaii News* office. She stopped to snap a placard 'Preserve Our Natural Beauty', which was trampled on the ground. A little girl in a muu-muu was standing next to the placard, lost for the moment and crying loudly, a crown of flowers tipped to one side of her head. Catherine took her picture and bent down to comfort her but the child was quickly scooped up by her father, who smiled at Catherine.

'Thanks, she'll be just fine now. This is great isn't it?' The little girl was hoisted onto her father's shoulders and they disappeared back into the crowd.

Vince Akana was anxious to hear about the photos that Catherine had taken.

'Taki isn't back yet, it's all still going on. What'd you get? I heard some of the speeches of the rally on the radio.'

Catherine carefully took the film from the camera, handed Vince the two exposed rolls and read off the notes she'd hastily made.

'I tried to move around and be the back of the crowd as I saw Mr Kitamura was focusing on the main action at the front.'

'Sounds good, sounds good. Daisy hasn't come back yet to write her story. I'll rush these through, take a look and give you a buzz. If I'm using any I'll let you know.'

'I'll buy the paper tomorrow,' said Catherine.

'Great. Thanks. And send me an invoice if any of yours appear, eh?' Vince dashed into the darkroom and Catherine walked outside to take the bus home.

Bradley was late home full of apologies about the game. He asked how her day was, but it was a polite enquiry and he jumped in the shower before she could answer. They walked over to the Bensens' large ground-floor condo for supper with some of Bradley's colleagues and their wives. As the cocktail hour dragged on, Catherine wished she could see the television news to see what coverage the rally had been given. No-one mentioned anything about the rally during supper, so she guessed no-one had been in the capitol area downtown that day. They mostly chatted about the upcoming Christmas craft fair, who was going back home for the Christmas vacation and the pull-out from Vietnam.

On the way home Catherine asked tentatively, 'So what are we doing about Christmas? Can we go to Australia? Mum and Dad are so keen for us to come out.'

'Catherine, darling, I'm sorry. On Friday I agreed to work through Christmas so some of the families could have leave. We just had the trip at Thanksgiving. We'll go to Australia later. March perhaps. How's that?'

'Oh, I see. Well, that's nice of you. I suppose with kids it's good to be with family. It'll still be warm at *Heatherbrae* in March.'

'Let's wait and see. I should be able to get some leave before I go to sea.' He reached over and squeezed her knee. 'Anyway, you said you liked it here and an Hawaiian Christmas will be different.'

Catherine perked up. 'Yes, that's an idea. I'm sure Kiann'e and her family would love to have us share it with them. That'd be such fun . . .'

'Oh no, if we're here it's only right that we spend it with the rest of our base family. The Goodwins will throw a lavish function. They bring in turkey, mistletoe, fresh pine trees, the works.'

'We could go to the Palm Grove! How fabulous that would be! Just for a day or so over the break,' suggested Catherine, thrilled with her idea. 'Wouldn't you rather have a more informal, family fun party with my friends?'

'Catherine, I won't have leave to go anywhere over Christmas. I'll be lucky if I even get all of Christmas Day off. We don't always have a lot of say in these things. We have to do what's expected of us. It's my career. You know that.'

'Yes. How could I forget?' she said tightly.

The Sunday edition of the *Hawaii News* had the photograph of the little Hawaiian girl crying and at her feet the crumpled placard 'Preserve Our Natural Beauty'. The headline above stated in bold type 'TEARS FOR OUR LOST LAND'.

Catherine was thrilled that her first professional picture was on the front page. She was about to wake Bradley to show him but then she opened the paper to see what else was in it. On page three there was another big picture of the leaders performing the old chant and quite prominently in the background she saw herself. Thankfully most of her face was covered by her hands and the camera but a close look would identify her to anyone who knew her well. She closed the paper and hid it. The other papers had given the event less prominence and their coverage had included some negative comments from others, including bystanders, tourists and a city official. She decided not to mention her part in the rally to Bradley and hoped no-one would recognise her although she didn't think any of his colleagues would read the *Hawaii News* anyway, as it didn't carry mainland news and sports results.

Christmas, then, was settled. They'd stay in Honolulu and join the Goodwins and other navy couples for Christmas luncheon. There was a separate function arranged for the single men and a dinner dance for everyone in the evening after church services. Carols would be held by candlelight in the park at Fort De Russy on Christmas Eve.

Catherine's parents were disappointed and she bought lots of gifts at the PX like the other wives were doing.

Bradley complained about her buying bulky and heavy items to mail to Australia, which was expensive in comparison to the rates to the mainland. She phoned her parents on Christmas Eve, which was Christmas Day at *Heatherbrae*, and the phone was passed around to all the friends and neighbours.

'Send us some of that liquid sunshine you have,' shouted Rob down the line. 'It's drier than Hades here.'

'We miss you, darling, but the time till you get here will go in a flash,' said her mother.

'It's going to be so dry, never mind, we have the pool,' sighed Catherine. 'I wanted Bradley to see it at its best.'

Christmas was predictable. The men wore dress whites for the Christmas meal held at scattered tables in the enclosed informal entertaining area of the Goodwins' home. The room had been kept air conditioned round the clock to preserve the fresh pine tree. One of the Christmas wreaths they'd made for the craft festival hung on the front door. Decorations of large glass ornaments covered in silver 'snow' and figures of Santa and elves were displayed on coffee tables along with macadamia nuts in monkey pod bowls. Christmas cards covered the top of a bookcase. Each table had festive runners of red and green laid along the white cloths with formal flower arrangements tied with Christmas ribbon.

The commander said grace, conversation centred around complimenting Mrs Goodwin on the food and waiting for the naval steward to refill the tiny crystal wine glasses.

No gifts were exchanged. The Goodwins had asked that donations be made to the naval children's charity. After the meal the ladies withdrew to the screened and air conditioned sunroom and the men to the patio pool room. Catherine couldn't wait to escape.

*

'It was excruciating,' she wailed to Kiann'e.

'You would have so loved our Christmas Day. We started the morning at the beach, a sort of breakfast picnic, then everyone pitches in for the big family luau . . . We cooked for days. M'ma came from Kauai and brought her special ingredients, Uncle Henry did the pig . . . we played games, it was fun. Maybe next year?'

'I doubt it. I can't believe how everyone at the base just mixes with the same people. It's like we're living in a foreign country and no-one speaks the local language,' sighed Catherine.

'There is a bit of a cultural gap. But then everyone comes together at public functions. You should bring all of Bradley's friends down to Kapiolani Park for the children's hula competition. The bands and dancers come from all over the Islands. Everyone brings a picnic, makes a day of it. There're stalls where people sell what they've made – some amazing things you never see in the shops – shells, carvings, quilts, woven grass hats, mats, bowls. You come anyway,' said Kiann'e.

'I'll try to persuade Bradley. I'm sure the wives would love it.'

Catherine was right. The other wives did want to come and they dragged their husbands along to the park for the big day of the hula competition. Just the same, they went in the morning and didn't take lunch as they didn't expect to stay very long and someone suggested they have lunch at one of the hotels in Waikiki.

However by midday when local families were bringing out their food, cooking on their hibachis and settling down during the lunch break to sing and play their ukuleles and guitars, Bradley's group was hungry. Bradley suggested they buy food from a stall and they all ate sitting on the grass. They watched families playing games with their children, pets tied to a tree in the shade, one family were bottle feeding a box of squeaking orphaned piglets. Catherine was amused to see all their friends had bought something from the stalls and taken photos of the 'darling little hula hula dancers'.

'Yes, it has been a nice day,' agreed Bradley. 'It was all very cute. A once-a-year thing. Jim suggested we go and see the new Don Ho show next Saturday night. In fact maybe we could get Don Ho to sign some of his LPs as gifts to take to your family next month.'

'I think you have to be here to appreciate Hawaiian music. But why not? Probably a more sensible gift than an aloha shirt for my dad,' said Catherine.

'And what will we bring back as gifts from your neck of the woods?' he asked. 'The Goodwins might appreciate a little touch of Australiana.'

'I can just see a big cowskin in their formal sitting room,' laughed Catherine. 'No, I know. Slim Dusty records. He's a big country and western singer at home. Swap him for the Don Ho records.'

Catherine was excited to be going home with Bradley for a two-week visit. A few days in Sydney being escorted around by Mollie and a week at *Heatherbrae* were going to be wonderful. Soon Bradley would be at sea and Catherine planned to finish her photography course and start printing her own pictures. Vince had told her she could use the *News* darkroom when available and he was prepared to pay her for any good photos. Bradley seemed happy with this arrangement as he realised that, while it was not exactly a proper job, it would keep Catherine happy while he was away. To Catherine, Vince's offer was a doorway to discovering more about the Islands.

7

CATHERINE TRIED TO SLEEP on the long flight back to Hawaii after their visit to *Heatherbrae*. She had mixed feelings. She glanced out the window and saw thick clouds and knew beneath them there was only the Pacific Ocean stretching between Australia and the tiny dots of the Hawaiian Islands. She felt the threads that bound her to her home country slowly stretching and she thought that there would come a point when she'd let Australia go and the Islands would draw her into their embrace.

But in this limbo her thoughts were with her family. The visit hadn't been all she'd hoped. It was still the end of a searing summer. The farm and landscape were brown, the creeks and the river dangerously low. The flies had driven Bradley mad and while he was charming and polite, Catherine could read him well enough to know he was bored and felt he had nothing in common with her family or their friends. But everyone liked him, thought him sophisticated and charming and said how lucky Catherine was to have married him.

The visit got off to a great start. They'd had a few days in Sydney with Mollie who broke the news that she had just got engaged. So they'd had dinner with Mollie and Jason, who was a stockbroker, which suited Mollie for, while she might claim to be a free spirit, she liked to do it with money.

Alone with Catherine, Mollie told her they were madly saving to buy a house but they'd love to go to Kauai and stay at the Palm Grove some day and she planned to keep working 'until kids come along. Of course I adore Jason,' she added, 'but he's just an average Aussie bloke, isn't he? Not a dazzler like your Bradley. God, he's so good looking.'

Mollie seemed to have her life planned out and this made Catherine realise how many upheavals she and Bradley were likely to have in the future. She had talked to navy wives who'd moved around the world, sometimes being uprooted at short notice and who had never felt they had a permanent home of their own. Their kids hated being moved from schools and friends and with husbands at sea, the wives were lonely and the burden of the family and home fell on their shoulders.

While Bradley was in Administration he'd assured Catherine he'd be shore based most of the time, but now that seemed to have changed and she wondered how she would cope with his long absences. It was all so different from what she'd grown up with. Bradley was sympathetic about the poor weather conditions at home, but he really couldn't understand how awful a drought could be for everyone. She was upset and concerned. She could see how hard her father was working and the terrible plight of Rob, who's father's property *Craigmore* was in dire straits.

In the brief time she had to talk with Rob alone, he'd told her that his father had run the place down terribly but wouldn't let him make any changes to modernise or reassess the management of it. Putting money into race horses had been a bigger concern for his father than putting money into his property. Rob's sisters had no interest in the place, nor did Barbara who, now that they were married, tried to spend as much time as possible going to Sydney to see her parents and friends.

'It's only country people like us, born here, growing up here, that really understand what this is all about,' said Rob. 'The economy is doing okay, wool and cattle prices are good. Mind you, what the meat sells for in shops is way, way more than we're getting. But our feed isn't good, the land needs revitalising somehow. Dad won't listen to my "way out" rubbish-talk of course.'

Catherine missed the yarns with her father and his neighbours and their cronies about farming, the land, cattle, life in general. But she understood that it probably was boring for Bradley, just as she'd been bored by his father's talk about the golf club, a favourite new restaurant and his sports games. She knew, too, she would miss the cups of tea and long talks with her mother when she returned to the Islands. They seemed to talk about everything. It was such a contrast to conversations with Angela and Deidre, which never got beyond clothes, shopping sales, going out to lunch and some light-hearted reminiscences about Bradley and his siblings.

As if reading her thoughts, Bradley took her hand. 'Missing everyone back at home already?'

She nodded, suddenly choked up. 'Not just the family. *Heatherbrae* and the country is so much a part of me. I know you didn't see it at its best, but it is beautiful.'

'I imagine so. I thought the sunset barbecue fire at the top of your knoll was lovely.'

'Until the mozzies came out,' she reminded him. Bradley had been eaten alive despite liberally dousing himself in insect repellent.

'Well, I did see lots of wallabies.' He hesitated. 'But really, Catherine, growing up there, what on earth did you *do*?'

She stared at him in amazement. 'I told you. We rode horses, helped on the farm, went to the cattle sales, the ag show, bush races, picnics, dances. And that's not even leaving the district. We went to Sydney and to other towns. I found Sydney less fun than being in the country. Bush kids know how to have a good time. We made our own fun.'

'But it's so rural. Aren't you happier in a city like Honolulu where you can have both? The mountains, the sea. And then we have Waikiki on our doorstep. It seemed to me your friends were quite envious of your life, Catherine.'

'They were. And I know I'm lucky, Bradley. It's just I do miss old friends, my home . . . and I can't help wondering what our life's going to be like. Not owning a home, being settled.'

'Catherine! We own an apartment. And what's all this about being settled? You were the one that wanted the gypsy life. You were so carefree, flexible, willing to take on the world. Where's that Catherine?'

She knew he was right. He hadn't wanted to marry a girl who lived near his mother, had lunch with their parents every Sunday, saw the same people, same places all the time. He wanted someone who loved to travel, someone happy to move each time the navy told them to. 'I guess I'm just homesick, saying goodbye and all. And not knowing where we'll be after Hawaii.'

'Enjoy Hawaii, we could end up in a lot worse places.'

'I know that. I truly love Hawaii. I feel a great attachment to the Islands already. Especially after the rally.'

'What rally?'

'Oh. When I was downtown taking photos . . . I saw a bit of a rally with a lot of Hawaiian people.' She stumbled over her words, cursing her slip.

'That Hawaiian land thing? Did you know some of the protesters? Was Kiann'e there?'

Catherine nodded meekly.

'I'm surprised at Kiann'e's being so . . . radical. She is different from the girl who dances at the Moonflower. So what happened?'

'You knew about the rally?'

'It was discussed in the office. Apparently there was criticism of the military. So where were you?'

'Taking photos of the Iolani Palace and downtown. So I took a few of the rally. Actually, I sold one to the newspaper,' she said defiantly.

'You what? Hell, I hope no-one saw you. Your name wasn't mentioned, was it?' asked Bradley in alarm.

'You mean, a photo credit? I don't think I'm at that level yet.'

'Catherine, this is serious. What paper was it?'

'The *Hawaii News*.'

'That trashy paper? You know that's a mouthpiece for the separatists. They've started with land issues, they're against development – and remember tourism is the life-blood of the Islands – and before you know it they'll be pushing for secession, independence or some such nonsense.'

'Bradley! People just want the right to stay on their own land. Wouldn't you?'

'Catherine, I'm not going to discuss this with you. I'm stopping this conversation right now. But just let me say this, you cannot fraternise with politically affiliated or contentious people who are expressing sentiments and essentially taking an anti-American stance. We cannot take sides when we are an arm of the government.'

'You. Not me, Bradley.'

'You're my wife, America is your home now. Good Lord, you're taking out citizenship,' he snapped in an angry, low voice. 'You're supposed to be thinking of us, our future. These foolish ideas and friends are damaging to us. Please consider that.'

Catherine was tempted to snap back, but saw the stewardess approaching with the meal trolley and so kept quiet.

They ate their meal in silence, then Bradley opened his book and settled himself with a pillow and was soon asleep. Catherine continued to stare at the blank world of clouds outside the plane. She could understand Bradley's point of view. But she could hear Mollie's voice saying, 'Stand up for yourself. Get liberated, Cathy.'

Catherine had been surprised to find that Mollie was now involved in 'women's lib' and despite her plans for her and Jason's future, she'd told Catherine, 'He's had to accept that I want a say in our plans – where to live, my working, starting a family, my money, his money.'

Mollie's outspoken attitude had made Catherine realise how much of her life she had relinquished to Bradley. But she'd loyally told Mollie, 'Bradley is so organised, such a planner, so sensible, and so amenable and fair. I'm quite happy to let him run things.'

'That's because you're an only child, Cathy. You've been looked after and spoiled and Bradley is doing the same.' Catherine had not replied to such an unjust remark, but she did think about Mollie's forthright attitude to marriage.

Catherine dozed and when she awoke they were getting ready for the descent into Honolulu. Her spirits rose. She began to think about the island's beauty, Kiann'e and her friends, starting her photography course, her early morning swim in crystal water.

When they left the plane the sight of the palm trees, the soft breeze, the warmth of the air and the smiles of the local people, the ease with which they went through customs, the calls of aloha, leis being given, people embracing . . . She took Bradley's hand.

'I'm glad to be home.'

They skimmed through the mail and Catherine grimaced as she read several formal invitations to morning teas, luncheons and a meeting of the Wives' Club. She rang Kiann'e.

'You're back! We've missed you. A swim tomorrow? What are you doing for lunch?' asked Kiann'e, sounding delighted to hear from her.

'Oh, we couldn't possibly face going out today, thanks. But I can't wait to see you in the morning. How's everything?'

'Good, good. Lester misses you. Are you jet lagged?'

'It's been a long trip. I'll tell you all about it tomorrow.' Catherine was keen to share her feelings and tell Kiann'e all about her visit home. 'But I'm really glad to be back.'

They went to the commissary for provisions, Bradley called some colleagues and as they were unpacking and sorting laundry, there was a knock at their door.

'Who would that be?' said Bradley. 'We really need an early night. I have to work tomorrow.' His face fell as he opened the door to find Albert, Kiann'e's teenage nephew, standing there with a large basket.

'Kiann'e and Aunty Lani sent this for Catherine.'

'Hi, Albert. What's this?' called Catherine behind Bradley.

'They thought you might be too tired to cook. They sent you a welcome home supper.'

'How lovely, come in.'

'Ah, that's okay. See ya.' He waved and left.

Bradley put the large basket on the table. 'Really,

Catherine, how embarrassing. We could go out to eat and we bought food. We're not on welfare and I don't want to be treated like family by these people.'

'These people are friends of mine, and I think this is so thoughtful. It's the aloha spirit, Bradley. Look, how yummy.' She began taking containers of food, some fruit and a cake from the basket.

That night they broke a rule and ate in front of the TV. Bradley had to admit that the food was good.

'I suppose you're seeing Kiann'e tomorrow. When you return the basket don't encourage any more food drops,' said Bradley.

Catherine ignored the comment and said breezily, 'I'm starting my photography course tomorrow evening. Can I take the car after I bring you home?'

Catherine caught up on the local news as she and Kiann'e walked the beach the next morning. She wanted to know how all her friends were and what they had been doing.

'My mother is pleased by the support the rally had. There could have been more in the news, but it's a start. They're trying to get a meeting with local council representatives. Lester has missed you. Now tell me about the visit. What did Bradley think?'

Catherine filled her in and told her of her disappointment with Bradley's reaction to Peel and *Heatherbrae*.

Kiann'e shook her head. 'That's too bad. He probably finds it too isolated and well, culturally foreign.'

'We speak English at least!'

'I mean that country life isn't for him. Maybe it's the space thing, he feels threatened by the wide open spaces! He's been living in small apartments, works in an office or else is on a cramped ship.'

Catherine laughed. 'Good theory, but I don't think

174

that's the cause. I'll adjust. I'm so glad I'm in Hawaii. I just hope we stay here a couple of years. Hey, I'm starting my course tonight.'

'Great. You should take a portrait of Lester. I think he misses the limelight a bit.'

'Good idea. And one of you, dancing on the beach at sunset. Not at the Moonflower, somewhere quieter . . . What about the beach opposite your aunty's land?'

'Fine by me. Figure out the camera first.'

Catherine loved her first photography class, though some of the more mathematical and technical aspects of it were not her forte. She showed Bradley what she'd been learning, taking several pictures of him as he browsed through a magazine.

'See, later on I can get extra lenses and filters for special effects, put stars in the sunlight on the ocean and . . .'

'Honey, you're doing the course, not me. I don't need a full recap of each lesson. And what do you want all those expensive extras for? The guy probably has a deal with a supplier and it's not as though you need to take professional photos.' He turned back to his magazine.

Catherine was tempted to make a comment about the offer from Vince to bring him photos for the *News*, but she didn't want to remind him of her participation in the rally.

As time slipped by, Catherine found she was busy from early morning till evening. She dropped Bradley outside his office, although it was close enough for him to walk, drove to Waikiki, swam and walked with Kiann'e, had coffee with Lester, then filled in the day with all her domestic chores. She had several gatherings with the Wives' Club, attended her photography classes, regularly popped in to see Vince at the paper and had started working on her major photography assignment.

'We have to do a series of portraits that tell a story . . . not just a straight head and shoulders type photo,' she explained to Bradley. 'Can I shoot you down at the harbour in your uniform?'

'I guess so. But really, Catherine, what are you going to do with all these pictures?'

'It's part of the course and it doesn't cost anything to print them. I'm learning darkroom techniques as well. We have to submit a portfolio of photos for our grade. But there is also a competition that all the class is entering.'

She was pleased with some of the shots she took of Bradley in his crisp white uniform, sunglasses and naval cap as he stood in sunshine, the shadow of a huge dark navy vessel looming behind him. The bollard with thick ropes on the wharf next to Bradley's immaculate white shoes was a study in contrasts.

She photographed Kiann'e in a sarong and lei, backlit by the setting sun with her long hair loose, dancing on the sand at the beach near her aunty's house. They were beautiful pictures but scarcely original ideas. Catherine took other pictures afterwards during the informal supper with family, of visitors and relatives who dropped by as Aunty Lani dished out food to everyone. She snapped the jolly Hawaiian woman ladling out food onto plates with a small girl tugging at her muu-muu.

Bradley also had decided to do a short course for admin staff. 'I thought if you're out a couple of nights a week you wouldn't mind if I did this course. It'll finish before I have to leave and it all helps towards further promotion.'

So while Bradley sat in the lecture room at the base, Catherine had dinner at Aunty Lani's with Kiann'e. She carried plates inside and helped with the clearing away.

'You're almost one of the family now,' said Aunty Lani. 'Here, take this leftover chicken curry home for your husband.'

'Thanks, Aunty. He'll love it. He goes to class straight after work so he'll be starving,' said Catherine.

'How's the picture taking going?' asked Uncle Henry.

'Good. I'm still looking for a few more people to photograph. There's a trip to Kauai for the winner of a photo competition and I'm dying to go back there.'

'Great, you know you can always stay with Beatrice. Take some pictures on Po'ipu Beach. Get some of those cute surfer boys,' chuckled Aunt Lani. 'Say, what about Lester? He's a good looking man even now. Oh, he was a looker when he first came here. All the girls were mad for him.'

'Have you known him a long time?'

'I met him in the thirties when I was very young. He was a legend even then. He was part of the group that hung around the Outrigger Canoe Club. He used to spend a lot of time in Kauai. But that's another story.'

'Is that where he met Eleanor? They must be good friends as she lets him live in her apartment,' said Catherine.

Aunt Lani didn't answer and busied herself in the kitchen.

'Did Lester work for Eleanor and her husband at the Palm Grove? What's the connection between them?' persisted Catherine, now curious.

'I couldn't say,' said Aunt Lani. 'Not our business. Lester is a good man. Here, you come back soon.' She handed Catherine the food to take home.

Catherine asked Kiann'e about Lester and Eleanor and Ed Lang the next morning.

'Who knows what the story is? There is something though, because Eleanor acted vague when I asked her. Vague as in evasive,' said Kiann'e. 'Anyway, if you want to photograph Lester, chat to him about his life. There's also probably a lot in the newspaper files, he was such a champion as well as designing boards and being active in getting surfing on the map.'

Lester was rather pleased at the idea of Catherine's taking his portrait, as much for the outing as the photography. She told him she'd pick him up on Thursday afternoon. In the meantime she went to see the librarian in the archive of the *Honolulu Advertiser* who pulled out clippings on Lester dating back over fifty years. Catherine sat in the little cutting library in the *Advertiser*'s offices crowded with filing cabinets, shelves filled with books of yellowing clippings and folders crammed with old press photographs.

There must have been some system to the chaos because the kindly librarian hauled out the file with Lester's name on it. 'We're starting to put things on microfiche now, before the old papers disintegrate,' she said. 'There could be old newsreel footage, early TV stuff, but you'd have to go to KGMB or somewhere to ask about that,' she suggested.

'This is great. Amazing,' said Catherine, poring over the fat folder of pictures of a handsome young Lester posing with Duke Kahanamoku and other surfers Catherine didn't recognise and in action himself. Slowly she began to see what Lester's public life had been like. Everything was centred on surfing. Shots of him on impossibly huge waves, a mere speck out the back of the waves, flipping over a curling wave, riding a long board at Waikiki with a girl on his shoulders, doing a headstand on a board with Diamond Head in the background when there had been few hotels along the beachfront. Other shots showed Lester wearing leis, with trophies and displaying an array of surfboards.

But what was his private life? Pretty girls posed with him but none of them appeared a second time in any picture. As Catherine flipped through the yellowing clippings she started to see what a contribution Lester had made to the Islands. He was indeed a true kama'aina. But he was an enigma. How could she sum this up in a photograph?

She talked it over with Kiann'e who reminded her that someone was always surfing somewhere on the island.

'You could take some pictures of the Australian boys who are always hanging around.'

'Oh, that's too hard. I know nothing about it,' said Catherine.

'And you're not too interested either, I can tell,' said Kiann'e.

'Nope. It's one aspect of Hawaii that doesn't turn me on.'

Kiann'e grinned. 'Wait till you see those surfer boys in action!'

But in spite of this suggestion, Catherine thought Kiann'e's idea to take a portrait of Lester was the best.

'You were quite the surfer hero in your time, Lester. I hadn't realised how famous you were. I saw some old newspaper clippings. You looked like a movie star.'

He merely smiled. 'Well, I did appear in a few films. Wasn't for me.' He dropped the subject.

Catherine saw an opportunity to prise open the shell around his past. 'Wow, Lester, that's pretty interesting. Tell me more.'

'Different times, back then, Catherine. Nobody's interested now.'

'Why didn't you ever marry, Lester?' asked Catherine.

He shrugged. 'I didn't have much to offer anyone. I'm not the type to settle in the suburbs, pay off a home.'

'You couldn't find a nice island girl? You are so happy here, the lifestyle suits you. And, my goodness, you were so handsome and then you became so famous the girls must have flocked to you.'

'Maybe that was part of the reason. Never any shortage of girls and I liked them all.'

'Lester, what a ladies' man you are!' laughed Catherine, thinking how little had changed. Kiann'e, even Beatrice herself, and who knows what other lady friends were still dancing attendance on him.

He took a scrapbook from a shelf and handed it to her. 'How about I put the coffee on?' he suggested.

Catherine began looking through the photos and newspaper cuttings, trying to equate the arthritic older man before her with the bronzed, stunning-looking figure in the pictures. 'Coffee, yes please, Lester. You look like a Greek god in these! And so fit.'

Lester looked over her shoulder. 'I feel a bit stiff today, but I lasted longer than most. I won a few championships in my late forties, though no-one knew my age.'

'You devil, Lester. I see what you mean. You look amazing.'

Catherine was astonished not just by how handsome and contemporary Lester looked, but by the quality of the old black and white photos. He was wearing fitted swim shorts in a lot of the pictures and if it hadn't been for the old-style white buckled belt around them, he could have been a surfer of today. There were a lot of photos of him posing on the beach standing against massive solid long boards, in action on the waves with Diamond Head in the background. But it was a series of studies using light and shade that caught her attention. Lester was posed on tiptoe, angled like a dancer in a brief knotted lava lava, like a nappy, she thought. Others were of him naked, back to the camera, lying on the sand. He had a lean, lightly muscled, well-proportioned body, an allover tan, the sunlight caught the light hairs on his arm, his sun-streaked blond hair fell over his face. One photo showed him on his side, back modestly to the camera, stretched naked on the sand, head resting on one bent arm, his other hand casually holding a large trophy – a cup for surfing or swimming, she assumed. The black and white pictures were of prize-winning quality, and looked as if they could have been taken yesterday.

'Who took these photos? They're excellent,' said Catherine.

'I took some myself, or I set them up and had a lady friend click the shutter.' He smiled.

'Lester, could I borrow this scrapbook if I promise to guard it with my life?'

'Why are you so interested in an old man?' he asked gently.

Catherine didn't have an immediate answer. 'I like you, Lester,' she said finally. 'And I think you'll be a great subject for the portrait competition.'

'What did you have in mind? I know what I'd do,' said Lester.

'At the beach? Outside the Outrigger Canoe Club where some of these were taken?' said Catherine.

'Got it in one, girl. Let's go.'

'Okay, you're ready?'

Lester wanted to change his clothes so Catherine washed the coffee cups and put them away. She couldn't resist a smile when Lester emerged from the bedroom wearing white shorts held up by a leather belt with a fancy silver and turquoise buckle and topped with a faded blue and white aloha shirt. He had sunglasses in his pocket and carried a perky cap. He slipped his feet into his sandals and took his stick.

'I'm right to go.'

The sun was still high in the early afternoon and Waikiki was crowded. At Lester's insistence she parked in the Outrigger Canoe Club.

'Mike, the manager, will let me in here. We can cut through to the beach,' said Lester as he headed towards the members only reception.

'Are you a member?' asked Catherine.

'Used to be fifty years ago. They know me.'

Catherine grabbed her camera bag and followed him. Lester gave the girl at the desk a big smile and said airily, 'Having my picture taken out the front, it won't take long.'

'Very well, Lester, you know the rules.' She smiled at Catherine

Lester had a few suggestions for photos: posing with an outrigger canoe pulled up on the beach; leaning against a gnarled banyan tree at the edge of the sand; and of course with a surfboard. He was a natural in front of the camera and Catherine took several pictures that she thought were good, but weren't *the* one. She looked towards the shore where several surfers were walking from the water carrying their boards. Lester studied them, squinting into the sun.

'Times change,' said Catherine. 'Those boards look different from the big heavy ones you used.'

'Yes, but some things never change,' said Lester softly. 'Soul surfers. That's what they call themselves now. These boys are in it for love and fulfilment, not winning and ego.' As the surfers came up the beach one of them spotted Lester leaning on his cane, and murmured to the others. They all headed towards the legend with the white hair and faded shirt as he wistfully watched them.

Catherine moved to one side and started shooting. The first surfer to greet Lester was Damien, the Australian she'd met at the rally. He looked awestruck. The other two boys, one with bleached-blond hair, the other Hawaiian, she didn't know. They all wanted to shake Lester's hand and ask questions. Clearly Lester had not been forgotten. One put his board down and came around to Catherine.

'Hi. How come you're here with Lester?'

'I'm doing some portraits of him.'

'Hey, could you do the boys one favour and take one picture of us all with him, please? He's one legend.'

'I know. He's incredible. And just a little while ago he was saying no-one is interested in him.'

'He's wrong there. You know him?' asked the blond surfer, clearly impressed.

'Yes,' said Catherine. 'Come on, I'll take your photo before he gets too tired.'

'It's for the boys, they'd love a copy of it.'

'We can arrange that,' said Catherine.

She took a formally posed shot of the group. Then, because Lester's legs were tired, they moved to the sea wall. Lester sat on a bench with his stick and the boys gathered around him.

Catherine wished she could tape the talk. The boys had a hundred questions, none of which she understood, about fin designs, weights, shapes, places and the breaks, the Pipeline, the waves on the North Shore.

'You wait till next winter, when the big waves come in,' Lester said to Catherine. 'That's the time to understand what surfing's all about. These boys, they like surfing fine, but the North Shore winter sorts them out. Only the wild watermen get out there in the winter waves.'

'Do you swim these days, Lester?' asked the Hawaiian boy.

For the first time, Lester's face fell. He'd been enjoying the young surfers' admiration, their passion, their mutual bond. 'Can't get up on these old legs. I swim in the pool at the apartment.'

'What about a surf sometime? Nothing beats the ocean, I'll take you out on one of the old big boards. What do you say, Lester?' said the blond surfer with a warm smile. 'Even for a body surf. Catch a few smallies.'

'We might well do that sometime, kid.'

Catherine could tell Lester was getting weary. 'Hey,

Lester, it's time, we'd better be making a move.' She turned to the surfers. 'How can I get in touch with you to give you a copy of the pictures if they turn out all right?' She fished in her handbag for a pen and scrap of paper.

The blond surfer wrote his phone number on it and handed it to her. 'I'm PJ and listen, I meant what I said. I'd be happy to take him into the ocean for a dip. Somewhere quiet, no people, nothing risky. He must miss it.'

Catherine had dismissed his earlier remark but now, as she looked at PJ, she realised that he understood Lester's limitations and was sincere in wanting to help him. With a slight shock she thought that PJ looked a bit like a young Lester. The same height and colouring, smooth gold skin, sun-frosted hair, sky-blue eyes and a serious sort of smile. There was salt crusted in his blond eyebrows and on his shoulders. He was staring at her, waiting for an answer.

'I'll call you.' She picked up her camera bag and took Lester's arm.

Damien tapped Catherine on the shoulder. 'Jeez, mate, it'd be so cool to have a photo with a ledge like Lester. I'll pay you for it.'

'It's okay, you've done me a favour. I think I have the photo I wanted. I'll contact PJ when I get the prints.'

'Groooovy. See you round, Cathy.'

She smiled as she helped Lester walk back into the club. Damien was a typical Aussie, abbreviating everything. Bradley had thought that it was a rather irritating trait, but to Catherine it sounded like home.

In the darkroom at the college Catherine and Paul held up the negatives in the glow of the red light globe. Catherine knew the shot she liked best of Lester: his head thrown back and an arm reaching out towards the ocean pointing to something. It was almost like a spiritual act as the awestruck and admiring surfers clustered, disciple-like, around him. With the surfboards, the strip of beach and a glimpse of the peak of Diamond Head, the expressions on their faces and the powerful face of Lester in the centre, the picture told the story.

'I'm calling it the *Changing of the Guard*. Or *Soul Surfers*. Maybe *The Old Man, the Sea and Soul Surfers*. I'm not sure, I'll toss around a few more titles.'

'It's a great shot. You can see he's such a grand old man still with enormous strength and a powerful personality. Well done. You're turning in some good work, Catherine.'

After she had printed the pictures of Lester she called around to show Vince at the *News*.

'Absolutely knockout, Catherine. Gee, I'd love to use this one. But obviously not until after your photo competition.' He studied them again, then rubbed his chin. 'Hmm, y'know you've been taking some good stuff. Interesting. Different. I suppose it's because you're new to the Islands.'

'Malihini eyes.' Catherine smiled.

'What say you do a regular picture for us? Places, people, anything that takes your fancy that has a bit of a story to it. Can you write a bit?'

'Enough, I guess. I'd love to do that. I often see people and want to photograph them and I feel a bit shy, but if it's for the paper I have an excuse to chat to them for a bit. How often would you want something?' Catherine was starting to feel very excited.

'Once a week, we'd run it in the Saturday paper, call it "Our Island, Our Home". We'd pay you the same rate as we have for the other photos of yours that we've used, if that's okay?'

Catherine nodded. 'This is sooo good, Vince. I can use this as a bit of an excuse to get out of some of the deadly Wives' Club things.'

'You can bring in the film and give it to the darkroom, by Thursday if you can, or you can develop it yourself if you want to.'

'How much do I have to write to go with it? A caption or a bit of detail?' asked Catherine.

'About two or three hundred words. Put in a quote if it's someone interesting. Let me see what you can do. We'll kick off with that shot of Lester, after the competition, whether it wins or not.'

Catherine shook his hand. 'Thanks, Vince. I've always wanted to do something like this. And write something. I'm sure that I can do something for you each week.'

'I'm not asking for a novel. Just keep it concise. And be sure to give us a bit of a selection. Couple of versions of the shot so I can choose one to work into the layout.'

'I can't wait to tell Bradley.'

'I'm surprised, well, that's handy for you. You must be coming along in that course,' said Bradley. 'I hope it doesn't take up too much time, though. And I wouldn't make a big deal of it at the Wives' Club. Working off base is always a bit of an issue.'

'I'll keep it to myself. I doubt any of them read the *Hawaii News*.' Catherine felt a bit deflated but she knew Kiann'e and her friends would be thrilled for her.

A few days later she rang the number the blond surfer, PJ, had given her.

'Hi, this is Catherine Connor. I took the photos of Lester and all you guys.'

'Right. How'd it come out?'

'I have some great shots. In fact, one might run in the *Hawaii News*.'

'Hey, the guys will get a kick out of that. Thanks a lot.'

'I'll leave them for you at the *News* offices. What's your name by the way?'

'It's Peter James. But PJ will do. Say, that Lester, what a terrific old man. I'd really like to take him for a quiet dip in the ocean. Do you think he'd like that?'

'He did say it would be a nice thing to do, but he kind of dismissed it as too hard,' said Catherine. 'He's pretty strong, and he's very determined. What would it involve?'

'Taking him somewhere where there's calm water, no waves to speak of. First time anyway. He was an Olympic swim champ, so he'll be okay once he's in the water and weightless. He'll just need a bit of assistance getting out of the water and up the beach.'

'I'd love to do that for him. That's really kind of you. I think he'd feel better if there wasn't a crowd. He's a very proud man, in a nice way. He was pretty chuffed at the attention from you all.'

'I'll arrange it. What's your number?'

Catherine gave him her phone number and then added, 'I nearly forgot, the reason I called was to get all your names and where you're from in case the paper uses the photo with all of you in.'

'You got me there,' laughed PJ. 'I'll have to call you back. Most of the boys have nicknames and I don't know their surnames!'

At the next Wives' Club meeting Catherine listened as the president ran through the agenda.

'We have donated the five hundred dollars raised for our children's charity from the handicraft fair. Perhaps we can begin a new project. Does anyone have any suggestions?'

Catherine lifted her hand. She'd had an idea for some

time, but it was a radical one. Nevertheless she plucked up courage and blurted it out. 'Well, yes. As we're living here amidst another community, perhaps it would be useful to learn a little more about the community we share. Learn a bit more about Hawaii . . . it has a fascinating history and culture,' said Catherine.

'That's a nice idea,' broke in Connie Goodwin. 'Of course, some of us have lived here for quite a while, Catherine. Does anyone have any ideas or suggestions?'

Catherine bit her lip.

Julia Bensen spoke up. 'An art class might be nice, or music – how about ukulele lessons, or even the hula?'

There was a round of laughter, followed by enthusiastic discussion about the hula.

'We loved those dancers we saw at the hula competition in Kapiolani Park that Catherine took us to,' said Julia.

'Why don't we put on a show? Raise money that way, have a bit of fun and give the money to an Hawaiian charity,' suggested Peta Harrison, wife of the head of the base transport division.

There was a flurry of agreement.

'But who's going to teach us?' Julia looked to Catherine.

Mrs Goodwin turned to Catherine. 'My dear, you seem to have some connections out there in the local entertainment scene, do you not?'

'I'll ask. Of course it's only fair they are paid, or we donate money to the charity of their choice.'

There was some discussion over the detail, which Catherine found boring. The decisions over who would do what, be responsible for what, report on what, drove her crazy. She wanted to jump up and say, 'For God's sake, I'll ask Kiann'e to come and give us lessons and we donate XYZ to some local charity. Let's move on.' But she held her tongue and it was finally resolved that Catherine would ask Kiann'e if she would give hula lessons and report back at the next meeting.

'Kiann'e, you don't have to if you don't want to. Or suggest someone else. But I tried, I really tried to get them interested in a project that would give them some sense of the history of the Islands . . . which I'm only just starting to learn,' wailed Catherine.

'It's okay. There are hula classes and hula classes. They'll get a lot more with me than they expect,' said Kiann'e. 'Hula tells stories, we'll creep the knowledge in – to music. Of course, you'll be there.'

After Kiann'e's first lesson, the wives clustered around Catherine.

'Wasn't that wonderful? It's so . . . ooh, seductive.'

'Much more so than rock and roll, or modern dance. Wait till I show my husband this!'

'No preview. Make them wait for the big show when we're really good,' said Julia, clearly excited by the prospect of something really different.

Several lessons later, as Kiann'e drove her home, Catherine thanked her friend. 'You're too famous to be teaching a bunch of naval wives, and real amateurs at that, the sacred dances of your people. They don't appreciate it. You're so good to do this.'

'Actually it's important to let people know there's much more to hula than just these movements. The hula has a language of its own and if it speaks, even just a little, to these women so that they understand this is a means of passing down and interpreting our culture, then it's worth it. And I do think that some of them appreciate its significance.'

'It just seems there is so much more we could be learning about the old chants, the royal family of Hawaii. And, of course, so much more we could contribute. Still, this is certainly a good start,' said Catherine.

Kiann'e was right. Many of the naval wives doing the hula classes became very keen about what they were doing. They pressed Kiann'e about the dresses she wore, wanting to have similar ones made.

Kiann'e explained, 'The big loose muu-muu is like a Mother Hubbard, brought in by the missionaries to cover up all the women. If the traditional dances were performed the missionaries had the women and men wear thick brown neck-to-ankle tights and tops under their ti-leaf skirts, pareos and cloaks. Now the long fitted dress I dance in is called a holomuu; the holoku is the same, long and fitted at the waist but with a train. And the short muu-muu is called a pokomuu.'

Some of the wives started bringing notebooks to write down the snippets of information they found interesting and over juice and coffee after class, Kiann'e was asked questions about dressmakers, leis and food.

'Catherine, this is such a good idea, it's all *so* interesting,' said Julia Bensen.

'Why don't we put on an Hawaiian feast when we do our show?' enthused Peta.

'A luau would be fun,' said Catherine. 'We could make it a fundraiser for one of the charities. Don't you think the Wives' Club should support a local Hawaiian charity?'

'Great idea. A luau and a chorus line of lovelies from the Wives' Club. The boys will love it,' said Julia.

'We'll need help with the food. Don't they cook it in the ground?' asked Peta.

'I have friends who might help,' said Catherine, rather amused. 'I'll talk to Kiann'e.'

Kiann'e was helpful but declined getting involved in

the luau and hula show for the Wives' Club. 'You run it, Catherine, you can handle it,' she winked. 'Seems you're becoming a bit of a star in the club.'

Catherine acknowledged the irony behind her remark. 'Yes. I suppose I am but, of course, it's only the younger wives who're interested.'

Although Kiann'e had refused to help with the show her aunt and uncle were more than happy to organise the luau. It was held down near the beach on the recreation grounds. Unfortunately, Uncle Henry ended up having to do kalua pig on a spit as they weren't allowed to dig the imu pit and roast the food in the traditional way because they were on naval land, but no-one seemed to mind.

The husbands and single men who'd been coerced into coming along had a ball. The food was delicious, the cheerful banter of Aunty Lani, Uncle Henry and nephew Albert made the evening a wonderful success. Catherine realised it was probably the first time many of these naval people had met the locals socially. However Mrs Goodwin couldn't help bossing and trying to run things. She started to treat Aunty Lani as staff, but Aunty Lani was quick to assert herself in a friendly manner.

'Now then, don't you try and tell me when we eat, ma'am. When the kau kau ready, we eat. You sit back and enjoy yourself.'

Catherine had designed the invitations and insisted that everyone wear Hawaiian dress. Mrs Goodwin had made a token effort but the young wives, armed with Kiann'e's directions, were all in attractive muu-muus and holomuus and looked stunning.

After the food had been served onto paper plates everyone found a seat on the grass or on collapsible chairs, or spread themselves out on mats or just stood around the bar to watch the show.

Bradley stood at the back with Commander Goodwin

feeling rather embarrassed that Catherine had instigated the event. But he could see there was a good turn out and the occasion would probably raise an excellent sum to go to some charity that the Wives' Club had agreed on. While it was rather casual, the food was certainly tasty and people seemed to be having a good time.

Commander Goodwin nudged him, 'I'm a bit apprehensive at how the evening's entertainment might go. I don't like our ladies making a spectacle of themselves.'

'Not many here outside the Navy,' said Bradley, glancing round at all the familiar faces.

One of the single junior officers had got into the spirit of the night and created an uproar when he appeared in a long colourful muu-muu, worn with his navy regulation shoes, and flower headdress to compere the show.

'Aloha, ladies and gentlemen, Commander and Mrs Goodwin! Welcome to the Whacky Wahines Spectacular. They dance for your pleasure, to enchant and entertain you – and for a great cause.' He cued Albert who was running the tape deck and the slack key Hawaiian guitar crackled through the loudspeaker as the line-up of wives, led by Catherine, walked demurely to the centre of the stage area on the grass. They were all dressed in matching long holomuus in red and white, made by one of the women handy with a sewing machine. They also wore white and cream leis threaded with green fern and matching hair crowns, organised for them by Kiann'e. There was a moment of stunned silence as the audience realised how lovely they looked. They stood in a line, hands lowered to one side, eyes downcast as the music and lyrics of 'A Little Brown Gal in a Little Grass Shack' began. They went into their now well-rehearsed routine.

The audience loved it and applauded madly. The performers went through their repertoire and while some were not as rhythmic or as graceful as Hawaiian dancers, they were all enthusiastic and kept together well enough. Bradley was quite surprised, not only at how tasteful it all was but at what a good and natural Hawaiian dancer Catherine was. She was undoubtedly the star of the show, the leader of the troupe, and her lessons with Kiann'e had certainly paid off.

'I'm rather impressed,' murmured Commander Goodwin to Bradley when the dancers had finished.

There were calls for an encore before the compere appeared to ask for a final thank you for the Wacky Wahines.

'So what are we going to do next, Catherine?' asked Julia. 'This has been such fun.'

'Oh, I thought a cooking course combining the foods of Hawaii and the customs of traditional feasts,' she said flippantly.

'Great!' came a chorus. 'Sounds good.'

Catherine laughed, but then realised they'd taken her seriously. She thought she'd better talk to Aunty Lani and Kiann'e about doing something that might be more rewarding – for both the American women and the Hawaiian society they were surrounded by.

'Yes, it was a bit of fun,' agreed Bradley when they got home. 'But it should remain a one-off performance.'

'The ladies want me to get something else happening.'

'That's nice. I'm pleased to see you're having some fun with the other wives. But tread carefully, Catherine. Be aware of our position, there is something of a hierarchy and you don't want to step on any toes. I'm not entirely sure that Mrs Goodwin and some of the other senior ladies were as enthusiastic as you are. And perhaps not too much emphasis on Hawaiiana? You are new to the Islands yourself, remember.'

'Yes, Bradley. I know that, which is why I'm keen to learn as much as I can about this place.'

He took her in his arms. 'It's good you're keeping busy. The Commander told me tonight I'll be going to sea in seven days.'

With the knowledge of looming separation, Bradley made love to her, murmuring, 'This is nice. We should do it more often!' And was soon asleep.

Catherine felt emotionally confused. She knew that she would miss Bradley while he was away at sea, but it had also occurred to her that their sex life had become a bit predictable and a bit too intermittent. There wasn't the heat, rush or passion of the stolen moments that they'd shared in the beginning. She hoped that after the enforced break the romance would return.

THE WATERMAN

The young man was swimming in a blue lagoon surrounded by rocks where a channel led to deeper water and a reef. Palm trees leant overhead and all looked idyllic. Then there was a splash. The young man thrashed, disappearing beneath the surface as if yanked by a large hand. In seconds he resurfaced, wildly throwing punches at the dark triangular fin beside him.

Over and over they rolled, lean, tanned arms grasping the long, grey shape, lethal jaws momentarily flashing above the water as the young man jabbed at the evil narrow eyes and then, pulling a knife from his waist, slashed and stabbed until his enemy sank from sight, wounded and dying.

With his knife between his teeth the young man swam to the beach and staggered onto the shore and, wearing only a torn loincloth, slumped onto the sand.

'Cut!'

'Great, great. Somebody rescue the shark, for gosh sake.'

A man in a plaid shirt wearing a straw hat and carrying a megaphone walked onto the sand. Behind him stood a group of people, around them were power cables, large lights, several canvas chairs and on a tripod sat a movie camera shaded by a large umbrella.

A girl ran forward and handed the young man a towel. He wiped his face and dark orange make-up stained the towel. As he strode up the beach the star of the film, Ramon Navarro, lounging in a chair with his name on the back, gave him a brief salute.

'You sure killed that monster.'

The young man laughed with everyone else as the props man hauled the dead rubber shark onto the sand.

The day's work over, the young man showered, rinsing off the extra skin colour, wishing he could remove the black dye from his hair. He was mentally adding up the days he'd worked and he realised that though it was boring, it was easy work and good money.

Again, a guardian angel had stepped from the wings to rescue him just when he was wondering where his next meal was coming from. He realised that while the Olympic Games might have brought him some fame, they had not brought him money. He'd been back on lifeguard duty at Santa Monica beach when a young woman with an expensive camera had asked to take his picture. He had figured this was as good an approach as any. Girls and women often hung around with him on some pretext or other.

But she had been quite professional, asking him to pose against the rescue boat. She had asked him to lift his chin and stare into the distance to show off his firm jawline and aquiline nose. Then she'd asked him to pose in his swimming shorts with a surfboard. The young man had never tried one of the boards that a few people were bringing to the beach, but he borrowed a narrow-tailed redwood board and stood against it and then, for fun, he laid it on the sand and did a handstand on it.

He'd thought no more about the pictures until the girl reappeared and handed him a card with the name of a Hollywood studio printed on it and asked him to come and audition for a bit part and for work as a movie stand-in. He found the screen test an odd experience, posing, turning side to side, reacting to directions and showing a range of expressions. But whatever he did they must have liked it because here he was in Cape Florida acting the part of a south seas native, his skin darkened with make-up, the muscles on his arms and torso oiled, his hair dyed black.

The story was about a missionary who arrived in the Islands with his comely daughter, played by silent-screen star Alice Terry in a blonde wig, who falls in love with the handsome son of a native chief, Ramon Navarro. However she is also courted by a rough bar owner who forsakes his coarse trade, closes his saloon and finds salvation thanks to her father. She realises that she cannot marry either of these men and so she catches the steamer back to America leaving the chief's son broken hearted and he flings himself over a waterfall.

The young man thought the whole story rather silly, but he played his small role, collected his pay and returned to Santa Monica.

Over the next six months he was called back to the studio for other small parts and some stunt work. He remained unimpressed with the shallowness of the film world and if he hadn't needed the money he wouldn't have bothered with it. He continued to swim and exercise, and through his coach at the club he was introduced to a new health regime where he was encouraged to eat fruit and vegetables and develop his muscles along the lines of dynamic tension devised by health promoter Charles Atlas.

His legs became muscular and his arms strong but his physique was well proportioned – a smooth, golden, hairless chest, tanned legs. His thick, fair, sun-streaked hair was tousled, falling over his forehead unless tamed and slicked back with hair oil. Blue eyes, long sandy lashes and a wide shy smile with white teeth all helped make him an eye-catching, superb figure of a man.

With his white drill pants rolled above his ankles, bare feet and long-sleeved white cotton-knit crew-neck sweater, he had a style of studied beach casualness. And while he was a modest and shy young man around people, preferring to keep his own company, there were always

admiring women around him at the beach. Nevertheless,
he remained self-absorbed, not ready to step into a world
that included other people who might put demands on
him. He was still to find what made him truly happy and
complete.

8

CATHERINE STOOD ON HER small lanai looking at Pearl Harbor – clear, blue, clean. She sipped her tea, proper strong black Australian tea that her mother had sent. It was her first morning without Bradley and she was trying to assess how she felt.

The previous day he'd said a private goodbye to her in the garden outside their apartment where no-one could see them. He'd hugged her tightly and gave her a long hard kiss. Then he had put on his cap and walked across the clipped green lawn to join two other officers to drive to their ship.

'It gets a bit chaotic at the dock, some of the women get emotional, best we say our farewells in private,' he told her.

'I'd quite like to see the ship leave,' said Catherine who was rather disappointed by this quiet goodbye.

'You'll see us go through the harbour from the apartment,' smiled Bradley. 'Bird's eye view.'

It felt strange to be alone in the apartment knowing that she had it to herself for weeks to come with no Bradley, no meals to cook for him, no commitments apart from her own routine. But she enjoyed her busy life and she felt settled and happy in Hawaii.

She looked forward to her swim with Kiann'e each morning. It was different from *Heatherbrae* where most mornings she leapt from bed and pulled on jeans to go for an early morning ride on Parker. Now her daily swim cleared her head, invigorated her and allowed her to plan her day. She knew she would hate the way Mollie's day began with a shrill alarm, a gulped tea and quick piece of toast and a race to catch the bus into the city.

She was thankful Bradley didn't eat breakfast, made his own coffee the way he liked it and sent his uniform to the cleaners. Nor did he object when Catherine had explained how much she valued her early mornings at the beach in the shadow of Diamond Head where the sand was unmarked, the water warm, crystal clear and calm and always so inviting. She looked forward to coffee with Lester, planning her photo essay for the paper, thinking about her duties with the Wives' Club and deliberating on what to prepare for dinner. The company of Kiann'e was a bonus. They didn't intrude on each other's tranquillity until, refreshed and heading back towards Lester's apartment, they would begin to chat.

Catherine finished her tea and wondered what Bradley was doing now that the ship had left the harbour. He'd looked so handsome in his white uniform as he'd walked away from her that morning. But she'd had the feeling that with each step he took across that lawn he was already moving into a different world that she didn't know and couldn't share.

It took only a short while to tidy the apartment and then she rang PJ.

'So is it still okay to bring Lester over?'

'I'm ready and waiting. I have just the spot. Meet me outside the Diamond Head Hotel. It's too rocky and too shallow near his apartment.'

Lester was dressed in swim shorts and his favourite aloha shirt was unbuttoned revealing a tanned chest sprinkled with white hairs, the skin sagging where once there'd been muscles. He gave her a quick smile.

'How're you this morning, Lester?" she asked.

'Well, honey, I've been better. Now, who's the young turk who had this idea?'

'His name is PJ. He's originally from California, I think. Been here quite a while. He's nice, admires you hugely. He seems to understand what the ocean means to you.' Catherine knew Lester spent many hours watching the sea from his lanai or a deck chair by the pool. To her the empty ocean seemed boring unless there were boats, or people on the beach or in the water, but obviously to Lester just gazing at it gave him some inner satisfaction.

'Just so long as he doesn't want to show me what a good surfer he is. Ask for tips, rave about the new modern boards,' said Lester firmly.

'Oh no. Anyway he said there wouldn't be a big swell, just smallish waves or something,' said Catherine.

Lester didn't answer, in fact he looked rather inscrutable and Catherine wondered what he was thinking.

They drove past elegant homes hidden behind high gates among lush trees at the ocean cliff edge where wealthy mainlanders had established an exclusive colony.

Lester glanced up at Diamond Head. 'When I first came here we used to hike up to Diamond Head. Punchbowl Lookout too. I had some good times here.'

'What's your favourite place?' asked Catherine, thinking it might make a good photograph.

Lester looked at her as if he was making sure she really didn't know the answer. 'The ocean.'

Catherine mentally added her unspoken comment. 'Of course.'

PJ was waiting in the small parking lot at the edge of the beach, standing by an old panel van with cream and wooden trim. Catherine could see the van held surfboards, towels and a mattress in the back. PJ, in a pair of long surfing shorts, gave a wave and opened the car door for Lester.

PJ and Lester walked to the edge of the sand and studied the water. A line of low breakers rolled lazily towards the shore. A deeper channel cut between the breaking surf and a sandbar. Lester leant on his stick as PJ pointed at the waves.

Catherine watched them, both similar in body shape and height. Lester's silver hair had once been as fair as PJ's sun-bleached curls, both had sun-soaked skin but where PJ's was taut and smooth, Lester's skin was baked into grooves and wrinkles like the whorls on the surface of the sea. They spoke together quietly, pausing occasionally to study the ocean. Catherine felt reluctant to intrude so she quietly took her camera from the car and began taking some distance shots instead.

Then the two men started to walk towards the water. For a moment or two Lester found it difficult to walk on the sand as his stick was useless. PJ casually tucked his board under his arm next to Lester so the old man could lightly rest his hand on its shiny bright surface for support. Closer to the water PJ laid down his board and dropped his towel. Lester took off his shirt and PJ glanced back at Catherine who was following them and then, together, the two watermen entered the sea.

Catherine's heart lurched at the sight of Lester's thin legs supporting him as he took his first steps into the water. Even though there was no strong undertow and the waves had trickled to a ripple by the time they slapped onto the beach, Lester seemed unsteady. PJ stood still letting Lester test the water and then pointed to the channel. Lester nodded and PJ took his hand and together, as a parent leads a child, they made their way across the knee-deep water over the sandbar. They reached the deeper dark water sliding between the shallow sandbar and the breaking waves and suddenly Lester dropped PJ's hand and dived into the channel, popped up and swam a few strokes, turned and swam easily along the channel parallel to shore, PJ following.

Even from a distance Catherine could sense Lester's elation. This was obviously better than swimming in the small pool at his apartment. The two men trod water side by side and then, by apparent agreement, Lester duck dived and swam under a breaking wave. Catherine caught her breath but the old man was young again, swimming strongly then turning to watch the line of waves before choosing one and in three arm strokes was on it, gliding into the channel in the white foam. PJ leapt up jubilantly pumping the air with an arm.

Lester swam back and caught several more waves before moving back to the channel and floating on his back to rest. PJ waded quickly across the bar, ran to the sand, grabbed his surfboard and paddled back to Lester.

He helped Lester onto the board and as Catherine watched through the lens of her camera, PJ pushed Lester back towards the waves. Lester dug his arms into the water and pulled the board towards the break. PJ swam beside him and then Lester turned the board towards the beach. PJ held onto it, treading water as they waited.

They picked an even, long-rolling wave, its fullness

curled within it waiting to unfurl like a flag on the smoother water. Lester began stroking, PJ gave an added push and the old man and the board cleaved neatly through the water, Lester guiding its direction with one arm so it cut across the face of the wave as it raced over the channel before dissipating on the shallow sand bar. PJ caught a following wave and reached Lester as he lay on the board, his cheek resting against the gritty wax. Catherine put her camera on PJ's towel and waded out to them.

'Hey, Lester! Fantastic! How was that?'

He didn't answer but looked for PJ who was quickly beside him.

'Roll, Lester.' As Lester rolled into the water, PJ motioned to Catherine. 'Grab the board.'

She was surprised at how light it was and as PJ helped Lester regain his feet and his balance on the sand bar, she waded through the water beside them. At the water's edge Lester lowered himself to the sand and PJ dropped beside him. Catherine carried the board up the beach and put it down carefully beside her camera.

'Yeah, it felt good,' Lester was telling PJ. 'Wish my legs could hold me up better, can't jump up easy like I used to. Something you never thought about, you just stood up.'

'Yeah, when something's natural that's how it is. But you caught a few today.'

'Been a long time since I can say that,' agreed Lester. 'Thank you, young man.' Lester smiled at Catherine. 'You want to learn to surf?'

'No. But you made it look fun.'

'Take my board out,' offered PJ.

'No, thanks. I might just get wet in the channel.' She waded across the bar, stepped into the cooler current in the channel and swam along, noticing that there was a bit of a pull and the swim must have taken a lot of energy out of Lester. She saw a patch of light-green water and stroked towards it. It was a clear patch that looked different from the rest of the channel, but once she reached it she realised it was much deeper and faster flowing.

She tried to stand but it was way over her head, she looked back and saw she was further out to sea than she'd imagined. She caught her breath in sudden panic, turned around and started swimming fiercely, but found she was swimming against the current, which was taking her backwards quicker than she could swim. She looked for PJ but he had his back to her as he helped Lester up the beach towards the parking lot.

Catherine now tried heading straight towards shore aiming for the sandbar, but as she kicked and flailed she found she wasn't making any progress and she was running out of breath. 'Tread water, call for help,' she told herself.

But PJ still had his back to her and there wasn't anyone else in sight. She felt as though she was on a rapidly moving walkway that was taking her swiftly along the channel. Ahead she could see tossing water and breaking waves. Perhaps if she let herself be taken to the waves she could catch one and glide closer in as Lester had done. But she knew she was in entirely the wrong position, these waves were not smoothly rolling onto the sandbar but looked menacing and she just knew this current would pull her towards the reef.

PJ and Lester had picked a spot that was safe but she had now gone too far out and the currents had suddenly changed. She was getting short of breath as she struggled and her head went under and she swallowed water.

'Oh no, God, no, don't let me drown, out here, alone . . .'

It was her worst fear. She might be a competent swimmer in calm water, but she was completely inexperienced in the open sea. She spluttered then gulped for air.

'PJ! PJ!' she screamed.

But she was now so far out that she couldn't make out the distant figures on the beach. She knew she must be a long way down the channel now, her legs and arms were so tired. If only the pulling, pulling water would let her go. The water was more turbulent. Where the drag of the current had been below the surface, a secret, dangerous unseen thing, the water was now rougher, slapping in her face.

It suddenly seemed easier to relax, give in and let go. She closed her eyes. But then she seemed to hear a voice shouting at her and she knew she mustn't give in. Gamely she started thrashing against the water, forcing her arms and legs to churn in a last effort to get to calmer water.

But it was useless, she knew she was wasting energy, getting nowhere. She lifted her head.

'Stop swimming!' came a shout.

Catherine looked up to see PJ's face looming in front of her. She was so relieved that she stopped flailing.

His surfboard sped close to her and he held out an arm. 'Hold on to my board! Take my hand,' he shouted.

Catherine grabbed at his hand, clinging on desperately as he came alongside and reached for his board. She found it too slippery and she lost her grip and felt herself slip from his grasp.

But PJ's board bobbed next to her again and he reached over. 'Grab my ankle and the board if you can!'

She found his foot and the narrow end of the board and held on tightly, trying not to pull PJ off as he dug his arms into the water and pulled towards the shore. She closed her eyes, feeling the power of PJ's strokes carrying them both through the water.

Then suddenly there was no more current, they were in calm, shimmering, harmless water and she could see the shore and PJ's panel van appearing closer.

PJ slid off his board and stood up and helped Catherine to her feet, but her knees were shaking and she felt so weak, she stumbled. PJ put one arm around her, picked up his board with the other and helped her to the sand where she crumpled and sat in a shaking heap.

He sat beside her as she caught her breath, then lifted her head.

'Thanks.' She coughed.

'Just breathe slowly and deeply. You're fine. No big deal.'

She was shaking and as she looked out at the sparkling sea, she shook her head. 'I'm never going back in there again.'

'You picked a bad patch. It happens. Try not to fight these things.' He touched her shoulder. 'You're fine. Ready to head back to the car?'

'I suppose so. I hope my legs hold me up.'

He jumped up, picked up his board and her camera, held out his hand and pulled her to her feet. Holding her hand, he led her back along the beach.

Lester had his shirt and sunnies on and was sitting by the car.

'I feel so stupid, Lester. That was scary,' she managed to say. She found her towel and rubbed her hair, hiding her face.

'Good lesson to learn. Respect the sea,' said Lester.

'Do you ride a horse?' asked PJ.

Catherine nodded. 'Yes, I have one of my own.'

'When you fall off, best thing is to get straight back on, right?' said PJ.

'So they say. And yes, I did,' said Catherine feeling better and calmer now.

'Okay. Let's go.' PJ picked up his board.

'What! Back in there? No way.'

'With me and the board. You can't be scared of the ocean. You just got to understand it. C'mon,' said PJ calmly.

Catherine shook her head. 'I don't think so.'

'If you don't go, Hawaii will never be the same for you. Trust PJ,' advised Lester.

PJ took her hand and silently they walked back across the sand towards the ocean, which now looked so benign, so safe, so inviting that Catherine wanted to shout at it as though it were a creature that had frightened her.

PJ held tightly onto her hand until they reached the shallows and then he pushed the board into the water and stood beside it. 'Get on, just lie flat.'

Catherine lay on the board as PJ waded beside her pushing the board into the deeper water. As soon as they hit the channel and PJ was forced to tread water, she began to shake.

'Just keep still, try to feel as one with the board. Feel how it's moving with the sea, you're all one. Go with it, don't fight. Put your head down, close your eyes. I'm holding on to you, you won't go anywhere.'

She lay on the board as it bobbed gently, restrained by PJ. The sun was warm on her back, water trickled across the board under her body. She felt herself begin to relax.

'I'm turning the board, keep your eyes closed,' said PJ softly. 'Okay, now look up.'

She lifted her head as he thrust the board like a javelin from his grasp. For a split second she felt suspended and then she felt the rush of water, heard it, but before she could glance back, the board was picked up and pushed smoothly and swiftly forward; the beach, the dark hills and PJ's van zoomed closer towards her.

It was exhilarating, the sense of power and speed. She assumed she wasn't going very fast and that the wave wasn't very big but, like Lester, she felt elated.

The board slowed and stopped, bobbing on the shallow sandbar. She rolled off and stood up in knee-deep water and saw PJ splashing towards her, a large grin on his face.

She picked up the board and together they waded to the sand.

'So how was that?' asked Lester.

'You're both right. That was great. It felt terrific. But that's it. I'm not learning to surf, I'm not going into the ocean alone again.'

The two surfers were smiling at her and nodding.

'Okay,' said PJ easily.

'Thanks, PJ,' said Catherine. 'Would you like to join us for some lunch? I owe you that at least. Where'd you like to go, Lester?'

'Back home,' he said.

'I have a few things to do, thanks,' said PJ. He touched Lester's arm. 'We'll do it again, hey? Hit the waves, have a bit of a swim, sit in the sun. Suit you to hang out a bit, Lester?'

'Only if you have the time and don't mind an old man and his thoughts,' said Lester gruffly.

'It's an honour. You're still a legend. I'd enjoy just hanging loose with you.' PJ smiled at Catherine. 'See you round. Give me a call. Give Lester my number.'

Catherine nodded. 'Hope we see you again.'

'You will.' He picked up his board. 'Might head out to Rocky Point, see you, guys.'

Catherine was about to ask Lester how he felt about his swim, but the expression on his face as he gazed at the ocean stopped her. There was an intensity in his eyes, but also a sadness and something else she couldn't fathom that almost shocked her. She'd found Lester so easygoing and friendly, his life a seemingly open book by newspaper accounts, that she never imagined there could be a side to him that hid pain, anger, dark secrets.

By the time they returned to his apartment and he'd settled in a chair on his lanai as Catherine made them both a sandwich, he was back to his old self. Sometime, she thought to herself, I really want to talk to him about the old days.

A group of the Wives' Club were gathered in Catherine's sitting room, some spilling out onto the lanai. She was glad Mrs Goodwin hadn't been able to attend today's meeting to discuss a suitable charity for the club to support as they were looking for a new project. Mrs Goodwin's presence always made Catherine feel as though she was in school. Julia Bensen topped up coffee cups as Catherine handed round a plate of Mrs Hing's malasadas and freshly baked pineapple cream pies.

'I think it would be nice to do something for the local community, don't you?' suggested Catherine. 'A children's play and activity centre perhaps. A place that specialises in Hawaiian culture where they can learn dances and songs and stories, and mainland kids could also go along and join in.'

The women stared at her, a silence falling over the group.

'I'm sure they do that in their schools. Or families show them that sort of thing,' said Amy Cord.

'Our hula show was fun. Learning the dances,' said Julia thoughtfully. 'Maybe our kids would get a kick out of doing the same thing.'

'I was thinking of a sort of cultural exchange. We could show them how we do some things, they teach us how they do some things. It'd be great to connect with the locals. Win a few hearts and minds,' said Catherine with a smile. 'After all, there have been a few . . . incidents. Bradley told me there are a lot of hapa streetkids whose fathers were servicemen based out at Manakuli Point.'

'What's a hapa kid?' asked a newcomer.

'Mixed races,' said Julia. 'Left over from men who

210

have been stationed in Hawaii. There are thousands of single men on an aircraft carrier who go wild when they get into Waikiki or downtown. You can bet those kids are never going to see their fathers again.'

'It's not our boys' fault, really. You can't blame them for being red-blooded. Some of the local girls are a bit, well, loose,' protested Amy.

'That's a bit harsh, surely,' said Catherine, amazed at the turn in the conversation. 'Hawaii is touted as the melting pot of the Pacific – Japanese, Chinese, Filipinos, whites, they've intermarried and had children.'

'And you know who gets treated worst? It's not the hapa kids. It's the white kids,' said Amy. 'Especially in school. D'you know some of the girls get harassed in the bathrooms? My friend's little girl refuses to go to the toilet all day. Another time her brother came home and said tomorrow was "Kill Haole Day". When she went to the school the principal just said it was harmless fun. They've been put in private schools now.'

'Well then, a sharing of cultures might be a good thing,' said Catherine. 'Why don't we talk to Kiann'e about it?'

'We'd better ask Mrs Goodwin what she thinks,' said Julia.

'Why? Surely we can do a bit of sounding out beforehand so we have all the information when we discuss it,' said Catherine, wondering why these women were so scared of the commanding officer's wife. Then she remembered: their husbands' career prospects rested in not rocking the boat.

But Catherine didn't feel as wrapped up in Bradley's life as these women were in their husbands'. They always talked about what their husbands were doing, saying, thinking. They didn't appear to have lives of their own. Once again, Catherine was so glad she'd met Kiann'e, Aunty, Lester and Vince.

She raised the idea about the club's project with Kiann'e the next morning.

'Mmm, basically it's a good idea, but these things can be tricky. It can't be called a school or have a teaching component, but you could call it Hale Pihana Kanaka – a shared gathering place – where they learn to appreciate that everyone is different and we're all special and that'd be a positive thing. God knows there have been enough problems from the forces. Our people hate having the military bases here,' said Kiann'e.

Catherine slowly digested this. She felt like her life was divided into sections: her life with Bradley with its regimented, structured naval lifestyle and her involvement with the local people with whom she felt such a bond and whose company she far preferred to the naval wives.

'So do you think I should push this wheelbarrow for the club, or just sit back and let them run another handicraft stall or something?'

'Catherine, you have to realise that the other wives aren't like you. They know that they're only going to be here for a short stay and they aren't interested in the problems of Hawaii, even if the navy has done a lot to create them. They just want to help their husbands' careers and not worry about anything else because they'll soon be moving on. Even though you want to make a difference, you're not going to change the Navy. So what are your plans for today?'

'Mr Kitamura is in town, he and Paul want to see me. Something about my photography course.'

'You must know everything about a camera by now.'

'That's what Bradley says. He doesn't appreciate the challenge of learning all the finer points of things you can do with exposures. I'm now learning to print my own photos. Wish I had a darkroom at home.' She sighed. 'That's the downside of Bradley's career, not having a permanent home where I could set up a little studio, a workroom, a desk, that sort of thing. My mum has a lovely sewing room at home. It's her space, Dad never goes in there.'

'You have to weigh up the other advantages – travel, free housing, the commissary and PX. These things sound very attractive to people struggling to pay bills and live in an expensive tourist city,' said Kiann'e. 'They say the price of gasoline is going to shoot up with the Middle East oil crisis. The cost of freight is going to add a lot to the price of food brought in to the Islands.'

'Then we'll have to live on pineapples and sugar cane juice,' said Catherine.

'And coffee. Boy, I'm ready for a cup of Kona,' said Kiann'e.

Mr Kitamura rose and shook Catherine's hand, beaming at his favourite pupil. Paul was also smiling.

Mr Kitamura picked up an envelope and handed it to her. 'For you.'

'What's this all about?' She ripped open the envelope and drew out a formally printed certificate announcing she had won the Photographic Portrait Prize.

'My goodness! Wow, this is so great.'

'Congratulations,' said Paul. 'It was a terrific picture of the surfers. You have really captured the essence of the Hawaiian surfing culture. But most of all your use of light and shade to highlight the respect that the young surfers have for the old man is exceptional.'

'You can take your prize soon,' said Mr Kitamura, 'While we have a break between classes as it is a vacation week.'

'The prize!' repeated Catherine in a bit of a daze. She knew that she had spent a lot of time and effort into getting just the right photo, but she also knew that she was up against really stiff competition and she hadn't expected to win.

'Yes, a week on Kauai. Staying at the famous Palm Grove Hotel,' said Mr Kitamura with a big smile. 'Mrs Lang has been very kind. You will enjoy to be back on Kauai?'

'I might wait till my husband comes back from sea.'

Mr Kitamura looked uncomfortable. 'It would be more convenient to take this trip soon. Mrs Lang has put the room aside, our classes are on a break . . . Is it possible for you? To also take photos of the Garden Isle . . .'

'Oh, I understand,' said Catherine quickly. She wondered if she could get in touch with Bradley but then thought why did she need to ask his permission. It was a wonderful opportunity, she knew Eleanor at the Palm Grove, she'd look up Kiann'e's mother, Beatrice. She'd send Bradley a letter to explain and anyway, she knew Bradley wasn't all that keen on the Palm Grove.

'Of course. It sounds great. Really wonderful.'

'The *Hawaii News* wants to use your prize picture on the front page. So you could talk to Vince about that when you see him,' said Mr Kitamura.

'I'll ask Lester if that's okay with him,' said Catherine. 'I'm sure it will be.'

Vince greeted her effusively. 'Hey, what a star photographer we have working for us! Well done. Can you do a bit of a write up on Lester to go with it? Not the old stuff, everyone knows that, what he's up to now.'

'Well, he's not up to very much, Vince. He's an older man with bad knees and a bit of arthritis. But he did get out on a board recently.'

'Really? You get a shot of that?'

'I took some, but nothing worth using.' Catherine

felt Lester wouldn't want pictures of him being helped onto a board and lying down like a beginner being compared with the famous shots of him taking out surfing championships.

'All right, run this other shot of him with the young guy as well. Is he a relative?' asked Vince as he picked up a copy of Catherine's picture of Lester and PJ.

'No, PJ just met him. Though he's a fan of course. But they have a similar look don't they?' Catherine studied the picture and suddenly recalled the early photographs of the young and handsome Lester. 'PJ has more hair, Lester's is a bit more cropped and smooth.'

'That's the difference between the 1930s and the 1970s I guess. So when you heading for Kauai?'

'Pretty soon it seems. To fit in with the arrangements. Shame my husband is away. But I'll make it a working holiday, Vince.'

'Good for you. Whatever you feel like doing. You know folks there don't you?' When she nodded, he added, 'You're becoming quite a local. Give me a call if you get onto anything worth covering.'

Catherine rang Julia Bensen to tell her she'd miss the next meeting of the Wives' Club.

'You've won a trip? And you're going to Kauai? Won't Bradley be disappointed? And surely it won't be any fun on your own,' she said incredulously.

'It's sort of a working thing,' said Catherine. 'And I have friends there.'

'You do? I'd love to go over there, I'm told it's beautiful. Well, I'll let Mrs Goodwin know. Do you want me to bring up your idea about the meeting place for the kids?'

'No, if you don't mind. I might have more information when I come back,' said Catherine quickly. She knew that if she were not at the meeting to explain her idea, Mrs Goodwin would simply squash it.

As the island jewel of Kauai came into view from the plane, Catherine felt a ripple of excitement when she saw the postcard beauty of volcanic cliffs and forbidding dark-green forested hillsides, glittering waterfalls, secret coves of white sand, the bright blue water inside the ring of reef and the whipped-cream cresting waves. But glaringly sandwiched between the cliffs and the sea she saw the dazzling white buildings of a resort, a deep blue pool, artfully arranged palm trees and secluded bungalows. Then they were over the town and gliding to a halt at Lihue.

And there was the looming, smiling figure of Abel John in his familiar Palm Grove aloha shirt, striding towards her.

'Aloha, Catherine! It's good to see you back. I hear you're Kitamura's star pupil!' He dropped a fragrant lei over her shoulders, kissed her cheek, picked up her bag and headed for the car.

'I'm loving it! I'll be looking for ideas of places and people to photograph while I'm here. How's Eleanor and everyone?'

'She's good. Things da same.' A slight frown creased his face. 'Maybe that's part of the trouble.'

'What do you mean? Is the hotel not doing well?'

'It's not my place to speak stink but there are some big new places going up, big modern resorts that are biting into her business. The Palm Grove is old-style Hawaii now.'

'But that's what I love about it,' exclaimed Catherine.

'It's not what tourists want these days. You know what places are like in Honolulu. I'd hate to see that take over here. We all love what Mrs Lang has done to bring Hawaiian traditions to visitors. It's been important for us.'

'I won't say anything of course,' said Catherine, but she couldn't help remembering Bradley's comments on their honeymoon that the older hotel looked a bit frayed around the edges. 'So is there anything interesting happening on the island I could go and photograph?'

'You mean for tourists or just for us?' he asked. 'I hear you're going to see Beatrice. She'll tell you what's going on. And how about coming to my house, meet my family? Sure to be a luau happen sometime.'

'Well, thank you, Abel John, I'd like that.'

There was a card from Eleanor beside a basket of fruit in her room. 'Come for a drink before the fire-lighting ceremony. In my office. Wonderful to have you back at the Palm Grove.'

Eleanor sat at a long table covered in papers and notebooks and a vase of flowers. A large basket that she used as a handbag sat beside her. Reading glasses had slipped to the tip of her nose as she concentrated on writing in a ledger. As Catherine tapped at the door she looked up and came around the table, her arms outstretched.

'Dear girl, aloha. How clever of you to win this! It was a wonderful picture of Lester. I'm surprised you got him to the beach.' She hugged Catherine.

'He went surfing the other day. Gave him quite a thrill.'

'Really?' Eleanor bustled back to her desk and made some space. 'I'll order a drink for us then I'm sure you'll want to see the torch ceremony.'

'Of course. Are there many guests staying here at the moment?' asked Catherine, curious about what Abel John had told her but not wanting to mention his comments.

Eleanor rang through to her assistant and asked for two pineapple juice cocktails. She didn't answer until they were both seated. 'Not so many guests as we're used to. Things are in a bit of a state of flux at present. It's how the hotel business goes. Places come in and out of favour.'

'But the Palm Grove is an institution,' said Catherine.

'Yes, and we have our regulars, but we need to attract more new travellers.' She gave a smile. 'So after some deliberation I'm planning a little refurbishment.'

'A lick of paint, or something more?' said Catherine. In her walk through the palm trees after she'd settled in her room she'd seen some heavy equipment at the back of the ponds.

'Upgrading. Adding another tennis court and a new wing,' said Eleanor.

'Sounds expensive. But it won't change the ambiance here, right?'

Eleanor sighed. 'I hope not. But things are changing round here a little bit. I can't hold onto my island oasis forever. Actually, Catherine, I've had to take on a partner.'

'I see. Is that bad?' Catherine wasn't sure how to react as it sounded a sensible idea but Eleanor looked so sad.

'Ed and I bought the Palm Grove and the Moonflower in Honolulu and I've always been proud of the fact we did it together without shareholders. Ed was great at persuading investors to bankroll us and of course they got a good return. But finding the right person with money to go into business with isn't easy.' She sighed. 'It's a bit like a marriage. Now, how are you and Bradley going?'

'He's away at sea. But I have to confess that, while I miss him, it's kind of fun being my own boss and escaping the watchful eyes of the other wives. And Mrs Goodwin, the Commander's wife. Eleanor, it's like being in boarding school.' Catherine wrinkled her nose.

Eleanor laughed. 'This trip is a nice escape for you then. Is there anything special you'd like to do? You can borrow my car any time.'

'Thank you. I want to explore and take some photos. Abel John offered to take me to meet his family. And I promised Kiann'e I'd see her mother and the rest of her family.'

'Beatrice is involved in so many things. Don't get swept up in her passion and commitment too much. You have to be careful of your position as Bradley's wife and as a haole. I know, it took me a long time to be accepted by the locals and while I made this place a tribute to Hawaiian traditions and employ as many locals as I can, there is still some resentment. In your case you're considered to be part of the military, which has lots of money and little understanding of what Hawaii is really about.'

'I'm trying to come to grips with all that,' said Catherine.

'Those who know you appreciate that, but for some local people, uneducated, poor, ill informed, you represent what they don't have. But enough of this negative talk, come and enjoy the best of the island.' She glanced at her watch. 'We'd better go, it's the magic hour.'

Sitting amongst the sprinkling of guests as Kane, the young Hawaiian, ran through the palm trees lighting the flame torches, Catherine watched Eleanor charm, smile and greet people before picking up the microphone to explain the meaning and significance of the lighting of the torches. No-one would have guessed she had any worries in the world other than the comfort and care of her guests.

The next morning Catherine met Abel John who was taking her sightseeing while he ran a few errands for Eleanor and then later to his house for lunch. Catherine wasn't sure how much Eleanor had taken the affable Hawaiian into her confidence so she asked cautiously, 'I saw a lot of heavy equipment at the back of the ponds. Is there some construction underway?'

'Yes, they're going to excavate for another tennis court and more rooms. More modern style. People aren't happy about that.'

'Why? Because it changes the style and the mood of the Palm Grove?'

'Partly.' He frowned. 'Some of the old people say it's kapu land.'

'What do you mean by kapu?' asked Catherine.

'Forbidden, taboo. Things can be kapu for many reasons. Originally it was a system the chiefs, the rulers, used. Perhaps a gourd on a stick in the ground, or a special rock or shell placed in a spot which meant Keep Out. It could have been to stop fishing or hunting to make the land more good. Today something might be kapu by a written law as much as by local ali'i custom. Anyway, Eleanor wanted to build elsewhere when we told her, but that new business partner, he want there be one view of the ocean from the top floors.'

'Who is this new partner?' asked Catherine.

Abel John shrugged. 'Mainland guy. Some old associate of her husband's. He's got the money so he's got the power. He never comes over here. She meets him when he goes through Honolulu. I believe he's got investments in Alaska. She not tell me much, of course.'

Catherine was thoughtful. The tall Hawaiian was such a warm and friendly man, she knew Eleanor relied on him, trusted him and he was part of her inner circle. 'I suppose, being on her own, she hasn't got anyone to share confidences with anymore.'

'She talks to old Lester,' said Abel John, then changed the subject. 'Let's check out Pinetrees.'

'You like surfing?' asked Catherine.

Abel John turned and looked at her to see if she was serious. 'You don't *like* surfing, you are consumed, obsessed. It's a way of life and for me it's my heritage.

Only the ali'i were allowed to ride the waves, the sport of kings.'

'Bradley told me the sport is very old,' said Catherine as Abel John turned the car down a winding dirt road lined with banana trees and flowering shrubs.

'Have you seen the old prints Eleanor has around the hotel? They're copies from the Bishop Museum showing the old Hawaiians, including wahines, riding the waves on rough planks of wood cut from trees.'

'Times have changed then,' said Catherine.

'Yes, now it's you Australians who are the kings. They come in and really blasted the waves with their new-style boards, aggressive surfing. Shown the locals a thing or two!'

'Really? I didn't know that,' said Catherine in surprise.

'They like to come to the island and stay a few months. Come competition time, like, it's crazy. If the break is going off they'll probably be over at Pinetrees today. You might get some photos of the Aussies in action.'

'Sounds good.'

They passed an occasional house tucked amid thick greenery. One had a goat tethered in a front garden, another washing draped over a makeshift line, another bicycles and old cars parked on the grass.

Abel John pointed at the simple houses in their lush and tranquil privacy. 'I bet these go one day. Too close to the sea.'

'But we're miles from anywhere,' commented Catherine who'd been following their journey over the mountains to the far side of the island.

'Didn't you see some of the big new resort complexes when you flew in? That's the trend now, set up a community close to the water, surrounded by private grounds. Some are gated. They take guests straight from the airport to the hotel and half the time people never leave the complex! Good thing we still have the beaches where the surf is running. Too dangerous and long way for most tourists.'

Catherine understood what he meant when they came from the hills onto the coast road, still a dirt ribbon that followed the shoreline, until they came into a wide bay. The beach was a narrow strip between the road and the stretch of blue ocean and the long, right breaking waves off the reef made even Catherine catch her breath. But it was only when she spotted a surfer cutting sharply across the face of the wave, slicing the clean blue in a flashing streak, that she realised the size of the waves in relation to the speck of a man on the tiny surfboard.

'Gosh, you wouldn't want to come off in those waves! You'd get pounded to a pulp wouldn't you?' she exclaimed.

'You have to know what you're doing before surfing this spot when there's a big swell running,' agreed Abel John.

'It's certainly beautiful scenery,' said Catherine looking up at the thickly forested volcanic ravines.

'The best view is from a board out past the break as you sit there,' said Abel John. 'But you should take a boat trip along the Na Pali coast further north. That's amazing scenery. Steep jagged cliffs, stunningly beautiful. Very magical. There's no way of getting there except by boat. At least that part of our island might stay unchanged.'

Catherine was silent as they drove further on, Abel John keeping one eye on the waves. He then turned down a track and pulled over onto a grassy mound where several other cars were parked. Boards, towels, flippers and soft-drink bottles were dropped beside the vehicles.

Abel John pointed to the blackened remains of a fire on the sand. 'I'd say they been here a couple of days.'

'Who?' asked Catherine looking around. The place was desolate. Beautiful but isolated.

He pointed to the sea and she saw another couple of

surfers bobbing beyond the roll of giant waves. As she squinted into the distance she saw both riders suddenly take off on waves as if propelled by some unseen force and the next instant they were picked up by a surge of water that crested in white foam, turned over on itself and flung its great weight of water towards the shore. The specks were swept up as tiny corks in a great sea, lost to sight, then, to her amazement, they shot out at the head of the surging foam, zigzagging ahead of the wave as it dribbled and dispersed itself across the surface of the sea. So spectacular had the actions of the surfers been that Catherine realised she'd been holding her breath. The two surfers glided into shore, picked up their boards and stood on the beach where they seemed to be discussing the merits of their fast flight from break to sand.

When they turned and walked up the beach towards where she and Abel John were standing, she suddenly recognised them.

'PJ and Damien! What are they doing here on Kauai?' she asked Abel John.

'You know them?'

'Yes. I introduced PJ to Lester and I met Damien at the rally.'

'Damien is one of the hotshot Aussies I told you about.'

Damien spotted her and broke into a big smile. 'Hey, you get around!'

PJ gave her a nod. 'Hey, what are you doing in Kauai? Abel John showing you his favourite breaks?'

'I won a photo competition, the one I took of you guys and Lester. But I didn't think Abel John knew all these secret places. It's a totally new world to me,' said Catherine. 'How long are you here for, then?'

PJ shrugged. 'Depends on the waves.'

'I'm moving round. Got to see Molokai. Seeing it's my spiritual home,' offered Damien.

'How come?' Catherine asked the cheerful Aussie.

'My mum named me after Father Damien, the priest who helped all the lepers on Molokai. She learned about him in Sunday school or something. So as it's my name and I'm in Hawaii, got to go there, right?'

'I guess so,' laughed Catherine. 'Where're you both staying?'

PJ waved vaguely behind him. 'Staying with friends. Got a house back in there. Drop by any time.'

'I only have a week. I'll see how I go. Otherwise, catch you back in Honolulu.'

'Maybe. Say hi to Lester. Tell him I'm still on his trail.'

'You trying to outride Lester?' asked Abel John. 'He was one freak. One wild man. Don't kill yourself,' he advised.

PJ shook his head of sun-gold curls. 'What comes along, comes along.'

'Wait a few months. Those winter sets will test you,' said Abel John. 'We have to move wiki wiki, catch you guys later.'

PJ nodded his head towards the jungly growth across the road. 'Come by sometime. See a different side than what you're used to, Catherine.'

He was smiling, his even teeth looking whiter in his tanned face. His blue eyes held laughter, but there was a hint of a challenge in his voice.

'I might do that. Enjoy Molokai, Damien.'

'That's my motto. Enjoy. See ya.'

Abel John smiled at Catherine as he drove back across the island. 'You know PJ good?'

'No. He doesn't seem an easy person to know. He's quite reserved. What do you know about him?'

'He's a waterman. Connected to the sea, always looking for the next wave. I understand him but I can't do like him. I have family, a job, duties, work with my people. He doesn't want any of those responsibilities. They'd cramp his style.'

'Well, it sounds like you have a life. I couldn't imagine just spending my time surfing. I'd be bored.'

'Ah, you're wrong there. It never boring. Every day is one challenge. You go visit *Nirvana*. You might find it interesting.'

'*Nirvana*?'

'It one old house that was abandoned years ago. It now home to haole kids from the mainland – dropouts, draft dodgers, hippie flower-power people. And surfers. Serious surfers.'

'Doesn't sound my sort of scene at all.'

'Which is what PJ meant.' Abel John glanced at her. 'There's something about you, Catherine. People like you. You're different. See and experience what you can, while you can.'

Hanging unspoken was the assumption that she would not be in Hawaii forever.

'Eleanor offered me her car. I might take her up on it.'

Lunch at Abel John's was what Catherine now appreciated as typical Hawaiian hospitality and she immediately fitted in with the family. His young children, initially shy, soon were climbing over her, demanding hugs and stories and laughing at her funny accent. His wife, Helena, was pretty and short, dwarfed by her strongly built husband. After graduating from college she'd worked on the mainland but, feeling homesick, she came back to Kauai and fell in love with Abel John.

There was fish baked in a banana leaf and sprinkled with toasted coconut and fresh poi which Catherine enjoyed for a change finding it sweet, while the steamed and chopped taro leaves tasted like spinach. As lunch was being prepared, Abel John showed Catherine the large pond where they grew their taro, the big heart-shaped leaves standing out of the water with roots growing in the mud ready to be picked for the poi. Papaya and lime trees were laden and chickens pecked around the steps leading into their large wooden house where they ate at a long table on the open verandah.

Catherine couldn't imagine the other navy wives or her in-laws sitting around enjoying this. She wondered whether it was because her upbringing had taught her to accept people for who they were, rather than for what they did, that made her at ease like this. She took lots of photos, especially of the children and Helena preparing the food.

'We live simple. Used to be all you needed was a taro patch, fish from the sea, maybe a pig and some chickens,' said Abel John. 'People call Hawaiians lazy. But we know how to enjoy life, know what important. Our ohana, our beautiful island, catching a few good waves, sharing food with friends.' He dropped his baby boy into a hammock strung across the verandah. 'Things are changing fast in the Islands. Too fast. There'll come a time when it will get to bursting point. The old kahunas are worried. So take photographs, Catherine, before it is all gone.'

Helena smiled at Catherine. 'Life is always changing. If you hold on and try to keep the present moments frozen, you'll find you're frozen too. I tell Abel John we must accept these changes, hope there'll be a better future for our keiki. Move with the current, not dam its flow.' She spoke quietly, calmly and Catherine sensed the determination and strength in the tiny Hawaiian girl who the strapping Abel John had married. She imagined him out in the surf before working at the Palm Grove while she looked after their children, prepared food and ran their household.

As they returned to the Palm Grove she thanked Abel John for the invitation to join his family. 'They're beautiful. Helena seems very organised, very calm.'

He nodded and grinned. 'I be lucky. She lived on the mainland, could be living in a big house with some rich haole boy perhaps. But her heart is here. Once the Islands grab you, you will always return.'

'I get a sense of that,' agreed Catherine. 'Maybe it's to do with your roots, your growing up.' She didn't say any more but suddenly she found herself thinking of her family and *Heatherbrae*.

9

Catherine and Eleanor had a quiet dinner together in Eleanor's small bungalow at the Palm Grove. Eleanor began to reminisce, talking about her parents who fled Europe from Belgium after the chaos of the First World War.

'My mother was very unhappy at leaving her family for the strange world of America. She never really settled into New York, so we moved to a smaller town upstate which suited her better, though I think my father, who was a businessman, felt he could have been more successful in New York City. I don't remember Europe at all. I grew up as an American.'

'I suppose that will be the case with any children that Bradley and I have,' said Catherine wistfully. 'Though I plan to take them home every year if I can.'

'Sadly I couldn't have children . . .' Eleanor paused then added, 'I would have liked a large family, but that was not to be.'

'Oh, that's sad.' Catherine waited a moment, sipping her coffee. 'Eleanor, do you still feel really American?'

Eleanor laughed. 'Partly but I'm more Hawaiian now. This is my home. I only go to the mainland on business. But, you know, one day I'd love to go to Australia for a visit.'

'Then we'll do it! I'd adore you to see *Heatherbrae,* meet Mum and Dad. You'll love it. Different from here, but special, just the same.'

'Put it on the list of Things to Do One Day,' said Eleanor.

The next morning Catherine drove over to the other side of the island to where Abel John and she had met PJ and Damien. The beach was empty and there weren't any surfboard riders and, while the ocean didn't look as ferocious as it had been when she'd seen the surfers out there, there was no way she'd set foot in it.

One end of the beach finished in a jumble of rocks and a jutting cliff. In the other direction a thin ribbon of gravely sand ran between the coast and the water. She gazed inland, trying to work out where the house PJ had mentioned might be. All she could see was lush growth in the hills that rose steeply behind the coast, but as she studied the vegetation she began to make out banana trees, coconut palms, plumerias and a tree covered with brilliant gold and red flowers.

She slung her camera over her shoulder, locked the car, crossed the dirt road and walked a little distance and was rewarded by finding a narrow dirt track, just a car width wide, leading into the growth. She debated about going back for Eleanor's car but decided first to check where the track went. Within minutes she was out of sight of the coast road and the ocean. She was walking further into a tropical Eden.

She heard the house before she saw it, sounds of the melodic Carpenters singing 'Close to You'. Then she stopped transfixed at the tableaux before her. Two tow-headed, tanned little children, a girl in bright pink overalls and a boy wearing only a hot yellow swimsuit, were playing amid a jumbled garden surrounded by fruit trees: mangoes, papayas, limes and avocadoes. The children held a bucket and were tugging at beans on a vine. Around the profuse vegetable patch were bicycles, a wooden wheelbarrow and two old Chevy station wagons.

The house was a beach shack, certainly not modern, open sided, latticed and breezy. There were beds and hammocks on the verandahs and a circle of chairs in the garden. Heavily scented old flowering trees leant against the peeling wooden structure, the drift of fragrance reaching Catherine as she stood there. Surfboards were lined up, towels and clothes scattered on the trees to dry.

The children spotted her and the little girl ran to her.

'Hi. Who're you? We're having beans for dinner.'

'Sounds good. I'm Catherine, what's your name?'

'Pink. That's Ziggy. Where's your bag?'

'In the car at the beach. I haven't come to stay. Er, is your daddy here?'

'No. Just Sadie.' The little girl took her hand and pulled her towards the house.

Catherine kept looking around at the flowerpots in hanging macrame baskets, Asian statues, colourful hammocks and lots of fat candles that had dripped wax in thick melted puddles. A handpainted sign dangling crookedly above the front steps read *Nirvana*. As she stepped onto the cluttered verandah a woman not much older than herself appeared.

'Hi. Where've you walked from?'

'Oh, not far. I left my car at the beach. I wasn't sure where the house was.'

'Who're you looking for? Everyone has split.'

'Everyone? I'm Catherine, PJ suggested I drop by.' She couldn't help wondering if this interesting-looking woman was his girlfriend. Or wife. She realised that she had no knowledge of PJ's personal life at all.

'He'll be in the water. They all went to the Cannons. Come in, make yourself at home. I'm Sadie, this is Pink and Ziggy.'

Catherine stepped inside, her curiosity piqued. The little girl took her hand.

'C'mon, see my house.' She led Catherine past bedrooms and through a big family room to a smaller bedroom. It was filled with posters, pictures, ornaments, shells and driftwood. There was a bed on the floor and beside it, a small pink teepee.

Pink crawled inside. 'See, this is my bed. These are my dolls.'

Catherine peered inside at the bed cluttered with homemade animals and a Barbie doll in a ballet dress. 'Cute. And is this where Ziggy sleeps?'

'Yep. But he's not allowed in my teepee. C'mon.'

She dragged Catherine by the hand into the kitchen where Sadie was preparing a meal. A stripped long pine table was covered with earthenware bowls, big glazed jugs and piles of fruit and vegetables. The kitchen was filled with pots and plants, candles and pictures. There were at least a dozen mismatched chairs around the table. It all looked very unusual to Catherine. It was not home decor as she thought of it. This was a makeshift temporary home, but there was a warmth and casualness about it that, while messy, was very appealing.

'I'm making lunch, some of the others will be back soon. Stay and join us.'

'Are you sure? I'd like to,' answered Catherine, looking at the squash, pumpkins, papayas, pineapples and lots of food she didn't recognise. 'You seem to have enough.'

Catherine sat at the table and watched Sadie make a salad. Pink brought her a hand-written, hand-drawn story book done on thick paper. It was about a little boy and a dolphin.

'This is a lovely story, who did this?' asked Catherine.

'PJ. He's good at stories,' said Pink.

There was laughter and chatter and two women came into the house, their arms full. One carried a guitar, rolled-up straw mats, a pair of shoes and what looked like a bag of clothes, possibly laundry, thought Catherine. The other carried baskets with food and one basket that served as a cradle. One of the girls was pregnant, her suntanned baby belly protruding above a low-slung sarong and below a short little top. Catherine wasn't exactly shocked but she'd never seen a pregnant woman flaunt her body like this. The only maternity outfits she recalled were checked blouses with peter pan collars and a floppy bow worn over neat stretch slacks. She knew she would have to remember all these details to describe to Mollie – the girls' tangled long hair with flowers behind their ears, their long floating dresses and skirts, the unusual woven sandals on their feet, the bangles and necklaces, a little bolero embroidered with tiny mirrors over a sheer loose top and, while they didn't wear make-up, they looked healthy and exotic.

'This is Catherine. Friend of PJ's. She's stopping for lunch,' announced Sadie.

'She's *my* friend,' insisted Pink.

'Cool. Hi. Do you mind hanging onto Petal while we unload?' The baby in the basket was handed to Catherine, a small sweet bundle who had a spangled beanie on her head, tiny bangles on her chubby arms and a silver chain around one ankle.

'Is this your little sister?' Catherine asked Pink who was tickling the baby's toes and kissing her cheek.

'Petal is Summer's baby.'

Confused, Catherine glanced at Sadie.

'I'm Summer,' said the girl who'd handed the baby to Catherine. 'I'll put the cold stuff away before it melts.' She took some packages out to the verandah where Catherine had noticed two big refrigerators.

Soon the kitchen was buzzing with activity. Procol Harum was now on the record player as lunch was spread along the table. Salads, chunky loaves of homemade bread, brown rice, pasta, cheese and fruit. It looked delicious but it was not a repast that would be served up in a restaurant or hotel and certainly not by any of the navy wives.

'Do you mind if I take some photos?' Catherine took her camera off her shoulder. 'It's all so colourful.' She quickly explained her working holiday.

'Take my picture,' insisted Pink, striking a pose.

The women were curious about Catherine and as she moved around snapping the shutter they gently pulled her life story from her in a matter of minutes.

'The navy! Don't mention that around here. Doobie is on the run – you'd better not take his photo!' laughed Summer.

The pregnant girl, Ginger, started cutting the bread into fat slices. 'So how'd you meet a shadow like PJ?'

'Shadow? I don't know much about PJ at all, except he's a surfer and he wanted to help an old man I know.'

'Surfer! PJ's a king. Known as the shadow because he's always around, right behind you, but hardly ever makes a sound or talks much. He doesn't often bring a girl here.'

'Well, he hasn't exactly brought me, it was a drop in kind of thing. Ah, can I ask, are one of you connected to him? As a girlfriend?' said Catherine candidly.

Sadie started tossing the salad. 'This is a pretty free

and easygoing house. People come and go. Some of us have been here a while, PJ comes and goes. Occasionally he has a girl in tow. Not for long. We kind of share him,' said Sadie.

'Hey, don't get the wrong idea, Catherine! We don't sleep with him. He's not one of our group in that sense. He just likes to have a base here. Place to sleep, place to eat, place to keep his boards . . . then he's off and we have no idea where he is and then weeks later he just turns up,' said Summer.

'If you're keen on him, he's a hard man to pin down,' said Ginger softly. 'Many have tried. He's only interested in one thing.'

'The ocean?' said Catherine.

'Of course,' said the girls.

'He sounds just like someone else I know,' said Catherine. 'But I'm not pursuing him. I'm happily married. Our paths have sort of crossed because of old Lester.' She was embarrassed they thought she was some chick with the hots for the handsome and mysterious surfer. 'Would you mind if I got my car? I have some different camera lenses in there I want to use.'

'Do whatever you want. Now you're here, why not stay the night? Plenty of hammocks, places to crash,' said Sadie.

Pink went and flung her arms around Catherine's waist. 'Goodie! Stay tonight and we can talk stories.'

When she got to the car Catherine was tempted to get in and drive back to the Palm Grove. The whole scene at *Nirvana* was so far out, so different from anything she'd known, but she didn't sense anything sinister in the setting or the people. In fact she was drawn to them, curious about their lifestyle. It was just so very informal and unstructured. Didn't they have jobs? How did they all just live as though they were on one big perpetual family holiday? She decided to stay a little longer.

She parked Eleanor's car at *Nirvana*, glad that Eleanor had offered it to her for a few days. Along with her bag of camera accessories, Catherine looked in her basket and found she had her make-up bag, a beach towel, her bikini and a clean T-shirt, but she was unprepared for an overnight stay. She'd wait and see how the afternoon panned out. The women had made tea and one handed Catherine a mug but it was milky, spicy and sweet.

'Is this Hawaiian tea? It's different from Aussie tea,' said Catherine. 'But I like it.'

'It's Indian chai,' said Ginger. 'There's fresh lime juice if you'd rather? Or a papaya milkshake. We make them with coconut water.'

Their conversation was interrupted by the sound of sputtering motors with loud mufflers.

'Good, they're here for lunch.' Summer put a cushion on a chair for Ziggy and a plate in front of Pink.

PJ was the first to stroll in and Pink rushed to him, hugging his legs. He picked her up. 'Hey, Miss Pink, how'zit?'

'Catherine is taking my picture.'

He swung around and grinned at Catherine. 'You got here.'

'Yes. Everyone's been very hospitable.'

Two other men came in, filling the room with energy and laughter. They had long hair, faded shorts and T-shirts advertising Led Zeppelin and Primo beer. They sat at the table, ruffling the kids' hair. One picked up baby Petal, gave her a kiss and put her back in her basket.

'This is Catherine,' said Sadie.

'Hi. I'm Doobie.'

'Hey, Catherine. I'm Lief. Spelled L-i-e-f, but said leaf.'

'Hello,' she answered, amused to see the men starting to heap food onto their plates.

'Good waves?' asked Summer.

'Fair. Doobie got a decent tube or two.'

'Going out this afternoon?' asked Sadie. 'We hit the store so we don't need anything.'

'Groovy. Then we can kick back,' said Lief.

'We could show Catherine around. We thought we might go to the heiau, have a swim with the kids,' said Sadie. 'You'll like it, Catherine.'

'Okay, I'm happy to fit in with your plans.'

'They don't have plans,' said PJ. 'Things just evolve.'

Sadie smiled at Catherine. 'With kids sometimes evolution needs a bit of nudge. We'll make it a women's excursion to the Goddess pool.'

'I'll change into my bikini,' said Catherine.

'You won't need to,' said Ginger. 'It's the women's sacred bathing pool.'

Catherine was a bit nervous at the idea of naked bathing but the women were easy to get along with and as she'd already agreed to go, she didn't want to appear a stick in the mud. Pink chattered to her, which kept her distracted, as everyone else fell into easy conversation, passing food and laughing a lot.

Surreptitiously Catherine watched the interaction between them all but she couldn't figure out which man was with which woman. They all paid attention to the children and seemed comfortable with each other. There was a lot of joshing around, laughter and sometimes intense debate over music, politics, the war, surfing breaks and food, along with stories of great road trips.

It was a foreign language, a different world for Catherine. Her background seemed so sheltered, so one dimensional. When she heard the stories these people told she felt that she hadn't really lived. Or had fun. Or escaped. Even her time in London now seemed sedate and unadventurous. She sat and listened and laughed, hoping no-one would ask her to share any of her wild experiences.

After lunch the three women cleared away and prepared

a basket with things for the two children and the baby, gathered some cold drinks and towels and packed up an old Chevy station wagon. Pink and Ziggy were put in the rear with the basket and while Sadie drove with pregnant Ginger beside her, Summer and Catherine sat in the back seat.

They drove down the coast road, which narrowed as it wound along the deserted coastline until there was no more beach, just a rocky foreshore. They all sang along to 'Puff the Magic Dragon' and Catherine joined in.

'What kind of music do you like, Catherine?' asked Summer.

'I love Peter, Paul and Mary, even if it's a bit old-fashioned now.'

'The song's set on this island – Hanalei Bay. Everyone's got a different interpretation of what the lyrics really mean,' said Sadie.

Catherine was glad she could relate to some of their music at least. At lunch they had played a lot she was not familiar with. It was what Bradley called 'harsh, modern music'. Bradley didn't even like the Beatles or the Stones and he shook his head in dismay whenever she played them. 'My husband likes old show tunes, movie musicals. And Hawaiian music.'

'Don Ho or Rap Replinger?' asked Summer with a grin. 'He's not into Led Zeppelin or Marvin Gaye, then?'

'Er, I don't think so.'

Pink began to chirp, '*Tiny bubbles, make you feel warm all over . . .*'

They stopped the car close to a boulder-strewn beach by a small headland. Catherine couldn't imagine where they might go from here, but everyone got out, gathered their belongings and even little Ziggy was given a towel and small cloth bag was strung around his neck. Summer tied baby Petal in a cloth sling, and knotted it around her neck and across one shoulder leaving her hands free.

237

Catherine followed them along the edge of the rocky beach until they got to two large boulders that seemed impossible to pass. Ahead was a jutting impenetrable finger of sheer rock and thick undergrowth. Summer in the lead, the baby strapped to her, bent down and rolled away a rock lying between two larger ones to reveal a small passageway. Squeezing between the rocks Catherine saw that there was a sandy track etched between the undergrowth, leading to the rocky beach and the large flat rocks at the base of the headland. It was familiar territory to the women who talked as they walked, helping Pink and Ziggy over the rougher patches.

It seemed that they were heading to the rocky beach when suddenly there was a cleft in the cliff face and they walked onto sheltered broad flat rocks.

'It's like an open-air room,' breathed Catherine.

'But better, look, a pool,' said Ginger.

Already Ziggy was following Pink who jettisoned her bag and sandals and skipped surefooted towards the deep glistening pool trapped in the flat rocks. Further out the water of a lagoon glistened and around the tip of the cleft they could see the white water rushing over the reef.

'It's beautiful. We won't get swamped or cut off by the tide will we?' asked Catherine.

'Very rarely. It's in such a position that the water comes in through that tiny channel at high tide but never washes over it. Unless there's a cyclone,' said Summer, slipping out of her shirt and crochet bikini.

'How did you find this place?' wondered Catherine.

'An Hawaiian girl showed us. It's not to be broadcast, talked about for, you know, tourists,' cautioned Sadie.

'No way. Of course. I can tell this is a special place,' said Catherine beginning to disrobe as the others had already shed their clothing.

Ginger was the first to slide into the pool, cupping her

hands under her baby belly. Pink and Ziggy, also naked, jumped in beside her, splashing and giggling.

'It's not deep this end, you can stand up,' said Sadie. 'There's a deeper bit in the middle and a shallow ledge at that end.'

'For the birthing,' said Ginger. 'It's a sacred birthing pool. We call it the goddess pool . . . seeing we're all goddesses!' She laughed. 'I'm having my baby here.'

'I had Petal and Ziggy here,' said Summer.

Catherine, feeling pale and shy, slid quickly into the velvety water. 'Is that a good idea? I mean, I've sort of heard of water births but not, like, in a place like this. Will a doctor come out here?'

Sadie and Summer laughed. 'No. That's our job.'

Catherine didn't probe further, it was so far away from what she imagined childbirth to be like. She couldn't imagine any of the navy wives, used to their big military medical centre, giving birth in such a place either.

'Well, it's a great place to skinny dip. Do the men come here too?'

'Uh, uh. That's kapu, this is wahine territory,' said Sadie firmly. 'After the baby is born and we leave here, the father has his right to do his ceremony.'

'How come you know so much about local customs? I didn't think you'd been here that long,' said Catherine.

'We have good local friends. Once you're accepted as not just another haole, they open their doors and hearts to you,' said Summer.

'That's true,' said Catherine, thinking of Kiann'e and Abel John and even the formidable Beatrice.

'Socialising with us haoles can be seen as "acting high", trying to be better than their friends and neighbours, which doesn't go down well. It takes awhile to be accepted, so that you're fitting in with them rather than them trying to fit in with you.'

'We get on with the locals because we live like they do,' said Ginger. 'No offence, Catherine, but the rich mainlanders, the tourists and the military, usually don't get invited into local homes.'

'The naval people tend to keep to themselves, it's a world of its own,' agreed Catherine. 'Maybe that's why they've been tolerated so long.'

'That's changing,' sniffed Sadie.

'But you're different, inquisitive. You want to find out about other people,' said Summer. 'That's why we've taken to you.'

'You're not going to stay in that closed world are you?' asked Ginger bluntly.

'I'm married to a naval officer!' said Catherine.

The women were silent for a moment.

'You might want to rethink that,' said Sadie.

'You don't seem the type,' said Summer.

'Don't get bossed around, listen to you heart,' said Ginger floating on her back, her large belly looking like a small brown island. Summer held her baby in the water, swishing her back and forth.

Catherine was shocked. And hurt. She didn't want to say she couldn't possibly lead a life like these women, drifting from day to day with fluid relationships, no plans, no security, no apparent rock-solid partner.

'Bradley's different,' she began, then stopped as the three women broke into big grins.

'Don't make excuses for him,' said Sadie. 'Look, I'm sure he's a nice guy. You've told us you dated in a romantic place in an unreal setting, far from home. I bet he's really good looking. And those sexy uniforms. Who wouldn't fall for the guy?'

'That's not important. It's how we feel about each other,' protested Catherine.

'So? How do you feel about him?' asked Ginger.

'I love him! I married him.'

'Ooh, I've been there,' said Sadie. 'Didn't last. Thank God I woke up quickly to the fact that he was totally the wrong man for me.'

Catherine was getting annoyed. She'd just met these women, whose world was totally different from hers, and here they were telling her how to run her life, insinuating her marriage was a disaster and that Bradley was not the right husband for her.

'Well, I'm going to make my marriage work. Bradley is generous, loving, everything a girl could want. My friends at home think I'm so, so lucky.'

'He's the lucky one I'd say,' said Sadie. She reached over and touched Catherine's arm. 'You might think it's not our place to say anything, but we've all come through some rough times and we hate to see another woman go down the same path. You haven't lived enough, Catherine. Cut loose a bit.'

'I couldn't live like you do,' said Catherine.

The three women were unoffended.

'Times are changing compared to our mothers' day,' said Summer. 'Going on the pill, sleeping with anyone who takes your fancy, having children out of wedlock, or by different partners, getting high on pot, whatever. Didn't go on in their day.'

'Those things don't go on in my world either,' said Catherine. 'It's true, I haven't ever been a bit wild or tried anything unconventional. And I don't feel the need to do so. Though meeting you lot is a bit unusual!'

The girls laughed and Pink paddled to Catherine, trailing long strands of mossy green seaweed she'd pulled from the rocks. 'Look, a necklace.' She dropped longer strands over Catherine's head.

'Or a crown!' Ginger pulled up fat fleshy brown leaves of seaweed with clusters of grape-like pods filled with water and twisted them into a circle and handed one to each of them. 'C'mon, Ziggy, here's your crown. You can be king!'

Laughing, they splashed around, inventing a silly game and the subject of Bradley and Catherine's marriage was forgotten.

'What are you doing after Kauai?' Summer asked Ginger.

'Haven't decided. Doobie wants to try and surf some uninhabited breaks people are starting to talk about. Micronesia. South Africa. A bunch of them want to make a little film – searching for the perfect wave, or something.'

'Tricky with a baby and Ziggy,' said Sadie.

'I'll probably visit my mom for a month or so. Then see where we all end up. I might base myself somewhere closer to the guys. I've always wanted to visit a big game park.'

Catherine listened to the ping-pong talk of plans, marvelling at the flexibility of their lives, the lack of responsibility or worry about the future. She wanted to ask how they could afford this lifestyle but decided it'd be rude to ask.

'Okay, time to go. The kids are getting tired. Me too,' announced Ginger.

Catherine hopped out, wrapped a towel round herself and grabbed her camera to take a few photos of the women and kids still wearing their seaweed crowns and frolicking in the pool.

'These are just for me. I won't give any hints about where this place is,' she assured them.

When they were dressed Sadie opened her bag and took out a taro root, some flowers and some coins and handed them around. 'An offering to the goddess of the pool.' She threw the taro root into the deep centre and the others followed her, though Ziggy was a bit reluctant to let go of his shiny coin. Then they stood in a circle, holding hands, and Summer, who had a beautiful voice, sang a short Hawaiian chant.

'What's that mean?' asked Catherine as they all headed back along the path from the secret pool.

'I can't translate exactly. I learnt the words from our friend, but it's like a blessing. A thank you for letting us bathe in the sacred water and a prayer to keep our women and children safe.'

'You've been blessed too, Catherine,' said Sadie. 'So you'll be watched over on the island.'

On the way back, Sadie carefully replaced the stone in the centre of the boulders, obscuring the tiny track.

Nirvana was deserted when they returned. Surfboards were missing as well as the old van but the women didn't comment on this and as Summer took the baby and the two children in for a nap, Sadie put a large coffee pot on the old stove.

'Any suggestions about dinner? Anything you don't eat?'

Catherine shook her head. 'Not at all. Though I'm wondering if maybe I should start back . . . Eleanor could be wondering about the car . . . me taking off . . .'

'Is she your mother? Aren't you rambling round taking photos? Relax, Catherine. Maybe you should've gone with the guys. Got some good surfing shots.'

'I've taken a few of those.'

'Ah, you can't say you've been there and done that. Surfing, waves, the riders, it's an eternal smorgasbord,' said Sadie. 'I've put in my time waiting and watching.'

'Do you surf?' Catherine asked Sadie.

'No. I like swimming but I don't surf. Ginger does. Not at the moment, though. She thought it would be a way of, first, getting Doobie interested in her, then holding onto him. We're no beach chicks sitting chastely on the sand like Gidget,' she laughed. 'Ginger got his attention more than most and with the baby coming, he's hanging around. But, as you heard, finding some unknown surf heaven will win out every time.'

'How will she support the baby if, say, he takes off and leaves her?'

'He won't leave her, he just drifts in and out. He does okay for money. Some of the boys move hash and other stuff around the world. Officials don't seem to know about hollow boards,' said Sadie. 'Not my business, I don't pry.'

Catherine was still digesting this piece of information when there was the sound of a car.

'That's not the guys.' Sadie put a jug of hot milk on the table as the door opened and Abel John stuck his head inside.

'Anyone home? Hey, Sadie, hey, Catherine. Hoped you'd find this place. PJ around?'

'They're gone. We've been out, too. Coffee's on.'

Catherine jumped up and hugged Abel John. 'Great to see you. Is Eleanor okay, does she want the car back?'

'Course not. She said she'd loaned it to you for the duration.'

'Where've you been hanging, Abel John?' asked Sadie pouring another mug of her thick local coffee.

'Escaping. Been fishing. Got a few. As I was on this side I wondered if you guys could handle a decent chunk of mahimahi.'

Sadie winked at Catherine. 'The universe provides. We were just discussing what to cook for dinner. You staying?'

'Thanks. Have to get back to the family. Always something happening. And I need to check in at the Palm Grove.' He smiled at Catherine. 'Glad to see you're getting into the local groove. Say hi to PJ.'

He went out to his car followed by Sadie to collect the fish.

Summer appeared, rubbing her eyes. 'What's happening?'

'Mahimahi for dinner. Abel John has been fishing.'

'Groovy. You cooking, Catherine?'

'Er, not really. Happy to if you show me what to do.'

Sadie came in flourishing a big silver fish. 'What a beauty. We'll cook it over the open fire outside. What else will we have with it?'

'Salads?' offered Catherine, remembering all the fresh greens and vegetables that were left over from lunch.

'And baked yams. In the coals,' added Summer.

Catherine sat on the verandah as the women organised the children and made preparations for dinner. They'd handed her a glass of not very good red wine and told her to lay back. She assumed she'd be given chores later. She felt herself unwinding. She hadn't realised there was such tension inside her body. Staying at *Nirvana* was a bit like being in a big family, or with a bunch of school friends. How Mollie would love this. She'd be right in there arguing, chatting, laughing, cooking with the women.

As Catherine sipped her wine, knowing that Abel John would tell Eleanor that she was okay and with no family or husband to report to, she started to relish this taste of freedom. She put her feet up on the railing, closed her eyes and hummed along to Diana Ross singing 'Touch Me in The Morning'.

She jerked as a hand lightly touched her shoulder.

'Hey there.'

She looked up to see PJ smiling at her. 'Where'd you spring from?'

'Not far. Came back to get a different board. Thought you might like to come down. It's going to be a great sunset,' he said.

'Okay. I'll get my camera.'

'Don't hurry. Finish your wine. I'll grab some drinks to take down. Maybe some pupus.'

'We won't be too long? I'm supposed to help cook dinner.'

'It'll happen. Don't worry. The guys'll be back to eat.'

'I don't s'pose you can surf in the dark anyway,' commented Catherine as she collected her bag.

'Full moon is good. Inside the reef. Wouldn't risk the bities in the dark in deep water.'

'Sharks?'

He nodded. 'See you shortly.'

They drove to the opposite end of the rocky beach from the Goddess pool. PJ drove slowly, glancing at the sea or up at the green hills as if searching for something. He didn't talk much and Catherine felt comfortable, not feeling the necessity for making smalltalk or filling in the space between them.

PJ pointed as they came around a bend in the road. 'Out there. Word spreads when there's good waves peeling like that.'

There were a dozen or so board riders out where he pointed.

'Peeling? What's that?'

'When the wave breaks evenly from one end to the other along its length. It makes for a good long ride,' said PJ.

'Oh, I see. There must be a lot to learn. About the ocean, the waves, the best way to ride them, I suppose,' ventured Catherine.

PJ glanced at her. 'Yeah. And more. It's not just a sport, a physical thing, it becomes a mystical thing. Hypnotic, some say spiritual, it's a control thing, intellectual exercise, all kinds of things. Hard to explain to someone outside – only a surfer really knows.'

He parked the wagon and sat for a few moments watching several riders weave down the wave, kick out and paddle back up to the line where they waited for another set. 'Damien's out there. Some of the Aussies are pretty aggressive surfers. Think they have to keep proving themselves. Pro competitions are starting up everywhere now. It'll get big time for sure. Money, business will get into it and the whole thing will change. But the essence – the rider and the wave – that's the heart of it, that won't change.'

This had been a big speech for PJ. He got out and pulled out the two surfboards he'd brought along. 'You want to have a ride? I'll take you over the other end where it's not a heavy swell, be a decent ride into the beach. Got the big board.' He pointed at the long board. 'Be another hour before the sun goes down.'

She glanced at the board. 'I can't manage that and you won't be able to stand out there.' The waves at the end of the beach he was looking at were nowhere near the size of the waves further out where the surfers were. It looked too serious for him to just push her onto a wave back to shore.

Catherine was still nervous of the ocean and the experience of nearly drowning in the channel remained very real to her. The sea was alive, a breathing, temperamental, unpredictable creature, a stranger to her.

'I was glad when you went out with me after your experience in the channel. This time come in just for fun. Trust me.' He gave her a smile, half hesitant, half teasing, slightly wistful.

'Okay. How're we going to do this?' She stripped down to her bikini.

'Tandem. This board can take both of us. Just hang on.'

She followed him into the water. The evening was balmy, the tradewinds had dropped, the sky was mellow as the sun began its slide into night. She lay on the long wooden board, grasping the sides, centring her weight, moving into the position PJ directed. He pushed the board through the water and as it deepened he swung himself onto it, straddling her body as he knelt and began paddling them both out towards the white rim of waves.

They sped along easily, water trickling over the board and wetting her underside. It became deeper and the push of the dissipating waves more forceful so that PJ had to lower himself onto the board to dig his arms into the water more strongly. The board shot forward and Catherine breathed with the rhythm of PJ's strokes. His body, now wet, lay on top of hers, she felt his skin on hers, could feel his muscles on her back, his breath close to her ear as he dipped and pulled them towards the break.

Then he turned the board and sat up, legs dangling over the sides as he watched over his shoulder. The board moved gently, she was at eye level with the sea. The water whispered to her. The reassuring touch of PJ's body, the stillness and quietness gave her a feeling of suspended calmness.

'Here we go!' He began paddling firmly and Catherine felt them lifted, poised in the air for a second before beginning to surge forward. 'Hang on, lift your head and shoulders!'

Catherine arched her body, aware only of the rushing water on either side of her. PJ seemed to have disappeared, she couldn't feel him and she glanced over her shoulder to see that he had jumped to his feet and, with arms outstretched, was guiding the board through the wave. She looked at the beach rushing towards them, the dark shape of the hills lit by the golden sky and felt she was flying.

The ride seemed to last forever, she never wanted it to stop. As soon as they slowed and PJ dropped to his knees to paddle into the shallow water, she wanted to turn around and do it all again. It had been exhilarating, and more. It had felt erotic with the touch of PJ's body on hers and with the surge of the wave, the speed, the thrill, the ride was intoxicating. But PJ helped her off and dragged the board onto the beach.

'Are you starting to get a feel for what it's all about?' There was that smile again.

She nodded, shaking her wet hair. 'Fantastic. Thanks.'

He picked up his short board. 'I'm heading out to the break. You might get some good shots from higher up the beach.'

Lightly he sprang onto the board and sped through the water, and it looked to Catherine as if he were one with the light turquoise board and water. A bird, a fish, he was part of the sea, at home and happy, always looking for the challenge ahead among the waves she was yet to understand.

She pulled her clothes over her body where she could still feel the weight and power of PJ on top of her. Slowly she picked up her camera. She climbed to a small green point and propped herself against a boulder to steady the camera as she used the long zoom lens to try to capture more closely the action of the boys on their boards, silhouetted against the setting sun.

By the time she made her way back down to the beach, there was a small driftwood fire blazing with a group around it, surfboards – their silent partners – lying close by. Bottles were being passed, cigarettes flared and voices relived the moments of the past few hours.

She felt shy at breaking into this intimate circle of young men who shared the bond, a communal oneness, of their individual experiences with a common element. She stood back and took a picture of the circle of lean figures in front of the sparking wood, the glowing clouds hovering on the horizon.

PJ spotted her and waved her over, shifting his body to make a spot for her. She sat on the cool sand, trying to recognise the faces lit by sunset and driftwood fire – Lief,

Doobie, others she'd noticed at other times on other beaches, and Damien.

'Hi, Damien! Didn't know you were here,' she said giving him a big smile.

The normally cheerful Aussie gave her a wave but was restrained, a bit withdrawn. He seemed to be in some intense conversation with a fellow next to him. Catherine realised that she was an interloper here, an outsider, not just because she was a woman but because she was not part of this culture. She sat quietly, feeling chastised, out of place. PJ noticed her mood and gently touched her arm, giving it a squeeze. He didn't look at her, but continued giving all his attention to Lief who was talking about a wipe out.

Catherine wished she could leave. She was an intruder in this private male post mortem.

Suddenly she was aware there was a shared cigarette being passed. PJ murmured, 'Do you smoke?'

'Nope, never took it up.' But across the fire she saw Damien drag deeply on a smoke, cupping it in his hands, inhaling deeply and passing it to the man beside him. She caught her breath as she realised they were smoking pot, hash, marijuana!

The reefer was passed. PJ took a drag and casually handed it to her. Already the girls had made her feel unworldly and naïve and since she didn't want the men to think that about her as well she took the smoke and copying the way she'd seen others take a toke and hold their breath, she took a long drag, trying not gag. She coughed slightly and someone handed her a bottle and she took a hefty swig of the claret.

She sat quietly as the joint was passed around and watched Damien busily rolling fresh smokes.

Then she stared into the flames of the small fire, tuning out of the talk and bursts of laughter. Pictures began to flare and form . . . a bushfire at *Heatherbrae* where gum trees had exploded into flame, scenes of the war in Vietnam she'd seen on television, Bradley's face flickering for an instant, then a volcano was erupting.

She became aware that PJ was nudging her.

'What do you see?' he whispered. 'In the fire?'

'A volcano going off!' And she started to laugh. Suddenly it seemed terrifically funny.

Catherine had little recall of the drive back with PJ except they talked and laughed a lot. Dinner was underway and several more people had dropped by and with music blaring, food and drinks circulating, the night had turned into a party. As the evening wore on Lief played his guitar and Summer sang, and the mood became more mellow. Some people were in deep intense discussions, others simply sat alone, lost in their own trip. Several of the women were gossiping and there was much laughter. No-one was being a host or hostess, everyone did their own thing. It was relaxed but stimulating and fun. Catherine had drifted between various groups, people were friendly but nothing was expected of her and she felt wonderfully contented. She kept remembering the board ride and it began to assume huge proportions, the wave was bigger, the ride faster, PJ's touch more intense. She could feel his skin on hers as though it was burning. She rubbed her arms.

'Are you cold? Okay?' PJ sat beside her.

'Hot, not cold. I was thinking of that ride on the board with you. I'd like to do it again.'

'Any time.' He smiled in the soft light from the lanterns strung around the verandah. 'Be careful. You might get hooked.'

'I need a walk.' The music, candles, incense were suddenly cloying.

PJ took her hand and pulled her to her feet. 'Good idea.'

They walked in the moonlight along the narrow dirt

road. She breathed deeply. The perfume from the night flowers seemed almost overpowering, she could hear the surf out on the reef and the call of a night bird on the hill. She held PJ's hand tightly as all her senses seemed so fine-tuned, so alert, her nerve ends close to the surface. She'd never felt so alive. Or so happy.

'I have no idea why I feel so . . . great,' she said.

PJ chuckled. 'It's the pot. Don't tell me that you've never smoked before.'

They got to the beach and Catherine suddenly dropped his hand and sprinted along the sand, skipping, dancing and twirling until she fell over, laughing in delight.

PJ reached her and took her outstretched hand. 'You all right?'

'Fine, never better. Let's go for a swim!' she danced towards the water's edge and PJ followed her.

Catherine waded into the water, her cotton skirt getting wet, sticking to her legs, before she tripped and sat in the water's edge with a splash. PJ sat in the water beside her. They looked up at the moon. And it seemed the most natural thing in the world for PJ to lean over and take her in his arms and kiss her.

PJ's kiss electrified her. She kissed him back wildly as if afraid to lose the sensations rolling through her body. Together they fell back, half in the water, half on the wet sand. She pulled him on top of her, clinging to him, trying to absorb his body so it flowed into her own.

She didn't recall their lips or their touch parting as clothes were ripped and pulled until they were naked, the coarse wet grains of sand grazing and sticking to their bodies as Catherine lay on top of PJ and he drew her to him, before rolling her beneath him where she clung to him as they made fierce love.

Catherine didn't know it, didn't hear it, as she moaned and howled aloud, her hair sunk in the sand, a wavelet trickling under her burning body as PJ continued making love to her as if it was a final act, a desperate, wild save-me-before-I-die plea, too pleasurable to let go.

Later, she remembered they swam, they laughed, they kissed, naked in the sea before calmly, quietly, walking back to *Nirvana*. Candles burned, the music was low, there was a murmur of voices in the darkness. No-one seemed to notice or care about the bedraggled figures moving slowly around the verandah, looking for towels and drying their sandy bodies before sliding into a hammock together, to fall asleep entwined and satiated.

In the morning, Catherine awoke with a dry mouth, her skin irritated by sand and initially only vague memories of the previous night. She sat up and Pink was beside the hammock. She could smell coffee and something baking. The sun was shining and a bird was singing.

'Hi, Catherine. You've been asleep.'

'Hi, Pink. I certainly have. Is it late?'

'I don't know.'

'Where is everyone?'

'Around. What're you doing today?'

'Gosh, Pink, I'll have to go back to my hotel.'

'Coffee?' called Summer.

'Sounds good.' Catherine swung her legs over the hammock looking at her dishevelled skirt and sandy T-shirt. Summer handed her a mug of coffee and made no comment about her appearance or the previous night.

'Sadie's baked banana bread. Plenty of eggs. Help yourself. I'm taking Ziggy to the beach,' said Summer. 'Get him out of Pink's hair while she has a lesson.'

'Thanks. What lesson is that?'

'Sadie is teaching her to read and write. Can't start too early.'

Catherine went to the outdoor bathroom and brushed her hair, put on some make-up and tried to piece together the night before. Only Lief was around, so she assumed the other boys had all gone surfing. She was glad PJ wasn't there, she didn't know how to face him. But it was a momentary sense of awkwardness.

Fragments of their lovemaking flashed through her mind and made her tremble. Had it been as mind-blowingly wonderful as she thought or had the pot confused her and made it all seem more magical and passionate than it was? She knew she could claim that she'd smoked and drunk too much and had had no control of her actions. But who was she going to make excuses to? The women seemed unfazed, Sadie had waved, pointed at the breakfast table and mouthed 'Help yourself' as she listened to Pink recite the alphabet. Somehow Catherine knew PJ would be frank and honest and not expect her to demean what had happened by saying she didn't know what she was doing. And Bradley didn't and wouldn't ever know. For the moment she had no guilt. This was not the setting, place or people to make excuses for what had happened. It had happened. It wouldn't happen again. Move on.

Over breakfast Lief, Summer and Catherine talked about their early schooling experiences, Lief passed on the news that a chopper had been flying low through the valley and that there was talk of a hotel being built on their side of the coast.

'Development for Japanese tourists apparently. Be a pain in the ass if it goes ahead. It will bring too many tourists. We might have to move on from Hawaii, to Indonesia, to other islands.'

'Would you do that? Just up and move and live somewhere else to surf where it's unspoiled?' asked Catherine. 'At least here you have the quiet part of the coast but over the other side of the island is civilisation.'

'It's what we've all been doing, moving around where

the wind takes us,' said Summer. 'But with kids, you need doctors and stuff.'

'Enjoy it while we can, I say,' said Lief. 'I'm heading out. See you, Catherine.'

He left and Catherine helped wash up. 'I'd better be going. I'm supposed to see some Hawaiian friends. Thanks for letting me stay.'

Summer shrugged. 'Any time. I'm sure we'll see you again.' She gave Catherine a hug.

Catherine wasn't sure whether her comment was just a casual remark or whether she was hinting Catherine would no doubt be back to see PJ.

Catherine said goodbye to Sadie and kissed Pink. 'See you again, Pink. Thanks, Sadie. I feel I've known you all for ages.'

'It's how it is. Come by before you leave the island.'

'I'll try. I only have a few days left. And a lot to do.'

Before she left, Catherine took a few more photos of *Nirvana* nestled in its lush surrounds, a place where people cruised in, stayed a while and moved on. She wouldn't forget it easily.

No-one saw her return to the Palm Grove. Her room was spotless and neat, the bed still folded down for the night with a flower on the pillow. She tugged at the sheets, rumpled the bed and stepped into the shower. As the water ran over her, rinsing away the sand, she started to tremble and suddenly she had her face in her hands, weeping uncontrollably.

10

IT WAS COOL IN the coconut grove. There were few early morning risers about. Catherine wandered by the ponds where the wild ducks paddled among the water lilies. The Palm Grove buildings might need a freshen up but the grounds and the grove were beautiful, mysterious, romantic. Catherine imagined them to be like the secluded gardens of a maharajah's palace, the grounds built for a prince and his concubines, or, perhaps, she thought, they were perfect for a dreamy Hawaii Hollywood movie set.

It was a calming place, with the serenity of still water, stately palm trees and silence, save for an occasional bird sweeping through the grove and the sounds of Eleanor's caged exotic birds.

It had taken a day to start to deal with the enormity of her encounter with PJ. It was as though it had been a dream, except – if she allowed herself – she could still feel his physical imprint on her skin and in her body and she quivered at the recall. But no matter what she felt and no matter what the circumstances, the bald, damaging fact remained. She'd been unfaithful to Bradley. She tried to put the whole thing out of her head, pretend it had never happened. But sneaking into the pores of her skin came the remembered sensations of PJ's touch and the exquisite power of his lovemaking, something more wonderful than anything she'd ever experienced before. But, she thought, it will never happen again. I'll never ever let Bradley down again.

A long canoe, paddled by one of the torch lighters standing in his malo, slid along the canal under flowering trees. Sitting in its centre was Mouse, the Hawaiian gardener and balladeer, strumming his guitar and singing an Hawaiian love song. He gave Catherine a quick wave and she remembered that a sunrise wedding was to have taken place under a flower-bedecked canopy by the main pond. The wedding breakfast must be underway and Mouse was providing part of the entertainment.

Catherine felt a sudden tear trickle down her cheek, shocking herself. It was so little time ago that she and Bradley were here, newlyweds . . . looking forward to a future together, lives entwined, adoring each other . . . At least that's what she had believed then. How could she have made love to another man such a short time later? She berated herself. What had happened to her?

She longed for someone to talk to about this, to reassure her that she wasn't a shallow, unfaithful wife. Mollie? But as much as they'd shared everything, Catherine couldn't bring herself to do that. She didn't want to admit to her best friend that even the most romantic-seeming marriage could have rents in it already. And, she acknowledged, there was the matter of pride. Bradley had seemed such a catch in their eyes at home. Mollie would tell her she was being a fool, forget what had happened with PJ, everyone makes a mistake sometime and just get on with life with Bradley.

And PJ probably considered their lovemaking a one night stand, great for the moment, but she was sure he would have moved on the next day, no regrets, no commitment.

I have to get on with my life, she told herself firmly. Forget PJ. It was a mantra she filed away. 'Forget PJ. Forget PJ . . .'

Catherine decided that the best way to do this was to take some photos. She returned to her room for her camera and, following the sound of the music, she came to the main lagoon where guests were gathered, the bride and groom seated on big wicker chairs beneath the canopy watching the hula show.

The girl dancers knelt around the edge of the lagoon, singing and throwing flowers into the water while the solo dancer, standing on a floating bamboo raft in the centre of the lagoon in her ti-leaf skirt with leis around her neck, ankles and wrists, swayed gently to a classical hula. Then Mouse paddled in to harmonise with the singers. Through the camera lens Catherine caught sight of Eleanor in the background, quietly overseeing the food being laid out on long tables under the palms.

This would be a wedding this couple would never forget. Would they be back here for important anniversaries long into the future, wondered Catherine sadly.

She caught up with Mouse after breakfast. Dressed in a white shirt and slacks with a red cummerbund and lei, he had escorted the bridal party to their cars. As the last of the vintage Cadillacs swept away, he loosened his shirt, released the snap on the red band around his waist and walked to Catherine.

'Don't feel comfortable starting day in straightjacket,' he said. 'Good to see you back. Want another horse ride?'

Catherine snapped a quick shot of the weathered man in front of her. Cleanshaven with his slicked down hair and pristine shirt, he looked quite different from the Mouse she'd met previously. 'What a great idea! I'd love to, Mouse. Do you have anywhere in mind, anywhere you have to go?'

'I'm off till sunset. Tell me where you want to go,' he offered.

'Do you know Beatrice Lo'Ohouiki? You know where she lives?'

'She mighty important lady. Big leader of our people. You know her?'

'Yes. I'm friends with her daughter Kiann'e and her sister Aunty Lani back on Oahu.'

Catherine was running out of holiday time and because she had not yet visited Kiann'e's mother she thought that this would be her project for today. Abel John assured her that the family were around and like most Hawaiian families, guests were always welcome, so Catherine could drop in any time.

'I'd like to visit her today,' said Catherine.

'We can ride to Lo'Ohouiki's house. You need some boots? We have them for guests.'

'Wonderful. I can't think of anything else I'd rather do right now,' said Catherine. Anything, she thought, to take her mind off what had happened between herself and PJ. When she thought about the wild freed animal that had emerged during her lovemaking with PJ, she was horrified. She didn't know herself at all.

Riding with Mouse again brought back memories of *Heatherbrae* and how much she missed being on Parker. They took the same route away from the Palm Grove as last time but, instead of going into the hills as they had before, they went around the high coast road.

Catherine thought back to her first intimidating encounter with Beatrice before the rally. While Aunty Lani was warm and homey, Beatrice was imperious, regal and authoritative but, like her sister, Beatrice also had warm and engaging qualities.

They came to a slope and Mouse pointed upland. 'We go mauka.'

The bluff rose above them and the horses broke into a canter as they rode towards the mountains. They followed a red dirt road that led eventually into a sheltered green valley of the abandoned fields of an old sugar plantation until they reached a double row of royal palms marking a driveway.

The winding driveway disappeared into lush gardens, very overgrown and obviously many years old. Giant traveller's palms stood like huge green fans beside ironwood and ohia trees and a massive poinciana bowed beneath the spread of its magnificent branches sprinkled with firey red flowers. Catherine was expecting Beatrice's residence to be a small farm perhaps, a tropical haven, but there before them loomed a grand white wooden two-storey house with shutters, elegant columns and two wings of buildings on either side.

'It's a mansion!' exclaimed Catherine as they reined in the horses.

'This one time the plantation manager's home. Before that, some of the royal family lived here. A princess related to Lo'Ohouiki. Now she has family home again.'

'Maybe I should have made an appointment,' worried Catherine. But a man came towards them from the main entrance and signalled them to tether the horses to the side fence.

'You visit, I'll stay here with the horses.' Mouse reached for his cigarettes.

Catherine took a few pictures of the beautiful old home and its tangled garden. As she stepped onto the wide verandah an elegant haole woman in a muu-muu came to greet her.

'Aloha. You've come to see Mrs Lo'Ohouiki?'

'Yes. My name is Catherine Connor. I'm a friend of her daughter's.'

'Ah, yes, of course. Do come in. I'm Verna Oldham. Our meeting is nearly finished. You're in time for morning tea.'

'Oh dear, I hope I'm not interrupting.'

'Not at all.'

Catherine followed her down the hallway of polished wood hung with old photographs and paintings, past a large carved hallstand. The walls were covered in old-fashioned blue and cream regency striped wallpaper and there were large urns of ferns. It was very Victorian, very gracious. She longed to take photos. She wondered if Kiann'e had grown up here. She had always assumed that Kiann'e had grown up in a casual, fun, outdoor setting like Aunty Lani's. This home was very different.

Beatrice and four other ladies were seated in a sunroom in a couple of wicker chairs and on a long sofa. A polished carved koa wood table with a lace cloth was set for morning tea. The women were all dressed in formal muu-muus and leis. Beatrice stood up and welcomed Catherine.

'Catherine, what a lovely surprise. Ladies, this is a very good friend of Kiann'e's.'

Catherine was embraced by Beatrice who then introduced the other women. They looked like Americans but there was a lilt to their accents. They were older women, two wore flowers tucked into their hair and they had the look of long-time local residents.

'I do hope I'm not interrupting. Abel John suggested I just drop in . . .'

'Of course. You're welcome any time. Our door is always open. We were about to have coffee.'

'I'll bring in the pot,' said Verna.

Beatrice patted the sofa beside her and Catherine sat down.

'Excuse my jeans. I rode here from the Palm Grove.'

'How lovely. What fun,' responded the ladies.

'Catherine, this is the local Kauai chapter of the Daughters of Hawaii,' said Beatrice in an explanation of the gathering. 'The organisation was formed in 1903 and all our members must be able to trace their lineage back to at least 1880. The seven founders of the organisation were all born in the Islands of missionary parents.'

'Many of our ancestors were missionaries who married into Hawaiian society,' added Verna, beginning to pour the coffee.

'And what is the purpose of the organisation?' asked Catherine politely, realising that this was an elite group.

'The original Daughters came together because they were distressed at the disintegration of our traditional culture so they wanted to perpetuate the memory and spirit of Old Hawaii and preserve the names and correct pronunciation of the Hawaiian language,' explained Beatrice. 'Now we work with the community to protect historic and cultural sites. It's an ongoing project for us.'

'How wonderful. That's so important. Is this house historic?' asked Catherine.

'It is indeed. It belonged to one of my ancestors, a princess of the royal family. After she died the house fell into disrepair until a plantation manager and his wife decided to repair it, and live in it, and turn all the land around here into sugar cane crops because it seemed the most profitable export after all the sandalwood had been cut down. But they had a lot of bad luck and couldn't make the plantation pay. So my family reclaimed the house and my husband and I have raised our family here. Some of the descendants of the Chinese, Japanese and Filipino hands brought in to work in the fields still live in this area.'

'That's interesting. So this house is linked to the story of sugar in the Islands. What other places have been preserved?' asked Catherine, thinking this might make a great photo essay. She wondered if Mouse could show her the remains of the old sugar mills.

'Have you been to see Queen Emma's Summer Palace on Oahu?' asked one of the women. 'That was one of the first big projects our grandmothers tackled. It took years to recover many of her artefacts and belongings. '

'I'll make a point of it when I go back,' said Catherine. 'What other things do you do?'

'Well, we locate sacred sites and identify, restore and record their history. Then there are gardens, traditional agricultural sites, really anything pertaining to our way of life and culture that is threatened,' said Verna. 'We've just got the Hulihe'e Palace on the Big Island put on the National Register of Historic Sites,' she added proudly. 'Mind you, we're always after money to do these projects, so we run a lot of fundraisers and the like.'

Beatrice turned to Catherine. 'It's not just about the physical things. Culture and history is held by the people too, in our customs, language and beliefs. You understand how passionate I am about keeping traditional Hawaii as its own entity within the USA. We don't want our culture swallowed up by the mainlanders.'

'The Daughters are apolitical, though,' Verna hurriedly added.

'I think what you're doing sounds wonderful. I'd love to know more. I'll ask Kiann'e to suggest where I should go when I get back. And could I take a photo of you all? And the house, please, Beatrice?'

'Go ahead, honey. But first, our tea. Cream? Sugar? And some delicious cake.' Beatrice turned her attention to the table of food.

'Would your friend like some?' asked Verna. 'I'll go and ask him.'

Catherine enjoyed her morning tea and her conversation with the six very passionate ladies but she didn't want to keep Mouse waiting too long. She thanked Beatrice, farewelled the other ladies and as she walked outside she signalled to Mouse that she was ready to leave.

'Give Kiann'e a kiss for me. And Lani, too. I hope you come back to Kauai before you leave the Islands,' said Beatrice, who had escorted her outside.

'Oh, I'm not going anywhere yet!' said Catherine. 'And of course, I'll always be in touch with Kiann'e. She's made me feel so at home here.'

'She's being groomed, you know. She'll be playing an important part in the future of Hawaii,' said Beatrice. 'Treasure her friendship.'

'I do, indeed I do,' said Catherine. But she was startled by this comment and realised that Beatrice was referring to something other than her talented daughter being a dancer and passionate believer in Old Hawaii.

It was hot and still and Catherine could feel the sun burning the back of her neck as the horses walked side by side along the track back to the hotel. She discussed with Mouse the beautiful house and the magnificent old gardens. He nodded.

'I went there when it was sugar plantation. The manager's wife had party for us camp kids.'

'You lived in a sugar camp?'

He nodded. 'My grandfather, he come from South China to work for this sugar company. He live in Chinese camp.

It like a village from old country, my father tell me. The camps not mix much with other nationalities.'

'Why was that? Hawaii is now such a blend of different cultures and people.'

'I think them planters want mixed camps. Best way to mix 'em together. But language and customs hard to break down . . . it easier for workers who speak same language to talk with each other. Not feel homesick. Later system change. Workers could buy house or build on company land,' said Mouse.

'Do you have happy memories of growing up round here?' asked Catherine, lifting her camera to take a shot of Mouse on horseback.

'For sure. Every camp had own parties and traditions. We always let off firecrackers for celebrations.' Then Mouse sighed. 'Some haole families very rich. Now people say, one day, all the green fields will be gone and there'll be houses and hotels all round here.' He swept his arm in an arc embracing the fallow sugar cane fields, the wild and beautiful landscape. 'That's why we need Miss Beatrice. She's one fighting wahine.' They rode in silence, both wrapped in reflections of what had been.

Back at the Palm Grove, Catherine helped Mouse unsaddle the horses and groom them.

'You don't have to help me, Miss Catherine. This part of job.'

'I enjoy it. I miss being around a horse. And you've been so kind, Mouse. It's been an interesting morning.'

That evening Eleanor had dinner set up in her bungalow and she handed Catherine a glass of wine.

'Here's to you, my dear girl. It's been lovely having you around. Sorry I haven't been able to spend a lot of time with you.'

265

'Thanks, Eleanor. You work so hard here. When do you take a break?' They touched glasses.

'Wouldn't know what to do. Ed and I used to take a trip to Europe occasionally but since I've had the Palm Grove to operate by myself, as well as the Moonflower, there's no time for jaunts. Besides it's no fun travelling on your own.'

'But Eleanor, there must be friends you could travel with,' said Catherine.

'I guess so. I couldn't leave now anyway, what with all the work happening here and my new partner wanting to turn the Moonflower in Honolulu into a Japanese-style hotel for Japanese tourists. Doesn't suit it or me at all. It's an Hawaiian hotel. That's why they come here, for gosh sake. They can stay in Japanese hotels in Tokyo,' she said crossly. 'But enough of my woes. Have you had fun?'

'I've got some great photos I think. I don't know if fun is the right word . . .' She sipped her wine, wishing she could tell Eleanor about PJ.

'Interesting times, hey?' smiled Eleanor. 'You're enjoying your photography job?'

Catherine nodded.

'You like the Islands? Kauai?'

'I love all of Hawaii! Every island I've been to.'

'You have lots of friends?' persisted Eleanor.

'Yes. Local friends. The other wives are forced acquaintances, although a couple are quite nice.'

Eleanor studied her. 'So is there a problem with Bradley? You don't find that his being away means that you're growing in different directions?' she asked calmly.

'Eleanor! We've only been married a short while. How could we be bored with each other already?' exclaimed Catherine.

'Very easily, dear Catherine. How long did you know each other before getting engaged?'

'Not very long. But I think that when you know, you know.'

Eleanor shook her head. 'When you're in love you can talk yourself into anything. I knew Ed all through college.'

'So you were sweethearts from then?'

'No. We went our own ways. I made a few mistakes and then we found each other again by accident. We were very happy. I miss him a lot.' She began to serve the salad. 'Following your heart isn't always the right thing to do. But I have no regrets.' She smiled at Catherine. 'Remember that. Please help yourself to bread.'

'Were you ever . . . tempted? To be unfaithful?' Catherine asked cautiously.

'It took me a while to agree to marry Ed but once I made that choice, I stuck by him. Thick and thin. I'm glad I did.' She gave Catherine a steady look. 'I can look back now and feel proud of that.'

Catherine lowered her gaze, her insides twisting into a knot. Now she wished she hadn't taken the conversation in this direction.

Eleanor unfolded her napkin and lifted her fork, saying matter-of-factly, 'Of course not every marriage is as harmonious as Ed and mine's was. Sadly, it was too short.'

The next morning as Abel John put Catherine's bag in the car she hugged Eleanor goodbye.

'It's been such a wonderful week, I can't thank you enough, Eleanor.'

'Again, I apologise that I haven't been able to spend much time with you. But you seem to have kept yourself busy,' she said. 'Did you get some wonderful photographs?'

'I hope so. I'll send you some prints of pictures I took around here. Are you coming to Honolulu soon?'

'Possibly. Another round of meetings with my business

partner over the renovations and new buildings.' She wrinkled her nose. 'I'll let you know. We could get together with Lani. And please, say hello to Kiann'e for me.'

The plane banked giving the passengers a view of the magnificent Na Pali coastline. There were oohs and ahs as tourists admired the rugged cliffs rising steeply from the ocean. As the plane rose and clouds began to obscure the emerald jewel of the island in the deep blue sea, Catherine glimpsed a length of beach where white-crested waves rolled towards shore. Was that the beach she'd been with PJ? Was he down there, gliding effortlessly in on a smooth wave? Or had he travelled through the mountains to the other side of the island to find another beach and another perfect wave?

The apartment smelled musty, mildewy. Catherine dropped the mail and her bags and opened the lanai doors and front windows to air the small space. She'd have to go to the store and pick up some food. She turned her attention to the mail. There was a fat letter from her mother who always sent her clippings from the local paper and two letters from Bradley.

She made herself a cup of her favourite tea, which she'd missed on Kauai. Next time I go, I'll take Mum's tea with me, she thought. Then caught herself. Next time. When would she next go to Kauai? She pushed an unwelcome thought of PJ from her mind and opened Bradley's letters.

In his first letter, Bradley recounted the daily routine on board ship in his usual droll way, mentioning how nice his fellow officers were, asking if she had she heard from his parents and, as it was his mother's birthday, if she could please send a gift from them both and was she managing okay without him? He finished by saying how much he missed her. *I can't imagine life without you in it. You have made me so very, very happy. I love you. Bradley.*

Tears sprang to her eyes. God, how she hated herself. She'd never meant to hurt him. How could she have been so swept away with PJ? Thank heavens he didn't know.

The second letter was briefer and hinted at a possible change in orders, quite possibly a visit to New Zealand and Australia.

What did that mean? Would it mean that he would be away even longer? She rang Julia Bensen to ask what she knew about the manoeuvres, exercises, whatever exactly the men were doing as her husband, Jim, was on the same ship as Bradley.

'They're not allowed to tell us much at this stage. You know how it is, Catherine. But I think they're replacing a ship that's been re-deployed. Anyway, as soon as we know, we'll know.'

'Has Mrs Goodwin dropped any hints? I just wondered if you'd heard any gossip while I was away on Kauai.'

'How was Kauai? I'm going to suggest we go there when Jim has leave next. You made it sound so lovely.'

Was Julia being evasive or did she simply have no idea what was happening with their husbands, wondered Catherine. She suspected the latter. Navy wives always seemed to be the last to know anything. 'How was the last Wives' Club meeting?'

'The usual. Oh, Sandra Towle mentioned your idea about the children's culture club but Mrs Goodwin wasn't enthusiastic.'

'Oh, no! I wanted to raise it. Without all the background and a solid presentation, of course Mrs Goodwin was going to hit the idea on the head,' cried Catherine.

'She's not saying no without a reason,' came back Julia rather defensively. 'Everyone's always on the move and she didn't think it was fair to take on a major local project and then have to walk away from it. What if Bradley gets transferred? How are you going to be able to find someone who is as enthusiastic as you are to take your place in the project? No, I think Mrs Goodwin is right. We should stick to what we've been doing. It's easier.'

Catherine was thoughtful. 'I see. I suppose I haven't kept up with your ideas as well as I should.'

'Well, it's too bad you weren't here for the last meeting.'

Catherine heard the faint censure in her voice. 'I'll be there with bells on for the next one. So what's happening?'

'I hope you don't mind, but I volunteered your services for the July Fourth picnic. We always make a big thing of it. It'll be at Fort De Russy on the day, plus a cocktail party at the Goodwins' and fireworks in the evening.'

'Fine. What am I down for? Cooking hot dogs? The little league game?' she joked.

Julia remained serious. 'It's one of the most important days in the calendar, Catherine. To celebrate Independence Day and remind everyone how lucky we are to be in America. Oh, and there's a special church service early in the morning to be followed by a breakfast. That will probably be in the park too, as there's so much setting up to do.'

'Of course. It all sounds wonderful,' said Catherine trying to sound enthusiastic.

'We also thought you could take photographs. Souvenir shots you can sell to military families. We thought we'd set up a pretty sort of arbour seat with flags and red, white and blue balloons and a flower arch behind it, you know, Hawaiian looking, where families can pose together. Mrs Goodwin doesn't expect you to cover the cost of film or developing or anything like that, but we all think that the photos will make the club a lot of money and they can be sent to the navy newsletter and magazine as well.'

'Happy to help. Anything else?' asked Catherine biting back a facetious comment about having her life organised for her.

'There's a morning tea. Just a social at Melanie Lindsay's apartment on Thursday, but we'll probably talk about July Fourth plans. So we'll see you there? Ten a.m.'

'Lovely. I'll bring something.'

'Of course,' said Julia lightly. 'We so enjoy your malasadas.'

Catherine hung up the phone feeling cranky. She didn't want to go to the morning tea in the slightest and although she could get out of it by pleading a work assignment for the paper, she knew better. She'd go and dammit she'd take the best apple pie they'd ever tasted. Or something. Once she'd figured out where to buy it.

In the darkroom at the *News* office she pegged up her negatives and in the dim red light the images of *Nirvana*, the girls, Pink and Ziggy, Damien and the boys with boards sitting around the campfire at the beach . . . and PJ, all came to life. But instead of the wet black and white negatives, she saw again the bright sunlight, the sapphire ocean, the lush greenery, the brown bodies of the kids and PJ's deep blue eyes lit by his smile.

She spread the prints across Vince's desk.

'I might have gone overboard a bit. Seemed everything I looked at was worth a picture,' said Catherine as he slowly sifted through them.

'They're fantastic, Catherine. A whole different side to the postcard Kauai we always see. Of course, you'll have to write a piece to go with them all. We'll make some of them photo spreads. The people in them are right with that, aren't they?'

'They said so. So you think they're good?'

'Some are very good. But they're all interesting. Different. Great characters. Good work. Now, which ones do you want to use first?'

'I don't know. It's up to you, Vince.'

'Let me have a think. I'll let you know so you can start writing about them.'

The following morning Catherine took her prints up to show Lester.

'I've missed you, young lady. How was Kauai? Did you see Kiann'e's mother?'

'I did. I caught up with some of the surfer boys, too. Damien from Australia. And PJ.'

'Where?'

'Pinetrees.'

'Did you see Eleanor?'

'Of course.'

'She might come and see me for herself some time,' he said gruffly.

'I showed her the pictures I took of you and PJ. She thought you looked terrific.'

'She did, huh?' He looked pleased and Catherine smiled at his vanity.

'So what've you been up to?'

'Same old, same old. Kiann'e's been in and out. Busy. No time to take an old guy for a drive.'

'I can take you out, Lester, I really don't have that much to do. Where'd you like to go? I won't take you in the water, but we could go for a drive up the coast road. Maybe some places I haven't explored yet. We could take a picnic, how's that sound?'

The old man looked mollified. 'That'd be very nice. What's that you've got there?'

'These are some of the pictures I took on Kauai. I

thought you might like to have a look at them. I'll put the coffee on.'

When she came back with the tray of coffee things and a plate of his favourite cookies, Lester was staring out the window with a distant look in his eyes, the photos dropped into his lap.

Catherine poured his coffee, added sugar, stirred and put it on the table in front of him. 'What do you think?' When he didn't answer, she touched his hand. 'You okay? Here's your coffee.'

Lester blinked and took the mug she handed him.

'Did it bring back memories, Lester?'

'Kind of. I was never much of a social person. You must have had a good time. You know all those people?'

'Not really. But they were very hospitable. I liked the girls and their cute kids. But it's a different way of life from what I'm used to. I've never known anything like it,' said Catherine.

Lester gave her a long look. 'Life patterns change. You make changes.' He paused. 'Or you don't. Or you just go on as you always have,' he added enigmatically.

He shuffled through the pictures again and held up one of Damien cutting across a wave. 'Not a bad ride. I surfed the Tunnels and the Cannons a few times in my day on Kauai. Weren't called that then. Nobody went there much. Just a few of the locals.'

'I'll take you for a drive, Lester. Maybe Kiann'e'll come too.'

Late in the afternoon Kiann'e rang Catherine. 'Willi has a meeting tonight. Shall I bring around some dinner, or do you want to go out?'

'Come round here, that'd be great. Tell me what to

get. We have some wine,' said Catherine. 'I'd like to have a meal at home.'

'I'll bring lau lau . . . Aunty Lani made it, it's really special. Pork and butterfish steamed in a ti leaf. The rice too.'

'I'll buy ice cream for dessert then.'

The two girls curled up on the sofa after their meal, the ice cream bowls scraped clean, nursing their glasses of wine as Carole King's *Tapestry* album played softly.

'These pictures are fascinating. I love the ones of my mom's home, makes me homesick. Now tell me about these people,' said Kiann'e picking up the photos of *Nirvana*.

Catherine talked at length about the women, how unorthodox she found them, yet how free and uncomplicated their lives seemed. She talked about going to the goddess pool and confessed she'd had her first joint.

'You're joking!' laughed Kiann'e. 'What would Bradley think?'

'He's never going to know. And it's never going to happen again,' she said firmly.

'Ooh, did you have a wild trip? See shooting stars, go a bit mad?' teased Kiann'e. 'One joint isn't going to hurt you anyway.'

'I remember most of it. Kind of an out-of-body experience. It was . . . different. But I don't want to do it again. And that's not going to happen anyway.'

'Bradley doesn't seem the type to smoke grass, that's for sure. I bet he never made love to you in the back seat of a car either,' giggled Kiann'e.

'No. He didn't. He didn't have a car until we got here. We courted in taxis. Not that we ever did anything in the back of taxi,' Catherine hastily added.

'So are you going to tell me?'

'Tell you what?' asked Catherine.

'There's something you're not telling me,' said Kiann'e. 'That's okay if you don't want to.'

'I've told you I smoked a joint and passed out in a hammock at some virtual strangers' house. That's a secret Bradley will never hear.' She jumped to her feet. 'Coffee?'

Catherine realised she had quite a big job on her hands writing even a small article to go with her Kauai pictures. She needed a lot more information. Research. She was learning. While in the library at the *Advertiser* she asked the helpful librarian about famous dessert dishes of Hawaii.

'I don't mean traditional luau things. A hapa-haole creation,' said Catherine. 'I have to take something to a morning tea where a bunch of women all try to outdo each other. Me buying Mrs Hing's malasadas every month is going a bit stale.'

The librarian laughed. 'Let's go through old copies of *Honolulu Magazine*. Or better yet, I'll ask my mother-in-law. She's a fantastic cook. Her haupia cake is fab.'

Catherine sat quietly at the morning tea as most members of the Wives' Club crammed into the small sitting room and terrace of Melanie Lindsay's ground-floor apartment on the base. It looked like every other unit in the complex, thought Catherine. It would be easy to come home in the dark and walk into the wrong apartment without realising it.

Melanie and Julia were acting as co-hostesses, while Mrs Goodwin sat demurely in the centre of the room in the most comfortable chair. Not a hair was ever out of place, not even if a gale had been blowing, thought Catherine. Mrs Goodwin's hands with their neatly clipped pale pink nails were folded in her lap, her ankles were crossed and she smiled serenely like a school principal watching her graduating class of young ladies perform as expected.

Catherine's fresh pink guava chiffon cake topped with lillkoi frosting – which Catherine considered Hawaiian passionfruit – had been baked by the librarian's mother-in-law. It was a big hit.

'You're very quiet, Catherine,' commented one of the women. 'You've been such a leader lately. We missed you at the last get together.'

'Yes, Catherine. Are you well? You look a little tired. Perhaps you're doing too much,' said Mrs Goodwin.

'Maybe I'm too relaxed. I've just had a week's holiday in Kauai,' shot back Catherine with a smile.

'What a shame you couldn't share it with Bradley. Now, shall we discuss July Fourth? Melanie, please start.' Mrs Goodwin turned her attention to their hostess who put down a plate of brownies and hurriedly reached for a sheet of paper to read out the points she'd made.

Catherine tuned out as the women ran through the minutiae of food and volunteers and ribbons and prizes and banners and music. She wondered what Beatrice thought of the irony of a day when the US celebrated its independence when Beatrice, and others, wanted Hawaii to be independent from America.

As if reading her mind, or because she had heard about Catherine's appearance at the rally, or possibly because of her friendship with Kiann'e, Mrs Goodwin looked at Catherine as she said firmly, 'We are here to maintain good relations and friendship between the mainland states and Hawaii. We all have a role to play. We know that, unfortunately, there are elements who do not appreciate the protection and advantages of having our defence presence here. And there are local people who don't want to be part of our wonderful American way of life. But they are only a minority. So it is up to us to wave the flag and share and show what it means to be American and how proud we are to be part of the greatest country on earth.'

This speech brought a round of applause, which Catherine joined with a polite clap.

'After the morning service and breakfast there will be a barbecue and softball games for the enlisted men and children. The Marine Corps Naval Air Station men at Kaneohe will set up the evening fireworks, which can be viewed from several places.'

'Where do they set off the fireworks?' asked Julia.

'I believe from a small island – Rabbit Island – off-shore,' said Mrs Goodwin. 'The local people come to the beach to see them as well of course.'

'Sounds fun,' said Catherine, wondering if Mrs Goodwin went to see the fireworks with the local people. Somehow she doubted it.

Mrs Goodwin rose. 'I'll leave the nuts and bolts to you girls to work on. We have invited several local schools to participate in the formal part of the proceedings and I'm sure it's going to be a wonderful day.'

There followed a flurry of discussion, lists passed around, jobs assigned.

Catherine went back to the apartment on her own. She felt such an outsider. Her enthusiasm to get the Wives' Club more involved in local issues had diminished. They were in a world of their own, an island within an island and a temporary one at that. Would she ever fit in? Did she want to?

Would all the places that Bradley would be assigned to, be like this? She remembered now his quiet remarks to her about being able to make a life and home wherever they might be would only be possible with the support of the 'navy family'. God, how claustrophobic it felt to her.

Nor could she imagine settling into any other place in the same way as she had here in the Hawaiian Islands. Maybe it would have been better if she'd been sent as a new wife to an ugly hardship post where she'd have been grateful for the support of the other wives.

She tried to be honest with herself. She thought that she would still like to explore, participate and engage with any local community even if she had difficulties like language. It just wasn't in her nature to retreat within the safety of her husband's world. Even though she'd come from quite a cloistered society – a small, far-flung rural township – her curiosity about people and their world, a certain fearlessness, an Aussie egalitarianism, a desire to take big bites of her new life and new surroundings, had led her to dive into life in Hawaii.

But a remark by one of the wives about Catherine taking a job in Hawaii had unnerved her. 'Well, enjoy it because you can't do that everywhere, especially outside America.'

She'd have to sit down and talk seriously to Bradley about these issues when he came home, though quite what they could change about their circumstances defeated her for the moment. In the meantime, she was going to enjoy every second of her time in Hawaii – her job, her friends and her lifestyle.

She wrote Bradley a newsy letter about her trip to Kauai, her new photo-essay assignment and a lot of detail of her involvement with the Wives' Club and the upcoming Fourth of July celebrations.

A couple of days later there was another letter from Bradley. It was brief, stark in its news, ending:

Nothing much else to report from shipside. But the news seems to be that we can expect to be away longer than anticipated. I'm afraid, Catherine, dear, I'll be gone several more weeks at least. I do hope you are managing okay – it sounds like you're certainly keeping busy! Keep in close touch with Mrs Goodwin and if you need anything she's the one to see. I love and miss you. Bradley.

Oh. She sighed and refolded the letter. Thank heavens she had a project to keep her busy. She had managed to spread the assignment out over several days to fill in her time so she didn't feel she had nothing to do.

She rang Kiann'e and told her Bradley might be away much longer.

'Don't be lonely, Catherine. Come and have dinner tonight at Aunty Lani's. And I'll see you in the morning for a swim.'

'I don't feel lonely. I feel so lucky to know you all,' Catherine said.

After weeks of endless conversations and meetings to finalise the July Fourth celebrations, the big day arrived and Catherine did her duty by handing out flags, tying red, white and blue balloons to the food stands and then setting up her photographic stand. It proved to be a great success and she worked for hours taking photos of military and naval families to send back home. Heavens, she thought, it is going to take me ages next week to develop them all and send them to the right people.

'We'll save you a spot with us to watch the game,' Julia called out later that afternoon. Catherine thanked her but she couldn't raise much enthusiasm for the softball games. She felt that she had made more than enough contribution to the success of the day and she hoped she could sneak away. She apologised for not being able to make the Goodwins' celebratory cocktail party telling Mrs Goodwin that she would have to start developing the photos right away to get them all done. Mrs Goodwin seemed impressed by her dedication to her task.

Pleased with her escape, she went to Kailua Beach Park, where she joined Kiann'e, Aunty Lani and her family and friends to have a picnic and watch the fireworks.

It was a gorgeous evening and families were scattered in groups along the park, at the water's edge and on the beach. The smoke from portable hibachis drifted into the twilight as food was chargrilled and young children chased each other in excitement before being called to sit down and eat. Some people had their ukuleles out and had started singing. There was a lovely sense of community and Catherine and Albert, in charge of turning the satay sticks over the coals on the hibachi, chatted and laughed as he recounted an adventure he had had chasing a runaway pig back at home.

'This reminds me of barbecues at *Heatherbrae*,' said Catherine.

When the fireworks started, sent across the water by the marines on the small dot of an island just off the coast, there were cries of delight from the crowd. Catherine sat beside Kiann'e holding a glass of wine in a plastic cup, watching the pink and green and silver rockets burst into showering stars. The sand between her toes, the smell of the ocean, the softness of the breeze suddenly brought back memories of being with PJ. And, gazing at the soaring fireworks lighting up the night, she remembered exactly how he'd made her body feel and she trembled.

'Are you cold?' asked Kiann'e.

'No. Maybe I'll go for a walk.' Catherine felt overwhelmed and had to get away from Kiann'e's concern. She was shocked at how, many weeks later and out of nowhere, the 'PJ effect', had struck her.

The fireworks had finished and while some families were packing up with their young children, other groups were settling in for a bit of a party. Catherine drew a deep breath and headed back to help Aunty Lani and the gang pack up. She was glad she'd driven herself and as soon as she could, she hugged everyone goodbye and headed for her car.

'Catherine! Howdy. Happy July Fourth.'

Catherine was putting her picnic basket in the back seat and she spun around in surprise. Walking towards her was Sadie, looking as Catherine remembered her, rather like a gypsy.

'You just arriving?' Sadie asked. 'You've missed the fireworks.'

'No, been here for hours. Just leaving actually. What're you doing here?' Catherine glanced around, catching her breath, half expecting to see PJ, as Sadie gave her a hug.

'Oh, I've come over to Oahu for a bit. Might stay, might move on. Just hanging with some friends out on the North Shore. They brought their kids in for the fireworks. You on your own?'

'No. Our group is packing up. What about you? Is Summer here? And how's Ginger?'

'They're groovy. Still on Kauai. Ginger's nesting. She had a little girl. She and Doobie called her Angel. As for me, I got wanderlust again. As you do.' She grinned. 'Want to catch up?'

'Yes, of course. Here, I'll give you my number.' Catherine was rattled. Sadie belonged to an episode in her life she thought she'd put behind her. But tonight had shown her how close to the surface her feelings about PJ remained.

'Great. I'll call you when I'm coming into town. Or why don't you come over to Sunset Beach? I'm in someone's house while they're away. Well, a room of it. Great location near the beach.'

'No, no, thanks. Could we meet in Waikiki?'

Sadie wrinkled her nose. 'I avoid the tourist traps. Let's decide later. I'll call you.'

Catherine couldn't sleep, memories and images of her time at *Nirvana*, mostly her time with PJ, kept flashing into her mind. Bradley had been amused at what a sound and solid sleeper she was – head on the pillow and out cold for seven hours – but now she felt the safe and secure world around her was being shaken and rattled and it seemed as though sleep would never come.

Sadie and Catherine arranged to meet at a coffee house at Kahala Mall, which seemed to Catherine the last place Sadie would frequent. Catherine wandered through the quiet mall with its soft lighting, piped music and carpet underfoot. She found a bookshop and then saw the coffee house and spotted Sadie wearing a long skirt, her curls tied up in a colourful bandana.

'Hi, Sadie. Have I kept you waiting?'

'No, no. I had to collect some books and get some food. Tea? Coffee?'

'A regular coffee. I never drank coffee much till I came here. So what are you doing with yourself?' asked Catherine.

'I'm actually heading back to California. Either Ojai or Big Sur. Then to India. Or I might go to India first. See what the maharishi and TM is all about.'

'TM? Remind me again?'

'Transcendental meditation. A technique to relax, attain inner happiness and fulfilment,' Sadie explained. 'No drugs, no alcohol, no religion. Seven simple steps. Sounds good to me. I'm ready to travel again.'

'On your own?'

'My journeys start out that way. I make friends as I go. What about you?'

'I'm not travelling for some time. I'm staying here, my husband is at sea. But I like Hawaii. And I have a part-time job.'

'Ah, the photography. How'd your Kauai pictures come out?'

'Good. I have some cute ones of Ziggy and Pink. Do you have an address for Summer and Ginger?'

'Sure. And the guys. They float a bit, but they generally go back to *Nirvana* between surfing safaris.'

Catherine avoided eye contact as she fished in her bag for a notepad. She'd send a set of prints to Summer and ask her to share them round.

Sadie hadn't once mentioned PJ but she asked Catherine a couple of awkward questions.

'So, you're happy? Marriage all it's cracked up to be? Holding onto your independence?'

Catherine adopted Sadie's flippant tone. 'Yep. Husband away for weeks, maybe months, I'm doing my own thing. Ditched the boring navy wives. Really trying to scratch below the surface of postcard Hawaii.'

'Great for you, honey.' Sadie dropped her bantering tone, leant across the table and put her hand over Catherine's. 'Try everything. Never be afraid, never have regrets. The guy I adored was killed in Vietnam but that hasn't stopped me doing all the things we dreamt of doing, loving whomever I want. I love and walk away. Whatever it takes to get you through the nights, babe. There are guys that are safe and there are guys that drive you wild. For now, I'm choosing to walk on the wild side. Like John Lennon said, "Life isn't a dress rehearsal."' Sadie smiled, but Catherine thought there was a shadow of sadness behind the bravado.

Driving back to her apartment after the long and stimulating conversation with Sadie, Catherine started to feel a bit trapped. She was tied to Bradley's life. She couldn't go to India or start to learn about so many things that were out there. Sadie believed the world was changing, this truly was a new dawn, old barriers, conventions, were crumbling.

Catherine arrived home and for once the magic of Hawaii couldn't cheer her.

Extract from The Biography of

THE WATERMAN

The first wave is never forgotten. In between swimming events and bit parts in movies, the young man still worked as a lifeguard and swimming instructor now at a swank swim club further south of the city. The strip of beach was frequented by film industry people and wealthy families. One morning at the beach he uncovered a discarded surfboard – a beaten-up redwood plank – which he took out into the surf and tried to ride with no success. In fact his topsy-turvy pearl dive pummelling that pushed him deep underwater scared him and he vowed to stick to swimming.

But a few days later he tried again when two-foot waves were rolling in. Suddenly he caught a wave, jumped to his feet and found himself riding across the ocean. The board ploughed ahead of the wave, on and on, and it seemed forever to the elated young man. He was doing what he'd always dreamed of since seeing the newsreel of the Waikiki board riders.

He was now in the grip of a passion more intense than any he would ever know. The time had come. A brief stint on another movie and then he spent his money on a steamship ticket to the Islands.

The days at sea passed pleasantly. The young man became known for the amount of food he ate at every meal. Food had always seemed in short supply in his life so he made the most of the voyage, building himself up for whatever lay ahead. He strode the decks, breathing deeply the clear sea air.

In Honolulu he headed straight to Waikiki, a village removed from the port and downtown's bright lights. He found a perfect strip of beach near two hotels – one of them, the Moana, seemed very glamorous – and some buildings under haphazard construction between the palms, pandanus, ohia and hau trees. The glittering water washed over the coral reef where perfect waves glided endlessly to the fine white sand. A few surfers and beach boys idled on the sand. And standing guard, protecting their playground, rose the stern sphinx of Diamond Head.

He hung around the Outrigger Canoe Club and he met one of Duke's brothers, also a swimming champion who was quick to introduce the young man with the impressive swimming record to the other surfers. He was taken out tandem surf riding and spent time with the beach boys who made a few dollars from tourists showing them how to surf. This was their career, their way of life – surfing.

Like them, the young man had found his vocation. He now lived to surf. The friendship, the sharing, the bond was like coming home. And home for this young man became the constant sun, the softness of the tradewinds, the cleanness of the colours . . . water so blue, clouds so white, foliage as green as emeralds, the hypnotic sway of palm trees and always, the call of the surf.

He lived simply. Food was in abundance in the garden of the house he shared with other surfers – avocados, mangoes, papayas, bananas. It was healthy, simple and quiet. He had no need of drugs or alcohol or noisy company. Everywhere he looked he saw beauty. From flowers, ferns and stately palms, to the mischievous dark eyes of the wahines, the friendly smiles of the native Hawaiians.

And it was his association, his easy friendship, with Duke and his family, the beach boys and the locals that awakened in him a curiosity about the origins and history of the island people. His work in the film industry had given him an interest in photography and now his camera captured the true Hawaii. Its unspoiled, uncrowded beaches, traditional hula dancers, barefoot boys scaling coconut palms, the outriggers cleaving through the waves bringing home a catch of fish, and always, the surfboard riders, waiting and watching for the next wave.

As he spent more and more time with the local Hawaiians and learnt something of the history of their ancient art of surfboard riding, his intellectual interest grew and he started to study Hawaiian customs and culture in the library and the museum.

The young man was intrigued by the stories of the ancient chiefs, the kings and queens, the royal lineage of the Islands. In the museum he found, hanging on a stone outer wall, two old Hawaiian olo boards, used by the chiefs. It was a tradition hundreds of years old. These were the first kings of the surf who, accompanied by their naked women surfing beside them, played at beaches reserved for them alone. Then came the missionaries who banned the activity until the kapu was finally lifted and the surf became a world for all.

The young man asked if he could study the old boards and was directed to the bowels of the museum where some of the earliest boards were stacked, forgotten. He examined the boards, under their layers of paint and caulking, and realised that these boards were quite ancient.

The young man formed a plan: he was determined to recreate the boards and discover how these massive pieces of wood rode in the waves, how they could be adapted and changed. Suddenly his passion had a new edge and a thousand ideas began to bubble in his head. At night he sketched, measured and drew up plans. He became a familiar sight working on boards beneath the palm trees of Waikiki. By day he was in the water, trying out his innovative boards, catching waves, learning the moods, the flow of the water through channels behind the jagged coral reefs exposed at low tide. He watched how the swells built up and began to understand the waters of Waikiki.

He continued to learn more about the waves, the tides, the swells, the weather patterns of the Islands.

But the greatest knowledge was that he had found the art of life – a way to live his life doing what inspired and moved him most – surfing.

11

CATHERINE AND LESTER STROLLED slowly along Kalakaua
Avenue enjoying the morning air. Lester had one arm
linked through Catherine's, his hand leaning lightly on his
walking stick. He looked quite rakish with a fresh hibiscus
tucked in his straw hat, dark glasses and an open aloha
shirt over a favourite T-shirt.

'Let's go into the Moana Hotel courtyard, under the
banyan tree,' suggested Catherine. 'It was Bradley's and
my favourite spot when I first came here.'

'When you were courting. It is a romantic spot. I
might have stolen a kiss or two under that banyan myself,'
he smiled.

'You old devil, Lester. You never talk about your
girlfriends,' said Catherine. It was a subject he evaded and
again he quickly changed the topic.

'Ah, it was for publicity pictures, that sort of thing. They were always dragging a pretty girl off the beach to pose with me and a board,' he said modestly.

Lester ordered juice. 'I've had my caffeine hit for the day.' He settled himself so he faced the beach. Lester wanted to talk about Kauai, as he had fond memories of surfing that island's north shore and knew Beatrice's home, although it was then the plantation manager's house.

'I don't think I'd ever seen any place as beautiful as Kauai. They haven't ruined it like this island, have they?'

'Not at all, though Eleanor tells me there are plans for some new big resorts. But there aren't the high rises and big community developments like here in Honolulu, thank goodness.'

'Not enough people on Kauai, I guess,' said Lester. Catherine sipped her cappuccino and suddenly Lester waved. 'Hey!'

Catherine looked across at the beach to see PJ, in swim shorts, strolling across the sand carrying a board, a woman in a sarong beside him.

'Hey, PJ!' called Lester and PJ turned and grinned, giving them a wave.

PJ spoke to the woman who smiled and walked away. Resting his board against a spreading pandanus tree at the edge of the Moana courtyard, PJ joined them.

Lester got to his feet and went to shake his hand. 'Good to see you, buddy. What're doing here?'

'Teaching tourists.' PJ spotted Catherine hovering at the table. He lifted his hand. 'Catherine. Good to see you.'

She tried to act calmly despite feeling anything but. 'Hi, PJ. What brings you to Oahu?'

'Work. This time of year I try to make enough money for the rest of the year.' He gave a disarming smile. 'How did your photos turn out?'

'Really well, thanks.'

'So what's with the shorty?' Lester indicated the short board.

'As well as surf lessons and taking tourists out in the outrigger and kayaks, I've started to do a bit of shaping.'

'Mmm. Cutting down long boards?' asked Lester with interest.

'Yep. Making a few guns. Trying a few new ideas. Like a lot of the good shapers around – Diffenderfer, Curren, Downing, Ben Apia.'

'They're great surfers who became really good board shapers. Guns are boards for big waves,' Lester explained to Catherine. 'Who's riding for you?'

'I have one of the Bronzed Aussie team. But I also try the boards out of course. Those Aussie boys are ripping into the local scene. There's been some heavy vibes about them.'

'So I've heard. So where are you doing your shaping?'

Catherine kept quiet as the two surfers talked. Lester was rubbing the blunt nose of the board and was intensely interested in what PJ had to say.

PJ nodded behind them. 'Over the back, got a shed in a place on Lewers, near Seaside. Come over and have a look sometime. I'd like your feedback. You were pretty radical in your day with your designs.'

'Yeah, probably ahead of my time,' replied Lester. 'Say, come and have something to drink with us.'

'Thanks, Lester, better get on. Besides, don't feel dressed for coffee with a lady.' He smiled at Catherine, acknowledging her properly for the first time.

As they made direct eye contact, Catherine suddenly felt so embarrassed that she had to look away.

'But listen, Lester, you come and see me. Bring him over, Catherine.' PJ turned and picked up his board, gave a wave and trotted back along the beach.

Lester turned his attention to Catherine and downed the remains of his juice. 'Well, that'll be good. I'm keen to see what he's doing. He's got the feel for it.'

Catherine didn't ask what that meant. She was suddenly wondering why she was expected to take Lester to see PJ. Why couldn't PJ pick up Lester himself? For an instant she thought, does he want to see me and Lester is just an excuse? Then she decided no, it's easier for everyone if I bring Lester to the workshop. Just the same she was feeling quite confused. She stood up.

'Hey, Lester, I think we should make a move. I've just remembered I have a few errands to run.'

'As you say, Catherine.' He linked his arm through hers and to passers-by they appeared to be a father and daughter out for a morning stroll.

But Catherine delayed seeing Lester again, not sure that she was ready to face PJ. She told Kiann'e that she didn't feel up to their morning swim and was taking advantage of Bradley's absence to sleep in.

'You sure you're all right? Doesn't sound like you,' said Kiann'e. 'Do you want me to come by? Bring anything?'

'No. Thanks. I'm fine, really. See you Thursday, okay?'

'All right.' Kiann'e sounded dubious. 'Are you sure there's nothing bothering you?'

Catherine kept to herself for two days, staying in the apartment apart from a quick swim at the base pool at lunch time. On the second day she was surprised by a call from Bradley.

'Bradley! Ooh, I'm missing you so much, this is great to hear from you.'

'Miss you too, sweetheart. What're you up to?'

'At the moment, I'm staying home. Tidying the closets. I painted the bathroom cupboards. Just being a homebody,' she said with honesty.

'Well, that's nice. Have you seen Mrs Goodwin, the other girls?'

'Oh, yes. Fourth of July went off very well. I was busy. I was the official photographer.'

Bradley sounded pleased. Relieved even. 'Great, that's good, honey. So, no problems?'

'No. None.' Catherine recalled the pamphlet she'd read on being a supportive wife and that when contact was made with spouses serving overseas it was best not to elaborate on any trivial domestic issues. Always to be positive and cheerful. 'How're things with you? Where are you? When're you coming back?'

Bradley gave a small chuckle. 'We should know the answer to that pretty soon. But things are fine. All going smoothly. I can't chat for long, there are others wanting the line. Please call or send a note to my folks, let them know you spoke to me and all is well.'

'Sure, will do.'

'Love you, Catherine. Bye for now.' And he was gone before she had a chance to say another word.

Catherine knew Lester was itching to go and see what PJ was doing and guessed that he would soon be chasing her, so when the phone rang later that morning she smiled to herself.

'Hi, Lester.'

'It's not Lester, it's me. PJ.'

She took a quick breath. 'Oh, hi. I was expecting Lester to ring me.'

'That's why I'm calling. Could you bring him round sometime? I'm a bit too busy to pick him up and he obviously enjoys going out with you.'

'He's good company. Such an interesting man. I wish I could get him talking more about his life, though,' said

Catherine in a rush. 'So, what's your address? Does any time suit?' She wanted to sound as businesslike as possible so that PJ would know that she was really only interested in Lester's welfare and nothing more.

'Round the middle of the day. I give lessons most mornings and in the afternoon I like to have a surf.'

She wrote down the address. 'How about tomorrow?'

'That'd be fine. Damien wants to see him so he'll be hanging around.' He paused briefly. 'How are you?'

'Me? Good.'

'You're okay? Happy? I've thought about you a lot.'

Catherine felt like shouting at him. Really? Have you now? Well, I haven't thought about you and what we did at all! But instead she found herself saying, 'Kauai seems like a bit of a dream.'

'I hope it was a happy one. I'll see you tomorrow.' And he was gone.

She felt confused by his words. She knew that she shouldn't feel pleased that he had thought about her, but she was, yet at the same time she wanted to put that episode very much behind her.

When she arrived to collect Lester the next day, he was ready and waiting, impatient to get going.

He lifted an eyebrow. 'You look very pretty. Are we going somewhere special?'

'Not really. Just to see PJ. I might leave you with him while I run down to the paper and see Vince.'

'That's fine. I'm keen to see what PJ's doing.'

They drove into the small back streets behind the main tourist strip of Kalakaua Avenue and were suddenly in an old residential area full of small houses with overgrown gardens. One cottage had a thatched roof and all had sheds and garages which were being used to house small businesses or overflowing families. They drove slowly looking for the right number.

'There it is,' said Lester. 'Yep, sure is the right place.'

Several surfboards were propped against the front fence, one was resting in a stand outside. The garage beside the house had its doors open, its inside painted bright blue and filled with surfboards.

Catherine parked under a golden rain tree and helped Lester out of the car. Inside the garage PJ was wearing headphones and a mask and was wielding a high-whining power plane, pushing it in sweeping strokes along the length of a board. He didn't hear them approach. Catherine waved her hand to get his attention.

He turned off the plane and smiled at them. 'Hey, great to see you. Careful, there's a lot of rubbish round here. Let's go outside. I'll get you a seat.'

Lester was studying the boards as he came out of the shed with two chairs.

'Where do get your blanks?

'The Clarkes distributor, downtown. I'm shaping a few six sixes as well as some eight and nine footers.' He glanced at Catherine. 'Big boards for big waves.'

'I rode a nine-foot-six balsa at Waiemea in the monsters,' said Lester.

'Are these all for sale?' asked Catherine, amazed at the variations in the different boards.

'Some. I'm doing some special orders. Those in there are all mine.'

'Why do you need so many?' she asked, wondering how he could travel around with such an array.

'Different boards for different waves,' he shrugged.

'It's a bit like an artist having a lot of different brushes, or a golfer with different clubs,' explained Lester.

'I'll leave Lester to watch you work for a bit.' She glanced around at the boards, wrinkling her nose. 'What's that smell?'

'Polyester resin curing,' said PJ. 'Aren't you going to

take a look at my boards? They're coming along well, I have a new idea about using them in big waves.'

'Explain it to Lester, he's really interested,' she said.

'And you're not? Come for another surf. How about a lesson with me?'

'I'm a bit busy. Thanks.' She looked away from him. 'See you later, Lester.'

PJ touched her arm and she was forced to look at him. The intense blueness of his eyes seemed to shoot through her like a ray gun. 'I'd like to see you again,' he said quietly.

'I'm sure we'll keep bumping into each other,' she said lightly.

'That's not what I meant. Can I see you? Come by any evening. I'm always here working at night.'

'I have to go. I have to meet my editor.' She hurried to the car.

Catherine drove two blocks back into Waikiki, found a parking spot and treated herself to an ice-cream sundae. Then she poked her head into a couple of beach boutiques and finally drove back to PJ's.

Lester was standing with PJ in deep discussion. She watched them before getting out of the car, their heads together, running their hands along one of the boards, stroking the redwood stringers down the middle, fingering the sharp pointed nose then waving their arms to demonstrate the manoeuvres the board would perform in the water.

She joined them. 'Are these boards different from what you used to ride, Lester?'

He grinned. 'We started with sixteen-foot solid redwood. Then we used hollow boards. And later on we added the fins. I made a few refinements in my time.'

'Lester was a pioneer, a legend in design. And he's still got good ideas,' said PJ. 'I'd love to see some of your old drawings. You still got them?'

'Maybe. And photos. I loaned one of my albums to Catherine.'

PJ looked at her in surprise. 'Could I share them? Are you doing a story on Lester?'

'Well, no, not really. I needed some information to go with his portrait I did for the competition.'

'You know, Catherine, this guy is amazing. You could write a book about him.' PJ turned back to Lester and they continued talking about boards and waves.

Catherine sat on one of the chairs watching them, half listening. There was a plumeria tree next to the shed and she watched several of its perfect creamy flowers drop to the ground. She wondered if PJ lived in this house, shared it, or just used the shed.

'Hey, I think Lester's ready to go. Thanks for bringing him by. He's given me a few ideas, a few hints.' PJ smiled at her. 'Hope to see you soon.' He helped Lester to the car and Catherine trailed behind them.

All the way back to his apartment Lester chatted on about board making, how things changed and how some things just went in and out of fashion.

'Be good to watch PJ's new boards in action,' he said. 'Might be weeks or so before the waves are right, I'd say. Have you seen these storming Aussie surfers in action?'

'A little bit. I took some photos of them on Kauai.'

Lester folded his arms and settled in the seat. 'Yep. PJ's onto something with those boards. Reckon the locals will sit up and take notice soon enough.'

When he was back in his apartment and she was leaving, Lester called, 'Been a great day. Thanks, Catherine. Don't forget to show PJ that book of mine. But don't you leave it with him. Surfers can be a bit too casual sometimes.'

*

Kiann'e shook the water from her hair as she and Catherine towelled themselves dry enough to wear their sarongs. 'My mother spoke with Aunty Lani last night. She said that she enjoyed seeing you on Kauai and we were to be sure and take you around to see some of the old palaces and gardens that the Daughters of Hawaii have restored.'

'Yes, I'd like that. Perhaps I could do something for the paper,' said Catherine.

'I think those places have been written up a lot already. There must be more contemporary things to photograph.'

'I s'pose so. I have to find something interesting for this week's edition though.'

'Aunty Lani's having a luau this Saturday, she said for you to come along, bring any friends.'

'Any special reason?' asked Catherine.

Kiann'e smiled. 'Not really. Uncle Henry is going to kill a pig. And he's got some old musician friend visiting from Las Vegas. They played together in a band years ago. So that's enough reason.'

'I'd love to come.'

'Do you think we should take Lester along? I bet it's been ages since he was at a luau,' said Kiann'e suddenly.

'He'd love it, I'm sure. But you don't think it'll be too much for him, do you?' said Catherine.

'Not if he just stays a short while. Anyway, we could always arrange for someone to take him home early. The pig will go into the imu early in the morning. People will start arriving at midday and we'll probably pull it out early in the afternoon. The feast will go on for hours, so there're people coming and going all day.'

'Let's suggest it to Lester.'

Catherine had a busy day. She seemed to find a lot of things to do, so it was quite late by the time she drove past the bright lights and the happy hour crowd and turned into the darker, quieter streets where PJ worked. As she parked she saw several people silhouetted against the light spilling from the cluttered workspace. Walking into the garden, carrying Lester's album, she recognised Damien.

'Hey, Cath! Great to see you, mate. What're you up to?' His Aussie accent made Catherine feel warm.

'Bringing Lester's scrapbook round for PJ to have a browse through. He really wanted me to bring it. But maybe you're too busy . . .' She looked at PJ who was grinning broadly.

'A lady of her word. That's nice to know. We're just finishing up and then we were going to grab pizzas. Join us and we can all look at the old man's designs.'

'He was never as well known as the Duke though, was he?' asked Damien.

'Lester was less flamboyant, kept to himself. After all he was a haole from the mainland. The Duke was up front, out there, ambassador of Hawaii, the father of modern surfing and all that. But Lester was a cool cat who never pushed himself into the limelight,' said PJ. 'That how you see it, Catherine?'

'It's terrific he's still around. I'd like to spend more time with him,' said Damien.

'He thinks it's great that the Bronzed Aussies have come in and stirred up the locals,' said Catherine.

'Yeah, I nearly got thumped out there today. The buggers kept dropping in on me, just to piss me off. There've been a few bad incidents. Tyre slashing, brawls, boards damaged,' Damien said to PJ.

PJ turned to Catherine. 'Locals mostly like the Aussies. You should hear them trying to imitate the Aussie accent – mate, comes out mite – but sometimes it gets a bit deadly. Bit competitive. But hey, don't get the wrong idea about surfers.'

'Why would I?' she said lightly and PJ gave her a look.

'Hawaiians love good-hearted people. But you do the wrong thing to them and they don't forget. They'll hold it against your brother too. Harm them, harm their family,' he said. 'Say, come on inside. Here, brah, go collect the pizzas.' He handed Damien a few dollars and ushered Catherine inside.

'So you live here?' She glanced around at the messy house that was filled with surfing posters, body boards, flippers, snorkels, books, magazines, record albums and cushions and a big sofa in the main room. It looked like people were sleeping on makeshift beds all over the house.

'I just crash here when I'm working. People come and go. It's not as organised as *Nirvana*.'

She hadn't considered that the old beach house on Kauai was organised, but in comparison with this, it did have a lot more peace and charm. She couldn't understand how people could live like this. But she certainly didn't want to be reminded of *Nirvana*. Memories of her time there with PJ made her feel uncomfortable.

'Where are your things? Your belongings? You must be a bit of a gypsy,' she said.

He started to clear a space on the kitchen table. 'Ah *things*. Things tie you down. All my clothes fit in an airline bag. My baggage is my boards. But I sell them if I have to. Except for a few classics. I have a Dick Brewer . . . fantastic boards. I store them when I can't take them with me.'

'You mean surfboards can become collector's items?' asked Catherine incredulously.

'Sure thing. Who knows? Some of those boards in the yard out there might be collectible in twenty years time.' He laughed.

'Well, I hope you sign them,' said Catherine.

Two of the Australian boys travelling with Damien came in and introduced themselves and their girlfriends.

Catherine enjoyed their earthy Aussie humour, their energy and their enthusiasm for Hawaii.

'Beaut place, bloody beautiful. Great waves,' was the general consensus.

'We're going to Tahiti next.' There followed a discussion of the merits of various boards and surfing spots until Damien arrived with the pizzas.

'Man, I didn't get enough for you lot,' he exclaimed.

'That's okay, we're all heading out to the Chart House. You want to come, Damo?'

Damien hesitated. 'I just got a pizza.'

'Catherine and I can eat it. But we'll leave you some and you can have it cold later,' said PJ.

The three boys left in a flurry of laughter, the pretty, star-struck girls tagging along. Even though they were all around the same age as she was, Catherine suddenly felt very staid and boring.

'I'd better go,' she said.

'What for? We have pizzas. You have to help me eat them.' PJ put a plate in front of her and opened a pizza box. 'Or don't you want to be with me?'

'It smells great.' She reached for a slice, suddenly realising she was hungry.

He took a bite and then said, 'You didn't answer my question.'

'I'm here, aren't I? And I brought you Lester's notes and drawings.'

'Okay. Thanks,' he said easily.

Later Catherine put the leftover pizza in the fridge and cleared the table so PJ could spread out Lester's album.

'There're some beers if you'd like one.'

'No, thanks. I'll make some coffee while you start looking at those pictures. I did promise Lester I wouldn't leave them behind. They're very precious to him.' She didn't need to add that with a household of surfers coming and going they could easily get mislaid.

'Sure. I understand.' PJ opened a Primo beer and became immersed in the sketches and notes on board designs.

Catherine washed up and cleaned the kitchen for something to do. She made the coffee and flipped through a surfing magazine. What a strange world it is. How passionate they all are. She'd thought of surfing as simply going for a swim with a board. Now she was beginning to see it was so much more to these young men.

'Is it true that once you start surfing you never stop?' asked Catherine.

'Pretty much. You work your life around getting in a surf.'

'Not the other way around. Will surfing always come first in your life?'

'It is my life,' he said, slightly surprised and turned back to Lester's album.

Catherine took her coffee into the living room, turned on the TV and settled herself on the big sofa.

She had no idea how late it was, but PJ was gently rubbing her shoulder.

'Hey, sleepyhead.'

'God, sorry. I fell asleep.'

'You certainly did. That's the best bed in the house.'

'What time is it?' She rubbed her eyes.

'Two a.m.'

'What!'

'I didn't want to wake you until I finished going through Lester's stuff. I want to talk to him about some of his ideas, though.'

'I'd better be going.'

'Will you be okay driving through Waikiki at this hour? Don't stop till you're at your apartment,' said PJ seriously.

Catherine wasn't really worried about driving home late at night and the Base was probably the safest place in Hawaii, but she was concerned that someone would see her coming back alone this late at night and wonder what she had been doing. Suddenly going home didn't appeal to her. 'Actually, you're right. I don't think I want to drive home.'

'So stay here. Go back to sleep, I'll get you a cover. You want a drink? Water?'

Catherine slipped off her shoes and curled up, using a cushion as a pillow. PJ dropped a cotton quilt over her and set a glass of water on the floor.

'The boys will probably wake you up when they come in. I'll see you in the morning.' He stood looking down at her and Catherine had to resist the urge to lift her arms and reach out for him.

'Thanks, PJ.' She squeezed her eyes shut to block out the sight of him. He was so good looking in his casual beachy way, yet PJ seemed unaware of his appeal. As well as his classical good looks, unlike Bradley's clean-cut looks, PJ had a superb physique honed from surfing but there was a reserve, a mystery about him that was alluring. His smile held secrets, the intensity of his blue eyes always reminded her of the depths of the ocean. But she wasn't going to do anything other than look. She was married to another man and that had to be the end of it.

It took Catherine a long while to fall asleep again. She was surprised at what she was doing. What on earth would Bradley think? She hadn't had a single drink, the car hadn't broken down and although she really didn't want to be seen getting home so late, there wasn't really a valid reason for her to stay here. But she wasn't doing anything wrong nor had she any intention of doing anything but sleep. Perhaps she just didn't want to be alone anymore.

Eventually she must have drifted off. She heard the boys clump through the house to their rooms sometime during the night then she went straight back to a dreamless sleep.

She was curled up, her back to the room, when she slowly began to awaken. There was a touch on her hair . . . as light as breeze, a cat's paw, a bird's wing . . . She rolled over, sleepily smiling.

'Catherine, are you awake?' PJ spoke softly.

She rolled over to see PJ crouched beside the sofa. 'I'm awake now.' She saw the silvery dawn light outside the window. 'It's early. What's up?'

'I'm heading to the beach for the sunrise. Want to come for a surf? I've made coffee.'

'I can smell it.' She sat up. 'I guess so. Now I'm awake.'

He padded out to get the coffee and Catherine went and washed her face. In the kitchen PJ poured her a mug of coffee.

'I'll have to go back to my apartment and get my swimsuit.'

'There're girls' bikinis hanging around here. They're on the clothesline. Drink up and let's go. Don't want to miss it. I'll treat you to breakfast afterwards.'

PJ gave her one of his T-shirts to wear over the swimsuit she found. Catherine felt strange walking the two blocks to the beach in the half light, each of them carrying a surfboard through the empty streets. I can't believe I'm doing this, she thought.

PJ hummed to himself. 'Board not too heavy?' he asked as they turned down a side street towards the beach.

'Not really. Cumbersome. I'm not going to be able to manage this thing, y'know.'

'What's the Aussie expression? Give it a go? You might surprise yourself.' He took her hand. 'I'd really like you to try to get the feeling. Might help you understand me a bit.'

She was silent. The touch of his hand felt so natural and gave her a sense of closeness with him. A warmth, like that which occurs between two friends who have shared experiences, replaced some of the guilt from the episode on Kauai. Suddenly, getting in the water, on a surfboard, seemed to be really important to her.

It was still, but cool and she left PJ's T-shirt on so that the fibreglass surface on the nine-foot board wouldn't rub against her skin. They stood in the water as the board bobbed between them.

'See how beautifully it floats, like a sleek yacht. Every part of the board is curved, it's like a woman. From every angle, the top, the rocker, fore and aft, and the sides. Thin in front, thick in the centre then thin again out at the tail. It's a sensual curve. Like a wave.' He ran his hands along the board. 'Okay, now lie on the board. Get comfortable, feel it mould into your body. All you have to do is stroke, like a swim stroke, smoothly and rhythmically. I'll navigate us around the breaks to avoid paddling through them. Though they're only gentle waves, I just want you to get the feel of being in tune with the water.'

She nodded. 'But how do I stand up?'

'Good! Good. That's great you're thinking like that.'

'Well, isn't that what you're supposed to do? Isn't that what surfing is?' said Catherine.

'Sweetheart, it's a helluva lot more than just standing up. Body surfers, board surfers, just want to interact with the wave, get on, go for the ride.' He became serious. 'Both feet should hit the deck at the same time, but I don't want you to be thinking about which foot in front, landing together, what to do when. First we'll get out there and we'll study the waves, their timing, their pace. Waves roll at a constant pace, then there's an interval and that's when you turn around and get ready to paddle. When you feel the board being picked up, that's when you stand up, if you can. But go steady, don't think about it. Bend your knees, they're your shock absorbers, arms go out for balance. They're your wings to help you fly and look forward. The idea is you do it all together.' He readied the board for her. 'Hawaiian style is to ride all the way to the beach and step off without getting your hair wet.'

'Oh, right,' said Catherine, gingerly lying on the board. He made it sound so easy and she knew it wasn't.

PJ jumped onto his shorter board and began stroking smoothly ahead of her. Copying his movements, she was surprised at the ease and swiftness with which the board skimmed along. Expertly he weaved through the water, turning slightly every so often so that she wasn't going through the wash of breaking waves. She saw other surfers in the distance, some riding a shallow wave, others sitting on their boards, but mainly she concentrated on following PJ.

When they were out far enough, PJ sat upright and glanced back her. 'Turn your board around and we'll just sit here for a bit, okay?'

She wobbled as she sat upright, her legs dangling on either side of the board. PJ pointed towards the eastern sky.

'She'll be up shortly.'

They bobbed gently on the surface of the breathing water. The other surfers also paused, all watching for the moment the day awoke. The sheen on the water went from silver to bronze. Everything seemed suspended. No-one moved, even the surfboards appeared motionless in the lull between waves. And then the rim of the red gold ball was visible and, like an exhalation, the sky ran with colour, ripples ran across the sea, the roll of waves swelled, their crests tipped in pink.

Catherine looked at PJ silhouetted against the light rising behind Diamond Head and it seemed as though he was from another world. He was a creature of the sea, as if risen from it, or perhaps he had been always anchored here. Lester had mentioned the word 'waterman' and now she fully understood its meaning as she looked at PJ. He seemed to have a way of interpreting the sculpture of the ocean. Now she thought that this was how Lester felt about the bond with the ocean, with the waves.

PJ pointed at her. 'Lie prone. Try for the next one. Come up like a push-up and then on your feet. Have the picture in your head of how you want to be and rise up to that image. All there is to it,' he called.

She lay flat and started stroking automatically. Then she felt the board lift lightly as if a hand beneath the sea was supporting the board and thrusting it forward. For a second she closed her eyes and saw herself standing on the board, cruising on its crest, heading for shore. Without consciously thinking about it, she found she was on her feet, half crouching. Then her arms went out, she straightened and felt the rush of the board cutting through the water, a sensation of speed and, with her eyes glued to the beach, she felt the adrenalin start to pump.

Instinctively Catherine shifted her weight and the board cut across the face of the wave, slewed and she was off, under the water, but laughing, laughing as her face broke the surface.

PJ paddled after her board and brought it back to where she was treading water. 'Fantastic! You did it! How do you feel?' His face was alight with excitement.

'It was thrilling! I know I fell off quickly, but it felt like forever. It just happened,' she said breathlessly, grabbing her board and dragging herself back on it.

'The way you shifted your weight and planted your

feet. Right foot forward. You're a goofy foot! Ready to go again? We'll paddle through the break, just keep your head down, or else do a push-up so the wave goes between your body and the board.'

Catherine lost track of time and everything else except the challenge of finding the point where her board took off. And she could stand, knees bent, determinedly locking her eyes on the beach, which came closer with each ride until she found she was almost at the shore when the little wave collapsed and sank and her board slowed and she rolled into the water.

PJ was just behind her and he jumped off his board. 'You couldn't have got any more out of that wave. Nearly made it to the sand.' He gave her a wet hug. 'Let's eat.'

Catherine pulled off her waterlogged T-shirt and wrapped a towel around herself, shaking her wet hair.

'It's amazing. The whole sensation. It's like the wave is alive, it helps you, it felt . . . I can't explain it.'

He dropped his arm around her shoulder. 'You don't have to.'

They picked up their boards, PJ taking her longer one. She slipped her arm around his waist as they walked back along the beach where a few early morning walkers were strolling along the sand. A gardener was sweeping the terrace of the Royal Hawaiian Hotel, its pink facade glowing in the early morning sun.

Catherine couldn't stop talking about the whole experience. It was not just the thrill of the ride but the fact she'd actually stood up the first time. PJ listened with a half smile, occasionally nodding, or answering a question.

She was beginning to understand Lester's explanation of the passion, the obsession, the spiritual connection that watermen have with the sea. It was a self absorption that centred on only them and the wave, its rhythm, its force, its flow that was akin to being in an hypnotic state. Except – as only a surfer knows – you are dancing on waves.

She was ravenous and they ate a big breakfast, Catherine indulging herself with pancakes, bacon and maple syrup. It was a small outdoor café close to the beach and they propped their boards against the low rock wall while they ate. Catherine had pulled the damp T-shirt back on and had the beach towel wrapped around her waist.

They were finishing their coffee when she heard her name.

'Catherine?'

Surprised, she turned around to see Julia Bensen and another woman walking along the beach towards them. Julia looked frankly curious, glancing from the handsome blond surfer to the wet and dishevelled Catherine.

'Hi, Julia. Wonderful morning. You're up early,' said Catherine.

'Obviously not as early as you. What're you doing?' asked Julia staring at PJ, who smiled at her and picked up his coffee cup and drained it.

'I've had a surfing lesson. This is my instructor. We've been out since before sunrise,' said Catherine cheerily, trying not to look as uncomfortable as she felt.

'Really? Surfing lessons. What fun,' said the other woman.

'She's pretty damn good. Stood up first go,' said PJ.

'You are a busy person,' said Julia. 'I don't know how you find time to fit everything in.' She had a slightly accusing tone and Catherine knew she was referring to a recent Wives' Club event she'd missed.

'That's why we're out before sunrise,' said PJ. 'Excuse me, Catherine. I'll get the tab.' He walked inside to the counter.

'This will be a nice surprise for Bradley when he gets

back. Will he be taking lessons too?' asked Julia.

'No, he's a swimmer not a surfer. That's why I'm learning while he's away. What are you doing down here?'

'Oh, sorry. This is my friend Bonnie. She's visiting from Ohio. She's also an early riser,' said Julia.

'I live on a farm,' smiled Bonnie. 'And where're you from?'

'Australia. Actually, I live on a farm too, but I have some Australian surfer friends visiting here. They're travelling round the world surfing and will be back here for the big championships at the end of the year.' Catherine hoped Damien didn't suddenly appear to dispute their long friendship.

'Well, I hope we meet again. Good luck with the lessons.'

'Thanks. Enjoy your visit. See you, Julia. Next Tuesday, isn't it?' said Catherine, who'd had no intention of going to the Wives' Club tea but now thought better of it. No doubt Julia would mention all this in dispatches to her husband, Jim.

'That's right. Remember me to Bradley when you write.'

'Thanks. Same to Jim.'

Walking back through town where shops were beginning to open, PJ said, 'Navy wives, huh? You'll be the talk of the town no doubt.'

'Possibly. They never do anything exciting. Don't mix much outside the navy circle.'

'Not like our surfer gal here. Wait till I tell the boys how well you did.'

Damien was cooking breakfast as PJ told him about Catherine. 'Get away! Good on you! Not too many chicks have a go. And you're a bush girl too. So you coming out tomorrow?'

'I'm not sure, Damien. I don't want to take PJ away

from his surfing. And if I'm having lessons, I should pay you, PJ.'

'I enjoy your company. If you want a couple of lessons I'll trade you for some of your photos during the championships later in the year.'

'Sounds a good deal to me,' said Damien, sitting down to a pile of scrambled eggs.

Catherine quickly showered and got dressed. 'Thanks for the loan of the bikini. I'd better collect Lester's book.'

PJ put Lester's album on the back seat of Catherine's car and leant through the driver's window and kissed her lightly on the cheek.

'I'm proud of you. Come at the end of the day if you want to go out, when the wind has dropped.'

'I don't want to stay on baby waves forever,' she teased.

'Listen to you. Go and tell Lester how you felt this morning.'

'I think he'll be really pleased with me,' said Catherine. 'Thank you, PJ. You're very understanding.'

They stared at each other and PJ nodded, knowing she wasn't just referring to the surf lesson. He hadn't pushed her, he hadn't mentioned their lovemaking on Kauai, he hadn't made her feel uncomfortable. Their relationship had become a friendship laced with a past and an uncertain future. But Catherine felt safe. And although his kiss and touch had been warm and casual, she knew they were standing at a gateway. It would be her decision to go through it, or turn and walk away.

Catherine jumped around Lester's living room, showing him how she'd leapt to her feet on the board, posing as she pretended to ride an imaginary wave. He chuckled.

'So you're hooked now, I can tell. PJ sounds like a

good teacher. Some guys can't explain it well, they can only show you how they do it, which doesn't always help. Now you just have to get out there and keep cracking waves. You do want to do that, don't you?'

'It's a challenge. I like that. But it's the feeling . . . that being lifted up, being part of that energy . . . I can't explain. Well, you know what I mean.'

'I do,' he said softly. 'PJ's given you a gift you'll keep all your life. I tried to get a few gals interested in my time. A couple were really good. It's too bad more girls don't surf. They think they have to sit on the beach and admire the guys. And the guys like it that way! So, you going to get that husband of yours into it?'

'I don't think so. No way,' said Catherine. 'Gosh, I hope we don't get transferred to some landlocked place. That'd be awful. Anyway, we have a couple more years here.'

'I hope so! I'll miss you if you move away. Keep this as your home base.'

'I'm not going anywhere for a bit. Maybe you could come and sit at the beach and watch me have another go sometime? Then you could get out on a board with PJ again. We could all go together,' enthused Catherine.

'I'd enjoy that,' he said. 'But you'll find surfing is a very individual thing. So, you giving up your morning swims with Kiann'e and going surfing?'

'No. PJ suggested I go out with him at the end of the day after he's finished working and lessons and stuff.'

Kiann'e listened to Catherine's bubbling description of her surfing experience.

'You seemed to have surprised yourself. Is that because you come from the country? Or has PJ got a lot to do with it?'

'He's a terrific teacher.' And seeing Kiann'e's amused

look, she added, 'Of course he does! He's a real soul surfer . . .'

'So he's into grooving on the feeling and not surfing to get on the circuit? A lot of the local guys get a bit gnarley – to use their expression – about the outsiders coming in and surfing their breaks,' said Kiann'e. 'Abel John gets pretty heavy about it.'

'Like some of the Aussies who're doing so well. But they move on; seems that a lot of the Californians are moving here to stay. Anyway I think I might do a picture story on PJ and his boards for the paper.'

'Well, you're spending a lot of time with him. You saw him on Kauai too, didn't you?'

Catherine felt guilty about not being able to tell her about the episode with PJ. She wondered how much Kiann'e suspected about what had happened on Kauai and didn't want to ask. It wasn't fair to Bradley to talk about what had happened between her and PJ and she still suffered pangs of guilt when she thought about it. But her relationship with PJ was different now. They were just friends, no cause for embarrassment at all.

The two girls were heading back along the beach when they noticed a knot of people and equipment in front of an apartment block. As they got closer they could see stands with silver screens bouncing the sunlight onto two people standing over a body lying on the sand.

'God, has someone died? What's going on?' Catherine shaded her eyes to see better. 'They look like movie people. Oh, yes, they're filming *Hawaii Five-O*. Let's go watch.'

They joined several other beachgoers who had gathered to watch a scene being filmed for one of America's favourite TV shows, but as everyone seemed to be just standing around they moved on.

When they told Lester what had happened, he was disappointed he'd missed it all. 'I'm a big fan of the star,

Jack Lord, who plays Steve McGarrett. So what's news, young ladies?'

'I was thinking, Lester, would you like to come to Aunty's luau on Saturday?' asked Kiann'e.

'So long as it's just a smallish affair. Don't like big crowds anymore.'

'Great, Catherine and I will sort out collecting you.' Kiann'e turned to Catherine. 'Would you like to ask PJ? He'd be company for Lester. Maybe you guys could bring Lester and drop him back when he's ready.'

For Catherine, Aunty Lani and Uncle Henry's luau was as she'd come to expect and enjoy when she was with Hawaiians. Being thrown into the heart of a family with lots of people, lots of noise, laughter, music and food was fun and having PJ along, to look after Lester, was a bonus. PJ was happy to sit in the background with the old man, talking to those around them and smiling at Catherine as she helped Kiann'e pass plates of food and top up drinks.

After several hours, when the afternoon had waned and the ukuleles and slack-key guitars came out and people began to settle in for the evening, PJ took Catherine aside.

'Lester's tired now. He's had a ball, but he's ready to go home. I'll take him back. Okay?'

'Thanks, PJ. I'll pack up some leftover kalua pig and rice and poi for him. Hang on.'

'You know, you're really like family with these people. Sharing poi and so on . . . I hadn't pictured you like this,' said PJ. 'You're not the outsider I'd figured. But I understand why they like you so much. See you tomorrow. We might try a different board.'

'Great. I'll just say bye to Lester.'

Out in the front of the house Catherine gave the old

man a hug and Aunty Lani also farewelled him with a big embrace.

'It's been too long, Lester. I thought you'd become a hermit. You get these kids to bring you out more often. You're always welcome. Beatrice will be happy to know you came along.'

'Mahalo, Lani,' he answered.

Aunty and Catherine watched PJ carefully settle Lester in his old car and waved as they drove away.

'Two of a kind, I'd say,' said Aunty Lani.

'Yes. I'm so fond of Lester. I miss my dad,' sighed Catherine.

Aunty was thoughtful. 'You and Kiann'e are the closest thing Lester has to family. Introducing him to your surfing friend was wonderful.' She turned to Catherine. 'I like PJ but I bet he has the wandering spirit.'

'He's just a friend. I'm pretty well anchored in my life,' she answered.

Aunty Lani looked at her. 'Sometimes an anchor isn't what you need, but full sails filled with wind to travel through life. Don't get trapped in the harbour, dear girl.' And with that enigmatic statement she sailed off to where everyone was settling in the garden around the fire pit. The tiki torches were being lit as musicians banded together and Kiann'e was being urged to dance.

Reluctantly Catherine went to the Wives' Club morning tea. Julia brought along her friend Bonnie and when she was introduced around the group, Bonnie smiled at Catherine.

'Oh, we met at the beach the other morning when you were surfing.'

'Surfing? You surf?' commented Mrs Goodwin looking at Catherine in surprise. 'Oh, of course, you're Australian.'

'You mean on a surfboard or body surfing?' asked Melanie.

'She was there with a surfboard and a very handsome instructor,' said Julia. 'My, you must have been out early.'

'We were. Sunrise is one of the best times to surf, besides my days are so busy,' added Catherine quickly.

'I see,' said Mrs Goodwin. 'Shall we move on?'

As they were leaving, Mrs Goodwin stopped Catherine. 'Have you heard from Bradley recently?'

'Oh, yes. He's very diligent about writing.'

'As you are too, I'm sure. The men like to have regular news from home. However, I wouldn't necessarily mention these surfing lessons,' she said briskly. And seeing Catherine's surprised look, added, 'The old adage of keeping the home fires burning, not worrying our boys with trivial matters that could be misinterpreted and letting them know you are busy and involved with the other wives is very comforting for them.'

'So Bradley tells me,' answered Catherine sweetly. 'I'm looking forward to our next phone call. His main concern is that I keep busy, active and happy, and I'm doing just as he asks. Goodbye, Mrs Goodwin.'

Catherine stood at her kitchen window looking at busy Pearl Harbor. She missed the view from their lanai at the TradeWinds apartment. This place didn't feel like her own space, although with Bradley's absence she ate the food she wanted, when she wanted, she kept the hours she wanted and she realised, she was leading the life she wanted. She wondered if this was to be the pattern of her marriage. Would it be hard to readjust to living with Bradley again?

Come late afternoon, however, she couldn't settle to anything and threw on her swimsuit under a cotton shift and drove to Waikiki. PJ was sitting on the sand talking to Damien who waved to her as she came towards them.

'Ha, she can't keep away now,' laughed Damien. 'You'd better make a board for her, PJ.'

'I don't think so! What've you been up to, Damien?' said Catherine.

'Doing a few events, trying out PJ's new boards when we can find waves. Rocky Point, Little Sunset, V-Land. I'm heading to Maui for a few days, hear there's some mean tubes happening. So I'll see how his boards handle it over there. I want to take one of PJ's boards to Tahiti.'

'Do you ride your boards in competitions, PJ?' asked Catherine.

'I've surfed all over the world and while I'm not the best surfer, I surf for myself. These boys, they surf to win, but sometimes I ride in competitions too,' said PJ.

'There's starting to be money in surfing,' said Damien. 'Big-time pro money. Get the crowds in, pump up the boys. It'll be great.'

'There're too many pumped-up egos out there now,' said PJ. He looked at Catherine. 'To me surfing is an art, a way of life. Not something to be wrapped up and marketed like soap powder.'

'Ah, keep your hair on, PJ. You're sounding like an old bloke,' said Damien cheerfully. 'I'm off. See you in a week or so, brah, Catherine.'

'Why does he call you brah?'

'Braddah. He's my surfing brother. I thought you knew Hawaiian. Let's catch a few waves, shall we?' PJ pointed to a board. 'Take that one. I brought it along in case you showed up.' He smiled at Catherine and she smiled back, excited by the idea of tackling the waves again.

It was almost dark as they dried off and PJ put the boards in his car.

'Hot food is needed. You used a lot of energy out there.'

'Yes, falling off a lot,' sighed Catherine.

'C'mon, that's what learning is all about. It takes a while to read the waves. And the south end of Waikiki at Queens is bigger than you've been in. You did great. Really great.' He squeezed her hand. 'Let's pick up some food. What do you feel like?'

'I've been eating a bit of takeaway lately, being on my own. What say I organise something?' suggested Catherine.

'Don't know that we have much in the way of kitchen stuff. Keep it simple. Brown rice and salad.'

'That's certainly simple.'

'Once I went on a macrobiotic brown rice diet for a year. So did the local poi dog,' he said.

'By choice?'

'The dog, no. Me, yes. But you make whatever you like. I'm mellow about food these days.'

'I've been thinking about food at home. I miss Mum's shepherd's pie. I'll find something.'

PJ reached for his wallet but Catherine shook her head. 'My treat. You won't let me pay for lessons.'

'OK. I'll get some wine. See you back at my place.'

She decided against cooking anything elaborate, so brought back a variety of salads, rice dishes and Japanese soup as PJ was so clearly into healthy food. He'd made space on the table and poured the wine while music was playing.

'That's a nice song, what's that?' asked Catherine.

'"Moonlight Lady", written by a friend of mine on Kauai, Carlos Andrade. It's about the beautiful strong women working in the taro fields.'

'I'm loving Hawaiian music. Like the music that they played at Aunty Lani's. Not the hotel hula stuff.' She put the bowls of food on the table.

'It's influenced by reggae, blues, jazz and old Hawaiian traditions, which the locals are starting to wake up to again. Ever heard Gabby Pahinui?'

Catherine shook her head, thinking of the touristy Hawaiian music that Bradley liked.

'Hey, kid. What've you been listening to?' PJ got up to change the record.

They talked and talked, PJ told her his views about many things – music, surfing, food, lifestyle. He listened intently as Catherine talked about *Heatherbrae*, her horse, the difference in the landscape between home and the Islands and how she felt about both. They finished the bottle of wine, cleaned up, moved into the living room and sank into the old sofa.

Catherine glanced around at the clutter of record albums and books. There were two surfboards against a wall and surfing and music posters. 'How long are you going to be here, PJ? Is this shaping business a permanent thing?'

'Nothing's permanent in my life. Or in this world.'

'That's sad.'

'Why? It means there are always opportunities for change, for growth, for learning. Enjoyment.' He reached out an arm and drew her close to him. 'Nothing stays the same forever.' He lifted her face and lowered his mouth to hers.

Catherine shivered and drew back. 'No! Please, PJ. I can't.'

He slowly withdrew his arm. 'Whatever you say.'

They stared at each other. Catherine's mouth trembled.

'It's not right. Not fair to Bradley. It's my fault.'

'It's no-one's fault,' said PJ easily. 'Things happen that you can't help.'

'I want to keep seeing you. I want to be friends. I like surfing with you,' said Catherine, a slight desperation in her voice.

'You want to keep surfing?'

'Of course! Can we be surfing buddies?'

He squeezed her shoulder. 'For sure.' He got up and went to change the music again.

'I'd better go,' said Catherine.

'Come by any time. I'm your friend, Catherine.'

'Thanks, PJ.' He was being so nice, so calm, it was almost upsetting. 'Thanks for everything.' She stood staring at him, unsure what to say or do.

PJ walked to the door and gazed outside. 'New moon. Be nice in the morning. You up for a surf?'

Catherine felt her body relax. 'Yeah. Absolutely. I'll see you at Waikiki.'

'I'll bring your board. G'night, Catherine.'

He turned back inside and Catherine got in the car feeling more settled than she had in ages. Surfing buddies. It sounded good.

12

CATHERINE WAS HARDLY IN the apartment. She still met Kiann'e every morning for their swim, had a coffee with Lester and then filled her day with errands, photo shoots and a little writing before racing to meet PJ two or three afternoons a week for their sunset surf. Often they had dinner together with Damien and other surfers, either at the house or in Waikiki.

She listened to the boys' stories and anecdotes about surfing and understood their obsession more and more. Sometimes she and PJ were alone and she enjoyed his thoughtful and intriguing views on the world. His stories of the escapades, tragedies and triumphs of the surfing fraternity sounded to her more daring, mad, funny and wilder than any book or movie. What a cast of characters! They were all non-conformist in their choice of lifestyle and ranged from the hippie health fanatics to psychedelic drug-fuelled ego maniacs, from loners to the gregarious. But when it came to riding the waves, whether rivals or not, they were indistinguishable, all as one in loving the challenge and the thrill.

She was looking forward to the championships at Pipeline and Sunset later in the year. PJ told her she'd start to appreciate individual styles and how the different personalities would come to the fore. The Aussies had also asked her to be their official photographer and she hoped to do a photo spread for the paper that would be different from the usual coverage.

During the day Catherine and PJ went their own way. Catherine didn't ask what PJ was doing or what plans he had for the next day. He was not a planner and didn't like being committed to times or pre-arranged events except when they surfed together. How different he seemed from Bradley who liked to organise every minute of each day.

One evening as she returned to her apartment at the Base, a young military policeman walking past gave her a broad smile and nodded.

'Had a nice surf, Mrs Connor?'

'Very nice. Thank you.' She went inside resenting once again the small goldfish bowl in which she lived.

She opened all the doors and windows of the apartment and collected the mail. Seeing Bradley's handwriting, she decided to make a cup of tea before opening his letters. Most of the time he had chatty news or an amusing anecdote, but inevitably there'd be a checklist of things to do. Why couldn't he just trust her to run things as she saw fit and not have him double checking all the time? She wished he'd just let her be herself, do what she thought best.

Before she could open his letter, the phone rang. There was that brief pause on the line and she knew it was an overseas call. Bradley? Or home?

'Hello?'

'Cath, it's me! Hi!'

'Mollie! How fantastic to hear your voice. Is everything okay?'

'Yeah, yeah. Of course. Sorry I haven't called. Been busy.'

'I've missed hearing from you. What's happening?'

'Same old, same old. You pregnant or anything?'

'Of course not. What're you up to? How's Jason?'

'Good. Except he's going to London on business and won't take me with him. He's going to be away for two weeks and I've saved some money so I thought I'd come and see you! Is Bradley still away?'

'Yes. Couple more weeks, I guess.'

'Good. I'll stay with you and we can have fun. Is that all right?'

'Mollie . . . wonderful. I can't wait to see you! Now tell me all the news.'

They chatted quickly, conscious of the cost of the overseas phone call and Mollie's visit was quickly arranged. Catherine was excited by the idea of showing Mollie around and introducing her to all her friends, especially PJ – her surfing buddy. She knew Mollie would be impressed with the good-looking happy-go-lucky surfer and she hoped she would be equally impressed when she found out that her best friend could now surf. Fleetingly she realised she was glad that Bradley wouldn't be around because, without meaning to, he put a dampener on things. It would be much more fun to have Mollie all to herself. And of course, she planned to take her to the Wives' Club. In her heart Catherine wanted Mollie's feedback, some reassurance that she was justified in feeling as she did about the crushingly boring and oppressive group.

The letters from Bradley had little to say, his day-to-day news was limited, so the letters were short and filled with reminders of things for Catherine to do now and when he returned. There were bits of news of his family, things his crew mates did, which were primarily concerned with following sporting events and suggestions for a vacation on his next long leave. She wrote back hurriedly with the exciting news of Mollie's coming visit.

The next afternoon Catherine tried to explain to PJ how close she was to Mollie.

'Don't you have a really close friend, someone you've known for ages or you grew up with? Someone you just click with? That's almost like family?' she asked him.

He shook his head. 'No. Don't need them.'

'What about your surfing mates?'

'That's all they are. People I see in the water. I recognise the outline of someone's head, I know how they surf. I don't need to know anything else about them.' He smiled. 'It's okay, Catherine. I can pal around with the guys if I want to. I just don't really need people.'

Catherine paused, unsure how to react to this statement. 'Well, I'm so excited that my friend is coming. Mollie is such fun. You'll like her.'

'I'm going to meet Miss Mollie?'

'Of course, I want her to meet you when we go surfing.'

'So I'm your pet surfing instructor? Or your surfing buddy? One of the beach boys?' he teased her.

'And my good friend.'

'Am I giving her lessons too?'

'No, but thanks anyway.'

Catherine was a little frustrated that PJ didn't really understand how important Mollie's visit was to her and she picked up her board and ran down to the water, paddling furiously out to the line of breakers. She sat on her board staring back at Waikiki, the line of hotels, the palm trees, the tourists on the sand and, looming over all, Diamond Head.

A surfer paddled past and nodded to her, obviously surprised to see a girl surfing. Suddenly her annoyance melted and she turned to watch the waves as he was doing. Although this surfer was a stranger, the two shared a kinship and the knowledge that the sea, the waves, the sky were part of a bigger picture in which they were small, small dots. She focused her attention on what she was doing and went for the next wave.

By the time she paddled back in to the beach, PJ had gone home. The afternoon tradewinds lifted her hair and refreshed her. She loved the softness of the Hawaiian breeze, it calmed and warmed her. She walked back to PJ's and found him in the front yard wearing a face mask, pushing the grinder along the board to sand it down. She hosed off her board, washed the salt from her skin, the sand from her feet and turned off the water tap. PJ stopped what he was doing.

'How was it?'

'Good. I felt really good out there on my own.'

'Might be time you graduated from Waikiki. Let's take tomorrow off; I'll take you over to Little Sunset.'

'Ooh, I'm not sure I'm ready for anything too big.'

'I'm not talking monsters. Too early in the season for them, but you should tackle different breaks, go to a different point.'

'Great. I'll bring a picnic.'

Over the next few days, Catherine enjoyed getting the apartment ready for Mollie's visit. She stocked up the pantry and did a spring clean. The apartment had looked neglected and she realised how little time she'd spent there, but now it looked lived in again. On the morning of Mollie's arrival she filled the apartment with flowers and took a beautiful lei that Kiann'e had made out of the fridge.

*

There was no missing Mollie . . . face alight, eyes dancing, soft arms outspread. Mollie was rounder than last time Catherine had seen her but still a ball of familiar energy and excitement. The girls hugged, laughing and dancing.

'Hi, hi. Oh, wow, how beautiful!' Mollie admired the lei Catherine dropped over her shoulders. 'God, I'd forgotten how beautiful it all is. Couldn't believe it when we flew over the neighbouring islands . . . they're huge! Those cliffs, the beaches, the colour of the water.' She linked her arm through Catherine's. 'We're going to have a ball. No men . . . Be like old times. Everyone at home sends their love.'

They both talked and laughed, barely pausing for breath, all the way back to the base. Mollie did a double take at the guard at the entrance. 'Wow. What a doll. Those uniforms . . . They make any bloke look handsome. So how's Bradley?'

'As far as I know, just fine. He doesn't exactly gush in his letters. And we wives are not supposed to dump how we really feel.'

'You're kidding,' said Mollie. 'Who says? So how do you feel? I mean, do you miss him heaps and heaps?'

Catherine paused, 'Well, it's nice having my own space, but of course, I do . . .'

Mollie nudged her in the ribs. 'Go on . . . come on, you're having a ball. I know it!' And burst into laughter, making Catherine smile. 'Look where you're living! It's paradise! I can't wait to see it all again. Last time I was only here for such a short time.'

'The outer islands are even more beautiful. I just love Kauai – that's the Garden Isle. Come on, this is us. I'll help with your bag.'

Mollie looked subdued for the first time as she stared at the formal brick building of apartments with the square of green lawn in front, the Stars and Stripes flying, the immaculate white woodwork. 'It's not *Heatherbrae*, is it?'

They sat over tea after Mollie had showered and unpacked.

'So what're we going to do first?' asked Mollie. 'I'm sure you have a plan.'

'Bradley's the planner, I've got more into the go-with-the-current, see-what-happens kind of groove. But I thought you might like to go and see Kiann'e dance and we'll have a sunset cocktail at the Moonflower.'

'Shopping? Wasn't there a big mall near the water?'

'Ala Moana. Sure we can go there,' laughed Catherine. Mollie was always such a shopper. It'd be fun. Apart from buying groceries she hadn't been proper shopping since Bradley left.

After having a drink with Kiann'e between her shows, Mollie, who wasn't the least bit tired after her trip, insisted on doing a cocktail crawl around the smarter bars and restaurants, ending up at the Chart House for dinner.

'I suppose you miss doing this sort of thing now you're engaged, ' said Catherine.

'No way! Jason and I go out several nights a week. He likes to entertain clients. I refuse to do the entertaining at home. I enjoy having pals over but I'm not into playing hostess for his dinner parties.'

'Thanks for your idea of ordering in for my dinner party,' said Catherine. 'I felt guilty but it made it so much easier. Bradley wants me to do a cooking course.'

'Good grief, haven't you got better things to do with your time? I love the pictures you've been taking. Will I get to feature in the paper?' She struck a pose.

But there was no way Mollie was getting up early to walk and swim with Kiann'e so Catherine let her sleep.

'Mollie is very gregarious, but strong-willed I'd say,'

said Kiann'e the next morning. 'A good friend. She'd fight tooth and nail for you. You must miss her.'

'I do. Funny how we're such close friends yet we're so different, but she's like a sister to me.'

Kiann'e smiled. 'Family is good. Look at my huge family.' She touched Catherine's arm. 'And our extended family – like you.'

'Oh, Kiann'e, that makes me feel so . . . ' Catherine was quite overcome. Having Mollie around with all her warmth, humour, irritating habits, the memories she triggered, had made her aware of how her marriage to Bradley had isolated her from her old friends. 'It's a comfort to know you guys are around for me.'

'You know, Catherine, if you are ever in trouble, if anything ever happens . . . we're here for you,' said Kiann'e seriously.

'Thanks.' Catherine drew a breath to steady her voice. 'Let's hope nothing bad ever happens.'

'Bring Mollie around to Aunty's, we'll have a little party for her.'

After leaving Kiann'e, Catherine went past PJ's house to see if he was home and found him gluing two halves of a board and clamping them in place.

'Hi. Mollie's here.'

'That's good. You having fun?'

'We are actually. I can't wait for you to meet her. I thought I'd bring her and Lester around this afternoon while we have a surf.'

He gave a half smile. 'A surfing lesson, or a little bit of showing off?'

She laughed. 'Mollie will be pretty surprised. I don't think she quite believes I actually get out there on a board alone.'

'Bring her round at sunset. Are you sure she doesn't want a lesson? I'll bring a board.'

'Oh, no. She's not sporty. She's the party animal who shops.'

Later Catherine and Mollie picked up Lester and went to Waikiki.

The late afternoon sun glinted on the water, beachgoers were lazing in deckchairs and on beach towels enjoying the last of the day. Lester and Mollie settled themselves on the sand and Mollie began snapping photographs of Catherine.

'Look at you with your surfboard,' she laughed as Catherine pulled a top over her bikini and picked up her board. 'They'll love this at home. I'll send one to your parents and Rob.'

'Mollie, this is my friend PJ. Peter James.'

PJ smiled and shook hands with Mollie who glanced from PJ to Catherine, her eyes signalling, wow, what a great looker. 'Nice to meet you. Never thought my country cousin here would take to surfing.'

'I gather there's not much surf where Catherine's from,' said PJ.

'No, it's all turf,' laughed Mollie. 'I'm the city girl but I'm not ocean-going either. More the Pimms by the pool type.'

'Mollie, Lester will keep you company for a bit. Then we'll all have a drink and pupus.' Catherine picked up her board.

'Aren't you going in, Lester?' asked Mollie. 'I hear you're a legend.'

'Did you now?' He looked pleased. Mollie made him laugh. 'I prefer the other side of the island.'

'This'll do me. I can't believe Catherine lives here. Must be like being on perpetual holidays.' She put on her new white and gold sunglasses and leaned back closing her eyes.

Catherine wanted to show off her new surfing skills

for Mollie, but once she was out there in the surf concentrating on the two-foot swell, following calls from PJ, she forgot about everything else. When she finally went back to the beach, Mollie and Lester were deep in conversation and clearly enjoying each other's company.

'Coming for a drink, PJ?'

'I should get back and do some more work.'

'Aw c'mon, PJ, I haven't had a chance to talk to you,' cajoled Mollie.

Catherine nodded her head in agreement, so PJ gave in and agreed to come. The four of them settled at the beachside café and ordered freshly squeezed juices and spicy satay sticks. Mollie chatted to PJ about his life, his home, where he grew up, how he got into surfing and then turned her attention again to Lester who was more talkative than he'd been in weeks.

As they were leaving, PJ said goodbye. 'I'm off to Maui for a while. See you when I get back.'

Catherine tried not to look surprised. 'Maui? What's happening over there?'

'A few waves, I hope,' grinned PJ. 'Damien and a couple of the guys are taking some of my new boards over.'

'Sounds fun. How long are you going for?' asked Catherine, suddenly disappointed she'd miss their lessons and his company.

'Depends. Enjoy your visit, Mollie. See you when I get back.' He touched Lester on the shoulder and smiled at Catherine. 'Take it easy out there, don't surf on your own except on Waikiki.'

'Man, is he a hearthrob,' said Mollie as they drove away.

'You should see the pictures of Lester when he was a young surf god. Makes all the others look second rate,' said Catherine and Lester chuckled, but looked pleased.

*

That night as they sat over a glass of wine, Mollie gave Catherine a shrewd look.

'That PJ. He's an interesting man. A case of still waters running deep though. How well do you know him?'

'I don't think anyone knows PJ all that well. He's a bit of loner.'

'You seem to like him. Like there's a bit of a zing there? What's the story?' asked Mollie.

'There's no story, Mollie. He's nice and he's been very patient teaching me. We're good friends, surfing buddies. He's just easy to be with.'

'How come you wanted to learn to ride a surfboard for gosh sake? What's Bradley think?'

'He doesn't care what I do so long as I'm happy and active – and don't neglect my duties as a naval wife.' She wrinkled her nose. 'I guess Lester got me interested in surfing. More wine?'

'Why not?' Mollie watched Catherine pour the wine and changed the subject. 'So when do I get to meet the dreaded navy wives?'

'Day after tomorrow. There's a meeting and a tea. I've let them know I'm bringing a guest. They like to know ahead of time, for the name tag and so on.'

'Oh, so I'm expected. That means I can't take up a better offer?'

Catherine laughed. 'No, Mollie, you can't. I want you to experience the Wives' Club.'

The phone rang and Catherine was delighted to hear Eleanor's voice. 'Catherine, dear. How are you?'

'Eleanor! Lovely to hear from you. I'm well. Very well, I have my girlfriend visiting from Australia.'

'How nice. I'm here in Honolulu on business – can we all get together for dinner? Are you free tomorrow night? I can ask Kiann'e, too.'

'Wonderful. Oh, I'm so happy Mollie will be able to

meet you. She's not going to Kauai this trip, but I've told her so much about the Palm Grove, she's going to bring her fiancé and stay there,' said Catherine.

Eleanor sighed. 'Well, I hope we're still open for business. We appear to have a few problems.'

'Goodness, that sounds bad – you will tell me about it? How are Abel John and Mouse and everyone?'

'They're fine, they send their best. Shall we say drinks at the Moonflower at six and we'll have dinner after Kiann'e's show?'

'Wonderful. See you then.'

The four women sat in a quiet booth in the Hibiscus Room at the Moonflower. Kiann'e was explaining the history of the hula to Mollie who confessed she'd give anything to move so gracefully.

'Catherine is learning, she's very good,' said Kiann'e. 'But you have to learn the proper way, not the tourist way.'

'Cath, you're nearly half Hawaiian – surfing, hula dancing – what other hidden talents have you got?' laughed Mollie.

'There's lots to learn, isn't that right, Eleanor? You know so much about the Islands,' said Catherine. 'And that's what visitors want to know, isn't it?'

Eleanor had not been her usual self, she was quieter and seemed troubled about something.

So Catherine finally asked, 'What's happening at the Palm Grove?'

'It's a long story . . . I don't want to bore you with it, spoil our dinner.'

'C'mon, Eleanor, we're friends,' said Catherine.

'You seem very worried,' said Kiann'e.

'I am. I have to speak to your mother, but I know what

331

she'll say.' Eleanor sighed. 'We have been excavating for the new building at the back of the lagoon – on land that hasn't been touched in goodness knows how long – and the workmen came across something. Being Hawaiians, they called in a kahuna. Now sometimes I wish they were haole workers who'd just kept on bulldozing.'

'What's a kahuna?' Mollie asked solemnly.

'An elder. Like a priest,' said Catherine, anxious to hear Eleanor's story. 'What did they find?'

'Stones. A heiau. Well, they think it is . . .'

'What's a heiau?' asked Mollie quickly.

'It's an ancient temple, a sacred place,' answered Kiann'e, who then turned to Eleanor. 'Do they think the stones are part of a structure, a burial site, or have they been moved there?'

'It's too early to tell. Between you and me, Abel John is seeking advice from an archeologist who has been working on malae sites on some of the outer islands and in Tahiti and Samoa,' said Eleanor. 'It appears it's been there for a long time. No-one knows for sure when the first Hawaiians settled here. When the workmen dug out the palm trees and undergrowth and drained the swampy ground they found this muddy straight line which could be a wall or an altar.'

'How exciting,' breathed Mollie. 'So it's very old.'

'It would be exciting if it wasn't holding up the whole building project. The area could be taken over by the state if it's deemed to be historic.'

'My mother believes that the first Polynesians arrived in Hawaii in the third century from the Marquesa Islands,' said Kiann'e. 'Eleanor, this could be of great cultural significance.'

'That's just my problem,' said Eleanor briskly. 'I have a meeting with my investor tomorrow and he doesn't care about cultural sites, just dollars and schedules. He'll drive the bulldozers over the place himself to get the building up on time.'

'You'll have a riot on your hands if the old people hear about this,' warned Kiann'e.

'Please, not a word, Kiann'e,' said Eleanor, looking very serious.

'Couldn't you turn this ancient place into a tourist attraction?' asked Mollie.

'While I really admire Hawaiian culture, I have to admit that some old stones buried in mud isn't all that exciting for most tourists,' said Eleanor. 'Look, I don't want to put a dampener on our evening. Let's order dinner, the new chef here is excellent. We'll see what transpires at the meeting tomorrow.'

On the way home Mollie was thoughtful. 'Sounds like your friend Eleanor has a headache with her building plans.'

'Yes, apparently there are remains of ancient building sites all over the islands. The Hawaiians don't want them damaged but most developers don't care about Polynesian history,' said Catherine.

'How come you know this stuff?'

'Kiann'e and PJ have told me stories about the early Polynesians. How they sailed canoes across thousands of miles of ocean. PJ says they must have been brilliant readers of stars and tides and winds to settle on so many far-flung islands across the huge Pacific Ocean.'

'So he's not just interested in surfing?' said Mollie with a glance at Catherine as she drove.

'PJ is interested in lots of things,' said Catherine.

'And what are Bradley's theories on Polynesian navigation skills? Being in the navy, he must have a view?' said Mollie.

Catherine gave a little laugh. 'I don't think we've really discussed it.'

'I'll treat you to brunch after your swim tomorrow morning,' offered Mollie. She could see Catherine wanted to change the subject. 'And then it's off to the Wives' Club do. I can hardly wait.'

Mollie made a huge effort at Mrs Goodwin's to charm and gush. She adored the beautiful house, gorgeous gardens, how lovely all the ladies were, the delicious food, how lucky Catherine was to have this exciting life.

Catherine kicked Mollie under the table as they sipped their watery tea and nibbled the rich fudge brownies. She gave Mollie a look that said, Don't overdo it, kiddo.

But Mollie pressed on. 'You must have lived in so many fascinating places, Mrs Goodwin. And I suppose you've entertained no end of important people?'

'Commander Goodwin and I have had our share of influential people to entertain. Why last month we had the Under Secretary of the Navy passing through. These girls will learn what it means to set a fine table and make conversation with very different people from all over the world. It's our duty to let everyone know, by example, what a wonderful place the USA is.'

'Yes, I imagine, so,' said Mollie. 'Particularly Hawaii. This truly is paradise.'

A slight flicker passed across Mrs Goodwin's face. 'It's all very well having a first posting somewhere as comfortable as the Islands,' she glanced at Catherine, 'but one has to be prepared for some hardship assignments also.'

'But if you're on a base with all American mod cons and other American families, you wouldn't feel too isolated would you?' said Mollie.

'No, that's true. It is a blessing. We all try to support one another.'

'Just one big happy family,' smiled Mollie.

'Excuse me, the teapot needs replenishing.' Catherine hurriedly left the table before she burst out laughing or crying, or started hitting Mollie with the teapot.

Mollie did the rounds. Watching her chat, laugh, ask everyone lots of questions about their life in Hawaii, Catherine had to smile to herself. Mollie was certainly a larger-than-life person and was making a big impact on the other wives. They must think me so dull and wimpy in comparison, Catherine thought. Mollie sat quietly as Mrs Goodwin conducted the meeting and welcomed Mollie as their charming guest from Australia.

As they were leaving, Mrs Goodwin drew Catherine aside. 'Some happy news, my dear. It has been confirmed that Bradley will be returning in two weeks.'

Mollie was puzzled at Catherine's momentary pause and the brief look of dismay before her friend gathered herself and gave a bright smile.

'That's wonderful news. Thanks for letting me know, Mrs Goodwin.'

Normally Mollie would have probed Catherine about Bradley's homecoming but Catherine didn't seem to want to talk about it. Maybe there was trouble in paradise, she concluded.

'So what did you think?' Catherine edged the car away from the Goodwins' spotless garden and out into the traffic.

'My God! Worse than I thought. Where have those women *been* all their lives? Y'know not once did any of them ask me a single question about me. They don't go anywhere, do anything . . . I mean like you do. I mentioned you had such interesting friends here – thinking of Kiann'e, Lester, Eleanor – and they thought I meant *them*! Quite flattered they were. I think I've boosted your image quite a bit,' she finished.

'You certainly did. They thought you were such fun,

so cute, just darling, what a lovely gal . . .' mimicked Catherine.

'Oh dear, we sound very catty,' laughed Mollie. 'I'm sure they're all nice girls on their own, back at home. They're just all out of the same navy cookie cutter. Is that Mrs Goody-win, do you suppose? Cripes, I hope your next commanding officer's wife is a bit more liberal.'

Again Catherine felt that flicker, the pang, at the knowledge she would eventually be moving on from Hawaii. More of the same elsewhere, she supposed. 'I have a terrible feeling that there will be a lot more Mrs Goodwins in my life,' said Catherine. 'I just hope I can maintain the distance like I can here. Anyway, we're not leaving for some time. Who knows, Mrs G might move on, the Commander might retire and we'll get some groovy, interesting woman in her place.'

'I wouldn't count on it,' said Mollie. 'I'm glad we're heading over to Aunty Lani's. I think that's going to be more my cup of tea. Mug of poi. Whatever.'

Catherine laughed. Mollie always cheered her up. 'Pass on the poi. It's like wallpaper paste.'

As Catherine knew she would be, Mollie was a great hit with Kiann'e's family. There was much laughter, dancing, singing and eating. Eleanor dropped by and seemed a lot more relaxed.

Catherine took her aside. 'How did your meeting go? You look a bit more cheerful.'

'Well, you can't help feeling better when you're with this lot,' said Eleanor. 'Though I do feel a bit awkward after talking to my business partner. He is simply not sensitive to Hawaiian concerns over these rocks.'

'They're just rocks?'

'That's what he calls them. I've been speaking to Abel John and he says all the workmen will walk off the site if the stones are disturbed. Very kapu. There is even the

336

chance that bones will turn up, meaning it was a burial place. No-one wants to disturb ancestral spirits. If they're disturbed they'll bring some dreadful retribution down on us. But try explaining that to a mainland investor.' She sighed.

'I suppose you're stuck either way, aren't you? Pleasing the locals, or getting your new wing. Doesn't seem that you can have both.'

'To tell you the truth, Catherine, I liked the Palm Grove the way it's always been. I don't think we should try to compete with the big hotels and resorts. I think we should remain unique,' said Eleanor candidly.

'There are lots of people who like the magic and the Hawaiian style of the Palm Grove. Those new places are all the same,' said Catherine, trying to sound optimistic. Just the same, she remembered Bradley's criticism that Eleanor's place was a rather run-down old-fashioned style of hotel.

'I hope you're right. And I wish my partner could see that. Beatrice will get involved soon enough and he will get to hear the other side of the issue,' said Eleanor, looking rather heartened at the prospect. 'You enjoy Mollie's company, bring her over to Kauai next time she visits.'

'Yes, I will. She's planning on bringing her fiancé back, too.'

'And give Bradley my best when he returns.'

'Thanks, Eleanor.'

Catherine watched her friend being swept into Lani's enfolding embrace as they said goodbye. Eleanor put on her straw hat with fresh hibiscus around its crown and excused herself. How strong and determined she is, thought Catherine, but she certainly has a big problem.

Aunty Lani caught Catherine's eye. 'Big things happening over there at the Palm Grove. Eleanor is caught in the middle. And wait till my sister gets involved. There's

337

no way Beatrice'll let them build on top of a heiau. Could be an important place.'

'Like what? Are they all different?' asked Catherine.

'Of course. It could be a burial place of the ali'i, birthing stones for the chiefs, or the stones could have great healing mana.'

'How soon before they find out? The delays must be costing a bit.'

'Could be a story for your paper.'

'I'll wait till Eleanor lets me know. I think she wants to keep it quiet,' said Catherine.

Catherine was surprised at how upset she felt when it came time to farewell Mollie. They hugged fondly.

'Things are going to seem so dull when I get home,' said Mollie.

'You're joking. With your great social calendar!'

'Your life is a knockout – look where you're living for a start,' said Mollie. 'And you have such interesting friends. Your Hawaiian friends are just lovely. They seem like family for you.'

'It's true. But I miss Mum and Dad and *Heatherbrae* and Parker and my mates, especially you,' sighed Catherine.

'I'm sorry I missed Bradley, but it's been good to spend time with you, just like the old days,' smiled Mollie. She hesitated. 'Cath, is everything all right in your life? You know you can tell me anything . . . I just get a feeling . . . Bradley, those navy wives, your Hawaiian friends?'

Catherine quickly shook her head. 'No, no, not at all.'

'Well, it's your life, remember. Don't get locked into something and feel you have to stick with it 'cause it's the right thing to do. You're a long way from home, but home will always be there, no matter what.'

'I know. It's just . . . I was brought up to do the right thing. You know how it is. I'm fine, really I am. Life's great on the Islands.'

'Even if everything is hunky dory here in the Islands, things might change when you're someplace else. Bugger doing the right thing, look after number one I say,' said Mollie firmly.

'Oh, Mollie. C'mon. Bring Jason over when Bradley is here, we'll have fun.'

Mollie dug her friend in the ribs. 'We don't need those blokes around to have fun! Come back home for a visit before you get posted to Okinawa or the Philippines or some place! Take care.'

'You too, Mol.'

And she was gone through customs, a colourful figure gripping a straw basket, a large shopping bag and a sealed canister of leis.

The apartment seemed even more empty and depressing without Mollie. Kiann'e had gone to Kauai for a couple of days to visit her mother, so Catherine rang Lester and suggested that she bring him round some supper and they have a drink on his lanai, eat and watch some TV.

'Haven't you anything better to do, girl?' he asked. 'But I won't say no to that offer.'

The next morning was clear, the water sparkling, and in the first hours of the day everything looked just washed from a light shower of rain during the night. After her swim Catherine decided to go to PJ's and collect her board and have a surf. He'd told her to help herself while he was away and that if there wasn't anyone in the house, just to push the garage doors open.

As she approached the house she saw the workroom doors were open and an unfamiliar, beaten-up car painted in wild colours was parked in front. Music was playing. Catherine wandered through the open back door into the kitchen. A girl was sitting at the table eating a bowl of cereal. She glanced up at Catherine.

'Hi.'

'Hi,' said Catherine. 'I just came to borrow a board I've been using.'

'Go for it.' The girl continued to eat.

Catherine turned away and was heading out the door when she heard her name. She spun around to see a smiling, freshly showered PJ standing in the kitchen. 'You're back.' She looked at the girl. 'I'm sorry to barge in . . . I was going to take the board out . . .' Catherine felt a little pang of jealousy. Even though there was no reason that PJ shouldn't have a girlfriend, deep down she realised that she didn't want to share him.

'Great. I'd come with you, but I just got back from the beach and showered. Have to go downtown for some supplies.'

'I understand. I'll see you later, I guess.' She hurried out the front and stood on the lawn taking deep breaths.

PJ came up behind her. 'What's the rush? Is your pal still here?'

Catherine shook her head. 'Why didn't you tell me you were back? I just feel a bit strange walking in on you with that girl.'

PJ started to laugh. 'That's Damien's new girlfriend. He met her in Maui. We've only been back a day and I didn't want to spoil your time with your friend – you said how special she was to you.'

'So were you just going to hang out here and not let me know you were back?' asked Catherine.

'I figured you'd be around as soon as your friend had gone. You didn't give me a chance to call you.' He looked perplexed.

'I would've let you know when I was back.'

She stomped into the workroom to collect the board, now determined to go down to the beach, surprised at how upset she felt.

'Want to have dinner, catch up?' asked PJ.

'Sure. I'll bring something. See you later,' she said, somewhat mollified.

When she returned from the surf, PJ had gone and Damien was in the workroom with the girl.

'How was Maui?' asked Catherine.

'Far out. Too bad we had to come back, but there's a meeting with a possible sponsor lined up.'

Catherine didn't want to hang around, she'd wait to get all the news from PJ that evening. 'Gotta run, see you later.'

He was sitting on the beach in shorts and a T-shirt with a group of surfers, no doubt discussing the waves in Maui, thought Catherine. She was disappointed he wasn't alone, but she knew he couldn't control the people who wandered along the beach, and this part of Waikiki was always a popular gathering spot.

He saw her coming, carrying a large picnic basket, and stood up. As she reached him, the other surfers were drifting away.

'What are you bringing all that stuff down here for?'

'I thought we might have a sunset picnic.'

'No surfing?'

'I'm not exactly dressed for it, but sure, if you like,' she said.

'That's okay. I'm going out early in the morning with the guys to Makaha, anyway. Come along if you like, though the sets out there might be a bit big for you to manage,' he added.

'Ah, we'll see. I have to finish some work for the paper for next week's edition.'

'What've you got in here?' PJ began rifling through the neatly packed basket.

'Hang on, let me set it out. I got us a really nice bottle of wine.'

'Why don't we take it home then?'

'The sunset, PJ!' she admonished him.

He grinned. 'Right. I know a better place to see it. C'mon.' He picked up the basket. 'Where's your car?'

As they drove down Ala Wai Boulevard, PJ described his time on Maui, then they turned inland and started to climb up a high hill.

'What's this place?' asked Catherine.

'Puu Ualakaa State Park. Very beautiful.'

He pulled into a lookout where the length of the coastline from Diamond Head to the Waianae Ranges was spread below them.

'You've been here before,' she said.

'Any surfer knows the best places to view the coast,' he answered.

They ate the food and shared the wine as they watched the sunset. They didn't talk but sat there wrapped in their own thoughts. Catherine wished she did this kind of spontaneous thing more often. There were still so many places to discover on the Islands. As the molten glow of the sky faded to indigo, the lights of the city below them began to sparkle.

'I love it here. It's really magic. I see why you can't leave,' Catherine finally said.

'I don't feel tied to this place. Plenty of other magic islands. I don't have the history here that someone like Lester has. But I wouldn't trade this for big city or suburban life, that's for sure.'

'What are you going to do with your life, PJ?' she

asked. 'Is it possible to make a living from surfing, making boards, teaching tourists?'

'Anything is possible.' He grinned. 'I tend to take things day by day. Keeps life interesting.'

'This has been lovely. I've found somewhere new to come,' said Catherine as they packed up.

'I know the island pretty well now. I'll take you round a bit if you like.'

So for the next few days PJ took her places around the island – secret surfing spots, through the pineapple plantations to small towns, to tiny local restaurants run variously by Hawaiians, Japanese and Portuguese. Away from Honolulu, the island of Oahu was diverse – farms, plantations, waterfalls, ravines, valleys, and even a few decent-sized cattle ranches. It was fascinating and absolutely beautiful.

'How do you know these places? I wish I'd known about them before.' Catherine said.

'I figured we'd get around to it. I don't want you to think this island is just Waikiki. There's a lot more to Kauai too, I could show you. But I thought exploring Oahu first might give you some ideas for photos.'

'It sure has,' she exclaimed. 'I can find out more about the history from Aunty Lani and Kiann'e.'

Coming home from one of these expeditions, she was greeted with a phone message from Bradley.

'Hi, honey, you're never home, so hope you get this message okay. We'll be docking Friday. Check with the office. The Commander will have the exact time we're due in. Can't wait to see you.'

Julia must have got a message as well, as she rang Catherine.

'Exciting, isn't it? What are you planning for Bradley?'

'You mean when he gets home? Going out? A dinner?' asked Catherine.

'No, for his arrival. The girls generally dress up, make a sign, bring leis of course. Susie Mitchell took their dog to the dock last year draped in leis, even though animals aren't allowed. Of course the kids always make a big deal of the welcome home for their fathers.'

'I see. Well, I don't have an animal or a child, and I think Bradley would be embarrassed if I made a placard or something. What are you doing?'

'Wearing sexy underwear. Suspenders. Jim gets a giggle out of that stuff. There's a shop downtown . . .'

'Hey, spare me the details,' said Catherine lightly. Bradley didn't indulge in any racy foreplay or seduction. Bradley was, in fact, quite modest. He didn't like to be seen naked and liked the bathroom to himself when he showered and shaved. And as for making love on the beach . . . No, thought Catherine, I don't want to go there.

'Well, I heard it's probable they could be gone again in six weeks time so, as Mrs Goodwin says, it's nice to make an effort to welcome them home,' said Julia.

'Do you think Mrs Goodwin wears naughty red lace knickers to welcome home the Commander?' said Catherine, laughing at the thought.

'Catherine! That's a dreadful thing to say,' said Julia primly. 'I'll see you down at the port.'

The morning of Bradley's arrival, Catherine stood under the shower trying to liven herself up and muster the effort to look excited and happy at seeing him again. She just felt very flat and wondered if Bradley would like her racing out at sunrise to swim and then at sunset to surf. She tidied the apartment, restocked the empty fridge and pantry and put fresh flowers on the table. That'll do, she thought.

She saw the cluster of wives waiting and was surprised

at how some had turned up in jeans and casual suntops. Other women, like Julia, were in heels and good dresses or fitted skirts and tailored blouses, hairdos freshly coiffured and lacquered. Catherine had opted for a full-skirted sundress with spaghetti straps and small-heeled sandals. Her hair cascaded around her shoulders in soft curls and she'd put a flower in it. She wore the pearl necklace that Bradley had given her for their wedding. She hadn't paid this much attention to her clothes since he left.

Catherine stood to one side, holding the orchid and plumeria lei she'd brought for him. There were squeals and long embraces as the men came down the gangplank to the arms of their wives and girlfriends. And then Bradley appeared at the top of the gangplank, surveying the dock. She lifted her arm and waved at her husband, feeling a bit like she did when she'd first arrived in Honolulu from London. She felt unsure, hesitant, shy even, but she could see why she'd fallen in love with this tall handsome man in his crisply immaculate uniform. Bradley beamed and strode down the gangplank giving a smart salute to the officer on the dock. And in a few long strides he was before her, dropping his small bag and opening his arms. He kissed her tenderly and then held her at arms' length.

'Heavens, look how brown you are! And your hair is longer. You look fit and well. This surfing must agree with you.'

Catherine was confused. How did he know about her surfing? Julia must have told Jim. Or was it Mrs Goodwin?

Bradley took off his hat and she dropped the lei over his head. 'You look good, Bradley. Not as suntanned as I thought you'd be.'

'Darling, I don't usually work on the deck. Shall we?'

Catherine opened the driver's door but Bradley took the keys from her. 'I'll drive.'

They made small talk on the way home. He was vague about the specifics of their tour of duty, talked about the men, asked about news from home, enquired about her family and wanted to know about the Wives' Club activities. Catherine found herself struggling to find things to say about her life while he'd been away.

'It's only three o'clock, I thought we'd go out for a sunset cocktail and I made a reservation for dinner.' She knew he wasn't going to take her to bed as soon as they got into the apartment. Bradley was not keen on making love in the daytime. But it seemed strange having him back. She'd gotten used to her own company, doing things as she wanted.

'Sounds wonderful. I'll unpack and then pop over to see the Commander. I have a few things to do at the Base, but I'll be home and change in time for the sunset drinks. The Ilikai? Or the Royal Hawaiian?'

'How about the Moana?' said Catherine.

'Of course. It is our spot, isn't it.'

Bradley rang her a short time later. 'Jim and Julia are coming to dinner with us. Jim wants to go down to Chinatown to some authentic restaurant in the Hotel Street area. I said we'd meet them there after our drinks.'

'Well, that sounds fun,' said Catherine, thinking the location was rather adventuresome for the Bensens.

Bradley ordered their cocktails at the Moana and they chatted about a new couple who'd arrived at the Base. 'Nice pair. From Pennsylvania. He's working with me so you'll meet her at the Wives' Club.' Bradley, however, didn't seem very interested in what Catherine had been doing. He didn't ask about her photography or the fact that she was taking surfing lessons. As Bradley talked Catherine watched the waves and the people enjoying the

346

sunset on the beach. One or two of the beach boys waved to her as they walked past with their boards.

However by the time they finally found Wo Fats Restaurant in Chinatown, Bradley started to sound annoyed.

'We're going to be late. And I don't like leaving the car in the street here. Too many unsavoury characters wandering around. We try to keep our enlisted men out of this area. A lot of the bars and clubs are off limits to them. They get into trouble.'

His mood wasn't improved when he found that the Bensens had invited two other men to join them, who were old friends of Jim's from his home town. They were several drinks ahead of the others and this restaurant had been their idea.

'We've been in Asia, we know the food. We'll order and we all share,' said one of the men waving the long menu.

For once Bradley and Catherine were united in their opinion of the evening. The two men drank whisky while Jim and Bradley had beers and Catherine and Julia stuck to green tea. The men, Hank and Milton, were loud, told stories of their tour in 'Nam and made a lot of racist comments that began to rankle Catherine. Even Jim began to be embarrassed by their crassness. So while Hank and Milton debated over ordering dessert, Bradley asked for the tab.

'What say we hit a bar or two? I know a few good ones around here,' said Hank.

'I don't believe we'll join you,' said Bradley pulling money from his wallet and putting a generous amount on the table, which made Catherine realise how much he wanted to leave. Bradley was normally meticulous at dividing a shared bill.

'Hey, Jim, ol' buddy, you're not going to chicken out on us, are you?' demanded Milton.

Jim glanced at Julia, who was tight lipped. 'Thanks, guys, we'll leave you to it. This has been great . . . really different food.'

'You haven't lived till you've explored the delights of Chinatown, buddy,' grinned Milton.

'We'll leave you to it. Nice to meet you,' said Bradley leading Catherine away from the table as Jim and Julia got up to leave.

Bradley was unlocking the car when they heard raised voices. Their dining companions Milton and Hank were arguing with two Hawaiian boys.

'Piss off, mokes,' shouted Hank.

Catherine saw one of the Hawaiians throw a punch and then Milton leapt at the other and a scuffle broke out.

'Bradley, stop them,' exclaimed Catherine.

Jim and Julia quickly hurried over to Bradley and Catherine. 'This could get ugly. We'd better get out of here,' said Jim.

'They're your friends, can't you stop them?' asked Catherine as the fight now looked serious.

'Those guys can take care of themselves,' Jim replied. 'I think the best course is to get you two ladies out of here before we get caught up in it.'

'Jim, you look after Catherine and Julia and I'll go back into Wo Fats and call the police. I'll be as quick as I can.'

Several people had come out of a bar and were shouting at the four men. It looked like several locals were ready to join in the brawl.

'He's got a knife!' someone shouted.

Bradley returned almost at once. 'The police have already been called. We'll all go in my car,' he said as he started his engine. 'We'll get your car in the morning, Jim.'

'If they've got knives, someone could really get hurt.' Catherine cried.

'Those two are pretty good fighters,' said Jim shortly.

'But you see why we have to keep our young hotheads out of this area. Those redneck mokes like to stir them up.'

'I hate the way these Polynesians like to make trouble,' said Bradley taking a side street to avoid the swelling crowd.

'That's a pretty sweeping statement,' said Catherine curtly, wanting to add that it sounded racist.

'Don't protect them, Catherine. These people are not like your Hawaiian friends. These guys deliberately look for trouble.'

'We shouldn't have come downtown,' said Julia.

'The food was nice, even if we didn't get much of a say in ordering,' said Catherine.

'They ordered too much. I'm sorry we included them in our nice reunion dinner,' said Julia.

Jim cut her short. 'Well, they're from home but I didn't think that they would behave like that.'

'Well, I guess the police will sort it out. What time do you want to pick up your car, Jim?'

'That's okay, Julia can run me down in hers.' He laughed. 'Well, not literally run me down . . . You're not mad at me, are you, honey?'

Julia laughed and took his hand, relieved the drama had passed. 'I'm glad you're back.'

Back in their apartment Bradley dropped the car keys on the table. 'That was all very distasteful. Such a rough area. I hope Jim's car is all right; those Hawaiians could bash it up just for spite.'

'Those two friends of Jim's could have caused the fight, they were pretty sleazy.'

'Why must you take the locals' side before anyone else's?' asked Bradley in an exasperated voice. 'You are so one-eyed about this small town, Catherine. Come on, I brought you a gift.'

Catherine pretended to be mollified but she was angry

at Jim and Bradley's attitude. There was something about the two men Jim had brought along she didn't like and it occurred to her that Jim could be a bit of a redneck himself.

Bradley had brought her a pale pink angora cardigan embroidered with seed pearls and a gold charm bracelet with a heart on it. He promised to add to it on each special occasion.

'I thought we could go for a drive, take a picnic, tomorrow,' Catherine suggested.

'Oh, honey, I'll have to report to work tomorrow, but that's a nice idea. Maybe on the weekend.'

He made love to her and fell asleep on his side of the bed, contented that all was well in his world.

Two days later Bradley came home looking very pleased with himself. He opened the bottle of champagne he'd brought.

'Good news, Catherine.'

'Oh. What are we celebrating?' She reached for the glass he held out to her.

'A promotion. I've been given a job in the Defense Department, attaché to Admiral Peters. I applied for this posting weeks ago but I didn't tell you so it would be a surprise.'

'Congratulations,' said Catherine looking puzzled. 'What exactly does the promotion mean? Will you be at sea?'

'No, not anymore. It's a desk job at the Pentagon. We move to Washington DC at the end of the month. I'll be out of this town that doesn't appreciate the US Navy, going to somewhere that does.' He raised his glass. 'Oops, oh dear, you've spilled your champagne. Here, let me refill it.'

Catherine sat rigid as Bradley fussed with paper towels and topped up her glass. Numbly she clinked glasses and gave a tight smile, while inside her body every nerve end was screaming, no, no, no.

Extract from The Biography of

THE WATERMAN

The jazz era passed the young man by. He stayed in the Islands but Hollywood still called him and he continued to work in the occasional movie. One new production was set in Alaska, where he was employed as a stuntman. The glaciers, wild country and stormy rapids were beautiful but treacherous. He became concerned at the inadequacy and lack of safety precautions being taken by the film's producers.

When they'd first arrived the young man had taken a small boat above the rapids to run a safety cable across the river with ropes hanging from it, so that if a boat capsized the occupants could grab one of the lines before they were swept downstream towards the rapids. However bad weather and endless minor problems put the production weeks behind schedule. With the delays the weather was warming, the snow melting. The young man warned the producers that the river would soon become as mad as a runaway train and even he, as the best swimmer, could not guarantee people's safety.

His advice was ignored; getting the film in the can was paramount.

Inevitably, with the now explosive amount of water in the river, one of the boats with two stuntmen was swept away from shore. The men jumped, grasping at the cable over the river where they hung on desperately.

The young man was summoned and with a rope around his waist, plunged into the glacial water, hauling himself along the cable to reach the exhausted men. But the force of water was too strong and the men were swept away in the violent rapids.

Their deaths affected him greatly. He blamed himself

and was angered at the cavalier attitude of the film company towards safety.

The movie industry was changing. Sound had arrived but the young man was disillusioned and no longer wanted to be involved. When he returned to the Islands he found that everyone was affected by the Great Depression. Unemployment grew as workers from the sugar and pineapple plantations were laid off.

For a while he lived simply, eating bread and fruit and surfing by day, but eventually he was forced to sell his collection of medals and trophies to survive. He refused to be saddened by the loss of his trophies. They were only symbols. His achievements were noted in the history books and in his memory, but he did keep one small medal – the first prize he ever won.

Throughout the thirties, he continued with his board shaping and still inspired by the craft of the ancient Hawaiians, he used the old shapes and made hollow boards, drilling through the solid wood and covering the holes with a veneer to lighten the weight of the board. His next step was to form the board with hollow sections that made it lighter still.

In a board-paddling race down the Ala Wai canal he broke every record several years running, but when there were complaints that he had an unfair advantage – though he made no secret of how his boards were constructed – he refused to race anymore and concentrated on building boards for anybody to use. He also designed boards to suit specific conditions at particular beaches as he knew the peculiarities of all the surfing beaches.

He showed others what he was doing and the Duke built a board based on the old olo boards for himself. Very soon the paddleboard and hollow boards were appearing on beaches in other parts of the world. He didn't make money from these designs, other than making a few custom boards on request, but, because of the demand for these, he set up a small production factory in Waikiki.

Finding a fin from a damaged boat, he decided to experiment with fitting a fin to his board. He also tried attaching a sail and then a motor to create as light and as small a water machine as possible. While the fin became a big success, he couldn't interest anyone in sailing a board with the wind, or speeding across waves with a motor.

After the death of the two stuntmen in Alaska, he often thought about the need for making water safety a priority. He realised the value of the hollow paddleboard as a rescue craft, where one man could use it to support four or five people in trouble in the surf, or on a river or lake. He also designed floating safety rings and other devices and later rescue boards that could be left at remote beaches in case of an emergency.

His interest in photography continued to grow. He photographed his boards, his friends, the surf scene and himself but wished he could capture his boards in action. So he designed a special waterproof case to go around his camera and paddling out in the surf, he photographed the beach boys trying his new boards.

The waterman was now a well known figure on the beach and his name was known by board riders even in other parts of the world. But his own world remained Waikiki where he knew everyone by name and they him. And while he'd weathered the Depression and had buried himself in his surfing world, there was no escaping the dark clouds of war looming on the horizon. His island paradise was soon to become a focal point of the war in the Pacific.

13

Bradley left again within days of arriving home with his news. He told Catherine he had to fly to Washington DC to talk to his new boss and find out what arrangements needed to be made about their housing. He assured her the whole move would be simple. They could put their Hawaiian furniture into storage and take just their personal things and then she'd have the fun of redecorating their new home.

When Catherine had murmured that it seemed to be an expensive way of doing things, Bradley had airily informed her that one could rent whole furniture settings for a house, an apartment or even just a room right down to pictures and plants. Catherine was horrified. It seemed so impersonal. But Bradley explained that it was a very practical solution, especially if they were only to be there for a short tour of duty.

After Bradley left, Catherine found the walls were closing in on her. She paced, counting the steps from the lanai to the front door. She drew deep breaths. But nothing, nothing, could take away the pain, or change the facts – she was leaving the Islands. Leaving her friends, Kiann'e, Lester, Aunty Lani and PJ.

Why had Bradley made this decision without discussing it with her? Had someone said something to him about her spending time with PJ? But Catherine knew this was nonsense. Bradley had made the decision and assumed that she'd just go along with it. He was so dictatorial. Deep down she'd always known that this was so. Bradley made the decisions. He was always in charge and while he would explain what he planned to do, he never really asked her opinion. Consulting her was more a gesture of polite protocol after he'd made up his mind.

She'd never argued with his intentions. He presented them in such a way that it would appear churlish to disagree. Or ill informed or silly. She'd been happy enough just going along because somewhere in her head she'd been told, or assumed, that she was very lucky to have a man who did everything for her, made all the decisions and ran their lives smoothly and efficiently. Why on earth would she complain? But the more she thought about her marriage to Bradley the more she felt as though she was suffocating.

The first day she stayed alone, telling Lester she didn't feel well. Kiann'e was too busy to go swimming. The second morning Catherine got up early and drove down to Mrs Hing's for a just-baked custard malasada.

'You're up early. You're my first customer of the day, you bring me luck. I put in an extra one for your husband, he like guava one – no charge,' said Mrs Hing.

Catherine thanked her and walked across to the boat harbour to sit and eat the warm custard-filled donut-like confection. The sun was just up and the water was mirror-smooth, reflecting the quietly nodding boats. Everything looked so sparkling. She ate both malasadas and walked back to the car feeling the first warmth of the sun, the slight breeze faintly rustling the palm fronds. She wondered what the surf was like this morning.

This was how she liked to start each day. Moments of peace and calm, the knowledge she was in a beautiful and interesting place with friends and where she still had much to explore and learn. At the end of the day there were the stunning sunsets and the welcoming of another balmy tropical night. How could she leave this?

She thought that Washington DC would have no redeeming features despite the points of interest Bradley had described. Other than *Heatherbrae*, no place could touch her soul like the Islands. How could she leave this place and live in dour, unfriendly Washington? She'd heard navy people talk about it and she knew that a tour of duty there would be a penance for her no matter how prestigious the job was for Bradley.

The Base was quiet, no-one around and returning to the apartment, she felt smothered again. She had to get out into the air, be at the beach, get into the water, ride her board and feel the power of the wave taking her away, away . . . Catherine ran from the apartment, slamming the door.

How could this be happening? She drove in a daze. A local man waved her on, giving her right of way with a smile. Everything was so familiar, so warm, from the sunshine to the friendly people.

Catherine arrived at PJ's house and knew at once he wasn't there as 'Woody', his old panel van, was gone. There was no-one in the house to tell her which beach he'd gone to. It was often like that. Word somehow got around when the waves were up and at a remote and empty beach surfers would suddenly materialise. PJ would be one of them. She collected one of the boards that she'd used before, put it in her car and drove to find him.

It took her some time. She spotted Woody among several cars at the side of the road where there was a track through a pineapple plantation to the beach. She'd been to the spot once before with PJ. The workers in the fields had taken no notice of the bare-chested men carrying surfboards as they hopped and ran through the field dotted with kiave thorns. As the track wound through the opia trees which served as a windbreak at the edge of the field, Catherine could hear the thudding of the waves. There was a small sand dune and she scurried down it and saw the surfers' gear under the shade of a pandanus tree. She found Damien's small airline bag he used for towels, zinc cream, board wax and beside it lay PJ's towel, shoes and a shirt.

The waves were pretty big, the break quite a distance away and there looked to be a shallow sandbar which dissipated the waves as they ran onto the beach. On the right point, much further out and beyond her comfort zone, she saw two board riders tackling a decent-sized tube.

Catherine pulled on a T-shirt, took her board to the water, slid onto it and began paddling. When she reached the waves, they looked bigger than they did from the shore, but she did as PJ had taught her and waited and watched before choosing the right wave which gave her a short but exciting ride.

There were two surfers in the line up near her and she could tell they were watching her. She caught two more waves and then suddenly PJ was skimming towards her on his board.

'Hi. Howzit?'

'I couldn't stand being cooped up a moment longer.'

'Yep, know that feeling. You okay? We're going in for something to eat.'

'Thanks, maybe.' Her two malasadas were a long time ago.

As they waited for Damien and the others to come in, PJ looked at her and leant over and rubbed her back and shoulders with his towel.

'You're shivering. The sun'll warm you up in a minute.'

'I don't think I'll ever feel warm again,' she said.

Smiling, he wrapped his damp towel and his arm around her.

'Oh, PJ.' She buried her head in his shoulder and started to sob.

'Hey, hey, what's this? What's up?' He tilted her chin and looked at her stricken face.

'I'm leaving. Bradley's been transferred to the Pentagon. I can't go, I just can't.' The sobs came thick and fast.

PJ held her shaking shoulders.

Finally Catherine lifted her head. 'What will I do?'

PJ spoke gently. 'What do you want to do?'

She stared into his blue eyes. 'I don't want to go. I can't live in boring Washington DC! I can't leave all this.'

'Then you've decided, haven't you.' It was a statement.

'How can I? I mean, leave Bradley . . .' Now she said the words, the realisation of what she was thinking, feeling, saying, was out in the open.

PJ let her go. 'Catherine, it's your life. It's your choice.'

'It's such a hard decision,' she said miserably.

'If you ask me, I think you've made your decision.'

He began to towel his hair. 'Damien and Split are coming. Do you want to talk about this in front of them? Do you want to go back in the water?'

'No. What are you doing now? Can I talk about this with you? What will happen to us and the fun we've had?'

'Nothing need happen. It'll sort itself out. Right now I have to finish a board for Split.' He smiled warmly at her and said softly, 'I'll see you later, Catherine.'

'Hey, Catherine!' called Damien.

'Hi. Can't stay, see you guys later.' She nodded at the other surfers.

'I'll take your board back if you want,' offered PJ.

'Thanks.' Catherine bolted.

She drove back to the apartment and wondered what to do next. She didn't want to make an irrevocable decision . . . but she knew that she didn't want to make a life with Bradley in Washington DC. She didn't want to discuss it. She was even reluctant to talk to Mollie. Normally she'd have talked to her parents and best friend and, here, her Hawaiian 'family', including Lester, about a problem, but maybe they'd tell her to stay with her husband.

She had to get things straight in her mind. Perhaps if she and Bradley hadn't been posted to Hawaii first, if she hadn't been utterly beguiled by the Islands and formed such strong friendships, she might have settled more easily into the life of being a naval wife. But Catherine kept trying to imagine her life with Bradley in Washington, or in any other post, and slowly acknowledged that, no matter where they might live, nothing would change in their relationship.

She could hear her father's calm rational questions and comments. Yes, she'd been swept away by Bradley. He was handsome and utterly charming. Moreover, she'd liked the sound of an exotic life of travel and new experiences he'd offered her. And, yes, Hawaii was seductive. And, yes, the promise of living in such a place had given her relationship with Bradley an added dimension of romance and allure. All this was true she acknowledged, but there was also a downside.

Bradley ran Catherine's life. Set the parameters. He

wanted her to be a mature, sensible adult. But I'm not ready to be a sedate, sensible lady, she told herself. I want to do exciting things and be with interesting people. I want to get involved with rallies, surfing, take photos and write articles.

The arguments within her head and heart raged backwards and forwards. What to do next? What would she say to Bradley? Could she bear to face him? Would he listen to her? No, no, she'd never won an argument with Bradley. He would talk her out of this madness, this rashness, make her feel childish and foolish and she'd give in and then they'd go on and nothing would change. And she would feel so unhappy. And then it would be too late. She was sliding, sliding towards becoming like Julia Bensen, like her in-laws, Angela and Deidre, conforming, being an appendage and not a person. For a moment she remembered Aunt Meredith and wildly thought of calling her. But what was the point? It would be like calling Rob back home. Neither could make the decision for her, only point out the pros and cons and she'd already thought of them.

She decided to take a drive around Oahu. So many places held an attachment and a memory, others were places yet to visit and spend time. And she'd only scratched the surface. There were the other islands. She'd seen so little of Kauai and Maui, had yet to go to the Big Island, Lanai and Molokai. Kiann'e had talked about visiting the other smaller islands, even the mysterious island of Niihau, and now Catherine wondered if she would ever see them.

The sun was sinking when she found herself driving along the familiar road which led to Aunty Lani's and Uncle Henry's house. Catherine had not intended stopping until Uncle Henry appeared at the side of the road leading two small goats. He recognised her and waved and Catherine pulled over.

'You're coming to see us, how nice. How are you, Catherine?'

'Not bad, Uncle Henry. Are they your goats?'

'New keikis – their momma died so Lani and me got two new kids!'

'You've got a bit of a walk to the house, do you want a ride?' Catherine got out of the car.

'That'd be good. They're not so strong 'cause they're mighty hungry. Lani went to the store to get formula and bottles.'

'Oh, they're so little.' Catherine took the small soft leggy bundle that Henry handed her. 'Let's put them in the back seat and you sit between them, Uncle.'

Catherine and Uncle Henry carried the kids into the house and they settled themselves in the kitchen where Aunty Lani had set a padded box ready for the new arrivals. Catherine stroked the small creature on her lap. She studied the wet dark nose, the pale pink skin beneath the fuzz of silky hair, the fine eyelashes, the slim fragile legs and tiny hooves. 'How sweet they are. What's going to happen to them?'

'Oh, they'll hang around the place then we'll put them out in a field. If they eat Aunty's flowers they'll be in the imu, wiki wiki.'

'Oh no!'

'Just foolin',' laughed Uncle. 'You watch, Lani'll have these in bed with us if I'm not careful.'

'You be careful, Henry, or you'll be the one in the doghouse. Here we go . . . Catherine! Lovely to see you.' Lani gave Catherine a quick kiss and dumped the brown paper bag from the store on the bench. 'So you've been roped in to kid-sit.'

'Just happened to be passing, Aunty.'

'Just happened? Way out here? Well, that's handy. Here, let me fix these bottles and you can feed that little kid.'

361

Catherine sat in the sunshine on the back patio looking across the garden to the mountains with the sleeping kid on her lap. Behind her she could hear the surf breaking over the reef.

'They can sleep in that box in the kitchen,' said Aunty Lani in a resigned voice. 'This'll be like having two new babies.' She smiled at Catherine, stroking the sleeping kid. 'You look very maternal. You thinking of starting a family soon?'

Catherine's involuntary jerk startled the kid awake. 'No. Not at all!'

Aunty Lani gave her a penetrating look. 'You don't want children?'

'Not yet. Not . . .' Tears sprang to her eyes and she turned her head away.

'I'm sorry, Catherine, it's not my place to pry.' Aunty Lani busied herself.

'Things are in a bit of a mess . . . I just don't know what to do,' whispered Catherine.

Aunty Lani went to her and gently laid her hand on top of Catherine's head. 'Sleep on it. If you're having problems, or don't know what to do, rest awhile and let your mind clear. You'll see things differently in the morning. And, dear girl, only you can make whatever decision it is. Only you.'

Uncle Henry joined them from the garden. 'I think I've put together a fair ol' corral out there for those babies. Want to have a look?'

'Sure. I was just going to suggest that Catherine stay the night with us. Babysit that youngster. You up for a couple of night feeds, Catherine?'

'Oh, I . . . hadn't expected to stay . . . but if you need me . . .'

'We certainly do.' Aunty Lani bustled Uncle Henry inside with a look he recognised as 'don't say anything'.

'It's just us around tonight for a change, all the children are with friends and their cousins. If your husband is still away you can stop here, no-one will worry about you, will they? Be good to have time here, Catherine. It's a special place out here, a cradle between the mountains and the sea.' Aunty Lani sighed. 'We enjoy it while we can. If we're forced to move from here the magic will disappear under some sort of development. You rest here. You'll see things more clearly after a night in the shadow of the mountain. Take a walk mauka. Put your back to the sea,' she said softly.

Catherine helped Uncle Henry pick some vegetables, lock up the chickens and make up a batch of milk for the goats to see them through the night. Aunty Lani sang as she cooked. The long shadows reached down to the simple house as the day faded. Catherine felt calmer, peaceful. Except for the thump of the surf this reminded her of being home at *Heatherbrae* . . . safe, secure and loved.

She felt like a spoiled daughter. Aunty Lani insisted she take second helpings and Uncle Henry wanted to hear all about her father's property and her horse, Parker.

After dinner Aunty Lani sat in a rocking chair under a bright lamp to do her quilting. Uncle Henry sat outside in the dark smoking a cigarette and watching the moon rise.

'It's so clear. Maybe I'll take a short walk,' said Catherine.

'Here, walk with my torch. Just in case,' said Uncle Henry. 'There's nothing to be afraid of out there. But looking at the stars sometimes you don't watch where you put your feet,' he laughed. 'Head in the clouds, feet down a puka.'

Catherine circled the house, following narrow, well-trodden tracks behind it, until she came to the small stream that was fed from the springs in the hills. She sat down and looked at the water bubbling over rocks and imagined that when the rain washed down from the misty peaks and all the waterfalls were running, this stream probably tripled in size.

She knew that all her friends would be busy. PJ would be in his house with friends and visitors – there was always a surfer passing through from Australia or the mainland. Kiann'e would be dancing and knowing that her husband was proud of what she did. Eleanor would be graciously greeting her guests and Abel John would be at home with his family around him. Would they miss her? Would they think about her when she was gone? And Bradley? Was he thinking of her, now wrapped up in his career and his plans for Washington?

As Catherine sat there, hugging her knees, across the stream she thought she heard a rustle and she straightened up, reaching for the torch. But before she turned it on she hesitated. What was that in the trees? Was it mist, moonlight suddenly shining through tree branches, a stray white animal?

For a moment she thought she saw the figure of a woman with long white hair wearing a shimmering dress, but she was transparent because Catherine could see the shapes of the dark trees through her. The image hovered and swayed and Catherine suddenly smelled a powerful perfume, richly sweet, that she thought was familiar. She closed her eyes and inhaled deeply. When she opened them, the apparition and the rustle were gone, but just a faint trace of the perfume lingered.

Catherine didn't feel afraid. She got up and turned the torch on and followed its wavering beam back to the house. Strangely she felt comforted, calm and slightly sad, knowing the moment for indecision had passed.

During the night Catherine fed the kids and put them back in the padded box Aunty Lani had made, then she curled back under her cotton coverlet. Out of the window she saw the droop of silver-frosted palm fronds and heard the distant cry of a night bird. She felt so grateful to the Hawaiian couple who had taken her under their wing and treated her as family. As Catherine drifted to sleep she knew Hawaii was her second home. She would be all right here. And on the fringes of sleep came the knowledge that she and Bradley would never make a home together, even if they were married for forty years.

Aunty Lani and Uncle Henry were more than happy for Catherine to stay with them, especially as they sensed that she was unhappy about something.

'Please, Catherine, you know that you're always welcome here,' said Aunty. Catherine thanked them both for their kindness, but said that the night had cleared her head and she knew what she had to do.

Bradley was due back any day. He had said that he would call and let her know when exactly. So Catherine hung around the apartment and waited for his call, keeping herself busy by giving the place a thorough spring-clean. But when he rang she was hot and dishevelled and still not sure what to say. Every time she thought about the situation she had to put it to one side. How could she explain it to Bradley? She just had a growing knowledge this was not the life she wanted but how did she say this without it seeming rash, sudden, or irrational?

'Hello?'

'Catherine, it's me. I'm back.'

'Oh, hi. Back? You mean, back in the Islands?'

'Where else? I'm in the office. I got a ride back on a military aircraft. Didn't seem much point dragging you out to meet me at the airforce base at Hickham. I've got a few hours work to catch up on. How're you?'

Catherine drew a deep breath. 'Bradley . . . I'm . . . I've been thinking a lot and I'm sorry, I've come to a decision. About us . . .'

'What on earth are you talking about? What do you mean, about us? For goodness sake, Catherine, what's going on?'

'Bradley, this isn't easy. And this isn't sudden. It's been creeping up on me . . . I just can't stay with you. It's not fair to you, I'm just not cut out to be the wife you want . . .'

'Catherine! For God's sake! What is this rubbish? What are you saying, can't stay with me? Look, I'll be there as soon as I can. I'll borrow a car, something.'

'I'm sorry, Bradley.'

'Just stay there!' He was almost shouting.

Catherine tried to tidy herself. She thought she should change her clothes but she also thought for once she didn't want to look neat, pretty and well groomed as Bradley expected his wife to be. She tried to think of different scenarios about what to say and how to explain her feelings, but discarded them. She could only speak from her heart and hope that he would understand.

She sat on the balcony watching Pearl Harbor. Was it a failure on her part that she couldn't be like Julia Bensen and the other wives, who kept the home fires burning, were loyal and faithful and devoted their lives to their husbands' careers? What would they think and say once the word got around? Should she speak to Mrs Goodwin? Catherine quickly discarded that idea.

The front door opened and slammed shut. Bradley walked through the apartment and stood at the door behind her.

'What the hell is going on?'

Catherine turned around slowly and her heart twisted a little to see him standing there in his uniform, so tall and handsome. But his face was red and angry.

'I can't go with you to Washington. I can't go anywhere and lead the kind of life you expect me to. I'm suffocating, Bradley. It's not your fault . . .' she burst out.

'No, it certainly is not. Catherine . . .' He walked towards her but did not reach out to her. But his voice softened, sounding bewildered. 'This is crazy. You need to see a doctor or someone. What's brought this on? What've I done?'

'You haven't done anything, Bradley. It's just your life, your career. I see that now. And I know it's not for me.'

'Nonsense. You knew exactly what you were getting into – you *wanted* this! What's got into you? Don't you love me?'

She paused. 'I thought I did. You've been so good to me . . . I feel awful, I'm letting you down. But, Bradley, I'm terribly unhappy, I know it's not going to get better, you can't fix this. I think we should finish now, rather than drag it out . . .'

'Catherine. I love you. You're my wife. This is ridiculous. I go away for a few days and you decide to end our marriage? You're mad!'

'It's been coming for a while. You know I've never fitted in with the others, with your way of life.'

'You might have said something, given me some clue that you felt like this. Marriage is a partnership, Catherine,' he said bitterly.

'I did say things and you treated me like a child.'

'Look at how you're behaving!'

'Bradley, what do you want me to do? Call your parents, speak to Mrs Goodwin, pretend I've got some illness and disappear?'

'Don't you dare mention any of this to anyone. You just come to your senses and get on with things. We'll work this out. I have to go back to Washington. I've already found us a nice place to live. Why don't you go home for a holiday? Have you spoken to your parents?'

When she shook her head, he took this as a good sign

and became placatory. 'You need a holiday. Tell me, what do you want to do?'

'I don't want to lead you on. I've thought hard about this. We're just not right for each other. We made a mad, terrible mistake.'

'I didn't make a mistake. I thought I'd found a wife who'd make me happy. Whom I'd make happy. We've been married for such a short time. Give our marriage a chance. I thought you were stronger than this, Catherine.'

'I am. It's taking a lot of strength to do this.' She turned her head away. 'A lot of things have shown me that we aren't meant to be together. I'm sorry, Bradley. Sorry and sad.'

He paced around the apartment, shaking his head and wiping a hand over his eyes. 'I am not going to lower myself to ask if there's someone else. I refuse to believe there could be. If you want to go and stay with those Hawaiian people, then do so. We'll talk about this later. I have to get the car back.' He looked at her with a frown. 'You are causing a lot of problems, Catherine. I hope you'll have come to your senses by the time I get back. I'm turning around and going straight back to Washington, which is a good thing because I don't care for your company right now.' He strode from the apartment and the door banged behind him.

Catherine let out her breath and spoke to the empty apartment. 'You don't want to even try to understand, to discuss this. I'm a naughty girl and I'll be punished and then we'll go on as though nothing happened, because then I'll be a good little wife.'

Should she call her parents? They would likely advise her to come home and think things over, or stay and go to Washington, persevere and give her marriage a chance. But now she knew, even more firmly than before, that while leaving was hard, it was the only thing for her to do.

What to do now? She tried to imagine how Bradley must be feeling. He'd had no warning, no time to prepare for this. She had to let him save face. He could say she was working over on Kauai until he had everything set up in Washington, though she supposed other wives would have gone with their husbands to help. But everyone knew that Bradley liked to organise everything so it wouldn't seem too unusual for her to remain in the Islands. She sat on the lanai a little while, then slowly she tidied away her coffee cup. She was about to go out when the phone rang. She knew it was Bradley.

'Catherine. This is ridiculous. Please collect me as usual and we'll go out to dinner and discuss how we can solve this.'

Short of Bradley quitting his career and changing his personality she couldn't think of a way of solving things, but all she said was, 'I owe you that. I know it's a shock. I think that this has been building up for months.'

'Well, you might have given me some inkling! I thought we were perfectly happy.' Bradley sounded confused.

'You were happy. But it's taken me a while to work out why I feel the way I do.'

'I suppose it's those friends of yours. I tell you, Catherine, don't consider staying here without me for one moment. The navy will take over the apartment and I will not have my wife wandering around without me.'

'I thought we were going to discuss things. That's the trouble, Bradley, you just tell me what to do. You never ask what I might want to do.'

'I have been exceedingly generous and tolerant of your wishes . . . the photo job, gallivanting around with those local people, neglecting your duties, doing exactly what you want.'

Catherine sighed. 'I suppose you're right. I guess I wasn't prepared to conform, to be like all those other women.'

'My mother told me this would happen – it's a cultural thing.'

'What? You told me you loathed all those suburban, superficial, stick-in-the-mud women you'd grown up with, went through college with. You liked the fact I was different,' snapped Catherine.

'Well, you've certainly changed. You're rebellious, quite non-conformist. It's embarrassing.'

'This isn't getting us anywhere. Why don't we leave dinner tonight. Let's meet tomorrow. I'll ask Kiann'e if I can stay with her tonight and you can stay here. Let's sleep on things,' said Catherine in a tired voice.

'Will that change your mind?'

'No. It won't.'

'So there's nothing to discuss. Your mind is made up.'

Catherine nodded at the phone and wondered, aren't you going to fight for me? Tell me you love me more than life itself, can't be without me? . . . then stifled the thought. She didn't want that from Bradley. It would only make this all the more difficult. 'Bradley, there's a lot to discuss. I really want you to understand how I feel.'

'You knew what you were getting into when you married me.'

'No, I didn't! It all sounded exotic and romantic and an adventure. Now sometimes I feel like I'm in boarding school! Mrs Goodwin the headmistress, prefects around . . . I'm always being watched, everyone knows everybody else's business. I go to the Wives' Club meetings feeling like I haven't done my homework and I'm going to be punished, kept in after class.'

'Don't be ridiculous. Perhaps you haven't been pulling your weight like the other women. Perhaps you were too busy chasing around the Islands for that newspaper.'

'Bradley! It's a job! Only a small, part-time one, but it gives me a sense of fulfillment, gives me a life of my own.'

'We don't need the money and you have a job – my wife. My career is your career.'

'For God's sake, it's not the nineteen-fifties, it's the seventies. Women's roles are changing.' Though not in the navy and not quickly enough, Catherine thought to herself.

'Very well, Catherine. I'll speak to you tomorrow. I will, of course, have to discuss this with Commander Goodwin.'

'Whatever you think best, though frankly I don't see it's any of his business at this stage. He will, of course, talk to Connie Goodwin and then everyone on Base will know. Is that what you want?'

'Well, I guess that can't be helped. And you do realise, there will be no sympathy or help for you. You go down this path and you're on your own, Catherine.'

'I'll speak to you tomorrow, Bradley. All I can say is I am so, so sorry. I loved you, I thought my life would be different. Hawaii is beautiful and being a naval wife isn't always going to be as nice as here. This makes me realise that if I can't be happy here as an adjunct to your career I certainly won't be happy doing it anywhere else.'

'You should just go back to your country town, Catherine. That's where you really belong.' He hung up the phone.

'Kiann'e? It's Catherine. Yes, yes, he's back. But there's a problem. I need to get away from Bradley for a while. I was wondering if I could come over and stay with you tonight?'

'Of course. Oh dear. I'm sorry. Anything Willi and I can do, just shout. Do you want to come over now?'

'I'll come over later this afternoon if that's all right.'

'Come when you want, stay as long as you want. If you want to talk, or not, that's fine too.'

An hour later Catherine had packed her clothes and a few favourite treasures, her photographs, camera and notebooks, into two suitcases. She lugged them downstairs, making sure that no-one was around, put them into the car and drove off. She wanted to see PJ and Lester before going to Kiann'e's.

PJ was busy planing a board. When he realised that Catherine was standing watching him he turned it off, pulled the handkerchief from over his mouth and looked at her for a moment before asking,

'How are things?'

Catherine shrugged. 'Hard. I've told Bradley that I'm leaving him. He didn't have a clue about how I was feeling. I suppose I should have said something earlier. But he doesn't understand how smothered my life is . . . and will continue to be if I stay with him and be a navy wife.'

'Mmm. So what are you going to do?'

'A bit unsure. I'm trying to talk to him. He's not being very understanding. Defensive, which is not surprising. For the moment I told him I'd go and stay with Kiann'e . . .'

PJ nodded. 'Good idea. You do what you think best. Do what you want to do, Catherine.' He ran his hands over the board he was working on.

Do what you want to do. Was that what she wanted? That was the crux of the issue – her freedom.

'I suppose there have always been expectations for me. That I'd get married. Be someone's wife. I had a few months in London with a bunch of girlfriends and then I met Bradley. But since being here, knowing you lot, sharing things, trying new things, it's made me realise how sheltered my life has been.'

'You don't have to do what other people say. You can find your own way and not lean on, or be led, by others,' said PJ. 'You'll know when you've found your place in the world. Standing on your own two feet . . . that's what it's all about, isn't it?'

'Yes. I suppose so. Scary though.'

He smiled at her. 'You're stronger than you think. And you deserve more. I'm not encouraging you or influencing you, just telling it like it is. But if you're around, hey, I'm here.'

'I know. I feel I've got a bit out of practice making my own decisions, but I feel good that I can start doing that now.'

She left PJ and drove over to see Lester.

'To what do I owe the pleasure of an afternoon visit? I just had a nap. Glass of OJ?'

'How about we go out for afternoon tea, Lester? Tea and cake or sandwiches at the Moana.'

His face lit up. 'I'd like that. You're a good buddy, Catherine.'

Impulsively Catherine hugged him. 'I love yarning with you, Lester. C'mon, a trade, you tell me some more stories of the old days around Waikiki and I'll treat us.'

'You gotta deal, sweetie.'

Lester had swept her along with his stories of the Waikiki beach boys, the early days of tourism, the growing popularity of surfing and the characters who had washed ashore on the Islands. There was one uncomfortable, or odd, moment when he asked about her husband coming back from sea and Catherine answered, 'Bradley just arrived back. But he's leaving for Washington in a few days – a desk job at the Pentagon.'

Lester looked stricken. 'So you'll be off then.' He shook his head. 'Desk job. On the mainland. Not my cup of tea.'

'Nor mine,' said Catherine. 'I don't want to leave Hawaii.'

Lester gazed across the beach and said thoughtfully, 'Things creep up on you. Before you know it you've made a decision that sets the path for the rest of your life. You gotta be pretty sure it's where you want to go. On the other hand, you don't always know what it is you want or where to go either.'

Catherine smiled wryly. 'That's not very helpful, Lester.'

'You askin' me? Askin' my advice?' He shook his head emphatically. 'Don't. I made too many damn mistakes.'

Catherine was feeling a lot better when she reached Kiann'e's house later that afternoon. Kiann'e was watching for her and came straight out when Catherine pulled up and gave her a big hug.

'Hi. Come inside. Those are your bags? Seems that you've packed more than for one night. It's lucky I don't have a show this evening and Willi is working late. We can do whatever we want.'

Catherine grabbed her suitcases and she and Kiann'e carried them into the house. 'Do you feel like that? That you can do whatever you want? I mean, how do you and Willi work things out?' Catherine asked.

Kiann'e laughed. 'He's so easygoing. I never interfere or ask much about his work . . . I mean, industrial engineering isn't my thing. And he has to put up with all my family and my mother's campaigning. He wasn't born in the Islands so he doesn't feel strongly about the issues as we do, but if I'm passionate about something he goes along with that. He's very good natured. Well, you'd have to be to put up with a mother-in-law like Beatrice, wouldn't you?'

'I have hardly any contact with my mother-in-law and we have nothing in common. She's always charming, over-the-top complimentary and so on, but I feel that she

374

really doesn't think that I do enough to further Bradley's career. I just don't fit in.'

'To her ambitions or to Bradley's?' asked Kiann'e.

'Seems to be one and the same. Honestly, Kiann'e, how could I have thought Bradley and I were on the same wavelength . . .' Catherine's voice trailed off.

'Ah. Is that the problem? Are you going to put space between you two?'

Catherine sank onto the sofa. 'I thought I knew him . . . The sad part is, he thinks that everything is fine and dandy. He can't see a problem when his dictatorial attitude has become a huge issue for me. And I can't see any way to change things.'

'It can take a while to see what a person's really like, what their priorities and values are because, let's face it, in the beginning you're attracted to all the wrong things. Well, the surface things. You had a romantic whirlwind courtship and you two didn't do the hard yards.'

'But we talked about things. Bradley can be so charming. But he was looking at me as being part of his life and doing what he wanted and I wanted to share things but still have some life of my own. It's the freedom to find out more about myself and know what I'm capable of doing,' said Catherine sounding exasperated. 'Being with Bradley, I feel my life is over and the chance to do all these things has gone.'

'You don't have to stop growing, exploring, experimenting because you're married,' said Kiann'e. 'It's who you're married to that makes that still possible. Do you think I could be looking at the road my mother and a lot of loyal Hawaiians want me to travel if Willi didn't think it was a good thing? He knows I might end up in politics, or working as a lobbyist, or wherever I'm needed for my people. He's not Hawaiian but he understands how important my culture is to me.'

Catherine nodded. 'Can't two people make a life together without one having to take the back seat? It's not fair.'

Kiann'e, seeing her friend was near tears, touched Catherine's hand. 'That's what you have to decide together. Willi has a successful business. He quietly goes along doing his thing and because people see and know me and my family here, they don't realise he has a very full and interesting life outside of our life together. But while we have different interests, we respect what each other's doing.'

'That's the difference, then,' said Catherine sadly.

'At least you see that now.' When Catherine nodded, Kiann'e said, 'This is a big step, a hard one. How have you left things with Bradley?'

'I said I'd talk to him tomorrow. I tried to make him understand on the phone and we agreed to sleep on things. He's always so good at persuading me his way is best. I can never win an argument with him.'

'But you've decided in your heart that this isn't going to work,' Kiann'e said sympathetically and Catherine nodded again. 'You're afraid he'll talk you out of it?'

'Am I being horrible? I'm a terrible person.' Catherine started to cry.

'You didn't deliberately want this to happen. But the marriage isn't what you thought it would be and frankly, you guys didn't have enough time to find out how compatible you were. If you are sure, totally sure, that the marriage can't work then a clean break now is far better, I think, than letting things drag on.'

'The sad thing is, I can't see any way we can try to make it work. His career is the most important issue to him and he won't give that up for me. And why should he? He says I knew what he did when we got married. But, well, it sounded different from how it turned out.'

'And people don't change their personality easily,

either,' said Kiann'e. 'Let's have dinner. And if you are really sure, Bradley won't be able to talk you out of doing what you think is best. For both of you.'

Kiann'e let Catherine talk and work through her thoughts and feelings aloud, and then as they were getting ready for bed, she asked, 'Have you thought through the next step? What you'll do? Go home?'

'This is all so sudden, I haven't spoken to my parents. Anyway, I don't want to go home. I want to stay in the Islands. I was thinking of going to Kauai. Maybe stay with Eleanor, if she can give me a cheap rate, even do some work for her.'

'You can stay with my mother,' said Kiann'e.

'Thanks. I just need a bit of space. Be on my own a bit.'

'Try to sleep. You've looked at this situation every which way and you keep coming back to the same result. See what transpires tomorrow.' Kiann'e hugged Catherine.

To her surprise, Catherine slept soundly. Perhaps talking with Kiann'e helped. At breakfast time she phoned Bradley.

'Bradley? When do you want to meet?'

His voice was cool. 'Later. I have things to do this morning. I'll meet you for coffee at three p.m. At the Plantation House on Kamehameha Drive.'

There was no discussion. He'd chosen a large rambling restaurant that was a tourist showcase of how a plantation once looked. There were shops, a little museum, rides, a formal reception area for weddings, a patio restaurant and coffee house. She'd been there once for a function with the Wives' Club and guessed that he'd chosen the out-of-the-way place because it would be unlikely anyone they knew would see them.

Catherine thanked Kiann'e who told her she was welcome to stay as long as she wanted.

Before she met Bradley she thought she would go back to their apartment to pick up a couple of things that, in her haste to leave, she had forgotten. She drove into the Base and was glad that neither Julia Bensen nor any of their other neighbours were around. But when she tried her key in the door it wouldn't open. Catherine jiggled and then to her shock realised it was a new lock. Bradley had changed the lock on the door! She was stunned, angry and then felt like laughing. How childish.

When she got to the coffee house Bradley was sitting in a far corner. The restaurant was empty save for an older couple who looked like tourists. The lunch crowd had gone. He half rose out of his seat as she pulled out a chair and sat down. The waitress handed them a menu but Bradley waved her away. 'Just bring us coffee, thanks.'

'Could I have a juice, please? Pineapple is fine,' said Catherine as the waitress moved away.

They stared at each other.

'Why did you change the lock?' said Catherine.

'There's no reason for you to be there. You've taken your things and moved out. I'll arrange for whatever else you want out of the apartment to be sent to Kiann'e's.'

'I thought we were here to discuss things.'

'You've obviously made up your mind,' he said bitterly.

'I guess I have. It's not how I wanted things to work out.'

'I'm very disappointed in you, Catherine. This is all very difficult for me. Embarrassing. Though I don't imagine people will be too surprised.'

'Oh? What people? Though I can guess,' she sighed.

'We could talk to the padre, to see if you will change your mind, but you seem very determined,' he said.

'Do you see a solution?' Catherine asked.

'Other than your joining me in Washington and starting afresh and agreeing to do the right thing?' he countered.

'That's not exactly an option. Nor meeting halfway,' said Catherine. 'It's your way or nothing, Bradley. Can't you see that?'

It was a repeat of the previous conversations they'd had. Bradley remained stony-faced, cold-voiced and unmoved, refusing to accept, understand or acknowledge her point of view.

'Just tell me this,' he finally asked, a slight crack in his voice for the first time. 'Is it me? Was there anything wrong with how I treated you? Was I a bad husband, a bad lover?'

Catherine didn't want to hurt Bradley's feelings any more than she had. She shook her head. 'No, Bradley, you were a perfect husband. For someone else. Not me. We made a mistake,' she said softly.

'I didn't make a mistake. I thought we'd be very happy. You will have to live with the consequences of this . . . madness,' he finished. He pushed his coffee cup to one side.

'So what happens now?' asked Catherine. Then caught herself. She was letting Bradley make the decisions again. 'I plan to go to Kauai for a while.'

'There is the question of money. And the car. I've made arrangements to sell the car to someone in my office. So I'd appreciate your leaving the car in the parking spot and giving the keys to the guard at the gate. I'll leave some money in our joint account to tide you over for a few weeks. If you want your freedom, Catherine, you'll have to support yourself.'

'I guess I can buy a secondhand car,' she said, determined to show Bradley that she could look after herself.

Bradley stood up. 'I'm going back to the mainland tomorrow or the next day. I will break this news to my parents.'

'Do you want me to speak to them?'

'Of course not. They're no longer your family, Catherine.'

'You make it sound like we're divorced.'

'Isn't that what you want?'

'I hadn't thought it through,' said Catherine, realising she hadn't looked that far ahead.

'Seems to me you've done a lot of thinking and this is the result.' Bradley dropped some money on the table.

So it's my fault, Catherine thought to herself. Bradley can be virtuous, the injured one. As he stood up Catherine felt a moment of panic – so was this really the end of her marriage, was this how she would remember him, striding out of a dark empty coffee shop? 'Bradley . . . I don't know what to say . . .' Tears sprang to her eyes.

'You've said enough. We both have. Goodbye, Catherine.' He turned and walked out the door. He did not look back and she didn't follow him. She slumped in her seat as the waitress picked up the money and wiped the table.

'Can I get you something?'

Catherine shook her head and reached for the glass of water. 'No. Thank you.'

She didn't want to see anyone, speak to anyone. She drove out to windswept Makaha and tramped along the empty stretch of beach. Sand whipped and stung her legs. The surf was choppy, no-one was around. She was on her own.

14

It was only at the beach that Catherine found a sense of tranquility during this upheaval in her life. She moved in with Kiann'e and Willi and they were considerate and left her to her own devices during the day. She asked Kiann'e if she'd mind cancelling their morning walk and swim for a little while as she wanted an early surf instead. The challenge and the beauty of being with the gold-tipped waves at sunrise gave her a feeling of equilibrium and helped her cope with her decision.

She felt very lost, especially after a phone call from Julia Bensen. Julia was quite cool and official, saying that she was calling on behalf of the Wives' Club and asking Catherine please to notify Mrs Goodwin in writing of her resignation.

Catherine felt betrayed. Bradley had made it clear

that she was not to tell any of their naval friends about their problems, but obviously he felt no need to do likewise. Now the navy wives would only hear his side of the story.

'Oh. I hadn't thought of resigning,' said Catherine, although she wouldn't miss the club activities. 'But I hope I can still see you, Julia.'

'I'm afraid that's not really possible, Catherine. We're all very shocked. Sad, too, of course.'

For me or Bradley, thought Catherine. 'I'm no longer welcome at any navy functions? I've let the side down, sort of thing?'

'Commander and Mrs Goodwin told us you were no longer part of the navy family. We assume you'll be going back to Australia. After all, Bradley has gone to Washington. Just as well you didn't have any kids,' she added.

'And did Mrs Goodwin, or my husband, I mean, Bradley, give you a reason for our separation?' asked Catherine tartly, thinking how glad she was that the bossy woman no longer had any say in her life.

Julia hesitated. 'Er, no, not really. I mean, she speculated . . . but it's happened, so you aren't exactly a navy wife anymore. I'm really sorry, Catherine,' she said awkwardly.

Catherine could well imagine what the speculation might be. They had all closed ranks, freezing her out. 'Well, I'm sorry we can't meet for coffee, or that you might want to hear how I feel. I thought we were friends.'

'Our husbands are friends and fellow officers, that's what our friendship was based on,' said Julia.

'Well, I can't say I'm sorry not to have Mrs Goodwin running my life anymore. I hope things work out for you, Julia. Who knows, our paths might cross again,' said Catherine briskly.

'I don't see how as Jim said that there was no chance of reconciliation. But good luck with things, Catherine.'

In spite herself, Catherine had to admit that Julia's final words had sounded quite sincere, but as she slowly hung up the phone, she was stung by the rest of her comments. How could Bradley discuss something with Jim and Julia without first discussing it with her? How quickly events rolled on, thought Catherine trying to put the uncomfortable conversation out of her mind.

Later she rang Mollie but before she could say anything, Mollie was in full flight, barely pausing for breath.

'I know, I know. I tried to call you at your apartment after your mother rang me. Your parents are very upset. Shocked, I suppose, but trying to take it in and understand. As am I.'

'It wasn't working . . .' started Catherine.

'Hey. This is me. I have to say I'm not entirely surprised. I saw your face when that woman told you that Bradley was coming home. But I'm really pleased that you stood up for yourself. Yes, strike a blow, get out, quick and clean. I have to admire you. You are pretty sure about this?'

Catherine almost smiled. 'Bit late if I'm not. I just got turfed out of the Wives' Club.'

'The pigs. Well, that's one good thing. At least you'll have that old battleaxe out of your life. What did she say?'

'She handed the dirty work over to my ex-friend Julia. I'm no longer part of the navy apparently.'

'You didn't join up when you married Bradley, for heaven's sake.'

'It was beginning to feel I had. Oh, Mollie, I feel so confused now. Have I done the right thing? I just couldn't face living in a place like Washington. Suddenly I could just see how my life was going to be, how I'd be under

Bradley's thumb, how it would never change and how I'd never be able to do things I want. Am I nuts?'

'Of course not, silly. So how's Bradley taking it?'

'He's hurt, shocked, but I'm sure he has masses of support. He left straight away to go to Washington, so I guess he felt uncomfortable.'

'His ego is dented I'll bet, but it shows that when it comes to a choice between his work and you, he chooses his job. So what are you going to do?'

'He's changed the locks on the apartment because it's naval property, so I can't get in.'

'He's what! That's pretty outrageous, Cath. I think that locking you out of your place, even if it does belong to the US government, is awful and spiteful. Where are you staying?'

'I'm staying with Kiann'e. Bradley's selling the car to some guy who just arrived. But I don't want to be pushed out of the Islands and I don't want to come home either, so I'm going to go to Kauai for a bit and think things through.'

'Sounds good to me – after all, it's your decision, your life. But of course you know you can come to Sydney. Stay here, any time, as long as you want. A big city might be a nice change.'

'Thanks, Mol. But I'd rather stay here, until my money runs out, anyway. I might have to ask Vince for a raise,' she tried to joke.

Kiann'e and Willi were out so Catherine answered the front door when she heard the bell ringing insistently.

A delivery man was standing there with a huge box. 'Sign, please. Whose birthday?' asked the man.

'I'm not sure.'

But as she signed the chit she saw the parcel was addressed to her. Catherine carried the box to the kitchen, snipped the tape and lifted the lid. Inside were a dozen long-stemmed roses, each rose end wrapped in a cylinder of water. Her first thought was they must have cost a fortune. Roses weren't grown commercially in Hawaii, so these must have been shipped in from the mainland.

There was a white box inside and a card. She opened the box and found an ornate glass bottle of expensive perfume. She drew the stopper from the bottle and sniffed and wrinkled her nose. The sickly sweetness was cloying. She would never wear anything so overpowering.

Finally, she opened the card.

Dearest Catherine,
You are my wife and I love you. Come home, stop this madness. Think what we have and the life we can have together. I am willing to forgive you. I hope we can start over.
Yours,
Bradley x

If Bradley's extravagant gesture had meant to win her over, he had, yet again, not tried to understand her point of view.

'Bradley! You don't understand! You still don't!' she shouted. 'Forgive me! You expect me to crawl back to you and go on as before. Well, I won't! I can't!'

She ran into the garden and sat crying until she couldn't cry any more.

Later she threw the roses in the car and drove to Waikiki. She stopped by Mrs Hing's and put them on the counter.

'I thought you might like these, Mrs Hing.'

'Oh my heavens, oh my goodness. They're beautiful. So expensive. Why you give this away?'

'I'm allergic to roses,' said Catherine stonily.

'Oh my, oh my. Here, you take.' Mrs Hing began putting a selection of malasadas in a bag.

'That's enough, that's fine, thank you,' said Catherine and fled the little shop.

'These are good,' said Lester biting into his third malasada.

'Mrs Hing's finest,' said Catherine and managed a smile.

He finished eating, took a sip of his coffee and gave Catherine a good hard look. 'So you've told me you're going to Kauai for a bit. Now, do you want to tell me why?'

'Oh, Lester. It's sad. Hard and sad. Bradley and I have broken up.'

'Ah, are you sure? You're still deciding?'

'No,' sighed Catherine. 'He's on the mainland and he sent me roses and an expensive bottle of perfume. I didn't want them. Everything I dislike. It was such a cliché. And he wrote a card that was supposed to make me apologise and crawl back to the box of my marriage. You know, a tiny, inexpensive, thoughtful gift would have meant so much more.'

Lester nodded. 'I never seemed to have money to buy my gal costly gifts. I made her a shell necklace once. She liked that.'

'What am I going to do, Lester?'

'Go to Kauai. Take deep breaths. Get in the water. Watch the sun rise and set.'

Catherine smiled. 'Not the sort of advice I'm getting from my folks back home.'

'They love you, honey, they'd be worried. You'll be fine. You never seemed wildly happy or in love to my mind anyway.'

'Oh. Well, I suppose once you're married, settled in a routine, getting on with things . . . that's how it is, right?'

'Don't ask me, I never got married. But I never fell out of love either.' He brushed the crumbs from his shirt and changed the subject. 'You better hang onto your job at the paper. I'll miss our talks, and who's going to take me out and about for a bit of a surf?'

'PJ still has his business here. You know he'll always be around in between surfing jaunts. Kiann'e will still be by every day or so. And I'll be back. I have no plans, Lester,' she said, suddenly feeling unnerved at the prospect.

'Best way to be,' said Lester firmly.

'Come on, let's go for a drive and do some shopping.'

Catherine called in to the *Hawaii News* and after telling Vince she was spending some time in Kauai she collected extra rolls of film and a couple of reporter's notebooks.

'I'll try to find some stories for you. Thanks, Vince.'

'It's hard to get colour pieces from the outer islands. We're supposed to be a paper about all the islands, not just Oahu, so I'll look forward to being able to expand our stories. If you can't develop the films, just send them to me. Have fun.'

She drove to PJ's house, but he wasn't home. Catherine wrote a note for him, put it on the kitchen table and anchored it with a bottle of kimchee sauce.

Hi PJ, I'm heading to Kauai for a bit. Is it okay to take my surfboard with me? Or can I borrow one from your friends over there? I'll probably stay with Kiann'e's mother, Beatrice, or see if I can do a deal with the Palm Grove. I'll meet you by the Outrigger Club at 6 tomorrow. Catherine.

The following morning PJ was waiting for her.

'Hi. You obviously got my note.' She dropped her

towel on the sand and put down her board. 'I'll leave this behind if you need it.'

He nodded his head. 'Plenty of boards over there you can use.' He gave her a quizzical look. 'How come you're going to Kauai, too?'

'I don't want to be around here. There are people I'd rather not see and memories I'd rather forget. What do you mean "too"?'

'I'm going over. Couple of people coming in to the Islands I want to meet. Maybe sell some boards. Surf should start to come up soon. Why don't you stay at *Nirvana*? Plenty of room. Ginger is there with her baby.'

'Really? And Doobie? Leif and the kids?'

'I heard Doobie disappeared. Things were getting a bit heavy. He'll roll back in.'

'Oh, poor Ginger.'

He shrugged. 'You know how it is. People come, people go. He'll turn up again.'

'I do need somewhere to stay till I find my feet. I was going to talk to Eleanor.'

'Nice if you have the money.'

'I don't. I thought I could work for her. Surf in between times.'

'There'll be plenty of boards there. Leave that one here.' He gave her a steady look. 'You all right? Seems you've turned your life upside down a bit.'

'Seems so. I thought Kauai might help, be a kind of transition into my new life, whatever that is. I'll be chasing a few stories for the paper, as well,' she said, trying to keep her voice calm. She suddenly felt teary.

'Plenty "talk story" on the Garden Island. Ready to hit the water?'

She nodded, picked up her board and followed PJ.

The surf soothed her. Today the waves did not challenge her but rose soft and swollen, creamy crests that slowly unfolded in a slope before breaking apart to dribble onto the wet sand. She rode easily, sliding across the gentle waves and after an hour she coasted back in to the beach. She sat on the sand and watched the knot of surfers and further out, on his own, the unmistakable shape of PJ.

It seemed strange just to make plans on a whim. She'd got out of the habit. Bradley had always arranged everything but once she'd booked her airline ticket she felt a slight rush of confidence. Just the same, she did miss Bradley being around. This feeling surprised her, but she felt that she knew his habits and they had a system of sharing their life. Bradley was a man set in his ways. He liked routine. Perhaps she, too, needed order and purpose in her life.

'I'm going to see how Kauai works out,' she told Kiann'e. 'I could stay at *Nirvana*.'

'Sounds from what you've told me you'd have lots of company,' agreed Kiann'e. 'But you know my mother and Eleanor are there as a backup.'

Catherine rang Eleanor to break her news.

'I'm sorry to hear about your marriage. If you're absolutely sure that you're doing the right thing, then you're wise to move on and not be miserable for years. You're young, you have a whole life ahead of you. Get out and live a bit, Catherine. When are you coming over? I'll get Abel John to meet you.'

'Eleanor, that's kind of you, but really that's too much trouble. I thought I'd stay out on the north shore again.'

'With those hippie people that Abel John knows? Is that really your scene? How are you going to support yourself? What will you do for money? You know you can stay here if you like. At least come and have a meal with me.'

'Yes, I'd like to. I'm going to do a few stories for the paper. And I've got a bit of money put aside, but I was hoping that I could work for you, doing something. I don't know what.'

'Well, let me think about it. Mr Kitamura does all our photography, so I can't use you in that department, but I'll try to think of something for you.'

'Thank you, Eleanor, I'm grateful. How's the new wing progressing?' asked Catherine.

Eleanor sighed. 'Not well. I'll talk to you when I see you. Now give me your flight time and Abel John will be there.'

Seeing the tall, smiling Hawaiian striding towards her outside the little airport terminal gave Catherine a great sense of relief. She hugged him.

'Abel John, you're so kind. It's like seeing ohana again!'

'How you holding up? I hear you've split with your husband.'

'Yes. I'm feeling better about it just by being here.' She took a deep breath. There was the familiar perfume in the air, the tropical colours and warm breath of the tradewind, a sense of dropping out of a city – even casual Honolulu – into a secret oasis.

He threw her bag into the back of his old car. 'All your worldly goods, Catherine?'

'Just about. I've left most of my things with Kiann'e, so I'm travelling light, starting over. Just need a surfboard. PJ told me there'd be plenty to borrow.'

'That's for sure. I've got several at my place. So you going over to *Nirvana*?'

'I thought I might. Do you know who's there?'

'Ginger and Summer and the keikis. Leif is on the Big Island, working as a paniolo, rounding up cattle for a big ranch. A guy from South Africa was at *Nirvana* but I think he's gone to Lombok. Indonesia is the new spot to surf. And PJ is coming. Few people hanging out for his boards.'

'Sounds a bit muddled,' said Catherine unsurely. 'Might be okay for a night or two until I find somewhere more organised.'

Abel John drove out of Lihue Airport and said, 'There is another place that might suit you better. Friend of Helena's is looking for someone to take care of her little place while she goes to Europe for couple of weeks. It's not fancy, bit of a shop with a studio apartment upstairs. It's on the south shore, so no good surfing there. But it won't cost you anything. Kinda interesting little town. She has an old car and I'm sure she'd let you use that, too. Want to have a look?'

'Sure. Why not?' Catherine suddenly felt her spirits lifting. Take it as it comes. Having a place of her own if it were safe and clean would be wonderful. The thought of *Nirvana*, filled with people and not much privacy, made her feel a bit uncomfortable. Abel John turned onto Highway 50.

'How's your family, Abel John?'

He grinned. 'Beautiful. Helena and those keikis are beautiful. My big boy and I fish together now. That's a special father–son thing to do.'

As they drove out to the coast, they passed landmarks that were familiar to her: a roadside café, a particular pineapple field, a jagged rock formation on a point with a windswept tree, a white house smothered in bougainvillea surrounded by hibiscus and plumeria trees. An abandoned kombi van covered in rusting graffiti was still parked in the middle of a paddock, just as it had been the last time she'd driven by.

Abel John sensed her mood. 'Glad to be back, huh?'

'Yes. And I've only island hopped forty minutes from Honolulu. Imagine coming straight from some crowded city on the mainland to this piece of paradise.'

'Or from a farm in country Australia,' he kidded.

Catherine laughed. 'Yes. It's another world, that's for sure. But each is beautiful, special, even familiar, in its own way.'

'You know when you've done the right thing, girl,' he said softly. 'It's a big step.' He glanced at her. 'You go through another door, see what's out there.'

'It's a bit scary. But I don't want to run home to my parents just yet. Have to stand on my own two feet, right?'

'You still got ohana – big family – here. We can be calabash cousins, eh, Catherine?'

'Thanks, Abel John.'

They turned off the highway onto a dirt road by a fence buried under scarlet bougainvillea and Catherine couldn't resist a gasp of delight as they drove into a little township.

'Nice surprise uh?' said Abel John. 'Reminds me of a street down ol' Mexico way.'

'It looks sleepy,' laughed Catherine. 'But I love it.'

Drooping red and orange poincianas and hibiscus bushes screened old houses. Tall trumpet and tulip trees and a yellow acacia shaded the dusty road. Scarlet blooms of bougainvillea and creamy plumeria were sprinkled along a wooden sidewalk. Some of the shopfronts with living quarters above were shuttered and closed, long empty. There was a dark and cluttered emporium that looked as though no customer had crossed the threshold for a century. Other buildings seemed to have seen several lives in various incarnations. There was a general store with a postbox outside, a café, a movie theatre no longer in use and a Chinese temple, its peeling gold facade set back with a small courtyard in front. In the road a dog lazily scratched its hindquarters and on a balcony with lopsided green shutters sat a skinny cat. There were several cars parked along the street but no one seemed to be about, though piano music could be heard from inside a house.

As Abel John stopped behind a big gold Oldsmobile, Catherine was struck by what she instantly thought of as a patchwork house. Its multicoloured mix of bright orange shutters, turquoise door and window frames, mushroom pink wooden facade and two large bright-pink flower pots filled with geraniums on either side of the door were eye-catching even in such a colourful street. The verandah posts supporting an upstairs balcony were painted in swirling stripes like a gaudy barber's pole.

Catherine realised that it was an art gallery as, through the double glass windows, she saw bold canvases, some hanging, some on easels and others stacked against walls. A sign above the door announced it was *The Joss House.*

The door was open and Abel John ushered her inside.

Catherine looked at the paintings, which were mostly of Hawaiian subjects – big flowers, dark-eyed girls in brightly patterned pareos, colourful birds, beaches, cliffs and waterfalls.

A woman came through a bead curtain from the rear and looked to Catherine to be as colourful as the paintings. She had wild red hair, bright pink lipstick, green eyeshadow, deeply suntanned skin and wore a wildly patterned sarong. She had bare feet, lots of jewellery and a flower in her hair. As soon as she opened her mouth, Catherine realised that she was from New York.

'Abel John! This is a nice surprise. Glad to see you before I leave.' She kissed his cheek and turned to Catherine and held out her hand.

'I'm Miranda.'

'I'm Catherine. Are these your wonderful paintings?'

'Sure are. Can't find anyone else's stuff to fill the place. I'm going to Europe tomorrow, might bring back some works from there. No one round here seems to want the local colour, so to speak. Do you paint?'

'No, sorry. That's a shame about your work, it's terrific. Though I suppose local people feel they can step outside and see the real thing,' said Catherine politely.

'True. Though who's going to want to buy scenes of Venice or Florence, either? Not that we get a lot of tourists through here to buy anything, anyway!' she laughed.

'Catherine has been living on Oahu and wants to spend some time here and check out the local scene. She's a photographer – and writer,' said Abel John.

Before he could continue, Miranda grasped Catherine's hand. 'A writer! A photographer! This is exactly where you should be!' She looked at Abel John. 'You've found me a housesitter?'

'That's what I figure,' he said amicably. 'Catherine's a very responsible person and needs a place to stay for a bit. Thought you two could work something out.'

Miranda smiled at Catherine. 'He's a doll, ain't he? C'mon in. I'll show you around. The place comes with a canary, a precious pot plant – not that kinda pot, it's a peace lily – and the Olds. You drive? Where are you from?'

'I'm Australian. You mean the car out there is yours?'

'No-one else'd be seen dead in it!' laughed Miranda.

'Could I put a surfboard in it? I'll be careful about sand,' said Catherine.

'She surfs too!' exclaimed Miranda. 'You Aussies are something else. Come on upstairs and have something to drink. When can you move in?'

'Now. Her stuff, not much, is in the car,' said Abel

394

John quickly. 'Sorry about the short notice. Catherine needs a place to stay and I remembered you.'

There was a main bedroom with an ensuite, an alcove bed-sitting room, a lounge room with a dining area that opened onto the narrow balcony looking down on the street and a tiny kitchen. It was all painted lime green, the shutters dark green, the furniture was ornate Asian black-lacquered bamboo with inlaid gold and pearl trim, upholstered in bright red.

'Wow, this is very exotic,' said Catherine.

'A bit Indochine. Suits the history of the place. This building was once an opium den,' explained Miranda.

'Hanapepe was the hot spot, a big town back in the nineteenth century. Lot of Chinese merchants, rice farmers and coffee plantations,' said Abel John. 'So this was an Asian town with opium dens and joss houses.'

'Now there are a few locals and us drop-out haoles. You'll meet them,' added Miranda. 'That is, if you're ready to move in now and you don't mind sleeping on the couch in the alcove for tonight.'

'I guess so,' said Catherine, glancing at Abel John.

'I'll go get your bag.'

After Abel John had left, Miranda made Catherine some coffee and Catherine found herself shyly explaining that her marriage breakdown was the reason that she had come to Kauai.

Miranda laughed. 'Ah, well, stuff happens, right? Move on, honeybun,' she said nonchalantly. 'Now you know where the coffee pot is, how about we tackle the car? Did you say you had a surfboard to collect?'

'It's over on the north shore. Maybe I should leave it there and surf on that side. I have friends there too.'

'Let's go anyway. I have to show you how the car works. It has a few idiosyncrasies. Why don't you keep your board here, when you get it, then you can go where you please. There're plenty of other places to surf on this island. Be a free agent,' she said.

As she drove the big gold Oldsmobile, Catherine had to agree with Miranda that a convertible was the best way to travel in the Islands.

'Can't have any secrets with this car – everyone recognises it, so don't go anywhere you shouldn't.' Miranda roared at her own joke.

Catherine showed her new friend the turn-off to *Nirvana*. 'You mightn't want me to take the car along this dirt road, though it's grassy at the end.'

'The car goes where we tell it. Put your foot down, honey.'

Catherine drove cautiously and felt a tug of recognition as the rambling beach shack came into view with its usual array of kombi vans and panel vans, surfboards, beach gear, towels and toys in the front yard.

'Well, this is a picture,' commented Miranda.

The children came tumbling out of the house followed by Ginger holding her new baby. Pink and Ziggy squealed in delight as they recognised Catherine. Petal toddled forward.

'Wow, great to see you, Catherine. What a car,' exclaimed Ginger.

'It belongs to Miranda. This is Ginger. And that's Summer.' Catherine went and hugged Summer who had come outside at all the commotion.

'Come in. Come in. You staying?' asked Summer.

'That's kind of you, but Abel John suggested I house-sit for Miranda in Hanapepe for a bit.'

Summer smiled. 'Hanapepe's a cute place. Anything happening there now? I haven't been by for ages.'

'Not much. Might change one day,' said Miranda.

'Miranda is a fabulous artist. You should come over and see her work,' said Catherine.

'We might just do that. Hey, kids, stop climbing over that car.'

'They won't do any harm,' Miranda assured the women. 'Catherine has the keys.'

Miranda fitted right in and over chai and homemade cake the girls laughed and talked.

'So you've really got into surfing, Catherine? Great isn't it? We'll have to go out together some time,' said Ginger. 'Do you want to borrow a board for a while?'

By the time they drove back to Hanapepe with Catherine's board angled across the back seat, Miranda was talking about spending some time at *Nirvana* when she got back from Europe to paint the kids.

'That scene would make a great painting. So full of colour and life.'

'I'm surprised Abel John hasn't introduced you to the people at *Nirvana* before,' said Catherine.

'We tend to move in our own little circles, which only overlap when a floater like you comes along,' said Miranda.

'A floater? You mean a drifter?' said Catherine. 'That's how I feel at the moment. But that's okay.'

The next day Catherine drove Miranda to Lihue Airport. As the Aloha Airlines flight landed and Miranda prepared to board, Catherine saw PJ walking across the tarmac.

She tapped him on the shoulder as he pulled his bag off the trolley. 'Howdy, stranger.'

He broke into a wide grin. 'Hey, you beat me here. Find a board? Say, you're not leaving already, are you?'

'No. I'm well settled, I'm dropping my friend here. She's flying to Europe and I'm staying in her house. Come and meet Miranda.'

'You're a fast mover. So you're not out at the beach house?'

Miranda shook PJ's hand and shot Catherine a look. 'Where's this guy been hiding?'

'In the surf,' said Catherine.

'Darn, I knew I should have taken it up. See you guys when I get back. Not sure when . . . Thanks, Catherine. I'll phone you. You have fun now.' She waved and walked to the plane.

'Do you want a ride?' asked Catherine. 'I have Miranda's car.'

As they drove along the sunny coast road in the gold convertible, PJ's bag and board crammed in the back seat, Catherine found herself humming.

Time passed with days of early-morning surfing, sometimes hanging out at *Nirvana*, then a surf with PJ at Hanalei – which Catherine thought was one of the most beautiful parts of the island – then minding the gallery for a few hours – Miranda kept loose opening times – for the occasional visitor who dawdled in to look around. More often than not, visitors were locals on an errand on that side of the island who stopped to pass the time of day. Some older people told Catherine what the village was like in their childhoods and were glad to see nothing much had changed recently. Even the old swinging bridge was still across the river.

Catherine started making notes for possible articles for the *News*. Before Miranda had left, Catherine took a photo of the artist with her bold and bright Hawaiian canvases and she started to write a story on 'The Island New Yorker'. Then Catherine thought that perhaps she could expand the idea into a series on women who had bloomed on Kauai. She knew that Summer and Ginger would agree to be in it. Eleanor, of course, could be another candidate and, while she was well known as a hotelier, Catherine hoped to find a different, more unusual, angle to write about her. She phoned Eleanor to discuss her idea.

'Catherine, I'm so glad you called. I was wondering how you're getting on. Abel John said you're staying in Hanapepe – is it all right? You know you can move over here . . .'

'I'm fine for the moment, thanks, Eleanor. I'd love to see you. Do you have the time to come over?'

'I'll make time. I have some mail here for you that Kiann'e sent on. How about tomorrow? Late morning?'

Catherine watched Eleanor park the little Palm Grove truck out the front of *The Joss House* and stand and gaze along the street at the buildings. The door tinkled as she came inside and hugged Catherine.

'Not much has changed in Hanapepe since I was first here years ago. This gallery is a cute place. Wasn't it an opium den once? Oh, look at this art!' Eleanor walked around the little gallery and studio. 'I've heard about Miranda's work. Very dramatic.' She looked thoughtful. 'This would make wonderful fabric. I'll have to talk to Miranda when she comes back. Be stunning in the new wing . . . if it's ever done.'

'What's happening?'

'It's a stalemate over the stones and the heiau the workmen have found. They've downed tools. We've had experts over to have a look and it seems it's a site of significance. The men say that if we build there'll be some dreadful retribution.'

'And you believe in such Hawaiian spiritual things, don't you?' said Catherine.

'I do, I guess. But our investor partner certainly doesn't. He wants to bring in new workmen from the mainland if we have to and get the job done.'

'Abel John and the locals wouldn't like that. What are you going to do?' asked Catherine. Eleanor looked so tired and concerned.

'The business has to pick up, so I have to get the new wing finished. Hopefully Abel John can find some sort of compromise. Now, before I forget, your mail.' She handed Catherine several letters.

There was a welcome payment from the *News*, a circular and one from her mother.

Catherine skimmed through it quickly, fighting back tears. 'It's my mum. They're upset, of course, about Bradley and me. But so loving. I don't want to go back home. Not yet.'

'No, you're at something of a crossroads.' Eleanor patted Catherine's hand. 'You'll know what to do when the time comes. I'd better go back. Come over for lunch or a drink anytime. Have a look at the hole in the ground.' She rolled her eyes.

Later, at sunset, as Catherine sat on the beach towelling herself dry and watching the last of the surfers come in, PJ joined her.

'You look pensive.'

'Bit down in the dumps. Had a letter from my mother, pleading with me to come home, asking me what am I going to do with my life and so on.'

'Bit heavy. What're you doing tomorrow?'

'Putting in a couple of hours in the gallery. What're you doing?'

'I was going to suggest we go to Pakala, it has a good left point break, or else try Poipu. They're close to Hanapepe. Looks like it's going to rain here and it's generally dry on your south-west side.'

'Great. Come to *The Joss House*. See Miranda's art. We could have dinner at Molo's down the road later. It's a great little café – nice food, pretty cheap.'

'Sounds good to me.'

PJ arrived early the next afternoon and they set off for the beach. There were a few surfers out and Catherine

400

found the left point at Pakala quite challenging. PJ complimented her on how well she did. They sat on the beach and she was relieved that they talked about lots of things other than Bradley. Her marriage, her past and the future were never mentioned.

Back at Miranda's, while PJ showered and changed, Catherine set out coffee on the balcony.

She handed him a mug. 'Why don't you have a look at Miranda's art downstairs while I have my shower?'

PJ was very taken by Miranda's paintings and he spent a long time examining each one.

When Catherine joined him downstairs he said, 'I know where that is. That's a nice touch. Mmm, I like that one. They're happy pictures,' he summed up. 'Little fragments of the Islands.' He surprised Catherine by adding, 'I've always wanted to paint.'

'Really? What kind of painting?' She was surprised.

'Watercolours.' He grinned. 'I don't know about technique, but when you're out there on the water, in the waves, under water, you get a different perspective of the world . . . watery, runny, liquid . . . like everything is melting . . .' He stopped. 'Well, you understand what I mean, don't you?'

'I think I do,' said Catherine slowly. 'It's the fluidity. Nothing is what it seems, everything changes from instant to instant. Soft one moment, surging the next.'

They were both silent, thinking.

Then PJ touched her hand. 'I'm glad you've got into the ocean. Trying the surfing. It helps you understand who I am,' he said awkwardly.

She nodded. 'Surfing is not something you can explain. You have to do it. Even badly.' She gave a small laugh.

'You're doing just fine. I'm really proud of you, country girl.' He smiled and leant over and lightly kissed her cheek.

Catherine closed her eyes, catching her breath for a moment. 'Let's eat. Molo's making something special for us.'

They walked along the wooden boardwalk to Molo's café and found four other people sitting around a communal table.

The food was delicious, the company eclectic and Catherine saw another side to PJ who talked to everyone about travel, food and life in the Islands. Then Molo talked about his ancestors and how they had lived in the hidden valleys of Na Pali.

He turned to PJ. 'Why don't you take Catherine to the Na Pali coast. I think it's the most beautiful part of all of Hawaii.'

'Need a boat for that,' said PJ.

'You can borrow mine. Or I can show you the way in over the mountain. Very secret. Very rugged. Some say the valley is haunted by a lost civilisation.'

'Ooh, rugged and haunted, I don't think so,' said Catherine. 'But a boat trip along the coast would be nice.'

'Be my guest,' said Molo to PJ.

It was late as they walked in the dark the few doors back to *The Joss House*.

PJ took Catherine's hand. 'Would you like go see Na Pali?'

'Yes, please. But I don't really want to hike over some abyss into a spooky valley.'

'It's quite a story. An archeological team went in some years back.' PJ began to tell her the story and Catherine held his hand tightly as the tale unfolded. They went through the gallery and upstairs to sit on the balcony and, as PJ talked, she lit a candle and poured them both a glass of wine.

The candle sputtered, a chime tinkled as a breeze stirred the balmy night. PJ leant over and blew out the remains of the candle. Catherine picked up their glasses and took them inside. PJ brought in the bottle and as Catherine rinsed her glass he lifted her hair and kissed the nape of her neck.

Slowly she turned to face him, melting against him, fitting easily into his body. PJ kissed her face and throat and hair. Slow, lazy kisses. They felt comfortable, connected. Catherine wound her arms about him, drawing her face to his. His kiss was suddenly hard, insistent.

'I want you, Catherine,' he said in a husky voice.

'Me too,' she breathed.

And it was so easy, so simple. Compared to the wild passion of their beach encounter, which now seemed an eternity ago, this coming together was unhurried, caring, tenderly caressing.

The night passed. Dawn was ignored as they held and loved each other with no thought of time or commitments, until, laughing, they dragged themselves to the kitchen for coffee.

Wrapped in a sheet, Catherine sipped the milky brew as PJ toasted bread.

He handed Catherine a piece of toast. 'You up for a surf?'

'Of course.' She licked the dripping butter and smiled at PJ. Catherine looked out at the blue and gold day. She had nothing better to do in the world.

The nights were dreamless. But she slept with the knowledge of PJ twined around her, their bodies linked. She was first to awaken and she hardly dared breathe so as not to disturb the moment. She loved his golden skin, his tangled blond curls that tasted of the sea. She counted every freckle, watched the thick layer of his eyelashes and longed for him to wake so she could touch his perfect mouth.

How different this was to the bed she shared with Bradley where an ocean of crisp white sheet had separated their bodies. Bradley had been a light sleeper and if she moved too much or touched him, his sleep was disturbed. Save for an occasional questing foot reaching across the divide, a hesitant invitation to make love, they could have been sleeping in separate rooms.

Catherine glanced at the lengths of hand-painted silk that hung at the windows. The morning light glimmered through them sending dancing colours across the bed. PJ started to wake up, tightening his arms around her, searching for her lips, seeking warmth and sustenance.

The days since their dinner at Molo's blurred together. PJ spent most nights with Catherine and the multicoloured *Joss House* had become a haven for them. After their early morning surf and breakfast they were both out and about. PJ had set up a workshop at *Nirvana* and started shaping boards to suit the local conditions for a new group of surfers who'd arrived. Catherine shut the studio for a siesta break, as the other places along the street did, and went out with her camera to explore Kauai.

The more she explored the island the more she thought of it as the most beautiful place she'd ever seen. Sometimes she imagined she was seeing a landscape no human had seen: great valleys and gorges like the Grand Canyon, impenetrable mountains and hidden valleys where waterfalls, lost tribes, unknown plants and animals might be living, trapped in their own world.

One day, PJ borrowed Molo's boat and they sailed along the Na Pali coast, with its breathtaking, untouched and frighteningly beautiful, sculptured, lush mountains rising from the sea. They landed on one of a few tiny crescent beaches below the cliffs and swam naked, made love on the sand and sailed away unseen. Catherine felt that the time they spent there was swiftly obliterated. They were just specks of sand in the millennia that had formed the island.

One day Catherine called in to see Eleanor at the Palm Grove but she was away, so she found Abel John and asked if she could go over to the site of the new wing. Together they walked past the great grove of coconut palm trees, with their name plaques at their base, past the rows of water lily ponds and man-made canals to where a swamp was screened by panels of hessian. As they stepped inside the screen, Catherine was confronted by muddy ponds that had been dredged from the slippery murky grey sand and mud.

'It's a coastal swamp they thought would be easy to dredge and fill,' said Abel John. 'But the backhoe started to hit a lot of rocks and once bones was seen in the sludge, everything came to a stop.'

'It's a graveyard?'

'More. Look over here. We started draining it to see what was here and found that.' He pointed to a neat rock wall formation. 'The way it lines up, the way the stones are laid, there's no doubt it's a sacred heiau.'

'An ancient temple?' Catherine reached in her bag for her camera, but Abel John stopped her.

'It's more than that. It's a whole settlement we think. We've had people from the University of Hawaii here and photos and samples went to the mainland. Plenty of archeologists have been here. Kahunas have blessed the site and the thinking is that it could be over a thousand years old.'

'What happened to it?'

He pointed to the ocean. 'A war between invaders or a tsunami possibly.'

'A tidal wave! How exciting, how are they going to know the whole story?' asked Catherine. Suddenly, in her mind's eye, this muddy area took shape as she imagined a village of round wooden houses, canoes and outriggers

405

pulled up on the beach, the stone structures of a temple and perhaps sacrificial altars, fires burning, children playing. 'It'd make a wonderful tourist attraction! A re-creation of an ancient village!'

'Nice thought,' said Abel John drily. 'It'd take ages to excavate, save and re-create. The old kahunas believe this could be a sacred place sung about in ancient chants. Stones hold magical powers. No way will they let this be re-buried under a tennis court and hotel rooms.'

'Oh dear, what's Eleanor going to do? This is on hotel land isn't it?'

'That no mean anything if it's certified as a place of cultural heritage. The legal people will be in next, I bet. That partner of hers, the guy with the money, won't want to let it go without a fight.'

'But even if it's not re-created, or whatever, it's an interesting place to visit. Surely people would want to come here and learn more about it,' began Catherine.

'And stay in one other hotel? The Palm Grove needs business. Anyway, there's more to it.' He hesitated. 'There're all kind of superstitious rumours flying around. The long and the short of is that, if Eleanor damages, digs, does anything, there'll be some almighty stink.'

'Poor Eleanor. I wish I could write about this for the paper.'

'Best not. C'mon. How're things at *The Joss House*?'

'I can't thank you enough. It's been wonderful,' said Catherine.

Abel John looked at her sparkling eyes, happy smile and pink cheeks and didn't comment. They turned back to the main buildings.

As Catherine was walking to the car she saw Eleanor in the parking lot in animated conversation with Beatrice. She called out and joined them. 'Beatrice! Eleanor! How lovely to see you both.'

Eleanor smiled but she looked very tense and tired. 'Hi, Catherine.'

'Dear girl, how nice to see you,' said Beatrice kissing her cheek.

'I've just seen the excavation down by the pond of the old . . . settlement,' said Catherine.

'We've just been discussing it,' said Eleanor tightly.

'It's a heiau all right. A very sacred place, which simply can't be disturbed,' said Beatrice firmly to Eleanor.

'We've been over and over this, Beatrice. It's now out of my hands, my business partner is insistent we push ahead. I've told him we'll preserve the stones, I understand their significance.'

'Eleanor, we've known each other for years. But I promise you, my people and this site have to come before anything else. He can build somewhere else . . .'

'There isn't anywhere else,' began Eleanor, sounding exasperated.

'Has your business partner seen the area? Perhaps if he came and saw it . . .' suggested Catherine, worried that she was intruding on what was obviously a sensitive discussion.

'Of course he won't,' said Eleanor. 'I'm the fall guy here.'

'Then tell him he won't escape either way. Move those stones or harm that sacred site and there will be an almighty price to pay. Some catastrophe, the gods and spirits will come down on those who defy the warnings,' declared Beatrice ominously.

'Abel John says the workmen won't touch them,' said Catherine.

'My partner has invested a lot in this, I know that he's going to bring in mainlanders.'

'Then as your friend, I suggest you leave this place alone,' said Beatrice firmly. 'That is my last word.' She turned to Catherine. 'Kiann'e said you were here, please come and see me.'

'I will,' Catherine said as Beatrice waved to her driver waiting by her old car.

Beatrice smiled sadly. 'Eleanor, dear, please. Listen to what I say.'

They watched Beatrice ease herself into the car, taking off her straw hat with its fresh flowers tucked around the crown and drive away.

'The royal decree. We have been told,' sniffed Eleanor tartly.

'Are you going to do what she says? It sounds pretty serious,' said Catherine.

'Like I said, I have no choice in the matter. How can I give up the Palm Grove? It's my life. I'll stay with it, no matter what happens. I just don't like losing my friends to do it.'

That night, curled in bed together, Catherine described the buried settlement to PJ. 'You don't think that the bones have anything to do with human sacrifice, do you?'

'No, I think you're letting your imagination run away. But it could be a sacred burial place where people's ancestors have gone into the night to the spirit world,' said PJ. 'I've heard stories from old watermen about stones that represent departed chiefs. They stand and face the sea, towards the land beyond the horizon.'

They lay quietly and Catherine suddenly recalled the images in her head of PJ, standing silent and still on a beach watching, watching the horizon.

'Do you believe there's something out there, across the sea, the land of Hanalei, some other place?' she asked quietly.

'I do. If the sea doesn't claim me, I want my ashes thrown across the waves,' he answered.

Catherine shivered. 'That's awful talk.'

He held her close and they drifted to sleep and in her dreams she heard the distant roar of surf breaking on a reef and the eventual slap of a shredded wave dying on the shore.

Extract from The Biography of

THE WATERMAN

He sat in the shade of a coconut palm watching the surf. The sea, the sun, the sand, the brush of the tradewinds, all were the same. But everything else had changed since the Islands had been plunged into war.

It had been a Sunday morning and he had just come in from the surf when the sky filled with Japanese planes as they began their lethal attack. Noise and chaos followed. Clouds of black smoke filled the air as the American ships in Pearl Harbor were bombed. Now, around the town were sandbags, rolls of barbed wire, men and women in uniform. More warships crowded the harbour, airforce bombers took off day and night and everyone had learnt to accept curfew times and blackouts. Even some food items were rationed and produce was requisitioned from the local farms.

He regretted that his mild arthritis, a legacy from his time as a stuntman, had meant that his efforts to join the forces had been rejected. Now the imposed changes to Hawaii were rocking his way of life and his peace of mind. He debated about going back to the desert, where the vastness of the lonely prairie gave him the same sense of solitude that surfing gave him. But travel was difficult in these times and his funds were low.

As he sat on the edge of the sand, thinking about these changes, a soldier and a girl walked along the sea wall.

'Hey, buddy,' the soldier said, 'careful a coconut doesn't fall on your head!' They passed by laughing.

At sunset, normally a favourite time for the water-man, he got up, pulled a white cotton sweater over his navy swimsuit, slipped his feet into zoris and began walking home.

Along the beachfront he saw a pretty woman in a nurse's uniform sitting on the sea wall, holding her shoes in one hand and wiggling her bare toes in the sand. They caught each other's eye and smiled.

'Enjoying the sunset?' he asked.

'Trying to. If you keep looking out to sea from here, you could almost believe the world was safe. Normal.'

'I was just thinking the same thing. Don't look behind you at the reality.' He smiled. 'You from the mainland?'

'Yes. I'm working here at Tripler Army Hospital.'

'Ah. Must be tough sometimes.'

'Yes, it can be. But times like this . . . helps put things back into perspective.'

'Then I won't intrude. Good evening.'

'G'bye. Good luck,' she answered.

The woman's face, her soft eyes and sweet smile, kept returning to his mind at unexpected moments. So he was only half surprised when he saw her again at sunset two days later. This time she was walking, wearing a cotton dress, her hair unpinned, softly falling to her shoulders.

'Hello again,' he said. 'How are things with you today?'

'Why, hello. The world's still here, so things are good. Yes, it has been good,' she added. 'Two of my charges have left the hospital, not fully recovered but on the path.'

'Have they been sent home or back to their units?' he asked, falling into step beside her as they walked along the beach.

'One has gone home on leave, the other to convalesce. So, you live here?'

They talked, their conversation covering the distance of Waikiki.

At the Outrigger Canoe Club he paused. 'Would you like to have a drink here at the club?'

It was now a place frequented by wealthy locals and

high-ranking military officers because the war had changed the Waikiki scene. Some of the young local surfers preferred to be on the other side of the island developing their surfing skills, but he was cautious when speaking of those who lived to surf when the rest of the world was fighting. And over time he found himself staying on the leeward side at Waikiki, spending more time with the gentle nurse.

It was an unspoken, informal arrangement – they began meeting at the beach on the evenings she was free. She talked of the dedicated people she worked with and her family and about growing up on the east coast. She quickly learned he was a reticent man, a good listener, but one who didn't talk about himself.

But she became fascinated, intrigued, when he talked about the sea, surfing, the Islands, the people, the culture.

So he began slowly introducing her to his favourite places. At Waikiki when the beach boys were around they talked story about growing up in Hawaii. Their graciousness and humour appealed to her and she came to understand what the aloha spirit meant.

He took her out on his board, riding tandem, but she preferred to sit on the beach and watch him, hour after hour, absorbed in riding the waves. It was as though he was reading the water until he knew every shiver and surge, every wrinkle, fold and form. He understood the waves' mood and momentum before he ventured among them.

And so they became lovers.

When they were together, they closed out the world. For them, the war, the battles happening in other places, didn't exist.

He had never let anyone intrude into his life before. Sometimes he felt afraid and vulnerable at the immensity of his feelings. Other times he was fearful that there'd be demands, a day of reckoning and that she'd expect something he couldn't give. But for now, with a war raging, they lived for the moment, wrapped in each other's arms.

One day she came to him with a sad face and he knew something was very wrong.

He tried to comprehend what she was telling him: that she was leaving for the mainland because now that victory was in sight, many of the nurses were being sent home. She wouldn't stay because she couldn't see a future for them together.

She was sad though. She said that she loved the Islands, she loved him.

He was bewildered but in his heart he knew she was right. He couldn't give up his life and the ocean here, even for her.

So it was over. She wanted no goodbyes.

All he could find to say was, 'Well, you know where to find me.'

He came in from the dark and turned on a low light on the small table. He smoothed the sheet of paper several times, as if caressing it, before lifting his pen. He had thought long and hard about committing the right words to paper. He was unsure of what to say. But he knew he must try if he was to convince her of his love and his wish to be with her. If only she could understand and agree to a life together in the Islands. As he wrote he poured out his feelings, surprising himself. But when he reread the finished letter he tried to imagine how she would react, but what was he offering her? His heart, his love, a dream.

He walked around the room, came back and read the letter again and realised that while he offered her his love he was not relinquishing his love for the ocean and his

413

way of life . . . an offer she had already rejected. He knew it was hopeless. Calmly he folded the letter, put it in the envelope and tucked it into the back of a scrapbook.

He went outside and the sound of the waves in the darkness comforted him.

15

How easily and sweetly each day slipped into the next. It felt to Catherine that there had never been a time in her life like this, a time without plans or commitments, simply enjoying every minute of every day. From the moment she opened her eyes, she had no thoughts other than of PJ.

She was surrounded by beauty unlike anything she'd ever imagined, from the dramatic to the romantic, the poetic to the homespun. Kauai was a like a dream. It seemed everyone she saw gave her a special smile, tinged with a knowledge, an acknowledgment, of her joyfulness. Strangers' smiles made her pause and wonder, do they know? Do they know how free I feel, how happy I am, how in love I am?

PJ occupied all of her. She missed him when he was away from her, she felt so close to him, not only during their entwined nights, but in the things they did together. As well as surfing they'd taken to hiking through the damp, lush valleys, swimming in waterfall pools, fishing, taking Molo's little boat out to skim along the calmer parts of the coast. In the evenings they sat on the small balcony of *The Joss House* or occasionally called into Molo's for an inexpensive dinner.

If they were surfing on the north shore they hung out at *Nirvana* for several hours and while PJ worked on his boards, Catherine played with Pink and Ziggy and helped Summer and Ginger in the garden or joined them all on a picnic and a swim in the goddess pool. She took lots of photos depicting their idyllic, if unusual, life where they lived as much as they could in rhythm with nature.

At *Nirvana* everyone talked about new ways of doing things co-operatively, living on communal land, sharing the work of growing their food and raising and teaching their children, bringing in money to share with the group and allowing everyone's creative talents to blossom. There was always time to sit and make music, play with the children, bake bread and never a day went by without a surf.

Fleetingly, thoughts of Bradley would flutter across the sunshine of Catherine's day like a small dark cloud. But she pushed these moments of sadness to one side. The thought of what her life might have been with Bradley in Washington seemed a world away. She felt an occasional pang that perhaps she should write to his family, but knew very well there would be no warmth or understanding from them. They were probably angry about what she'd done to their son. It crossed her mind that the only person who might have some awareness of why she couldn't remain married to Bradley would be Aunt Meredith.

Instead, Catherine wrote chatty, happy letters to her parents enclosing pictures of Kauai and copies of what she was writing for the paper. She did not mention PJ, only that she had a group of supportive, fun and caring friends to spend time with. Her mother had stopped asking about her plans and when was she coming home.

One morning PJ asked Catherine to come and stay on the other side of the island as he'd heard the waves were running. Steve, another surfer friend, lived there in a small farm house. Steve sold a few boards but also, between the rows of sugar cane in his small field, he grew healthy marijuana plants. He asked PJ to shape some boards for him, offering him the use of his beach shack in return.

The shack was a cottage once used by field workers and it was filthy as well as decrepit. Catherine and PJ cooked outside over an open fire and she likened the experience to roughing it on a camping trip. The few times they went to Steve's farm house Catherine was uncomfortable, disliking the heavy drug use and strange people who drifted in and out. It didn't have the happy, casual, creative feel of *Nirvana*. The music was wild heavy metal, there was cocaine and heroin being used as well as marijuana and there was an aggression and unfriendliness she didn't care for. The people were using surfing as an excuse to drop out and Catherine knew they were not serious soul surfers.

Catherine was glad when they returned to Miranda's little gallery. PJ told Catherine that he had made money on the boards and he'd done a deal with Steve to shape more, but he seemed in no hurry to do so. Catherine was pleased as she had no desire ever to see Steve and his cohorts again. She was comfortable with their life on this side of the island.

One afternoon as she pottered around the gallery after a couple had left with a small painting, the phone rang and Miranda's laughter bounced down the phone line.

'Everything is great,' Catherine assured her. 'Just sold

a small oil of hibiscus and shells. Your work is selling really well.'

'Fantastic. Can you stay on a while longer?'

'Of course. You having a good time in Venice?'

'Am I what! I've met the most glorious guy. We are having a ball. So . . . figured I might as well play as long as I can.'

'That's fine by me,' said Catherine. 'Is he Italian?'

'Venetian, sweetie. He's a gondolier!'

'Really! He must be handsome. Does he wear a striped T-shirt and sing love songs?' laughed Catherine.

'He does for me. Actually he owns a fleet of gondolas . . . quite the little tourist operator. A touch younger than me, but that's how I like it. If you can stay on, that's great, if you have to leave, ask Molo to get someone to help in the gallery a few hours.'

'I'm not going anywhere. Have fun, Miranda.'

'Ciao, bella!'

'Miranda rang from Venice. You'll never guess what she's up to!' exclaimed Catherine to PJ later.

'Sock it to me,' he grinned.

'She's madly in love with a gondolier and is staying on a while longer.'

He shrugged. 'She sounds quite a gal.'

'But it means we can stay on here longer too,' said Catherine.

'Makes life easy. I was talking to some of the boys and they're thinking of heading to the Mentawai Islands off Sumatra which has unreal breaks. Be a good test for the new boards. It's totally rugged,' he added. 'Just sleeping on the beach. Nothing there apparently. I thought I might take off with them for a while.'

'Sounds kind of exciting,' said Catherine carefully, wondering how long he'd known about this. 'When are you leaving? Will you be gone long?'

'No idea. One of the guys, Stewart, a New Zealander, has a movie camera and he's been making a surfing film. Been chasing waves for six months. He gets the word and he's off. Wants Damo and me to be in it.'

'Sounds . . . expensive. Well, time-consuming. But very interesting. Is there a big audience for a film about waves and surfing?' asked Catherine.

'Sure is. The surfing world is getting bigger. Far bigger than when Lester was in his prime. He'll get a kick out of seeing places he'll never get to surf.'

'Me too,' said Catherine. 'I'd better lock up the gallery.' She went downstairs knowing that she was excluded from this part of PJ's world. He would never ask her on this adventure. It was clearly just for serious male surfers.

The subject wasn't mentioned again. But suddenly a dozen surfers moved into *Nirvana*.

'The sea is up. Big sets coming in. Bring your camera. Damien wanted you to get shots of him and his Aussie mates,' said PJ. 'They'll be heading to Oahu to Waimea, Sunset, Pipeline in a few weeks.'

Catherine was at the beach before sunrise and spent hours focusing her lens on the specks riding the enormous, spectacular waves, often disappearing into the snarling white lip that doubled over on itself. Capturing the moment, the essence of the ferocious yet glorious surge of translucent water was, she felt, a bit like grasping at rainbows. She had to divide her attention between photographing the surfers and trying to capture the ephemeral and dynamic moods and movement of the ocean. Now, with some surfing experience, she tried to imagine what it must feel like out there, to be picked up, to be part of that explosion of water, to be in its heart, to experience the exhilaration, the sensuous pleasure as well as the fear and respect, and to know, as one surfer said to her, what it was like to be 'in the eye of god'.

She took it upon herself to drive to the nearest hamburger joint on the coast road and pack a box with sandwiches, fruit, drinks, cakes and snacks and take it back to the beach for the hungry surfers. They'd leave the water, flop on the sand, eat, discuss their rides, talk about where to surf next and either return to the water or head to a further point to check how the waves were breaking there. Catherine was always repaid and the boys were keen to know what she might have captured in her shots, especially if one was considered an epic ride.

Catherine learnt the capriciousness of waves from the solid reliable reef rollers to the here-today-gone-tomorrow sandbank breaks and the brightly lit, cathedral-like iridescent underwater 'green room' of a tube. She captured some frightening wipe outs, which, though dangerous, never dented a surfer's keenness.

Days like this just dissolved, time was fluid. Suddenly sunset loomed. The waves had diminished, but when the last stragglers came in from the surf, PJ was still out there, looking for a last wave. The sea was gilded, waves the colour of melting gold, he and his board a dark silhouette until the final wave that carried him towards her. She waited for him at the water's edge with his towel.

'Almost too dark for any more pictures. But you got one more ride in before night came,' she said. 'You were a long way out.'

'Magic time. Even out there the offshore wind carries the scent of flowers, cries of birds and somewhere an engine rumbling. A tractor in a field maybe.' He kissed her. 'And I imagined I could smell your perfume, your hair.'

That night he made tender love to her. His sweetness, his endearments brought tears to her eyes. Yet in his gentle lovemaking she experienced the most powerful sensations her body had known. Like waves sweeping over her, great

420

rolling, quivering, surging explosions rocked through her. She was drowning in his body. He wrapped his arms around her and held her as he drifted to sleep.

Catherine watched him sleep, breathing deeply and slowly, in the pale light shining through the window. She hadn't asked when he was heading off on his surfing safari. Soul surfers like PJ surfed from the heart, not for money, not for the adrenalin hit, not for kudos, not for recognition. It met some primeval need, it was a drug, an addiction.

The departure came suddenly, when Stewart the filmmaker finally decided that it was time to head out. Catherine found herself driving PJ, Damien and Leif in Miranda's car, while their bags, boards, Stewart and his camera and tripod and the other surfers crammed into two kombi vans. At tiny Lihue Airport there was a lot of laughter as the boys cracked jokes and farewelled friends.

Catherine's goodbye to PJ was not very private, nor very emotional. They hugged tightly, he stroked her hair and as the final boarding call was shouted by a flight attendant in the little terminal, they kissed fiercely. They drew apart and PJ hoisted his small bag onto his shoulder. His blue eyes were shining.

'You're excited about this trip, aren't you?' she said.

PJ nodded. 'Hardly anyone's surfed this spot. If it's as good as Stewart says and the film comes out, then everyone will know about it. But I think he has a few more places up his sleeve. He's been doing some heavy research. He's quite the adventurer.'

'All very Robinson Crusoe. Unspoiled paradises,' she said lightly. 'So I suppose getting word back to me will be tricky.'

'Yeah, don't count on it. No mail or phones out there on deserted islands, remote coastlines. But listen, even though you don't hear, you know I'll be okay. I'll think of you, Catherine.' He kissed her quickly. 'Gotta go. Want to make sure those boards aren't damaged when they load 'em. See ya. Take care!' He waved and hurried through the departure door.

Catherine watched him walk across the tarmac, dressed in sandals, cotton chinos and a blue shirt hanging loosely over a white T-shirt. It was the most formally dressed she'd ever seen him. His sunglasses were pushed up on his head over his cloud of long blond curls. At the plane's hold he talked to the handlers and watched the surfboards being loaded. He then raced up the steps to the plane without a backward glance to reassure the boys that the boards were safely stowed.

She was the last to leave the terminal building, standing alone at the window watching the small plane disappearing into blue sky until her eyes burned and she could only see spots. As she walked outside she passed a woman in a bright muu-muu threading leis at a low table covered in flowers. Her young daughter squatting beside her was sorting blossoms for her mother. Lengths of fragrant leis hung behind them. The woman smiled at Catherine.

'Aloha. Here, take one lei. Please, no look so sad.'

Catherine stopped and fumbled for her purse but the woman waved her hand away. 'Come.' She held up a lei and Catherine bent down as the woman slipped the flowers over her head. 'You throw dis one into the sea at sunset and your love will return.'

'Mahalo,' murmured Catherine, tears spilling from her eyes.

She didn't want to go to *Nirvana*, nor to Miranda's. She wanted a distraction. So she drove to see Beatrice as she'd been meaning to do for several weeks.

Beatrice welcomed her with a large embrace. 'Dear child. How are you? You have not decided to return to your husband?' She lifted her shoulders, her dark eyes were warm and her slight smile was philosophical. 'These things happen, okay? Far better you do this now than suffer in silence believing things will right themselves. All that means is your being a doormat longer and bearing the guilt and burden of domestic duties and children. It's much harder to leave when there are children.'

'Eleanor said much the same.'

'Yes. Well, she knows what she's talking about.' Beatrice turned inside the house. 'Come along, Verna is here. Tea and cakes time. We're throwing around a few ideas for the next meeting.' She slipped her feet from her zori at the door and Catherine followed suit. It was a local custom she'd adopted as a matter of course and supposed it had come from the Japanese influence in the Islands. Barefoot they padded down the polished-wood hallway. 'So what have you been up to?'

'We've been looking after an art gallery for someone on the other side of the island.'

'You say "we". Who might "we" be?'

Catherine paused, then said candidly, 'A mainlander called PJ. He's been here a long time. Taught me to surf. I was very attracted to him but didn't realise how much until Bradley left. Then we, kind of, got together.'

Beatrice glanced at Catherine but only said, 'Enjoy your freedom. That's what you've been after. Don't exchange one restricted life for t'other. You be in charge.'

'I'm still learning to take control,' said Catherine. 'It's a new experience. It hadn't ever occurred to me there was another way of doing things. Thinking for myself, I mean. My dad always looked after the practical matters and then I was married before I knew it and Bradley ran our lives.'

Beatrice nodded. 'A familiar story. Fortunately Kiann'e comes from a line of powerful women. All I'll say to you, Catherine, is don't waste this opportunity.'

As always there was a lot happening at Beatrice's home. People coming and going, talk of plans for lobbying and meeting with groups and individuals Beatrice thought could help their cause. Only once did Catherine hear mention of the Palm Grove and she realised the discussion was about the future of the heiau and the sacred stones that had been unearthed. Beatrice again warned that there would be retribution, divine or political, if the building for the new wing disturbed the sacred site. Catherine didn't say anything, but she was worried for Eleanor's sake. The owner of the Palm Grove was literally between a rock and a hard place.

The busy and stimulating day with Beatrice had taken her mind off PJ's departure so that by the time she got back to *The Joss House* she thought she would be fine about being on her own. But the moment she walked into the space she and PJ had shared, his absence came home to her. She looked at the tumbled bed where they'd made love. She picked up the coffee cup he'd used and drained its cold dregs, pressing her lips to where his had been. In the bathroom she picked up his still damp towel and lifted it to her face, burying her head in it, seeking the smell of his skin.

As the days passed Catherine couldn't stand the loneliness. She ached for PJ and hated being on her own. While he hadn't always been around, or she hadn't known exactly where he was or what he was doing, it didn't matter because she knew that, whether it be day or night, he'd eventually appear and take her in his arms.

She couldn't sleep as she reached for PJ's body. She missed sleeping entwined with his limbs, skin touching skin. His body was so familiar she imagined she could conjure him from thin air, from grains of sand and discover again the tang of salt on him, the citrusy smell of his hair, feel the golden sun that warmed his skin, the sinewy strength of a foot pushing against her own. But when she awoke, her bed was empty and cold.

The lei she had been given at the airport had wilted on the bedside table. Catherine remembered the directive to throw it into the sea so that her love would return. She wished she'd done it. Now she felt that her failure to do so was a bad omen. She just hoped that the filming expedition would soon be over and PJ would be back in her arms.

Over the next few weeks she had sold almost all of Miranda's paintings and the gallery started to look bare. She asked Molo if he knew whether Miranda had a stash of art anywhere else, but he shook his head.

'Nah, it's how she operates. She goes away, comes back and works like crazy, sells it and takes off again. No worry, Catherine. Just lock up the gallery. But stay upstairs of course. You one great saleswoman.'

'Her work sells itself,' said Catherine. 'Just a matter of people stumbling through the door.'

Still there'd been no word from PJ, so when Eleanor rang to say there was some mail for her that had been forwarded from Oahu, Catherine hoped that there might be a letter for her from PJ.

She drove to the Palm Grove and parked the gold car in front of reception. Narita, the Japanese waitress, called out to her.

'Wow, that's some car, Mrs Connor! How're you going?'

'Good, Narita. How're you? How're things here?'

Surprisingly the small Japanese woman, who was usually so cheerful, looked down and lifted her shoulders in a helpless gesture. 'Things are not so good. Miz L's going ahead with the building and it's causing lot of stink. No good.' She shook her head. 'You staying?'

'I'm not sure. I'd like to . . . I have to talk to Mrs Lang.

Maybe I could get some work and stay here.' She smiled and Narita giggled, dismissing the idea as a joke.

Eleanor greeted her warmly but she was preoccupied and looked drawn and much older.

'Good to see you. What are your plans?'

'I don't know. But I don't want to bother you. How're things going? Can I help you in anyway, Eleanor? Do anything here? I'm at a loose end.'

Eleanor gave her a quick, appraising look. 'We'll have to talk. Can you stay for dinner? Why not stay the night? Plenty of spare beds.' She gave a slight, hollow laugh. 'I have a few things happening right now. Now, here's your mail,' she said taking Catherine into her office and handing her several letters. 'Abel John is about. He'd love to see you. What say we meet after the torch-lighting ceremony for a drink and dinner? Stay the night, hang around a day or so. If you have no commitments, that is.'

'Free as a bird. I've sold nearly all of Miranda's art, so I'm looking for something to do.'

Eleanor took off her glasses and rose. 'Great. I'll get Talia to brush up a room for you. Be good to have some company.'

'You have a hotel full of people,' laughed Catherine.

'We're not full and I can't tell my woes to the guests,' she said, trying to joke.

'Eleanor, I'd really love to know what's happening with . . . everything.' Catherine was thinking of Beatrice's stern warning. Eleanor picked up her basket from her desk. Suddenly the feisty woman looked very vulnerable.

Catherine ordered a coffee on the terrace and read a letter from her mother. Things had been very busy in her father's legal practice and he was a bit worried that he couldn't spend as much time on the farm as he should. Rob had been a tremendous help but he was having problems of his own. 'I don't want to gossip, darling, but he's having financial worries, he told Dad. Between Barbara's spending and his father's racehorses, he's having a hard time.'

Catherine folded the letter and for the first time in ages she thought about *Heathrbrae* and the people at home that she loved. How comforting to know they'd always be there.

There was a note from Mollie with some photos of the new unit she and Jason were buying which had 'harbour glimpses'.

There was nothing from PJ.

One letter was fat and official looking. Catherine hoped it wasn't a bill. She had little money left, so she'd definitely have to talk to Eleanor about the possibility of some work. There was also a letter from California in large, firm handwriting. It was from Aunt Meredith and it was the first communication from Bradley's family she'd had since their separation.

Dear Catherine,
I am so dreadfully sad to hear the news about you and Bradley. But I have to say I am not overly surprised. You are too young, too untested. What I mean is, you haven't had a chance to test yourself against the forces of the great and glorious world out there. I thought you were good for Bradley. You are a loss to the family, but I understand how you must feel. I would very much like to keep in touch with you. Good luck to you.
Warmest wishes,
Meredith

Catherine folded the letter thinking that she too would like to maintain contact with the forthright Meredith. She reached for the last letter.

It took a moment or two for her to realise what she

was holding in her hands. The documents were from Bradley's attorney-at-law. Bradley had filed for divorce.

Catherine's hand started to shake as she read the dry, cold phrases. Their marriage had broken down, she read, due to 'irreconcilable differences'. There were details of the division of communal property which explained that what each partner had brought into the marriage remained with that person. So Bradley retained the little apartment in the TradeWinds and the few shares. She was to retain 'gifts such as jewelry'. A small cash settlement was to be negotiated.

Catherine was shocked at seeing her marriage reduced to a list of material possessions. But then she became angry. Bradley had, as usual, just gone ahead and set the wheels in motion with no warning or discussion. She would certainly have her father look at these legal documents. But as she drained her coffee and looked at the papers, all these feelings melted and resignation took its place. It was over. There was no point in fighting it. And for what? She had brought very little into the marriage in the way of acquisitions. Indeed, she had very little even now.

But PJ and life in the Islands had shown Catherine that there was another way of living, a different set of priorities. Unlike her parents' generation of the 1950s, Catherine's life, she thought, wouldn't be centred around thriftiness, hard work, always thinking of the future, their children's future and planning for retirement. It wouldn't be a life where the men made the money and decided what to do with it while the women stayed at home. No, the ideas of this seventies generation of free thinkers and women's liberationists with their blended families, living for the moment, had given Catherine a new outlook on life.

She neatly folded the documents along the crease lines and slipped them back into the envelope. Perhaps divorce from Bradley was the best option.

She walked outside and saw Mouse.

'Ay, Catherine! What you do?'

'I was about to drive back to Hanapepe and collect a few things. I'm staying the night, having dinner with Mrs L.'

'Ah, that good thing. She very worried. All 'bout this heiau. Bad thing, very bad. Say, you want to go for one ride?'

'Maybe tomorrow, Mouse. Early in the morning?'

'We go special place. West side. You been down Waimea Canyon?'

Catherine had passed the lookout and the majestic cliffs of the 'Grand Canyon of the Pacific' but she and PJ had never got around to exploring it. 'Yes, Mouse. I've never been in there. It looks spectacular.'

'I take you special place. We leave early, sunrise, okay?'

'Sure. I'll borrow some riding boots from the hotel. See you tomorrow.'

She headed towards the dedicated palm trees when she saw the tall, smiling figure of Abel John coming towards her.

'There you are, been looking for you. How things going?' He gave her a kiss on the cheek.

'Life is interesting. I just received my divorce papers.'

'Oh dear. Well, life goes on. How's PJ?'

Catherine bit her lip. 'I have no idea. He went to Indonesia surfing with a bunch of guys, to make a surfing film. I haven't heard from him. For weeks now.'

'Ah, Catherine. You must understand how it is with surfers by now. They could disappear for months. How things with you? In your heart?'

'I don't know what I feel, Abel John. Empty, I guess.'

'You must start for think of yourself. Not be in the shadows, waiting for life to happen. You make things happen. For you.'

'That's kind of what everyone tells me,' sighed Catherine. 'And your family?'

'All good. But here,' he shook his head, 'not so good. Come and see.'

Once they were through the coconut grove and the sheltered ponds and came to the clearing beyond the canals, Catherine stopped in shock. Heavy machinery and workmen were all over the place. A small mountain of dirt was heaped in one corner. Tapes and rope sectioned off muddy areas where a long stone wall stood beside other stone structures.

'They're not moving all this are they?'

'That business partner of Eleanor's gave the orders. Get the new wing up, move the stones and put them some place else. It's wrong, very wrong. This is sacred ground. A lot of powerful energy and spirits here. None of the Hawaiians will work here. These men were sent from Oahu and the mainland. Beatrice is raising a big stink.'

'What will happen, Abel John?'

'I don't know. I keep around to watch out for Eleanor. Just in case.'

'You're a good man, Abel John.'

Later at the torch-lighting ceremony, Catherine watched Abel John in his red lava lava, the torchlight flickering on his strong, dark body as he was paddled into the lagoon to blow the huge conch shell. She remembered how moved she'd been on her honeymoon when she'd first seen the lighting of the torches and the dancing, heard the conch-shell call, the chants and Eleanor's Hawaiian blessing to welcome the night. After what Abel John had said, she too, had an uneasy feeling.

At dinner Eleanor talked about her lack of options and how much she regretted taking on a business partner.

'But it was either that, stagnate or go backwards. Tourism is taking over the Islands. And even though I'm in the business, I don't like to see so much change.'

'And you're not worried about what Beatrice and Abel John say – about some kind of retribution over the disruption of the heiau?'

'What can I do? It's out of my hands now. Let's talk about something else. What're your plans? Seems you'd better be thinking of your own future.'

Catherine had told Eleanor about the divorce papers. 'I've grown up so much since coming to the Islands. I look at the world rather differently.'

'And this PJ? Where does he fit in?'

'He's captured my heart, Eleanor. I've never felt like this before. But he is a bit of a free spirit. But he'll have to settle down at some stage I suppose . . .'

Eleanor held up her hand, stopping Catherine. 'If he hears the words "settle down" he'll run a mile. Men like him, watermen, never grow up, never change. You have to accept that for your own sanity.'

'I can't just walk away, Eleanor,' said Catherine sadly. Then more brightly said, 'I'll talk it over with him when he comes back. See what we can arrange.'

Eleanor leant across the table and touched her hand. 'Believe me, Catherine. Remember this for what it is, a great romantic interlude. A love affair. Trust me. There's a wonderful man somewhere whom you'll marry, you'll have children, make a life together where you share everything equally, where your needs and ambitions are as important to him as his are to you. Don't sell yourself short, dear girl.'

Catherine didn't sleep well as Eleanor's words continued to ring in her head. At dawn she got up, tidied the room, dressed and crept outside in her riding boots. Night fragrances lingered, the stars were fading in the pre-dawn light.

She heard the snuffle of horses, the shaking of a head, the jangle of stirrups and bridle. Mouse was putting the two horses into the small horse float behind the old truck.

'Good morning. We can leave soon?'

'Sure, Mouse, though I wouldn't mind bringing a coffee.'

There were no cars or people about as they pulled into the deserted ranger's station and let the horses out. The sun was peeping over the horizon and creases of the rugged red canyon walls were etched in gold. By the time they rode along one of the trails heading down into the canyon the sun had risen, but the valley was still in shadow. The muted grey-blue and purple chasm was soon lit by sunlight turning the wet green growth into shades of shining emerald. Two thousand feet down they passed a sparkling endless cascade of water.

'Is this from Mount Waialeale?' asked Catherine.

'Sure is. They say wettest place on earth. The big Alakai swamp on top of the mountain . . . That one amazing place,' said Mouse.

'This is pretty stunning,' said Catherine.

It took them several hours to reach the floor of the canyon and they walked the horses along a sandy trail that would run with rushing water after heavy rain and which joined the Waimea River at the bottom of the gorge.

Catherine felt as though she was walking in the steps of creation and that she was the first human to see this rainforest. Startled birds swept through the canyon, lifted on updrafts, but mostly it was cool, still and silent.

They dismounted at lunchtime and ate the snacks and fruit Catherine had brought with her coffee. They drank from the stream and the water was icy and refreshing. Occasionally Mouse pointed out an unusual or rare plant or tree and Catherine took a photograph, but mostly they rode in silence, absorbed by the rugged beauty. She felt dwarfed, the immense scale of her surroundings reducing her own world to insignificance.

By late afternoon, as they rode back to where they'd left the truck and the horse float, Catherine had begun to think differently about her life. She hoped she could somehow start over, utilise all she now knew and she also hoped that PJ would be part of it. The journey into the canyon had given her a fresh perspective and a sense that she could take control and trust fate, the universe, the spirits, providence or whatever it was, which would guide her towards her tomorrows.

Two days later Catherine headed back to *Nirvana* to see who was there and if any of them had any news of the wandering surfers and PJ. It was the usual sprawl of people, children, food, music and laughter. She was welcomed as part of the extended family and she was glad of the company. Being among this surfing community made her feel very happy. There was a group from the mainland and South Africans there and when Catherine heard them talking about surfing Indo breaks, she asked them what they knew about Indonesia and if they knew the film guy, Stewart.

'Yah, man, I know these guys,' said a South African in his rolling drawl. 'They're going to my town. I gave them some tips of places no-one goes. 'Cept the sharks.' He laughed. 'But big waves this time of year. Real epic ones.'

Catherine finally managed to speak. 'You mean they've gone to South Africa? PJ? Stewart? Who else?'

'Yar. And a couple of Aussies. Be some wild trip. Should get some great waves. And good film shots. There was talk of them going to South America and maybe then to Tahiti. Seems they want to have a world surfing safari, hey?'

'Seems so,' Catherine managed to say and turned

away. She walked to the beach where she and PJ had first made love. Was that an eternity ago?

She found no solace there. Her breath came in short gasps as if she'd been punched. At first she worried that something had happened to PJ, but quickly dismissed the notion. Why, why couldn't PJ have contacted her, let her know that he would be away for months? But then, why would he? Why should he, came a voice in her head? There was no commitment, no claim on each other, no plans. Something Lester had once said, in a self-deprecating tone, about watermen: 'They march to the drum of the waves and hear no other voice.' Now she really understood what he meant. She was not as important to PJ as the ocean and the waves.

Catherine returned to the beach house to find Ginger and Summer. When they realised how distressed she was, the two women took her into a bedroom and sat on the bed.

'Are you so in love with PJ? Not just a rebound thing?' asked Ginger.

'You must know what these men are like, they never grow up, they'll never give up the surf,' added Summer.

'But look at you two, you've made a life with the men you love,' said Catherine, close to tears.

'Ah, doll, take a hard look,' said Ginger. 'Leif and Doobie come and go as they please. They love us, they love their kids. But what they want to do comes first. We count ourselves as lucky because they choose to come back.'

'And we choose to accept how they are,' said Summer. 'That's why Sadie left. She knew that and wasn't prepared to compromise. Ginger and me, we don't mind and we like it here. You, Catherine, couldn't live like us indefinitely, waiting for your man to turn up.'

Catherine thought about this. They were right. She

hadn't imagined that she and PJ would simply drift around the Islands indefinitely, an itinerant life. She assumed there would come a time when that would end and they'd start their real life. But now she saw how it would be. She couldn't change Bradley and now she knew that she couldn't change PJ. Tears trickled down her cheeks.

'He probably loves you, loves being with you, Catherine. But he loves his freedom more,' said Ginger gently.

'It hurts that he couldn't explain this to me,' said Catherine.

'It's how he is. He probably hasn't worked it out in his own head. He is self-absorbed and selfish without knowing it. If he comes back and you're here, he'll go on as before. If he comes back and you're gone, he won't blame you,' said Summer. 'Tough, but that's how watermen are.'

Catherine stared at the two women. 'So what do I do? I miss him. I want him.'

'Stay and drag it out until the end is inevitable. Or you live like we do, with kids, little money, happy, not appendages to husbands but never knowing where they are. You have to make the decision,' said Ginger.

Catherine nodded. 'Beatrice told me that I had should take charge of my life. And Eleanor said that I should let PJ go.'

'Listen to wise women,' said Summer.

They hugged Catherine and she knew they were right. The time to move on had come. But could she move on without PJ? She turned away, tears of unhappiness welling in her eyes.

In Hanapepe she packed up her things at *The Joss House*, gave Miranda's bird and plant to Molo, left a thank-you note on the fridge for Miranda, telling her that she'd moved to the Palm Grove and locked the front door.

Abel John picked up her bag and surfboard, put them in his pick-up truck and smiled at her. 'Ready?'

'No. Not really. But, well, trying to move on with things.'

'Good for you.' He helped her into the front seat.

Catherine wiped her face. 'My gosh it's hot. Steamy and clammy. And so still. Haven't felt it like this before.'

'Kona weather. When we lose the tradewinds. Lucky, it doesn't happen often. Oppressive though.'

'Yes. Do people get cranky and depressed because of it, or is it just me?'

'I think most people feel like you,' he said comfortingly.

Catherine was grateful to Eleanor for letting her stay at the Palm Grove in return for working as her office manager. She enjoyed the company of the other staff at the hotel and she loved having a proper, challenging job and an interesting routine, but she quickly realised that the place was not as full as it should have been.

It was a few weeks later and Catherine had barely fallen asleep when she was awakened by a pounding on the door of her bungalow.

'Catherine, get up, quick.'

She dashed to the door. 'Abel John, what's up? What's happened?'

'We've just been told there's been an underwater earthquake recorded in the eastern Pacific. There will be aftershocks and a tsunami maybe heading this way. Better be prepared to move inland, to higher ground. We are on low-lying land here and across from the beach so we can be flooded if there is one. We've organised trucks, cars and a bus to take guests out if it looks likely.'

'How will we know?'

436

'We'll get some kind of warning from the coastguard. Just be ready to grab anything important if you have to make a dash for it.'

'Oh. Righto. What can I do now?' It was so calm outside, no wind, no rain. It seemed weird.

'Get dressed and go to the office, see if you can help Eleanor.'

'Thanks, Abel John.'

Lights were coming on, people gathering outside, chatting, some were dragging bags to cars, others simply stood around saying, 'It's nothing. Don't worry. This sort of thing has happened many times. Too far away.'

'It wasn't a huge quake apparently,' said Eleanor briskly as she put documents into a folder. 'But it can do anything as it travels across the ocean. Better to be safe than sorry. Here, help me stack all these files up high in case we get a bit of water under the door.'

But an hour later as the kitchen was serving sandwiches and coffee in the dining room, Abel John returned looking grim. 'To be on the safe side, I think we should send guests up the hill. To Pokua Park. I told Helena to bring our kids over here, so get them into a car will you please, Catherine, when they arrive.'

'Of course. Where are you going, Abel John?'

'Around the beach and park along the shore just in case there're any campers, people sleeping on the beach who haven't heard the news.'

'Aren't the emergency people, the police checking the beach?' said Catherine.

'It was a pretty sloppy job, but I know where the kids like to go and they might have been missed by the authorities. It'll be fine. I'll see you later.'

He gave a big smile, gathered up his torch and, barefoot, in his colourful shorts, red T-shirt and baseball cap, jumped back into his pick-up and drove away.

Catherine was kept busy ushering people into vehicles, handing out packets of food and fruit and reassuring everyone that it was just a precaution, a bit of an adventure, nothing for them to be worried about. When she saw Abel John's wife, Helena, and their three children, Catherine smiled and said he'd be glad to know that they were safe.

'You better come away too, Catherine,' said Helena, looking worried. 'The tide has gone way out and that's a bad sign.'

'Where's Abel John? Is he back yet?'

Helena shook her head and tried not to show how concerned she felt as the children began to ask when their father was joining them.

'You go. I'll get my things and I'll see you up there. I might get a ride up the hill with Abel John,' said Catherine cheerfully.

As the small bus departed, Eleanor appeared beside her in the hotel buggy. 'We're running out of transport. I have a few things in here, Kitamura has taken some of my more important documents, just in case. You'd better hop in.'

'You're leaving the hotel?' said Catherine.

'Some of us should be with the guests. A lot of staff have gone home to move their families and secure homes, although those who live away from the coast aren't so worried. Grab your bag.'

Catherine had a cotton hold-all with her wallet, passport, jewellery and camera. She hopped in beside Eleanor and they trundled along the road behind the hotel. Some people were standing outside their homes, a few cars were also on the highway, driving towards the hills.

Up at the Pokua park no-one seemed to be taking the event too seriously. It was more like a late-night picnic. Catherine glanced at her watch. It was just after one a.m. Mr Kitamura joined her and handed her his binoculars.

'Too dark to see much. Get your eyes used to dark. Look at beach.'

Catherine thought she was looking at a silver stretch of sea but then she realised she was looking at a vast stretch of sand, exposed far beyond the normal waterline. 'Where's the water gone?' she whispered, handing the glasses back to Mr Kitamura.

There was a shout and someone pointed. Looking through the binoculars, Mr Kitamura said urgently. 'Wave coming. Not so big. It okay.'

In the moonlight Catherine could see the long, low wave travelling at great speed as it raced across the naked beach.

'It's going to cross the road. We'll get a bit of water in the hotel grounds for sure,' exclaimed Eleanor.

There were a few pinpoints of light. 'There're people taking photos! I should get closer,' said Catherine.

But Mr Kitamura shook his head. 'No. You stay.'

The excitement seemed to be over. People gathered together, finishing their food and suggesting that it was time to go down the hill back to the hotel. But Eleanor refused to allow any of the vehicles to leave until they had been given the all clear. Nevertheless, some people started to walk back down.

'What's that?' asked Catherine.

Mr Kitamura looked at Eleanor. 'Here it come, big one.'

There was a distant rumble of what seemed to be thunder in a cloudless sky.

'What's happening?' asked Catherine, suddenly fearful.

The noise that came to them standing on the hill was a dreadful sound that Catherine would never forget. The sound of a growling sea that swallowed and pushed all before it. In the grey night light, they could see the dark wall that suddenly appeared against the skyline. It grew larger as it rolled faster and faster towards the shore, overtaking the original film of water that had washed over the road. This wave pushed a wall of water several feet high further inland, overturning cars, before it was lost from sight among the coconut trees.

'My Lord, this is going to be disastrous. Tragic,' said Eleanor.

'What about the horses? The animals?' asked Catherine suddenly. 'Did Mouse move them?'

'Abel John told him to,' said Eleanor. 'But I think we're going to have a lot of damage.'

'Nobody go,' said Mr Kitamura sternly as the crowd had grown silent, moving together as they listened to the noise below.

'There could be more water coming. Though they say the second wave is the worst. I didn't need this,' said Eleanor in a trembling voice.

It was daylight when they got word that it was safe to go down. There was no electricity, so there had been no lights except for the emergency vehicles and a spotlight that had been rigged up.

Eleanor stopped her buggy blocks away from the hotel. As she and Catherine began to wade through water and debris toward the Palm Grove they realised what a disaster the tsunami had been. People were paddling surfboards, canoes and small dinghies along the low lying streets where the water hadn't escaped. Finally the two women were spotted by Kane who had one of the Palm Grove's long canoes and he helped them into it, shaking his head.

'Tings very bad, Mrs L. Much breaking. Coconuts all gone.'

Catherine took out her camera and, with tears spilling from her eyes, she focused on the battered remains of the hotel. Once the banks of the ponds and canals had been breached, the water had swept through the bungalows and buildings, washing away the gardens, uprooting and breaking the grove of palm trees. She couldn't see how this destruction would ever be repaired. They couldn't even get near the main building as the huge thatched roof had gone and the columns that had held it up were now leaning and collapsed. Furniture was scattered like a broken doll's house.

But then, as they skirted the main devastation, they came to the heiau area.

'The parts that the bulldozers haven't moved don't look as thought they've been touched,' said Catherine in surprise.

'They're stones, too damn heavy to move,' said Eleanor bitterly.

'This one sacred place. Night marchers come through here, scare every ting away,' said Kane. 'Powerful spirits here.'

Suddenly Catherine thought of Beatrice's warning. 'Has anyone seen Abel John?'

Eleanor looked up. 'He must be somewhere safe.'

All through the day the work to restore this section of the island to some normalcy continued. Although there was no electricity or phones, at least there had been sufficient time to evacuate people and there were no reports of casualties. Guests were moved to other hotels and guesthouses. It would be days before the water could be drained from the hotel grounds so a clean up could begin and Eleanor could start to assess what was salvageable.

Eleanor was grim. 'I don't know how I'll be able to start over.'

Beatrice arrived and found Eleanor and Catherine trying to work out what could be saved and what could not.

'We can stay with Beatrice I'm sure,' said Catherine to Eleanor.

'I can't leave here. I have to be near here,' said Eleanor. Then as Beatrice got out of her car, Eleanor stopped and looked at Beatrice's solemn, sad face.

'What has happened? What else could?' asked Eleanor.

'It's Abel John.'

'Where is he?' asked Catherine. 'Is he back at his place?'

Beatrice shook her head. 'Three bodies have been washed up.' She hesitated, then said, 'Abel John is dead. It is thought that he tried to rescue some trapped kids. They have all died.'

Eleanor's cry and Catherine's shocked gasp stopped Beatrice from speaking.

'Oh, no. No. His poor family,' said Catherine.

Beatrice looked sadly at Eleanor and Catherine. 'I did not wish for this retribution. It is a great, great loss.'

There was too much sadness. Yet still the sun shone, the sky was angelic blue, the sea calm, the surf flattened, holiday-makers lounged by waving palms in this picture-postcard paradise. But on the other side of Kauai, tears still fell. The death of big, strong, affable Abel John, respected and liked by all, was difficult to accept and comprehend.

Mourners, friends and family began gathering in the afternoon at Abel John's favourite beach for his final journey. It was a surfing beach, there were no houses, no amenities. From early in the morning friends had helped clear the wild scrub and kiawe bushes and set up thatched shelters and spread kapa mats for seating and eating. Women prepared food, children played quietly, aware of the gravity of the day.

The kahuna arrived to conduct the ceremony. Musicians, all friends of Abel John, came to play. His surfer friends, his friends from *Nirvana*, arrived with boards and everywhere were flowers and leis. Helena, in a muted coloured muu-muu, sat silent and withdrawn, her youngest child in her lap, the others sitting quietly close by. A flat-bed truck arrived with canoes stacked on it and when they were unloaded, the musicians used the flat bed as a stage. Beatrice and Lani and their families and a retinue of Abel John's friends settled themselves next to Helena. Hundreds of people lined the foreshore as the sun began to set and the kahuna gathered Abel John's family and friends in front of him. All fell silent.

The kahuna made a signal to start the ceremony and Abel John's elder son stepped forward. Dressed in his father's red lava lava, rolled over at the waist to shorten it, and wearing his father's kukui nut necklace, he carried the great conch shell his father had blown to begin the torch-lighting ceremony at the Palm Grove.

The kahuna gave the boy a nod and an encouraging smile. Everyone held their breath as if summoning their own lungs to give strength to the young boy so he could force air through the shell to give it voice. From somewhere deep inside his narrow chest, it was as if all the pain and sadness, the weight of being his father's son, exploded in a tremendous burst. His chest heaved, his cheeks filled, his face flushed and from the conch shell, held to the sky, there came a mighty, mournful cry that made the earth shudder and rose through the soles of feet to clench at the hearts of all there. For as long as he could, an impossible time it seemed, the boy held the note, until his breath escaped and was gone, like his father. He lowered the shell, bowed his head and waited for the final, final reverberation to drift away.

The silence was broken by the men, rising up and beginning their chant. It was a tribute to a great man, a good man, and they called to the chiefs and the gods to accept and honour Abel John. The drumming took over and then the women joined in, their voices harmonising with the resonant sound of the men.

To accompany the powerful yet lilting song, Kiann'e came forward to tell in dance the story of Abel John – his strength, his fishing and surfing prowess, his love of his wife, his gentleness with his children. And as they prayed, a flotilla of canoes and surfboards gathered at the water's edge. Solemnly, the kahuna led Helena, her daughter and baby son to a canoe being paddled by Kane. They all carried flowers. In a separate canoe Abel John's elder son sat holding a small open calabash containing his father's ashes.

The music on shore continued as everyone filed to the water's edge. They held flowers and watched the canoes, surrounded by the surfers paddling slowly on their boards, as they stroked towards the start of the wave break. The sun was sinking, throwing an embracing light across the sea to those on the beach.

The canoes stopped and drifted on the surface of the sea. The men sang quietly, the kahuna lifted his arms and prayed as Abel John's son slowly leant over the side of his canoe and set the koa wood calabash atop the water.

Crying gently, Helena took the lei from around her neck, kissed it and dropped it into the sea. Her daughter did the same. The baby was asleep, rocked by the canoe and unaware of the grief that surrounded him. The flowers floated towards the bobbing wooden bowl.

And as the sun sank below the horizon, a wave suddenly rose up and surged towards the group, lifting them as it rolled beneath the canoes, breaking after it passed. But the great breast of water carried with it the flowers and the calabash, upending Abel John's ashes and taking all beneath the sea.

'He is gone. It is over,' said the kahuna and they turned for shore where the watchers waited.

But the men who'd surfed with Abel John caught the

wave and rode it, calling and shouting in exhilaration. And as they rode they took off their leis and flung them into the water.

The feasting, the talk story, the music went till the moon rose and bright stars lit the night sky. Catherine was exhausted. She was worried about Eleanor. The fire and spirit seemed to have gone from her. The damage to the hotel complex was staggering, but where once she would have been determined to start over, the death of Abel John seemed to have diminished her. She blamed herself for his death because she hadn't stopped the destruction of the heiau and the removal of the sacred stones.

'That wasn't you! It was your partner! He insisted on doing it. He brought over the workmen. It was not your fault,' said Catherine firmly.

But Eleanor was deeply depressed and wouldn't be comforted.

As Catherine helped Beatrice into her car while they waited for Kiann'e, she sighed. 'Will things ever be the same again?'

The imposing older woman put an arm around her shoulders. 'No. Times have changed. It is how it is. Your life is changing, too. It is time to move on. Your time here is over. Go home. It is best.'

Catherine was silent as they drove away with Beatrice's royal command ringing in her head.

Kiann'e reached over and touched her hand. 'Don't be sad. Remember the happy times here.'

'Oh, I will. I always will,' said Catherine, feeling a sudden rush of powerful emotions and memories. 'Being in the Islands has changed me forever. Thanks for being my friend, Kiann'e.'

They smiled at each other in the dimness of the car, a wistful, sad, warm smile, each wondering when their paths in life would cross again.

16

SWEAT WAS A WET sheen on the horse's coat as Catherine rode to the top of the knoll where they stopped, the horse shaking its head from the exertion and exhilaration. She slid from the saddle and wiped her hand along its damp neck, fondling the horse she'd come to love as deeply as its sire, Parker.

'Well done, Pani. Think we might have broken our record.'

She tied the reins loosely to a tree and sat on her favourite rock on the knoll as the horse began to forage. As it always had, this place gave her a sense of peace and calmness after the turbulent last few days when her memories of Hawaii had resurfaced after years of being tucked away in a special box in her mind.

She heard the steady rumble of the four-wheel drive coming up the slope behind her.

'Were you two training for the Peel Cup? You bolted up here.' Rob got out and handed her a picnic basket. 'The girls have the Esky and the food. Thought you'd have the billy boiling by now.'

'I wanted to sit and enjoy the view. There's so much to think about.'

'Are you getting excited about going back to Hawaii after all this time, Mum?' asked Emily, putting down the heavy food hamper.

'Kind of. They say you shouldn't go back to places,' said Catherine. 'And I'm sure it'll be very different. Except for Kiann'e and Aunty Lani, I'm not sure who's left from my time there.'

'Your old newspaper pal, your boss, he's still around if he's involved with the book launch,' said Rob.

'That's true. Vince must be pushing seventy.'

Catherine smiled at her younger daughter. 'It's a shame you two can't come, Ellie, not very good timing for your end-of-semester exams or for Emily getting time off work.'

'I know, it can't be helped. Anyway, this is a trip for you and Dad to enjoy.'

Rob dropped his arm around Catherine's shoulders. 'I'm happy to tag along. When did we last have a holiday together, alone?'

'Three years ago. New Zealand. And after a week you wanted the girls to come and join us,' said Catherine. 'Was I such boring company?'

Rob kissed her cheek. 'You're never boring, my love. But it was such a beautiful place and all that snow . . .'

The girls started setting up the picnic and gathering twigs to light a fire.

'C'mon on, Mum, we're starving.'

'We could be saving ourselves a lot of trouble and eating down there at the barbecue and gardens we built up for our guests,' said Rob. 'And then Dave gets to do all the hard work.'

'No, no way, Dad. This is our special place. That's for the visitors. This is for us,' chorused the girls.

As her husband and daughters got the lunch ready, Catherine lingered at the lookout. While the landscape hadn't changed since she first came up here as a child, she was, as always, amazed when she gazed down at the changes to *Heatherbrae* itself and how it had gone from carrying stud cattle to, as Rob put it, 'feeding and watering holidaymakers'. How proud she was of what she and Rob had achieved, how they'd weathered tough and good times together.

'You okay?' Rob sat beside her and handed her a glass of wine as the fire crackled behind them and the girls began frying onions.

'I was thinking back to how it used to be. My twenty-first, when Dave fell in the pool and now he's working with us. What a shame your parents can't be here to enjoy this picnic with us.'

Rob's usually happy demeanor dropped for a moment. 'I thought I'd never forgive my father for losing *Craigmore,* but now I'm sorry he didn't live to see what we've done here. And poor Mum, even though she seems calm and happy, she has no idea what's going on. Half the time she doesn't know who I am or where she is.'

Catherine knew that his mother had never really understood what Rob's father was doing when he lost all their money on racehorses and finally had to sell *Craigmore.* And the loss of the property was the last straw in Rob's marriage. Barbara had never liked the country life and she liked it even less when there was no money.

'You know, I admire your dad so much,' Rob continued. 'How fantastically well he's done, not just with his cattle but in his law firm, too. He's been so generous in the way he's helped set this all up,' said Rob.

'He's thrilled you're here, running *Heatherbrae*. Mum's so happy the way things worked out.'

Rob leant against her. 'And you? No regrets? Pleased with what we've done?'

'Rob, I've been blissfully happy since the day I married you.' Catherine linked her arm through his.

'I kick myself for not grabbing you before you went overseas after your twenty-first. But I guess we had to make mistakes, marry the wrong people, learn a few lessons. But now . . . this Hawaii thing, I can't help wondering if I'm second best,' said Rob jokingly.

'Rubbish! Are you trying to make yourself out to be a pathetic creature?' said Catherine digging him in the ribs. 'You have made me more content than I ever dreamed possible. We have so much going for us.'

'Not to mention two gorgeous daughters,' he added, giving her a quick kiss.

'Did someone mention us? Mum, the salad is ready. Shall we throw the meat on the fire?' Ellie smiled at them. Both girls admired the devotion and love of their parents and each dreamed of being lucky enough to find a partner and have a marriage as solid and loving as Rob's and Catherine's. Their life was filled with fun and laughter as well as a deep love and respect.

As the smoke and aroma from their campfire wafted into the crisp blue sky, Catherine studied the distant scene where she and Rob had established their eco-farmstay resort. When cattle prices had slumped Rob and Catherine decided to try something new, inspired by Catherine's friend Eleanor. Together they did the figures, planned and built the romantic farmstay, which a new type of tourist soon discovered. The cosy cottages, hidden among gum trees, offered country space and peace, an opportunity for families to participate in rural life or just unwind and rethink the pace at which they lived in the city and reassess their priorities. Gradually more cottages – furnished with the attention to detail Catherine had learned from Eleanor – grew into a self-contained development. Keith and Rosemary had been very excited by the idea and had invested in it. They had then bought a place in town and started to travel, leaving *Heatherbrae* to Catherine and Rob.

Aware of Eleanor's sensitive inclusion of Hawaiian culture at the Palm Grove, Catherine had invited several local Aboriginal families, stockmen and elders to become part of *Heatherbrae's* farmstay staff. They were involved in all the aspects of the business, including Dave's campfire cookout, music, storytelling and taking visitors riding or on mini walkabouts.

There was a communal dining pavilion, swimming pool, outdoor barbecue and campfire area as well as an old-style bush camp and a small stage where there were informal singalongs, poetry readings, storytelling and dances. There were activities from art classes to nature rambles and many visitors liked to work on the farm with the animals. Catherine always drew on her experience and observations of the Palm Grove by trying to keep the atmosphere warm, friendly and natural. She had written and talked to Eleanor over the years as she and Rob had developed *Heatherbrae* into a first-class country retreat. Rob said it seemed that Eleanor's spirit hovered like a guardian angel over their development.

'So we'd better maintain her standards or else,' Catherine had laughingly told him. She thought of the warm and generous-spirited staff at the Palm Grove and hoped that those who worked for them at *Heatherbrae* felt like family and part of the enterprise too. Their old friend and neighbour Dave and his wife and family lived on the property. Catherine and Rob oversaw the entire running of the resort where they still ran a few stud cattle, as well as feed and some organic vegetables. Having listened to her Aboriginal head stockman talk about the old days and ways of nurturing the land, they began to experiment with conserving the water that flowed from a nearby natural spring.

Ellie came and sat next to Catherine. 'You look so far away, Mum. What are you thinking about? Hawaii?'

'Not at all. I was thinking about *Heatherbrae*. What your father and I have achieved. How happy I am.'

'Oh, Mum, that's lovely.' Ellie put her arm around Catherine's shoulders. 'But you will enjoy going back to the Islands won't you? We're so impressed with you writing a book.'

Catherine smiled. 'It is something, isn't it? I just hope he'd approve. Lester was modest and a bit of a loner, but he was very aware of his achievements. The hard part is going back knowing Eleanor isn't there anymore.'

'I wish I'd met her. I'm so pleased that you named me after her. She would have been so proud of you writing a book about Lester. Do you have any photos of her when she was young? I've only seen ones when you knew her.'

'No, I don't, come to think of it. She left a lot of her Hawaiian collection and some personal pieces to Beatrice and Lani for them to put in a museum.'

'What are you two talking about?' Emily sat down beside them.

'I guess we're talking about Eleanor and my book launch,' said Catherine. 'My book. I'm still not used to saying those words. I never thought it would ever be published.'

'Why did you write it if you didn't think it would get published?' asked practical Emily.

Catherine thought a moment. 'I'd put all those memories away for so long that when I got the parcel from Lester's estate a few years ago and found he'd left me all his albums, scrapbooks and the very first medal he won for swimming, I felt I owed it to him.'

'To tell his story . . . *The Waterman*. But why did he leave those things to you? Didn't he have anyone else?' wondered Ellie.

'No, Lester didn't have any family, although Eleanor and Ed had always been kind to him,' said Catherine. 'He might have left his things to her, but she died long before him. I don't think Eleanor ever got her light and joy back after that tsunami destroyed the Palm Grove and her life's work. Lester was way ahead of his time with being a fitness fanatic. Maybe that's why he lived well into his nineties, even if he did have really bad arthritis. But most of his contemporaries died before him.'

'He sounds a sad man,' commented Emily.

'Maybe to outsiders he seemed lonely. But I don't think he was, as long as he was close to the sea. He would have been very lonely stuck in some place for old people on the mainland,' said Catherine.

'Are there still watermen in Hawaii?' asked Ellie.

'Ah, there'll always be watermen,' said Catherine softly. 'The ocean is a great definer of men. Men will always challenge the power of the waves even though it is the sea that controls them.'

'Men trying to prove themselves,' said Emily.

'Only to themselves. The championships, the big money, the commercialism, that's new. And different from what watermen are about.' Catherine prodded her girls. 'Hey, what's happening with our lunch?'

In bed that night, Rob lay on his back, his hands under his head, staring at the ceiling. Catherine glanced at him and put her book down.

'Shall I turn out the light? You're not reading.'

She rested her head on his chest and he put his arm around her, smoothing her hair.

'Cath, I'm so proud of you. Having a book published is a wonderful achievement. I'm so excited about this trip. I'll see the places that you loved and I can't wait to meet Kiann'e and Aunty Lani. I feel I've known them all our marriage.'

'Rob, I love you so much, that's a lovely thing to say. Every day with you has been wonderful and it just gets better and better. How is that possible?'

'Ah, we must be getting used to each other.' He kissed her. 'Better get some sleep, we have to be up before six to meet that private plane bringing in a group of guests tomorrow.'

As the late afternoon golden light streamed into the screened sunroom that had been her mother's sewing and knitting space, Catherine put down her cup of tea and picked up the advance copy of her book – *The Waterman*.

The publisher had done a beautiful job of illustrating Lester's story with the photographs Lester had taken over the years. Catherine had gone through his albums and carefully selected the photographs she wanted for the book before sending them to her publisher who returned them to Kiann'e for safekeeping. It had been strange sifting through the photos at *Heatherbrae* where the winter frost on the garden and paddocks was a contrast to the pictures of sunny sand and surf.

Lester's photos of himself, so handsome, of the famous Waikiki beach boys, of the Duke, of surfers outside the Outrigger Canoe Club and of his collection of boards depicted a world that seemed very far away. His pictures, of old Waikiki; boys climbing coconut palms, the original hotels, hula dancers, some of the old plantation homes now gone, the outriggers filled with tourists, a fisherman casting a net, Hawaiian keikis playing in the tidal pools all captured an essence of the Islands. That appeal still survived and still attracted visitors. The stunning and serene beauty, the warmth of the people and the knowledge that the Islands were separated from the rest of the world and its worries by a great sea of blue, meant you became part of island life, drifting to its rhythm: the sway of palms, its music and song and its constant heartbeat – the throb of the waves.

Catherine had decided that she would take Lester's scrapbooks and albums back to Hawaii with her and give them to Kiann'e to see if they could be housed in an appropriate place. Dear old Aunty Lani might have a suggestion too. Although she was getting on, she'd promised to fly over from Kauai, where she now lived, for the book launch in Honolulu. She told Catherine that Uncle Henry mightn't be able to make it as he had good and bad days now and he was just as happy to stay on his porch in the sun. Catherine had promised to visit them both after the book launch.

Catherine put the book to one side and flipped through Lester's albums. She'd had copies made of her favourite pictures but there were blanks in the album not just where she'd taken out photos for the book. There were many other gaps where pictures had been removed over the years and she wondered why.

On her way to the bedroom she began to plan what to pack, remembering how warm, tropical and casual the Islands were, and found she was full of excitement and anticipation. What great fun she and Rob would have there. She had a pile of summer clothes piled on the bed when Rob raced in.

'Cath, darling, quick! Dave's come off that bloody mad horse. I think he's broken his leg.'

'Oh, no! Have you rung for the ambulance?'

'Yes. He seems to be holding up okay but I'm sure he's

454

going to be out of commission for a bit. Sandra will go to the hospital with him.'

'Rob, this is going to leave us very short handed, isn't it?'

'We've got that big group just in, so we have a full house.' Rob looked at Catherine. 'How would you feel if I didn't go to your book launch?'

'Disappointed, but you're right, the business comes first. But it's very upsetting.'

'Cath, I've got an idea,' said Rob suddenly. 'Why don't you ask Mollie to join you? Didn't she go there with you before?'

'Mollie came to visit a couple of times. She loved the Islands . . . that's a brilliant idea. I bet she'd love it. She met Lester. They both thought each other was great.'

'There you go then,' said Rob sounding relieved. 'Give her a call.'

'Fabulous! I'll drop everything,' shrieked Mollie. 'I was going to suggest I go over but Jason said I shouldn't horn in on you and Rob. Of course I should be there! My God, I think I still have the muu-muu I bought when I went to see you there. It's about the only thing I can get into these days. Ooh Waikiki, here we come. I'd love to see Kiann'e again.' Mollie bubbled over with plans and reminiscences. 'Say, Cathy, you should send Bradley a copy of the book. Where is he these days?'

'Still in Washington DC with his wife. I doubt he'd be interested, we haven't spoken in years. But I will send Aunt Meredith a copy. She's still going strong. She's a good old stick, I like her.'

'Yeah she was good fun when she came out here on that cruise a few years back and we had lunch with her,' said Mollie.

Meredith had always sent Christmas cards and followed Catherine's life closely over the years, so when she had come to Sydney on a cruise ship, Catherine had made the trip to Sydney to see her.

'It's been a wonderful trip. I thought it would be a great chance to visit Australia and hopefully see you. I'm so glad you could come,' Meredith exclaimed.

Catherine had taken Meredith around Sydney, introduced her to Emily and Ellie, who were both living there at the time and, the day before the ship sailed, Mollie had joined them all for a riotous lunch at a smart restaurant overlooking the harbour.

As they hugged goodbye Meredith held Catherine's hand. 'I'm so happy at the way your life has turned out, dear girl. You always had a spark and I worried Bradley might extinguish your fire. You just weren't right for each other. He's happy, with a compliant wife and children who always tiptoe around him and never raise their voices. Everything is just the way he wants it.'

As Catherine chuckled, Meredith added, 'Don't have regrets, Catherine. Your time in Hawaii was a growing time. I'm sure you learned a lot. You were brave to leave Bradley. But it was the right thing to do.'

'Looking back I know it was. I worried about hurting him and I thought I was punished because I left, but often these things that seem disasters at the time turn out well,' Catherine had said.

'So how do you feel about going back? Be a few memories there, eh girl?' said Mollie. 'Now to important stuff: what are you taking to wear? Is your book launch cocktails or morning tea? Are we going to Kauai? Maybe we should do a twirl around some of the other islands?'

Catherine laughed. 'We'll see, but, yes, Kauai is a must. Aunty Lani and Uncle Henry are there now. And

I must go back to Hanapepe and see if Miranda's *Joss House* is still there.'

'It's going to be a blast,' said Mollie emphatically.

At their first glimpse of the Islands from the plane, those green gems scalloped in sandy beaches and white-crested waves, Catherine grabbed Mollie's hand.

'Look, we're flying over Kauai.' And she found that even after all these years she could still identify peaks and valleys, the north shore beaches. The places PJ had showed her.

Honolulu Airport was bigger and glitzier and there was a troupe of singers and dancers to welcome them. There were big advertisements in glass cases for hotels showing luxurious high-rise glass towers that seemed to dwarf even Diamond Head.

'Holy cow, the joint has stepped up a bit,' said Mollie. 'Why isn't your publisher putting you up in the penthouse of one of those?'

'Because it's a small publishing house and I wanted to stay at the Moonflower. Oh, there's Kiann'e.' Catherine broke into a run to embrace her beautiful friend who was holding leis and smiling just as it had always been. Catherine buried her face in the creamy plumeria and pikake flowers, inhaling their perfume and was flooded with memories and sensations that enveloped her only in the Islands.

Mollie did the talking as they drove from the airport to Kiann'e's house. Even she was astounded by the changes to Oahu, the crowded freeways, high rises, apartment complexes crawling up the hillsides, the shopping malls and touristy restaurants and resorts. Catherine was glad Mollie was exclaiming for both of them. She was too overwhelmed to speak. There had been so much change, some places were unrecognisable, but others, so very familiar.

Once they were in the residential streets of Kiann'e's neighbourhood, Catherine drew a breath. 'Well, at least some things are still the same. You and Willi are still in the same house.'

'Yes. But I've also inherited Mother's house on Kauai. The Daughters of Hawaii restored it and it's a kind of living museum that holds special treasures. We still have meetings there and that's where the offices of the sovereignty movement are.'

'Have things moved forward much?' asked Catherine.

'Well, yes and no. Senator Akaka introduced a bill in 2000 to establish a process for native Hawaiians to gain recognition similar to that of native Americans but it keeps going back to the drawing board for modifications and changes and being "reinterpreted",' said Kiann'e. 'But the bill is the "foot in the door", so we hope reparations and reconciliation will come after that.'

'What's that about?' asked Mollie.

'This bill recognises the political obligation that the US government has to the people who continuously lived on these islands for hundreds of years. It is very sad, but it is true that the social ills in Hawaii today affect a disproportionate number of native Hawaiians,' said Kiann'e.

'Like what?' asked Catherine.

'Drugs, homelessness . . . disaffected youth, unemployment, it's all out of balance. Mother always predicted that this would happen,' she answered.

'Balance. I remember Abel John talking about that,' said Catherine. 'He talked about the balance between men and women, individuals and communities. That without the concept of balance society won't get anywhere. Like a canoe without a paddle or a sail. How're Helena and the kids?'

'Grown up of course. His elder son graduated from

university and he's working with us now. He'll be a leader. The younger ones don't remember their father. But the rest of us do,' said Kiann'e quietly.

Later that day Kiann'e drove Catherine and Mollie over to the Moonflower, where she still occasionally danced. For old times' sake they went to the Moonflower's dining room for dinner that evening with Willi and Kiann'e's two grown-up children.

'After my kids found out that I was coming here with Catherine, they made me promise to organise a family get-together here next year,' said Mollie.

'Be sure to let me know so we can meet them,' said Kiann'e.

The following day Catherine met her publisher who congratulated her on her book and explained the details of the launch party, which would be held on the big terrace of the Moonflower. Vince, now partially retired from the *Hawaii News*, had provided large blow-ups of the photos Catherine had taken for her articles all those years ago as well as big prints from the book about Lester as the backdrop to the ceremony.

'You know, Catherine, looking at the pictures of yours that Vince brought and reading your articles, I think there's another book that you might like to do: Hawaii in the seventies compared with the Islands today.'

'Sounds like you and Rob could come and stay for a month to do the research,' said Mollie when Catherine told her of her publisher's suggestion.

'I don't think so. Rob wouldn't like to be away from *Heatherbrae* for that long. Anyway, I think I'd rather remember the Islands as they were,' she said.

'Then how about we go on a bit of a tour around and see how Waikiki and the North Shore have changed,' suggested Mollie. 'And do a bit of a pub crawl like we did the last time.'

Catherine laughed. 'I don't know if I have the stamina to keep up with you.'

Mollie drove their rental car and Catherine, watching from the passenger's window, was amazed at the new development. While the old TradeWinds apartment building was still there, it was buried behind buildings and a motorway. There were more hotels squeezed into that area, but her old haunt, the Chart House, was still there.

'Let's go there for dinner one night,' said Mollie.

Waikiki was jammed with new buildings. As Mollie said, 'It's very touristy, but buzzy. Heck, it's fun.'

At Kapiolani Park they were lucky to find a parking spot so they walked through the park, past the statue of Queen Kapiolani. They saw a stand asking people to sign a petition for an Hawaiian candidate to represent Hawaii in Congress and at the rotunda there was an advertisement for a children's hula contest and show.

'I remember when I brought the Wives' Club to a hula show,' said Catherine. 'Bradley thought they'd hate it, but everyone loved it. I wonder what's happened to all those women.'

'None of them would have had a life like yours and Rob's,' said Mollie, linking her arm through Catherine's. 'So how do you feel about being back here?'

'Too early to tell. It's a bit overwhelming. I think Kauai will be the real test,' Catherine answered lightly.

At sunset, Mollie and Catherine sat beneath the banyan tree on the terrace of the classic Moana Hotel, refurbished yet again.

'Well, they can't change the sunset,' said Mollie.

'I have to say it was romantic here . . . I think this setting swept me off my feet as much as Bradley,' said Catherine.

'Before you marry someone you should go through the boring test,' said Mollie. 'Be somewhere boring, with boring people, where things get stuffed up. So you see each other in a real light in real life. I told my daughter to take that Gordon of hers off on a camping trip before she agreed to marry him.'

'Gordon! He's such a computer geek and cafe-latte type. A boulevardier,' laughed Catherine.

'Exactly. Trudy isn't exactly the outdoor type either so the whole trip was a disaster,' said Mollie gleefully. 'But they were able to laugh about it and coped so I figured they'd be all right together.' She sipped her cocktail. 'Can you believe I'm going to be a grandmother? Yikes. I don't look like a grandmother do I?' She struck a pose with a hand behind her head of wild curls. She wore a strapless long sundress over her ample bosom, big gold hoop earrings and had tucked a large hibiscus behind one ear. Mollie was shocked to find muu-muus were no longer de rigueur but swore she'd find something Hawaiian to wear at home.

'You're still larger than life, Mol,' said Catherine fondly.

'That's right, you need me to boss you around,' said Mollie firmly. 'Now, do you know what you're wearing and what you're going to say at your book shindig?'

As she had done so often before, Kiann'e said she'd make special leis for Catherine's book launch.

'I'll never forget the ones you made for her wedding,' said Mollie. 'They were divine.'

'My daughter helps me, she's learning the kaona, the old knowledge,' said Kiann'e. 'Would you like to come with us? It's a special time.'

'Sure, that'd be fun. Don't you think, Cath?' said Mollie.

'We have to go before sunrise,' said Kiann'e.

461

'Oh,' said Mollie, her enthusiasm wilting.

'It'll be fun. Interesting. Yes, we'd love to go with you,' said Catherine.

It was barely light and windy as they drove over the Pali the next morning and turned onto a side road into a valley. Kiann'e pulled off the road and handed Catherine and Mollie a flashlight and a woven basket.

'You might need this. Anika and I will go ahead.'

As soon as they entered the cool, damp rainforest, the women fell silent. Kiann'e's tall, beautiful daughter led the way, her steps sure in the dim light. Catherine and Mollie kept their eyes to the ground following the pool of yellow light from the flashlight so they didn't trip over thick roots, stones or plants on the path. It wasn't until Kiann'e and Anika stopped that they looked up and saw where they were. They'd come to a small stream singing over stones lined by mossy boulders. Tall trees reached towards the pearling sky. Anika looked to her mother.

Kiann'e lifted her hands and softly began to chant, her sweet voice rising upland as she called to the spirits across time. Anika crouched and picked a handful of small damp ferns and expertly braided them into a circlet and placed it on the waters of the stream as the notes of her mother's chant drifted across the valley.

'We are honouring the aina, our land, saying a mahalo, for allowing us to be here,' Kiann'e explained to Mollie.

They walked single file along the edge of the stream and Mollie touched Catherine's hand and whispered, 'I can smell them. The flowers.'

Kiann'e and Anika pointed out the ferns, seeds, strands of moss and, further along, the flowering trees.

'It's best the flowers are picked with the dew on them,' said Kiann'e.

As the sky lightened they gathered the flowers and ferns and carefully placed them in their baskets.

Kiann'e held up certain flowers, tucking a fern beneath one or curling a leaf and seed pod around a perfect cluster of pikake, already thinking of how she'd create each lei. 'Making lei is creating a connection between nature and us, it is a gift that speaks of many things. Hello, welcome, farewell, good luck, congratulations.'

'I wish they lasted longer,' said Mollie.

'Like many things, it is the intangible, the memory that stays with you.' Kiann'e smiled and held out a plumeria blossom. 'Smell and remember. Now each time you see and smell this flower you might remember being here, these moments.'

The sun had risen and its first rays penetrated the rainforest canopy sending shafts of misty light through the trees to sparkle on the stream. Dewdrops began to melt like tears. The women felt privileged to be there. Even Mollie's exuberance was subdued. On the way out of the valley with their baskets of flowers and greenery, Kiann'e and Anika talked about lei designs, the artistic interpretation of them, the art of blending each individual perfect bloom in a harmonious whole and the many various ways leis were strung, backed and put together.

Kiann'e and Anika left them at the hotel and waved goodbye. 'See you tonight!'

Mollie linked her arm through Catherine's. 'Well, that was worth getting up for. Thanks. Now let's have breakfast, it's still early!'

Catherine was in a daze as the book launch drew near and let Mollie take over. She had already been interviewed on radio and the *Hawaii News* had written a major feature about her and the book, complete with photo. Rob and the girls had rung to wish her luck.

Mollie handed her a glass of champagne as Catherine

fiddled with her hair. 'Here, a dressing drink. Stop fussing, you look gorgeous.'

'I'm not used to being the centre of attention. Vince said it'd be all right to keep my speech short. I'm so nervous. It's ridiculous.'

'Just thank everyone you can think of, say a few nice things about being back here. Don't tell them the whole place is ruined and how shocked you are by the traffic and the homeless people,' advised Mollie.

'Well, I am still in shock after going out to Makaha,' said Catherine. 'When I lived here, the North Shore was deserted. Just surfers and a few locals lived out there. Now it's jammed with the homeless, thousands of them.' She shook her head at the memory of the rows and rows of tents, camps and makeshift shelters strung along the beachfront for miles.

'If you're going to be homeless, Hawaii is better and warmer than New York City, that's for sure,' said Mollie.

'What's sad is so many of them are Hawaiians. They can't afford to live in their own state,' sighed Catherine.

'Yes, I know,' said Mollie. 'But come on, show time.'

Catherine was amazed when she saw how many people were gathered. Vince Akana as her old boss had appointed himself her official escort and took her around introducing her to guests. It turned out many were old friends, some she recognised, some she didn't.

When she saw the crowd, she was glad that Kiann'e had arranged a small get-together with Aunty Lani ahead of the formal function. Aunty Lani, still large and smiling but with grey hair, had hugged Catherine, tears streaming down her cheeks. Catherine had promised her they'd have to time to chat properly when she and Mollie went over to Kauai.

'Uncle, he getting on, but he want to see you. He remembers the time he got you to look after those baby goats.'

'I remember. I have a few goats at home,' said Catherine. And as Mollie shot her an amused glance, she added, 'Angora goats, Mollie.'

As she walked onto the terrace of the Moonflower, seeing the tiki torches flaring with the ocean behind, the flower arrangements and a small troupe of young dancers in ti-leaf skirts that Kiann'e had organised, Catherine was suddenly reminded of the Palm Grove.

A small, elderly Chinese woman came up and greeted Catherine with excitement. She looked familiar and as Catherine was trying to place her, she pumped Catherine's hand. 'Me Mrs Hing, malasada lady.'

Several other people that she had known from the newspaper came up to her and chatted about the old days until Mollie extricated her.

'Another old friend would like to say hello,' she said with a raised eyebrow and led her to a group where a striking brunette held out her hand.

'Congratulations, Catherine.'

'Julia! Julia Bensen, is it you? What're you doing here?' Catherine was surprised to see her and glanced quickly around. 'Are any of the Wives' Club here?'

'You'll be sorry to hear, no,' said Julia. 'You're not the only one who's moved on with your life. You have done very well.'

'It's a small book,' began Catherine modestly.

'I was talking about your life. Your friend Mollie has told me how successful – and happy – you are in Australia. We were all in awe of you, you know, so I always thought you'd do something special.'

'Me? I was terrified of all of you!' exclaimed Catherine. 'I always felt such a country bumpkin compared with how sophisticated you all were.'

'No, your independence, how you seemed to do just what you wanted, I think everyone was a bit jealous.'

'But what are you doing here? Where's Jim? Do you have a family?'

'Jim and I are divorced. He's married a bimbo, silly fool. Our kids are all grown up, so I thought back on my time here and I thought how much I liked Hawaii best. So I moved here. I've brought along a bunch of friends to meet you.' She indicated a group of women beside her.

Catherine smiled and nodded to them all. 'And Commander and Mrs Goodwin?'

'Long retired. The commander has passed on, but Mrs G is still active, as you can imagine, in the navy wives' groups in Washington DC. I don't think the young wives are quite as subservient as we were, though,' added Julia.

'Oh dear, I always felt that I failed Bradley badly,' said Catherine.

Julia looked down and then said candidly, 'Did you know Bradley really wanted you back? He told Jim that he'd do anything for you.'

'No, I didn't know that.'

'Yes. But the commander told him that he might have difficulty in getting another promotion if he did. I suspect that it was Mrs G's influence. She never liked you. Frankly, I think your openness, your independant ideas and how you stood up to her, challenged her position.'

'What an old witch,' said Mollie, stepping in as she saw the expression on Catherine's face. 'Come on, I think your publisher wants you. Speech time.'

Catherine squeezed Julia's hand. 'Thanks for coming. I hope you're happy.'

'Hey, I'm in Hawaii, how could I not be?' she said brightly.

As pupus were passed, her publisher, dressed in a new aloha shirt, glanced at his watch and raised a questioning eyebrow at Catherine. 'Ready?'

'I guess so.'

The music paused and, in the silence, guests gathered into a semicircle as the publisher went to the podium and lifted his hand. A spotlight fell on a young man who stepped forward. Catherine caught her breath. Silhouetted against the last of the sunset, the young man, dressed in a red lava lava and kukui nut necklace, a crown of maile leaves around his head, lifted a large conch shell. In that moment Catherine saw Abel John as the young man she had known. She realised that this must be his son.

As the haunting notes wavered and faded there was a crackling through the amplifiers and Eleanor's voice rang out, reciting her prayer to the night. Catherine, wrapped in memories, faced the sea as the sun disappeared below the horizon.

'Sorry, I should have told you,' said her publisher.

'That's fine,' said Catherine. 'I never realised that there was a recording of Eleanor saying the night prayer. How wonderful to hear her voice again.'

Catherine paid tribute to Lester in her speech. She told the audience of his time as an Olympian and as a stuntman, but most of all she told them about the beauty of the Islands, their myths and their magic and the spell that they cast over all who landed on them and how this place caught Lester's heart in particular. She told them of Lester's love of the ocean and how he had dedicated his life to it, capturing many of his memories in his magnificent photos.

'I hope,' she said, 'that he would approve of my telling his story.'

After her speech Catherine was surrounded by more well-wishers and the local press.

Later, as everyone settled down to enjoy the food and drinks, a tall woman with long hair, exotic jewellery, black slacks and a dramatic and colourful jacket came towards Catherine.

She recognised the woman immediately. 'Sadie! You too. I don't know if I can stand any more surprises.' They embraced warmly and Catherine asked after Ginger and Summer.

'Well, happy, last I heard. They're in a little place in California called Joshua Tree, all sharing a big old house, doing interesting, alternative things – as you'd expect.'

'And you, Sadie? Are you living here?'

'No. One of life's coincidences. I live in Europe, I travel a lot. I work and teach. I always try to stopover here, the old fascination. And I read about your book launch in the paper and recognised your photo. So you did it. Good for you.'

They smiled at each other.

'I've thought about you, wondered where your path took you,' said Catherine. 'Much further afield than my small patch of country Australia, it seems.'

'Yes, I'm a traveller. And a loner – but it's how I choose to be. But your life sounds rich, fulfilled and happy.'

'It is,' said Catherine.

Mollie joined them, curious about the interesting-looking woman. Catherine introduced them.

'Do you know what happened to any of your Aussie friends, the surfers? Damien was one I recall,' said Sadie.

'Ah, ask Mollie,' said Catherine.

'Well, I know that this might be a bit hard to believe, but years ago he joined my husband's stockbroking firm, then struck out on his own as a futures trader,' said Mollie and they all laughed. 'Damien is now making more money than he knows what to do with. Married with kids, five-star lifestyle at the beach. He stills surfs at dawn every day, I'm told.'

It was late when Mollie and Catherine collapsed on the balcony of their suite. Mollie lifted her glass of champagne.

'Here's to you, kid. Queen of the Islands. You sold

a bundle of books and we've met so many people that I think you know everyone here.'

'It's been overwhelming,' sighed Catherine. 'Now I can't wait to get to Kauai and leave all the hoopla behind. Though to tell you the truth, I'm nervous about what I'll find.'

The short hop to Kauai wasn't long enough for Catherine to readjust from the excitement of the book launch and modern Honolulu but she was pleased to see once again the familiar outline of the Garden Island.

Mollie glanced at her face and, seeing the impact the sight had on her good friend, she started to sing softly. 'Memory, all alone in the moonlight / I can smile at the old days / I was beautiful then / I remember the time I knew what happiness was / Let the memory live again.'

'Oh, cut it out, Mollie,' said Catherine.

'Ah, Cathy. We all have memories of old romances, old adventures. Most of us don't revisit them though, I guess.'

Mollie had made the arrangements and had booked them into an upmarket hotel out at Poipu. As she pulled the car into the private entrance of the hotel she exclaimed, 'Just as well there's valet parking, there's not an inch to park anywhere near the beach.'

'It's all reserved for apartments and hotels. Where do the locals get to park?' wondered Catherine. 'This used to be such a remote stretch of beach. We used to run through a pineapple plantation to get there. There was a gorgeous mansion on the point and the boys used to surf there and use the private beach and garden.'

'Talking of surfing, when are you going to see if you still have it, babe?' asked Mollie as she handed the car keys to the attendant.

Catherine smiled. 'Oh, I think that's all in the past.'

'Dare you. Bet they hire out surfboards here.

469

Anyway, I'm going to hit the pool, then lunch, then a siesta.'

'Oh, I can't wait to go to Hanapepe, it's not far.'

'C'mon, Cath, relax. It's been full on. Take time out first.'

Catherine knew Mollie was right. So, after settling into their luxurious suite they changed and set out to explore the lavish hotel and its grounds at the edge of the beach.

'I'm going in that pool. Look at it, it's even got a grotto and waterfall in the centre,' said Mollie, taking command of two chaise lounges under a thatched umbrella.

'I'm going for a walk, I might go in the ocean. Keep my place,' said Catherine.

She stood on the strip of beach in front of the hotel shading her eyes, watching the break and sets of waves. A hotel lifeguard smiled at her.

'Want to go for a canoe ride? Or hire a board?' he said lightly.

'What kind of board?' asked Catherine.

'Surfboard, lady. You know, for riding the waves.' He was young with a body that said, Look at me, I work out at the gym several times a day and think I'm a great hunk. He probably fancied himself as a model or actor and idly she wondered if steroids had contributed to his extreme body shape that was bronzed, hairless and oiled. Suddenly an image of PJ's beautiful, naturally proportioned body and halo of gold hair flashed into her mind.

'If you've got a seven or eight footer I wouldn't mind trying it out,' she said. 'Or a mini mal.'

He did a short double take. 'You know what you're doing? Don't go out too far, there's a bit of a swell off that point. You stay in close now, you hear?'

Catherine ignored him as the boy brought out a board for her to use. She looked at it carefully, running her hands along its length, checking the workmanship. It was mass produced with a cursory finish. Nothing like the hours of work Lester and PJ had put into their boards.

For a moment she thought what she was doing was insane and wished she hadn't risen to the bait of the arrogant young man. Nonetheless, as he was watching her from behind his mirrored glasses with an amused smirk, she picked up the board and carried it to the water's edge. She stood and waited, studying the water, and soon she forgot about the young man, the tourists, the shouting children and fixed her attention on the waves.

Then she was on the board paddling through the shallows, going through the small low break and out to where the sets were rising and rolling. The rhythm and balance had come back to her within minutes. Like riding a bike, she thought to herself. Your body remembers.

There were several men and two girls out there. They looked at Catherine but were far enough away not to pay her much attention. While she wasn't as fit as she once was, Catherine was still slim and she'd always been strong. With her hair pulled back in a pony tail, from a distance she could be any age.

She picked a modest wave and although she wobbled – her legs were not as powerful nor her feet as secure as in the past – she was up and rode a short distance before cutting back to get out further and try for a bigger wave now she had some confidence back.

She stayed in the waves for nearly an hour and by the time she paddled back into the beach and carried the board back to the lifeguard station her legs were shaking and her arms were aching but she was exhilarated. She signed for the board, ignoring the lifeguard's stare, before she went to find Mollie who was dozing beneath the umbrella. Beside her was an empty cocktail glass that had held some coconut concoction with a pineapple stick and cherry on an umbrella left in the bottom.

As Catherine settled on the other lounge Mollie opened an eye. 'So? Did you have a go?'

'I sure did. I'm wrecked,' she laughed.

Mollie sat up. 'You mean you went surfing and you didn't tell me? I wanted to take a picture. Go back out again.'

'No way. My surfing days are over. Once every thirty years is enough for me,' said Catherine. But she couldn't help grinning. 'But it felt good that I could still do it. I showed that lifeguard. What're you drinking?'

'Mauna Kea Fantasia. Killer cocktails. Not to be taken before surfing.' Mollie lifted her hand to a pretty waitress in shorts and an aloha shirt. 'Two more of these, please.'

'There's the turn-off. Heavens, it still looks pretty much the same, except that the road's paved.'

'Only just, the side bits aren't and there's not much of a footpath,' said Mollie, easing into the main street of Hanapepe. 'Heavens, more chickens! There are chooks all over this island. Outside shops, in parking lots, even along the beaches.'

'Yes, amazing. Stop here. Let's walk. Oh gosh.' Catherine was thrilled to find this tiny village more or less as she remembered. 'Oh, they've restored the old pool hall. And there are a few more galleries and shops.'

'It's pretty sleepy. But cute,' said Mollie getting out of the car to follow Catherine.

Catherine stopped and pointed to a pretty colourful two-storey house. 'That's *The Joss House*. And that little café used to be Molo's.'

Mollie trailed behind as Catherine went in and out of the shops and galleries that were open. There wasn't another person in the street. A few chickens pecked in the gutter. She asked the man behind the counter in the café did he know of Molo.

The man nodded. 'Yep. He's got a house on top of the hill, near the Japanese cemetery. But he's away on the mainland. Come back next month.'

'Can I leave him a note, please? Would you give it to him when you next see him?' Catherine scribbled a note on the pad the man gave her and he put it on the shelf.

'You old friend of Molo?'

'Yes. I stayed here once. Down the road in the old *Joss House*. Do you know Miranda? She had a gallery there. Very attractive woman, red curly hair.'

He shook his head. 'But there's a lot of ladies here. All them arty places run by single ladies.' He grinned.

'What's with the chickens everywhere?' asked Mollie.

'Dey all escape da farms in Hurricane Iniki in '92. You want chicken souvenir?' He pointed to postcards, mugs and tea towels decorated with chickens.

'We'll pass on the chooks, thanks,' said Mollie.

The old swinging bridge, recently repaired, dangled over the river but Mollie refused to walk across it. They marvelled at a house that was a collection of art pieces and eccentric architecture. An old black pick-up truck painted with raging flames along the bonnet and sides had its open back filled with dirt from which spilled trails of scarlet bougainvillea.

They drove up the hill and took more photos of the view out to the ocean.

'Anything else?' asked Mollie.

'I guess not,' said Catherine. 'I keep expecting to see the people I knew here looking exactly as they used to.'

'Well, at least this is one place that hasn't been buried under cement. Let's go and see Aunty Lani. They're hanging out to see you.'

473

It was a small house tucked next to a small plantation shadowed by high cliffs into which red and green whorls had been carved by the wind and rain. A lone coconut palm waved by the front gate.

As they turned in off the road, the old couple were waiting for them. Uncle Henry was stooped and grey haired and Aunty Lani as energetic as ever.

'I've been telling Uncle 'bout that party. He loves your book, Catherine.'

'I was so glad you came over,' said Catherine. 'Sorry you missed it, Uncle.'

He was smiling broadly, his eyes sparkling and he couldn't speak as he embraced her.

They settled themselves on the porch facing the magnificent mountains.

'You're not lonely out here, Aunty? You seem far away from things.' Catherine was thinking of their house near the beach back on Oahu which had always been filled with people, where there always seemed to be food or a party and music happening.

'This is the land they gave us. Because we are Hawaiian people,' said Aunty. 'This is our land now, no-one can take it away. We have a ninety-nine year lease, so even our children can live here.'

'That's if they want to live out here,' said Uncle Henry. 'We're not so far from Beatrice's house and we still got lotta friends here. Miss my kids on Oahu, though.'

'Kiann'e comes to visit a lot doesn't she?' said Catherine.

'Yep. She becoming a very important lady in the Islands now. She going to get us sovereignty. Now you girls eat up this haupia cake.'

The time flew by, Mollie made Uncle giggle like a schoolboy with her jokes and teasing. He kept slapping his knee and shaking his head.

'You bring dis girl back. She good medicine, Catherine.'

Mollie carried the plates inside and Uncle followed her. Catherine reached over and took Aunty Lani's hand. 'It's so good to see you. I hadn't realised how much I missed you all. I'm going to bring my girls over to the Islands to see you.'

'You do that. Maybe you write another book, eh?'

'I don't think so, Lani. I'll take some photos though.'

'That's a good thing you do that book. Poor ol' Lester. Too bad he never see it.'

'I think he knows. He must have left me his albums for that reason.' Catherine sighed. 'I think he must have been lonely in his old age. He lived such a long time. And no family. Though, you know, I found a letter in one of the scrapbooks. He really loved a lady once and he wrote her a letter, a beautiful letter, asking her to come back and marry him if she could only take him and how he lived in the Islands as he was. But he never posted it.' Catherine shook her head. 'So sad. I wonder who she was. There were blank spots in the photo albums, like he'd removed the pictures of someone. It must have been her.'

Lani stared at Catherine. 'You don' know? He always love that lady. And in her way she loved him. But they never meant to be together, oh no.'

'You know? Who was it? Who did Lester love so much?' asked Catherine curiously.

'Why, that be Eleanor, of course. They met in the war. But she was ambitious lady. She knew Lester never gonna change.'

Catherine drew a sharp breath. 'Yet she came back to the Islands.' Suddenly things she'd wondered about, things Lester and Eleanor had said, now made sense. 'And she married Ed. Was she happy with Ed? And she looked after Lester.'

'Ah, that much later. She and Ed were very happy.

Both business people. Lester never had business head. Ed understood Lester, he loved Eleanor and she adored her Ed. Lester was someone she knew at a certain time in her life.' Lani gave her a shrewd look. 'People come into your life, they go, life goes on, eh?'

'So that's why she let him live in that apartment. That's nice,' said Catherine.

'You been back to the Palm Grove?' asked Lani.

'No. That's our last stop.'

Lani patted her hand. 'Don't be sad. Remember how it used to be. And we got a lot of good pictures and memories, haven't we?'

'Pictures up here.' Catherine tapped her head.

Catherine remembered the last time she saw the Palm Grove and described again to Mollie the terrible tsunami, the water and the destruction of the hotel and the sadness at the loss of Abel John.

'He always said something awful would happen because they started to clear the heiau,' said Catherine.

'You sure it's on this road?'

'I think so, but there are so many buildings along this stretch of coast, I'm confused. Maybe it's behind that glass monstrosity,' said Catherine pointing to a large luxury resort.

Mollie turned the car between the massive lava rock gates that led to a driveway lined with young coconut palms. 'This looks like it.'

Catherine was too stunned to speak. At the entrance was a sign, 'The Palm Grove'. But there the likeness ended. Emerald lawns, fountains, a huge open-air glass and steel foyer filled with orchids that cascaded down a waterfall in the lobby confronted them. A concierge in an elaborate uniform came and opened the car door.

'Welcome to the Palm Grove, ladies.'

'Is this where the original Palm Grove hotel was?' asked Mollie.

'It is the same site. But the land has been filled and the grounds extended. It used to flood you know. Are you checking in?'

'No,' said Catherine. 'I used to come here a long time ago. Can we look around?'

'We'll have something to eat. Maybe a drink later,' said Mollie taking Catherine's arm and leading her into the foyer. 'My God, look at this place. It's stunning! Gorgeous. Look at the French antiques! Why aren't we staying here?'

'They probably charge thousands a night. Mollie, this is awful. I can't believe it!'

'It's divine! I love it. Plush, plush. Look at that pool. Ooh, this is movie-star stuff,' breathed Mollie, quite awestruck.

'But think back to what it was, what Eleanor created . . . But of course you never saw it.' Catherine stopped a passing staff member. 'Excuse me, is there anything left of the original Palm Grove hotel?'

The girl looked confused. 'Sorry, I'm new. The old area is out the back. Over there.'

'Well, thank heavens for that. Come on.' Catherine headed through the lobby in the direction the girl had pointed. Mollie trailed behind her taking in the décor with its life-size portraits of Hawaiian royalty and marble tables with huge crystal vases of flowers, the Aubusson carpets and deep comfortable furniture in beautiful silk fabrics.

'Can you imagine what the suites must be like?' breathed Mollie.

Catherine didn't answer. This was not like anything that Eleanor had tried to do. She followed the path through the grounds, surprised she couldn't see anything familiar, but then she saw a discreet sign pointing to 'the sacred grove and temple'. She strode past the day-spa area and through a small gateway in an old lava stone wall by a tiny waterlily pond. Then she stopped and stared.

This was the heiau, almost unrecognisable in its transformation. As Abel John would have wished, the sacred stones, the original temple walls and altar, had all been exposed in situ and sat amidst clipped lawns. Small plaques with artists' impressions of how it might have looked hundreds of years before were displayed before each group of stones. And at the far end was a thatched roundhouse where it seemed dances and ceremonies were held.

Mollie caught up to her. 'Hey, what a groovy place. They must hold weddings here.'

'It's the heiau. A sacred place,' said Catherine quietly. 'Even this has become a tourist attraction.'

'Where are the old palm trees? You know the ones with names on them that you told me about?' asked Mollie.

'I don't know. So much was destroyed in the tsunami, but I can't believe it's all gone. I'm so glad Eleanor can't see this.' Catherine stood there a moment longer, her eyes closed, then turned on her heel and walked away.

'Are we going to have a drink? It's hot and the bar looks amazing.'

'Mollie, I'd rather not. Let's drive a bit.'

Catherine directed Mollie out to her last stop on this odd pilgrimage and was relieved to find she remembered her way along the coast road. But there were cars and car parks at every possible location as well as expensive-looking homes. The road that had been a dirt track was now paved and part of a residential area. It was hard to recognise where *Nirvana* had been, but as they passed one sprawling suburban house with a large garden Catherine exclaimed, 'I think that's where it was. The trees look familiar. And the setting. Gosh.'

'Not exactly an out-of-the-way hippie dropout place now,' said Mollie. 'Where to?'

'One last shot and that's it.'

They parked off the road, locked the car and Catherine led the way along the beach. A wind had sprung up and there was no decent surf so the rocky beach was deserted save for a lone fisherman. At the end of the beach she found the path used by surfers to reach the rocky point.

'Where are we going? This doesn't go anywhere. Dead end ahead, Cath.'

Catherine didn't answer as she studied the rocks blocking the track and then gave a short cry. 'Here.' She pushed a rock and it rolled to one side. No track was visible, just short grass. Catherine plunged ahead. 'Follow me.'

And then, there it was, just as she remembered. The goddess pool. 'See, the tidal pool. It's a special women's place. And the tide is out. Let's go.'

'Go? Where?' asked Mollie. 'What're you doing?'

Catherine was peeling off her clothes. 'We have to go in. Come on.'

Naked, she picked her way across the rocky foreshore and settled herself in the clear water caught in the circle of rocks hidden by the cliffs.

'When in Rome . . . whatever.' Mollie followed and eased herself into the water and leant back. 'Hey, this is mad! I love it!'

The two friends splashed and giggled.

'This would be fun to do with the girls,' said Mollie. 'Y'know, you can kind of believe in all the myth and magic stuff about the Islands when you're here, in a place like this.'

Finally Catherine felt herself letting go of the old memories.

'Like Aunty Lani said, this was all part of a certain time in my life but I moved on and I've been so fortunate that I'm so happy. But I'm glad I came back. And I'm glad you're here too, Mol.'

They returned to Honolulu and, at Kiann'e's invitation, stayed at her house for their last two days.

Now, it's shopping time,' announced Mollie. 'Ala Moana, here we come.'

They were due to fly out in the evening. Catherine was shopped out, but Mollie had gone back to get some things she'd been undecided about and now wished she'd bought. They arranged to go to dinner with Kiann'e and Willi before Kiann'e took them to the airport. So while Mollie was in her final burst of shopping, Catherine caught the bus down into Waikiki. She felt like a tourist who'd had a fantastic holiday that was coming to an end.

No matter how they built and changed, razed and developed, nothing could spoil the Waikiki sunset. Catherine walked past the Royal Hawaiian Hotel and debated about having a drink on the terrace when a woman she didn't recognise approached her shyly and held up a copy of *The Waterman* and asked her to sign it.

'My name is Margaret. You don't know me, but I remember you,' she said. 'And I read about you and the book in the paper.'

'Oh, I'm sorry, where do we know each other from?' asked Catherine.

'I've worked at the Outrigger Canoe Club as a receptionist for years. I remember Lester well. It would be nice if some of his photos were hung in the club.'

'Yes, it would. I'll suggest that,' said Catherine and she signed the flyleaf.

'I remember you being around the club with PJ,' the woman added. 'When Lester was getting on in years.'

'Ah,' said Catherine. 'PJ. I wonder what happened to him?'

'Oh, he's good. He's still around. Y'know, I often think PJ became Lester. They're two of a kind, aren't they?'

'I wouldn't know. I lost touch with him years ago. Since I left the Islands,' said Catherine.

'He still surfs outside the club some mornings. He's amazingly fit.' She grinned. 'Still attracts the girls. Well, congrats again on the book. It's terrific. Thanks for signing it.'

'Mahalo, you're welcome,' said Catherine as the woman disappeared into the hotel.

Catherine walked along the beach towards Diamond Head, blotting out the cheek-by-jowl resort palaces and hotels that inched along the golden strip of Waikiki. She kept her eyes on the water, the waves and the changing end-of-day colours she remembered so well. There were a few surfers at Queens break, some dotted in clusters, waiting and watching, perhaps chatting. The swimmers had left the water. People were preparing for their evening activities.

The sun had set, so she turned to retrace her steps. But a figure riding a golden wave caught her eye and she stopped. Slowly she walked to the water's edge. He glided into the shallows and stepped off, pushing the board ahead of him before lifting it and walking onto the sand. He was certainly older, weathered, but his body was suntanned and trim. The thick hair, still curly, was silvery gold and there was about him an air of insouciance, of being contained, comfortable and oblivious to anyone around him.

He was going past her, but for a moment she couldn't speak.

'PJ?'

He slowed, turned to her curiously with a slight, questioning smile, his blue eyes bright as he stared at her.

'Hello, PJ.'

From the tone of her voice he sensed something was required of him.

'Hi.' Then, 'Do I know you?'

'It's me, Catherine.'

'Sorry, Catherine?'

'I was Catherine Connor. It's been a long time,' she finished lamely.

'A long time.' Then as if a fog lifted slightly, he said slowly, 'From Australia?'

She nodded. 'Last time I saw you, you were off to Mentawai for a few weeks.'

'Yeah, yeah. Wild waves there.'

'You were going to be in a surfing film,' she prompted.

'Yep, I've done a few of those,' he acknowledged.

She paused. He doesn't remember me.

'Have you been in the Islands since the seventies?' she asked.

'Off and on.' He looked away briefly.

'I've written a book about Lester.'

He smiled and she couldn't help wincing at the familiarity of his smile, his strange beauty.

'Lester, eh? Miss seeing the old fox. Looked after himself. He hung in there a good time. I'm trying to do the same. A book. He'd like that.'

'PJ! Come on.' A girl's voice called from behind Catherine.

'Photos. Lester took lots of pictures. Did you . . .?' A faint light started in his eyes.

A young woman in a short dress with brown limbs and long hair hurried along the sand. 'Come on, PJ. We'll be late.'

'Yes, I took lots of photos too.' Catherine glanced at the girl, who was staring at her, then looked back at PJ. 'You taught me to surf,' she finished.

'Good, that's good. Come down tomorrow, we'll have a surf.' The girl caught up to him and possessively took his hand, giving Catherine a smile that didn't touch her eyes.

The girl was probably the same age as Catherine had been when she'd loved PJ.

'Sorry, I'm leaving for Australia tomorrow.'

'Maybe next visit then.' He smiled at her. Did she imagine some tangled expression in his eyes, his smile?

'Sure. I'll look you up.'

'I'll be here. I'm never far from the beach.' The girl tugged at his arm and he turned away.

'Oh, I know that,' said Catherine, softly. 'I hope it makes you happy, PJ.'

But the girl was chattering and he didn't hear or acknowledge her remark.

It was dark now. The soft velvet night embraced the Islands as the moon rose, the stars began to shine and flowers perfumed the breeze.

She smiled to herself as she walked along the soft sand. Mollie would kill herself laughing at this encounter. But that was okay, Catherine was happy.

These Islands would always hold a place in a corner of her heart. But she wanted to go home now – to Rob, her girls and *Heatherbrae*.

The End